CW00793597

The
Marilyn
Diaries

WITH NEW AND EXPANDED DIARY ENTRIES

Charles Casillo

Hayworth Press

Copyright © 1999 – 2013 Charles Casillo

All Rights Reserved

All rights reserved. No part of this publication may be reproduced, distributed, or transmitted in any form or by any means, including photocopying, recording, or other electronic or mechanical methods, without the prior written permission of the publisher, except in the case of brief quotations embodied in critical reviews and certain other noncommercial uses permitted by copyright law.

3rd Edition

ISBN-13: 978-0615937755

Although *The Marilyn Diaries* is based on some factual events in the life of Marilyn Monroe, it is a work of fiction. Incidents recreated are not a description of what really happened nor are they the actual thoughts of Marilyn Monroe. All of the characters, whether real or imaginary names are used, are products of the author's imagination and are used fictitiously. The photograph of Marilyn Monroe and John F. Kennedy used in the introduction is a fantasy, photomontage.

For My Parents
Gloria and Ralph

Introduction

MARILYN MONROE AS FANTASY

Introduction

This is not the diary of Marilyn Monroe.

As far as we know, no such diary exists. Instead we have fragments of her life that, for years, people have pored over, investigated, analyzed and speculated about—in an attempt to discover who the real woman behind the public fantasy was.

Here was a celebrity who was able to capture the imagination and hearts of the public like no other actress before or since. No one has even come close. Yet many details of her life remain sketchy.

In the years since her death, Marilyn Monroe has almost become a work of fiction. A fairytale character who actually walked the earth. There have been so many biographies, photo books, rumors, memes, theories, movies based on her life, documentaries, false quotes and fictitious recreations that the accepted facts begin to meld with speculation, gossip and fantasy. It has become nearly impossible to decipher what is true, what is half-truth and what has been purely invented.

Yet she was a real person who, in spite of living most of her adult life in the public eye, had an intense and complex inner life that she revealed to no one.

In an attempt to understand the "real" Marilyn better, there are day-to-day, year-to-year documented facts that can be studied. It is possible to examine public records. We can listen to the few in-depth interviews she gave during her lifetime. We can read the recollections and observations of husbands, colleagues and her known friends. There is her image on film. Of course, there are the thousands of photographs to examine.

But moving on from these basic sources her story almost immediately begins to become jumbled and confusing.

Marilyn Monroe herself willingly added to the disorder of her biography. She famously said that she always knew she belonged to the public because she never belonged to anyone else. So she set out to create a fantasy figure that would most capture the attention of her beloved public. She started devising the myth early in her career, when she first changed her name from Norma Jeane Baker to Marilyn Monroe.

Some of the facts are indisputable. She was born illegitimate. She never knew her father. Her mother was mentally ill. She grew up in a series of foster homes and an orphanage. She married shortly after turning sixteen so she wouldn't have to return to the orphanage. And while her husband was serving in the Merchant Marines she began modeling. She went from successful model to starlet in a relatively short time. She divorced, changed her name and, as she approached superstardom, began a lifelong exercise in inventing herself for public consumption.

Her biography started to get muddled when she began to relay the events of her early life to reporters in the first stages of her stardom. In the early 1950s, Marilyn spoke about subjects that were then taboo. She instinctively knew the time was right.

She realized the public loves a Cinderella story. Marilyn cast herself as a modern-day Cinderella. But her version of Cinderella's saga was sordid and tragic. She played it up. Some say she exaggerated some of her hardships while completely leaving out a number of the violations against her. Most agreed that, whatever happened, her childhood damaged her.

What complicates her own narrative of her life is that, no matter how much she altered her history, there are seeds of truth in everything she revealed.

That a family member tried to smother her when she was a baby. That she was sexually abused. That her mother was institutionalized. Her dismal life of neglect and loneliness in foster care and the orphanage.

What her relationships were like with the men who helped her—or used her. The things she endured in her struggling years as a starlet. Why she posed nude for a calendar.

Some of these segments of her life were revised in some way by Marilyn—mostly to make a more provocative tale. Or to accurately convey the strong emotions she felt at the time. But how much of her biography she distorted could never be proven or disproven. In all likelihood the true, unrevealed story is the most compelling.

As her last publicist and close friend, Pat Newcomb, once said, "Marilyn Monroe never told anybody *everything*."

Part of the genius of Marilyn was that in her early publicity she used fragments from her real life—the kind of things that other personalities of her generation would rather cover up—as the "hook." This was a girl in her early twenties, instinctively launching one of the most brilliant celebrity publicity campaigns in history.

Denis Ferrara, a Monroe historian who always speaks intelligently and lucidly about the facts of her life, astutely observed that she was fascinating because she was the first truly, publicly, neurotic star.

You can find this in her earliest interviews and publicity. Was she sexy or psycho? A burning bush of ruthless ambition or a frightened, easily led child? Her display of herself was—for its time—shocking. Yet, as her screen persona jelled, she was no threat to women, although they still were put off by the voluptuousness of her body which she daringly displayed without a bra or girdle or panties.

She was mad and her madness had no precedent in movie history. No star had been like Marilyn. Nobody knew what to make of her. Just as she didn't know what to make of herself. The first naked star! That emphasis on her body would follow her always.

She was wild and slutty and abused—the abuse being a new factor in modern celebrity life—and at the same time she was incredibly innocent and childlike. During her lifetime, people got it, but they didn't know quite what they were getting. The body and wardrobe of a harlot. The face and manner of a lovely young girl. Who in that place and time was prepared? Some audience members became embarrassed and annoyed by her constantly emphasized bosoms and ass. But what was she to do? This is what the world wanted from her.

She was so perfect for that exact time and place. Outwardly sexual in her looks, yet on the screen playing characters who mostly were naively unaware of their sex appeal.

Right from the start, when you read the fan magazine stories of the day, Monroe is this big mystery. And the public relations buildup transformed her into a "legend" before she'd done anything legendary. Then she starred in *Niagara* and *Gentlemen Prefer Blondes* and so solidified every over-emphasized tale. She lived up to the buildup, but the build-up had served her up as less than human.

She push-pulled her audience—I'm this, but I'm really that. I'm that, but I'm really this. Take me seriously, and take my uplifted alabaster bosoms, too.

She was a product of her constricted time but also a free spirit who would have been happiest had she peaked in the 60s.

Marilyn is still loved because she was crazy in the most modern way—seeking herself. She even spoke in a kind of short-hand manner—don't you get it? Don't you get me?

From the beginning Marilyn was too good of a story to ignore, but she kept making it better and better. She flaunted her beauty, flaws, insecurities, mistakes, tragedies and sexuality in front of the public like priceless jewelry. Then she snatched it all back and returned it to the vault. Only to soon reveal something more fabulous, scandalous, shocking, or touching a few months later. Eventually she hid it again.

Then, in the middle of a multitude of mysterious intrigues and dramas, she died.

The world was shocked, devastated, confused and angered by her death. They had been waiting for her next chapter. Many of the questions of her life were left unanswered. That there were numerous controversial mysteries surrounding the details of her death added to the puzzle.

In the years since she died many biographers and historians and fans have tried to unravel the enigma that was Marilyn Monroe. At first, most biographers tried to stick as closely to the facts as possible and to the recollections of people who unquestionably knew her at one time or another.

The phenomenon surrounding her grew. But there remained a great deal of mystery.

In the following decades new generations of journalists set out to answer the many questions that still remained about Marilyn Monroe. But they wanted new "hooks" and more sensational revelations.

With the distance of time, some disreputable people stepped forward and added to the Monroe legend by lying about events in her life. It was not uncommon for someone who had a fleeting acquaintance with Marilyn, or something as simple as having a picture taken with her, to fabricate an entire relationship that supposedly lasted for years. To make themselves more interesting they invented Monroe-related anecdotes. A long list of men came forward making highly dubious claims of being her lover at one time or another. Some of them wrote their own books and appeared in Monroe documentaries. Movies were made using some of these allegations as source material. It's as if by claiming a connection with Marilyn they might carve a tiny place for themselves in history. Who was around to challenge their stories now?

Some biographers took these deceivers as the real deal and their concoctions as facts, which added to the ever more confusing Monroe mythology.

When I was working as a journalist in New York City, I was approached about doing a new book with a woman who had already written a popular memoir about working for Marilyn. I remember reading her memoir as a kid. It wasn't a particularly flattering portrait of Marilyn but there were some unusual and interesting tidbits. Well, now, years later, it was revealed to me, with some remorse, that the memoir was false. In fact, this former Monroe employee worked on the book with a ghostwriter who fabricated most of the material. Yet, because she seemed like a trustworthy source, writers to this day use anecdotes from her memoir in new biographies as long accepted facts.

With an abundance of fresh, yet questionable, information a new slew of authors began forming their personal opinions about who Marilyn Monroe truly was. They took the basic foundation of facts but incorporated the previous decade's doubtful revelations, particularly if the gossip fit into the thesis of their new book. Meanwhile they added a new layer of uncovered half-truths, theories and lies and presented the resulting portrait as the last word on Marilyn Monroe. But it seems there's always more to reveal.

The legend kept growing. Her name never left the headlines. Amidst the sensationalistic new biographies, an authentic letter of Marilyn's would emerge. A trove of her belongings discovered. Some new documents uncovered. A batch of previously unseen photos found—and she would once again allow us a peek into some previously unknown corner of her life. These kinds of discoveries added to her ever growing mythology. The insatiable appetite for more revelations about the goddess grew.

But by now, with so many telling and retellings and interpretations and speculations and deceptive investigations, her biography can be told in a myriad of ways. And it is. Anyone who is interested in the story of Marilyn Monroe is free to pick up a fact here, a rumor there, and an outright lie somewhere else—and they can pretty much invent her life anyway they choose.

Almost everyone thinks that their account of Marilyn is the indisputable "real" story. And people are surprisingly defensive about their interpretation of Marilyn Monroe. That's part of the reason why she lives on and on. Marilyn left behind just enough to allow anyone to create her into being exactly what they want her to be.

I don't think she would want it any other way.

I felt like she was mine.

When I was about eleven-years-old, I saw a photo of her in a magazine. I'm sure I was aware that there had once been a movie star named Marilyn Monroe but I don't remember ever having any particular interest in her. But something about the photo captivated me.

It was one of the many shots taken of her at the Manhattan premiere of *Some Like it Hot*. She was voluptuous. Glowing. Sensual. Smiling. The article that accompanied the photo, however, was not at all complimentary. Written by one of her last hairdressers, it detailed his memory of a sloppy, drugged-up, not particularly beautiful movie star, who had the ability to transform herself, for a public event, into the most physically exciting personality he'd ever encountered.

I kept going back to the photograph of her. I had a visceral reaction to it. The smile. The careful makeup. The glittery, body-hugging gown. There was something extraordinary hidden beneath the sparkling glamour. I intuitively sensed a great loneliness behind her expert mask. The photograph touched a secret place in me that I couldn't explain then and I wouldn't even try to now.

I can say that I felt like an outsider back then. A misfit. I was wearing my own mask. I intuitively knew that this spectacular woman, now dead, whose hair stylist was writing mean things about, had a hidden interior—a sadness, sensitivity and tragedy—that fed into and helped transform her magnificent exterior.

It was an immediate thing. I had to know more about her. I started seeking out her movies. Reading all the available biographies. Collecting vintage magazines.

In my neighborhood it was unusual for a boy my age to be so fascinated by a dead movie star but I couldn't help myself. I needed to know her. I started by reading the earliest accounts of her life and read the newer ones in the order that they appeared. In that way I discovered how her story was initially presented, grew, then split and ultimately splintered in hundreds of different directions.

I thought I was alone in my fascination. But in time I discovered that mine is actually a very common experience. Marilyn Monroe continues to have the power to seduce and enthrall even from beyond the grave.

Eventually I became knowledgeable regarding the many versions of her life and death. I also noted that her place in popular culture was stronger than ever. I saw the models and actresses imitate her famous photographs—almost every Monroe photo shoot has been recreated several times over. I saw movies, stage performances, drag shows—all based more on her public image than anything else. And although the imitators are often expert and lovely there is some vital, mysterious ingredient missing: a wildness, a charisma, a unique *somethingness* that has never again been generated since she left the earth. It is pure Monroe. She alone had the secret ingredient.

Her kind of sensitivity, vulnerability and magic can't be manufactured. It simply can't. It has to be authentic. It must be undeniable

Like all of us I began to develop my own personal version of what she was like—what she was "really" like—to me. I became just as adamant about who she was and just as protective of my image of her. I always wanted to defend her. I felt as if I was one of the few who truly understood her. Just as you probably feel that you hold a key to her mystery.

What if she left a diary?

There were always rumors that she had kept one. It was believed to have "disappeared" shortly after she died. I couldn't stop thinking about it, imagining what she might have revealed.

I always knew I would write about her. I just wasn't sure how. I was well aware that the only possible knowable truths about her lie somewhere between the fictions and the biographical facts. By now all the "takes" on Marilyn's life in the biographies, the novels, the movies and the plays combine to form the Marilyn Monroe each of us believe her to be.

Because she has become a fantasy figure to so many, I thought my personal interpretation of her could add something new to the narrative. I chose to write it in the guise of fiction in a diary format. Although I recreate some actual events in her life, her thoughts and actions are obviously imagined. All of the characters are presented fictitiously.

Back when I originally wrote *The Marilyn Diaries* there wasn't as many fictitious recreations of her private life, told from her point of view, as there are today. At the time I was most concerned about creating an illusion for the reader of peeking into a real diary. I thought it should be disjointed, somewhat sloppy, fragmented—the way I suspected Marilyn would have written it. I even kept in typos and misspellings. I felt it worked. Liz Smith called it "a classic."

In this updated and expanded edition I kept my original diary concept but I was less concerned with creating the realistic experience of reading a secret diary. This time I wanted to convey a broader, fuller spectrum of her inner thoughts and emotions as devised by my version of Marilyn: Complicated, intelligent, sensual, and vulnerable—with a lively, craving mind. A far cry from the luscious, bubble-headed caricature of her films and publicity. Nor is she the tragic, psychotic victim that legend has painted her to be.

It bothers me that when conjuring Marilyn so many people fall into the trap of portraying her as a stupid, breathless, baby doll—confusing Marilyn Monroe, the sharp, talented woman, with her onscreen persona—the sexy dumb blonde character she skillfully created for the movies. However, the way she spoke and acted on the screen was very different from the way she was in real life.

My Marilyn Monroe is a sensitive and talented artist wracked with fears and self-doubts that she is always striving to overcome. But she is also a woman shrewd and calculating enough to cast herself in the roles that people of her generation expect of her. A woman who delights in her sexuality but is compulsively planning ways to have her other qualities acknowledged. Someone who is used but who is also a master user— expertly devising masquerades to conceal her complexities. Sexually magnetic, ruthlessly ambitious, constantly fighting the demons left over from an excruciating past, but never losing that bewitching radiance that continues to seduce.

Obviously I will always love her.

There are countless interpretations of who Marilyn Monroe was, what she thought and how she lived. Everyone has their personal Marilyn.

This is mine.

The Diary

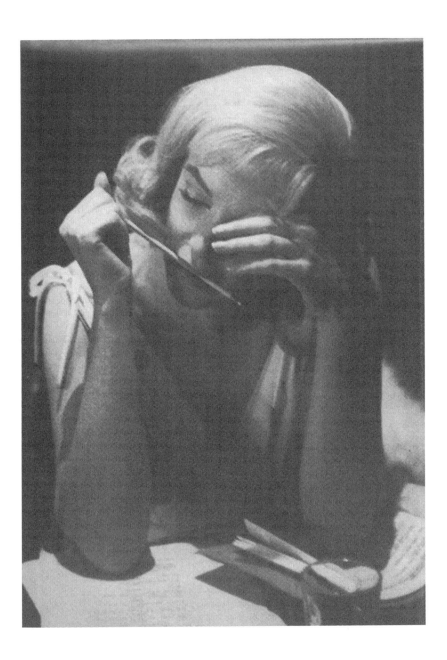

1960

July 15, 1960 (Los Angeles)

...and I just thought of something: all the best lines come to me during or immediately after sex and by the time I could write them down they're already gone. Maybe it's because the moments before orgasm heighten all of your senses so much that you're thinking more clearly and the thoughts are absolutely pure.

So I decided to start writing right now – before these feelings can float away.

To begin.

I'm writing this on July 15th in the seat of my limo on my way back to my hotel after having...how shall I put this? A tryst? Yes! A sexual tryst with Jack. Or shall I be more specific and say John Fitzgerald Kennedy?

While I'm writing this, in sexual afterglow, I won't focus on what's wrong about it. On guilt. On how we are both in marriages of sorts. On what a disastrous road this could lead me down.

The thing is, my life has been filled with questions in which the answer always seemed to be a simple "right" or "wrong." I've learned that it's not always so easy. After all, there are many subtexts within a story. If I always chose what looked "right" in other peoples' eyes I never would have gotten anywhere. It's always been so difficult to make any move at all because of the scrutiny I put myself under. So, I won't judge myself tonight. Not tonight. Instead I'll say, the night was lovely.

I'm glad to be alive today.

And oh what an exciting time to be alive! You find yourself saying, "This is a notable time in history and, gee, here I am! Living it!" The Democrats are in Los Angeles to choose their candidate for president, and they chose Jack of course, and it was the most triumphant day of his life and he wanted to see me! This remarkable man, destined for greatness, wanted me with him to share this moment of honor. And I was honored.

I watched him give his acceptance speech at the Coliseum and he said something like (I scribbled this down), "We're standing today on the edge of a new frontier – the frontier of the 1960s, a time of great opportunities and also some danger. I'm asking all of you to be pioneers..." And it was as if he were speaking directly to me. When his eyes did meet with mine it was like...I don't know what kind of feeling—torture, passion, admiration, desire—all mixed up together creating something totally new in me.

The speech thrilled me and gave me goose bumps. Here was the future leader of our country, I believe, asking all of us for our help and saying in essence, "Look, we're all in this together. We're going to have to work together if we want to move forward."

I said to myself: "This man has power. The power to improve the world and change lives. I could be worthwhile, if only he would love me."

Now let me just say this: the whole reason I was able to meet with Jack is because of my friendship with Peter and Pat Lawford. I've known Peter for years and when he married Pat Kennedy, Jack's sister, I became close friends with both of them. Peter's movie career hasn't exactly set the world on fire so it feels good to him to be attached to an important political family. Importance by proxy. That's Peter.

Pat would always tease me saying, "My brother, you know, the *senator*? He has a big crush on you." I would just sort of shrug and bat my eyes. But they had set up a party for Jack at their house on the beach in Santa Monica and he specifically asked them to invite me.

Well, Jack wanted me at the party, but they said to him ("they" being the people who advise him, his protectors and his entourage), "It wouldn't be good to arrive at a party with Marilyn Monroe while your wife is not present." The dodos – if his wife was going to be present he wouldn't want me there. I am married. Jack is married.

So it was set up that I would come to the Lawford party with Sammy Davis Jr., who is a very dear person to know. Jack wasn't back from the Coliseum yet but you could feel his presence all over the place; his powerful speech lingered in the air like a rare and intoxicating cologne that filled the room. He was the biggest star of the evening, even though there were the most important players in town in attendance. Well, I know how that feels. I was happy to hand over the crown to him.

Everyone at the party was excited and a-buzz. That's the kind of reaction the name "John F. Kennedy" brings. We feel that with him as president the world is in for a dramatic and important change. He cares about the people and civil rights and he's young and in tune with the youth of the country.

But the party that Pat and Peter set up was in a kind of stark contrast to the prestige and formality of his nomination. This was a real Hollywood party, even by Hollywood standards. The beautiful people were out in full force—drinking and laughing and dancing and there were naked bodies running all over the pool area jumping in and out of the water.

"It's like Babylon," I whispered to Sammy.

"We're standing on the edge of a new frontier, baby," Sammy said to me. And then he looked at me as if he was seeing me for the first time.

I was hoping he'd notice me because it would give me the boost in the ass of confidence I needed before Jack arrived. I was wearing a white dress that fit me like a fresh coat of glossy paint. I was sewn into it, my dear, the stitching going right up the crack of my ass to…uh…show it off to its best advantage.

"My God," he said, "You are spectacularly beautiful tonight. What would you have done with yourself if you weren't born so beautiful?"

As always, I took the question seriously and thought it over.

"God's not that cruel," I said finally. "He had to give me something to work with." And Sammy rubbed the small of my back. Once he was in love with me – Sammy was – and I sort of get the feeling he still is.

And then I saw Jack arrive at the top of the stairs, like some god peering down from Mount Olympus. Everyone was rushing up to him, touching him, shaking his hand, congratulating him, but he had locked eyes with me the moment he walked in and I could see he was slowly edging his way in my direction.

Me? I stood perfectly still – trembling — waiting for him. When he was standing in front of me, face to face, Sammy vanished instantly. That was part of the plan, I suppose. Jack took my hands and said, "I'm so glad you're here, Marilyn."

His voice was gone. Just a whisper, really. Damaged for the night—or longer—by the forcefulness of his speech at the Coliseum.

The moment I looked into his eyes my heart and entire body over-flowed with a feeling that—I don't know—it weakened me and filled me with passion and terror. I wanted him too much. It hurts to long for something too much for fear you might not get it.

I'm in love! (I think) and I might as well state it here and now.

Oh there has been a dry spell of love in my life. My marriage to Arthur? Over, over, over! It's been over for longer than I've even been willing to admit to myself. It's just a matter of time. Just the thought of him makes me sad. Or the thought of "us." I simply can't think about that now. I can't!

I've been wallowing in loneliness. It's been years, actually, since I felt this way about a man. But no man has ever presented me with such a total package. He has the good looks and dynamic sex appeal of Marlon Brando. He's entertaining and charismatic like Frank Sinatra. And very loving and protective towards me, the way Joe (DiMaggio) has always been. I've had the privilege of knowing some very outstanding men in my lifetime.

But he has all these qualities wrapped in one magnificent package. He's everything I've been looking for. I'm trying very hard not to get my hopes up or invest too much emotion in this because this feeling I have for him could swell up into desperation. And that, of course, would destroy everything. There are no saviors. I've learned that the hard way.

When Pat and Peter invited me to the party, saying, "Jack would really like you to be there," at first my old insecurities made me feel suspicious, of course. Whenever someone wants to be in my company so badly I always have to wonder what they expect to get out of it. It's like I can't believe that anyone could want me for "me." I'm trying to get over that kind of thinking now.

My psychiatrist, Dr. Greenson, says I must start seeing my worth – but, still, the feelings of inferiority are there. I'm well aware that there are times when people want me at their parties because I sort of glamour-up the guest list. Still, this party was too exciting to miss – I mean, being a piece of history and all.

Jack was eating the attention up. He loved being in the midst of all this Hollywood type of glitz and glitter. He is very "Hollywood" himself. Except for actors on a movie set, Jack is the first man I've ever seen wearing makeup; an orangey-kind of cover-up which is supposed to give the illusion of a healthy tan. He combs his lush hair constantly when he thinks no one is looking. I was looking. He is very vain, in a sexy way, and he was proud to have me at his side.

As we plunged into the crowd together he said to me, "Time to turn on the ol' B.P."

I asked, "B.P.?...what's that?

"Big Personality," he replied.

He confided to me that he actually hates being touched by strangers but it's something that he's taught himself to deal with. I understand that. Whenever I go somewhere there are always hands tugging at me, tearing at me. I suppose people have seen me on huge movie screens and they want to make sure I'm real. It's almost as if they think I was created by Walt Disney or some mad studio executive in a Hollywood lab.

We linked arms and walked around the party. He was pumped with pride, greeting people with cocky looks and confident movements that suggested hundreds of hours of practice in front of a mirror. Frankly, I'm not physically attracted to weak men. This added ingredient of bold narcissism in Jack turned me on even more.

I said to him, "Brains and beauty."

He looked at me quizzically.

I added, "You have them both."

He laughed hoarsely. "That's what I wanted to say to you."

Actually it really did frighten me, how much I was attracted to him. His eyes pierce into you, observing, taking you in. His face exudes a compelling private history. His comb-grooved hair is thick and full, as if he wouldn't consider allowing it to be thinning the way it is for most men in his age category. He has been handed things his whole life and so he has acquired the air of a man who doesn't take "no" for an answer.

And there's the danger factor: Jack wouldn't dream of ever truly wanting anyone. He, instead, would take what he could from them – making believe that they meant the world to him, that they were loved and that they were safe, and then discarding them when he was through. I sense that about him. He was bred for success. Now he thinks that he is superior to mere mortals, and he never lets anything (or anyone) stand in his way.

On the other hand, I felt that when you have his protection, you are protected totally and completely and no one would dare harm you. To be with a man like Jack would be like having a bullet proof shield, where insults and lies and gossip would bounce right off of you – unable to leave even the slightest scar.

With these contradictions, being involved with him would be like walking through mine fields. Why would I want to put myself in a relationship with a man that has such powerful and dangerous control over my emotions? Well, because he has cocksure elegance and confidence and brilliance and respect and power. Everything I ever wanted for myself.

Confidence is an aphrodisiac.

When I'm around somebody with this kind of personality I become more breathy, more helpless, more fragile. It's not planned but this is the role in which most people respond to me in and I fall into it by rote. It's not an act. It's very much a part of me. It's one of my "selves," you might say. And those strong personalities, like Jack has, call up this vulnerability in me. No matter how much I educate myself, improve myself, change myself—the helpless victim in me always finds a way to present herself.

We walked around the party greeting people. But he kept steering me into quiet corners so we could be alone. Oh, how I longed to make a witty remark but, alas, none came to me at the moment. And these things can't be forced lest you come off sounding stupid. Now, mind you, I can be as witty as the next girl but sometimes my mind goes blank and all I can manage to do is stand there, as fetching as possible, and let my looks do the talking, thereby (great word, huh?) inspiring those around me to be the witty ones. I know a clever remark when I hear one.

Jack, though, at this party turned to me and said, hoarsely "Oh my dear, you are so exquisite." Not exactly clever or witty, but exactly the kind of thing I wanted to hear from Mr. John F. Kennedy. So if my looks were doing the talking they were obviously saying the right things.

Later on, after midnight, he asked me if I would like to leave the party and walk along the beach. He needed to clear his head of politics and power-plays for the moment, but he didn't want to do it alone. He wanted me with him! We walked and walked along the shore. He was asking me questions about my life, my career, and my loves. He seemed genuinely interested in me as a person, as if I was the most important person in his life at the moment, and as a result I allowed him to peel off layers of my persona.

"Are you happy with the...uh...playwright?" he asked, dismissively.

It was kind of disrespectful to talk about Arthur Miller that way, my husband, considered by many to be the greatest of living playwrights. But I didn't defend him.

Instead, I told him my marriage to Arthur was finished. We both disappointed each other in so many ways. We were only staying together for the duration of the making of this movie he wrote for me. *The Misfits.* I told Jack that filming was starting in a couple of weeks. "It's not my usual kind or role," I said. "It's dark and dramatic. And I'm just terrified."

"Terrified of what?" Jack asked.

"That I won't be any good. That people won't like me in it. That I'll fail. I don't like the fact that what other people think of me matters so much. I hate it, actually. But I find that I always put my self-esteem in the hands of others. Which is a dangerous place to put it because I don't have any control over it."

"Don't let anyone have that kind of power over you," he said. And when he looked directly into my eyes he added, "Besides, how can *you* be *anything* but wonderful in *any* movie of *any* kind?"

I explained to him that, well, when you serve the public up one kind of image they kind of get used to it and they like it. They might not accept you if you show them something unexpected.

Jack said: "I think that would be a good way to keep them interested."

"I thought that too," I explained. "But the image of me is so potent now. They can't see me as anything else. For instance, if you were to go onstage at a political rally wearing a clown-nose, doing a vaudeville routine."

"I think I could pull that off," he shrugged with all the self-assurance in the world. And in that moment I believed he could.

I wish I had more faith in myself.

Still…still…There's no comedy in this script that Arthur wrote. I have little confidence in myself but I have even less faith in the screenplay. It's bleak and heavy with a lot of talk about life and death and mistrust and freedom. On the other hand, the good hand, Clark Gable and Montgomery Clift are going to be in it with me. And it's to be directed by John Huston. That gives me some hope.

Hope, hope, hope.

I found myself revealing things to Jack in a way I haven't been able to express to anyone. About how I had been babbling to the press, and anyone else who would listen, for so long about wanting to be a serious actress. And now here I am about to start work in a very dramatic story, working with the finest talents in the business. No matter how I do in it, when the film opens, some of the press will be waiting to make their little jokes about the silly sexpot who takes herself too seriously. Oh yes! The knives will be flying at me from every direction. They have been from the very beginning. Luckily I've become good at dodging them.

Jack said "You are more complicated than your image".

I said, "You make me feel like I'm more than just a decorative ornament."

He was staying that night at the Lawford guest cottage. He asked me if I'd like to join him there for a drink. I desperately wanted to be with him but everything in me told me not to go, that this man could complicate my life—which already has more complications than I can handle.

Plus, to add to the complexity of it all, I wasn't crazy about the idea of having another affair. Yes, Arthur and I are through but I already committed adultery once. I think…well…could it be because I feel I'm floundering and I want a man to anchor me…protect me…save me?

The last affair was with a man who was married too. Actually, it's not exactly over yet. This actor. Yves Montand. Well, he's the costar of the movie I just completed. *Let's Make Love.* I mean, it is over but I've been hanging on—hanging on to thin air it seems. Yves wants to go back to his wife. A woman who was also my friend. It all makes me feel soiled and mixed up and, well, bad. I *am* bad! What I thought might be my next big love turned out to be just one of those "movie" affairs that last for as long as the filming. The kind of affair I promised myself never to fall into. I imagine many lives are strewn with broken promises and I am no exception.

And I'm a human being too, with the same wants and desires as everyone else—most of all to be wanted and desired—and so I told Jack I would like to join him for a drink.

The room had been prepared for him. A little fire glowing in the fireplace. Lush bedding. Fresh flowers. As soon as we entered the room his hands reached for me, going for my ass first, which he stroked hard, as if he was looking for something inside of it, and I immediately lost any erotic feelings. When a man reaches for me he expects to feel "Marilyn Monroe." And that's all I am—only Marilyn Monroe. A woman. The same as any other. Well, more or less.

But he got so caught up in role playing that he forgot I'm an actual person. I was so terrified I might disappoint him. My men expect so much of me. They expect lights to flash and a musical soundtrack to swell up. "Wow an orgasm with Marilyn Monroe!" It's something they've fantasized about. It's nearly impossible to live up to a fantasy.

I wanted to say, "Jack, I'm so scared. I'm so tired. I need so desperately to feel safe." But I thought better of it and instead I remained silent.

Actually the best sex I have, the times I enjoy sex most and really let myself go, is when the person doesn't know who I am.

My doctor, my psychiatrist, is always saying, "Marilyn, go deeper. Dig into yourself. Look for patterns in your behavior. Search for reasons." And then he adds, "Write it down. Keep a journal. Write as if you are revealing your secrets to a best friend. Or, better yet, write as if no one will ever read it. You're up all night. Put your time to use instead of trying to fight sleep and maybe it will come easier."

When I first moved to New York City—I was already quite well known by then—I would put on a disguise and go to a Midtown bar on a Friday night. Not often. Once in a great while. When I needed to get myself away from myself. Why did I feel the need to test myself this way? Who knows? Maybe just as a way to prove to myself that I *am* still real.

I'd wear a black wig and change my makeup. I would put on a pair of horn-rimmed glasses. I even adjusted my way of walking, my body language—my entire attitude became different. I'm good at that. The burden of selfhood was gone. I was any woman. I was every woman.

This bar was like dozens of others in the neighborhood, filled with bosses, secretaries, and office workers having a few drinks at the end of the work week. But sexual desire makes everyone equal. And fueled by stingers and gin martinis the place filled up with sex. It floated around the room on a cloud of cigarette smoke. Sex was everywhere, in every glass, in every glance, in every attempt at small talk, every shift in positions. Sex, I guess, allowed them to leave the drudgery behind them, at least for the night. Everyone is looking for an escape from one thing or another and I understand that.

I'd start talking to an out of town salesman or a second rate lawyer. Not particularly good looking or extensively bright. I didn't want the pressure of having to keep up my end of an in-depth conversation. I didn't want too much information either. I didn't want to possess him, just experience him for a while.

We'd have some drinks and before too long he'd invite me to come and see his hotel room or his one room apartment. I always knew it was coming. The "getting picked up" part was uneventful. But it had a kind of sweetness and it would ultimately become exciting. I loved it when we were finally in bed and they would discover and delight in the beauty of my body (one guy said, "Well put together.") There was always a joyful surprise at how beautiful my body was under the drab clothing I was wearing. Well it is beautiful in a very normal sense of the word. But the beauty of the moment for me was that I didn't have anything to live up to—not even myself.

Once I was with this travelling salesman who had aspirations to be an actor. He looked like he was in his late thirties or early forties. He had a nice head of thick, jet black hair (dyed) and very blue eyes, but aside from that (and a terrible nose job) he was just a few degrees less than handsome. From a distance he looked fantastic. For most women there would be a disappointment with a closer look. That's what I liked about him.

He told me he had never been married. He said that he'd been taking acting classes and quoted some outrageous sum he was paying to study. Someone was taking him for a ride. But he seemed excited about it, so I didn't have the heart to tell him. As long as he was enjoying the ride. He said this acting "coach" had broken down his "type" to three categories: snippy executive, sinister criminal and nice father figure. These types couldn't be further apart and actually the only type I could see him playing was a sad, milquetoast drifter.

He asked me back to his cheesy hotel room.

He talked of his love of the movies. His admiration for Audrey Hepburn. His adoration of Marilyn Monroe (ha ha) and Elizabeth Taylor. He told me I was pretty enough to be an actress. "It's never too late," he said.

I didn't want to be smart for him. I wanted to be a dumb, stupid floozy and enjoy myself. And that's how he wanted me. I put myself in the right frame of mind. He kissed me. It was awful, as I knew it would be. I was aware of his tongue...cold and wet and horrible. But I had come this far with him, so I went to bed with him anyway. Then something happened. He became more and more excited, hungrier, more passionate. It was contagious. The more he enjoyed me the more I started enjoying him. It became mutual. Soon we both became vessels of desire. He did everything in his power to please me and ultimately he did.

I don't think this is wrong. I don't think it's a sin. People have called me an "angel" of sex. Maybe that's what I am. It's as if God is using me to reward someone, to bring a little happiness and a little tenderness into some nice person's life who normally doesn't have very much of that.

Afterwards he took out, I kid you not, a little pocket-size bottle of hydrogen peroxide, which he proceeded to gargle with and wipe down his "you-know-what" with, even though I had made him wear a rubber. "I hope you don't mind," he apologized. "But you can't be too careful." I guess I should have been offended but then I thought, well, it wasn't really *me* he was with anyway.

But, back with Jack in the comfortable guest room, I was myself. And not only that but I was myself at my very best. I controlled and created everything about *me*. I was aware of every movement I made, every smell my body gave off. I was aware of how my body felt under his hands and I could feel how much he was enjoying the exploration of me. Oh sure, yes, part of his excitement was that it was a fantasy come to life. A fantasy of "Marilyn." But I am Marilyn, so I was myself. If that makes any sense.

And as I became more and more aware of his excitement, his moaning, his probing, my erotic feelings came back. I became rough and demanding, only to grow tender again and soft as a baby. At times he was almost screaming. I could tell he is used to the missionary position with…"you know who."

Afterwards we lay very still, breathing hard. This was the second man with whom I committed adultery but I quickly brushed that thought away.

I thought instead of how nice it would be to die in this moment in an embrace that would never end. I mean, with the bed, and the fire, and his arms, and my head on his chest as a pillow. It might have been a way of preserving us that way. And the feeling. And the comfort. The two of us hurdling through the heavens for eternity holding each other. Just holding.

As a matter of fact, the feeling of wanting to die with him (and I thought it must be true love) on the bed in front of the fire was so strong, that I thought he must be feeling it too.

I wouldn't have to worry about going back to work and making, *The Misfits*, a script which taunts me with its wrongness. There'd be no more fear as to whether or not I'll be good in the next scene. Or how I'd look. They told me I should wear a wig in the film. I told them I don't want to wear a wig. "But," they urged, "It will be so much easier. You will be shooting in the Nevada desert. Any hairdo will frizz up and be ruined within minutes. It will never match from scene to scene. Think of all the time we'll save." So for the first time in a movie I will be wearing a wig.

On top of that, the costume tests showed I could stand to lose a few pounds. You always look heavier on camera. When they screened the tests I ran from the projection room crying.

If I were *finished*, these concerns wouldn't matter, none of them. I could sigh. The struggle would be over.

And for him there would be no more important decisions. He wouldn't have the pressure of having to become the next "great leader" or of ruling the world. We'd be at peace, frozen eternally in an exquisite moment of contentment.

Oh! He must be feeling it!

"I can stay like this with you forever," I said to him to test the waters and see if we were on the same wavelength. He stroked my hair and mumbled something back that I couldn't understand but sounded like, "lalalablahblahblah...campaign tomorrow." But whatever it was that he said it made me sure that there were no visions of suicide dancing in his head.

July 16, 1960

I was packing, readying myself for a flight to New York when Jack called me. "I can't stop thinking about you," he said.

My plan had been to fly to NYC for a week so I could rest in my apartment, see my acting teacher, Lee Strasberg, and just be alone and replenish myself for a few days before starting the new movie. Making *Let's Make Love* (and having a love affair with the leading man) has left me depleted and diminished and very worn out (feeling and looking.) I've had no time to get myself to an emotional place where I feel healthy enough, or strong enough, to start another picture. After all, I'm an actress not a machine.

But Arthur is already in Nevada getting things ready on *The Misfits* location. Everyone is ready to start shooting that film. I decided to stay in Los Angeles for another couple of days to be with Jack. I think being with him can restore me better than lying in bed worrying, alone in my New York apartment.

We agreed to meet for dinner at Romanoff's, which is Frank Sinatra's favorite place and, oh, how I hoped Frank would see me dining with

Jack. Boy, would he be jealous! He always says he's just waiting for my marriage with Arthur to be over and then he's going to make his move. And seeing me with Jack would make me even more desirable to Frank. But, alas, he was nowhere in sight.

For proprieties sake Peter came along and so did Jack's assistant, a very nice guy named Ken. Jack was in high spirits. At one point he was having a sort of casual conversation with Peter, and all the while his hand was slowly creeping up my thigh. It was thrills a mile a minute. His hand kept going higher and higher, until he reached the high point, and he felt that I was not wearing panties. He turned bright red and became quite flustered. I got into a giggling fit while Peter and Ken looked at us completely baffled.

Undated July 1960 Entry

My heart is with Jack, who is on a plane headed back to Washington for more campaign strategy planning and God knows what else. After our dinner the other night, we only had another couple of days left to spend together in Los Angeles before I had leave for New York and then I will be moving on to Reno to shoot the movie.

Jack said, "Meet me over at Lawford's house tomorrow afternoon."

When I got back to my hotel, I immediately called Pat. "Your brother," I told her, "wants me to meet him over at your place tomorrow."

"Of course he does, darling," she said. "I arranged the whole thing. Be here around noon-ish."

"What is she up to," I wondered. "Why is she so eager to push Jack and me together?" Not that I'm complaining, mind you. Just wondering.

Jack wasn't there yet when I arrived, so I spent some time by the pool with Peter and Pat. We sat on fluffy, cushioned green lounge chairs, mine carefully positioned so that I was in the shade – I want to make sure I'm all ivory and blonde and white for *The Misfits*.

Pat said, "Jack hasn't stopped talking about you since the party, darling."

"Ha ha," I replied. "With all that's going on in his life now – the election looming – and he can't stop thinking about me?"

Pat poured another margarita for herself from an elaborate pitcher sitting on the table between us, then she took a deep swallow and licked her lips free of salt and said, "I'm sure he's thinking 'First Lady' and how much more glamorous it would be to have you on his arm when he's sworn in."

"Oh," I said quickly, not daring to even consider such a thing. "Jacqueline is pretty glamorous herself."

"The statue!" Pat said.

Peter adjusted the silver sun reflector he was holding and said, "She may be glamorous, Charlie, but she ain't Marilyn Monroe."

"Charlie," is Peter's nickname for me

To stop Pat and Peter from talking any more – and putting any such ideas in my head – I pulled out this diary and started writing. I think it's very foolish for them to be putting foolish notions in my head, because once I get a notion stuck in my head, foolish or otherwise, it's very difficult for me to get it out. Imagine! Me as First Lady!!!

I thought I should write a little something here about my relationship with my friends, the married couple I was protecting myself from while they baked in the sun at my side: Peter Lawford and Pat Kennedy Lawford.

Peter and I have known each other since my starlet days. Even before I was famous Peter used to say, "Oh Marilyn, you're so gorgeous. You're so sexy. I love you. I want you!" He was already in movies and very handsome and distinguished but I never gave in to him, never went to bed with him, and now I say, "Thank God for that!"

On the outside he can look very suave and conservative, but there's something buried under the groomed hair and cologne and starched shirts; a snaky kind of perversion that slithers in and out during his guarded and unguarded moments. A little perversion can be appealing in some men but in Peter it has some sort of dangerous connotation. His snake is poisonous, you might say. And this was back in the days when I didn't trust anyone. Not that I trust anyone now…but even less so back then.

I was just starting out in show business and Peter saw that I was kind of floating around the scene, trying to break in, and he asked me out for a date. He was debonair – the British accent had a lot to do with that – and good looking and in the movies, so I said, "Sure." I figured if nothing else at least I'd get a lobster dinner out of it.

But when he arrived to pick me up I was positive he would change his mind. An English gentleman, such as he was, would not want to go out with a schlub like me. Him: Suit, tie, cuff links. He was immaculate. My apartment at that time was in a seedy section of Hollywood. I was running late and I answered the door in my ripped terry cloth robe—and my cute, little dog had just made a large and un-cute poop on the white rug. Peter looked around my apartment and let's just say I'm not the best housekeeper in the world. His expression said "GHASTLY," although his mouth didn't say a word.

"I'll be right out," I said, rolling my eyes in shame on my way to the bedroom to dress. I wore a simple white cocktail dress that was one of the few good articles of clothing I had. I often wore white because I thought it looked elegant in any situation. Plus, it suited me.

But he took me to a nice dinner in spite of his shock at the state of my living conditions and he never stopped complimenting me. He called me "Charlie," that first night. The nickname stuck.

When we got back to my place, dog poop or no dog poop, he wanted to come in and, even though by then I had decided I wasn't all that physically attracted to him, I felt too guilty to say "no" because, after all, he had spent a lot of money on a lobster dinner and some very good champagne too.

So I invited him in and he started kissing me and I was thinking, "Oh dear, how am I going to get out of this?" But I said, "Um, just a second, Peter, I have to go to the bathroom."

And to my great curiosity and greater surprise Peter said, "Oh, can I watch?"

I tried not to look shocked but I was...um...shocked! But then I thought, "Oh what the hell. I'm enough of an exhibitionist to allow it." I figured, well, maybe letting him watch me pee would be enough of a payback for dinner. So as casually as I could, I said, "Sure."

He followed me into the bathroom and I pulled down my panties as theatrically as I could, wiggling back and forth, so he'd really get his money's worth, so to speak (in those days I occasionally wore panties, especially on first dates.) I sat on the toilet and just sort of looked up at the ceiling and whistled and when I glanced at him leaning against the wall in rapt attention, I could tell that watching me tinkle really turned him on. When I was finished, before I could even get my panties up, he rushed over and started kissing me with his full force and passion.

For a second there I started to actually feel a bit of passion back for him – as I've said, the more desire the other person feels for me, the more I can enjoy myself – and it's always better to spend the night tenderly holding someone you like, rather than waking up cold and alone in the morning. But then he took my hand and guided it in a sort of smack across his face. You know? Like forcing me to smack him. And then he did it again. And then again – harder. "Uh oh," I thought. I suspected what he wanted.

Then he said. "Hit me," verifying my suspicion.

In the past I had known men who liked to be hurt, in various different ways, but I just simply could not bring myself to do it.

"I can't hit you, Peter," I replied.

"Why not?" he asked.

"Because I like you too much."

"But I want you to do it," he said. "It would feel good to me." And with that, perhaps to demonstrate, he started hitting himself. Well, I'm sure I don't have to explain to you how weird it was to be standing in my bathroom with my panties still around my ankles watching a grown man in a suit and tie and an English accent smack himself silly. *That's* Hollywood.

Finally I saw a way out of all of this. I said, "Peter, you're a very handsome man and I like you a lot, but I feel too tender towards you to ever get enjoyment out of hurting you. So I guess we're simply not compatible in the romantic department."

He said he guessed I was right. He said he understood. And then he casually suggested that I go to the bathroom on him! I would have liked to think he viewed me as a sophisticated lady of the world, but I guess my face betrayed me because he asked, "Am I shocking you?"

I didn't want to seem prudish and so I adjusted my dress and I said very quickly, with all the dignity I could muster, "No, you're not shocking me but I just never wanted to go to the bathroom on anyone, that's all." But, in truth, he was shocking me – as if there was any more shocks left in me to be had! I paused and then I asked, "Do you like that?"

"Absolutely," he said. "Last week I met this great black girl at a jazz club in New York who peed on me just for the experience of doing it on a movie star. You should try it."

A girl had to draw the line somewhere and this, I decided, would be where I would draw it.

"No," I said simply. "Just no."

He sighed dejectedly, lit a cigarette, exhaled smoke quickly and concluded I was right – we weren't compatible sexually.

That cleared the air, so to speak, and he left without bitterness towards me. After that night we became good friends, and friendship usually destroys any erotic potential a relationship has anyway. I guess you're wondering why I would be friends with such a man but really, he wasn't only an out-and-out pervert. There's more to Peter than that – outside of his strange bedroom preferences he can be very funny and kind and a lot of fun. But I would be lying if I didn't admit that I occasionally feel that dangerous snake in his personality slither out.

"He's queer," a girl I knew from my modeling days told me. I wasn't sure if she meant "queer" as in "strange" or "queer" as in homosexual.

"Homo," she said. "Oh yes. That's why he likes to be degraded. He's ashamed of himself for what he really craves."

Well, if he is "that way," I have to say in all fairness he continued to try and get me to go to bed with him from time to time.

After Peter married Pat Kennedy, my respect level for him rose considerably. Pat Kennedy, of the famous Boston Kennedy clan as everyone knew, was worth millions, and was considered quite a catch. And yet the Kennedys were all brought up strictly in the Catholic faith. Perhaps she would be a good influence on him. I couldn't imagine Peter asking her to pee on him. Although maybe her experience from being taught by nuns would allow her to give him a good spanking from time to time.

Eventually Peter introduced me to Pat. This is going back a ways. Hmm – let me think – 1954, I think it was. We hit it off right away, Pat and myself. Soon Pat became my primary relationship in that union. Oh, by the way, I'm talking FRIENDSHIP!

I've never had many girlfriends before. It was funny. People told me that she was in awe of me because I was a movie star. I was in awe of her because she was part of the rich and illustrious Kennedy family. I couldn't help but wonder what it was like. One winter night when Peter was out of town I spent the night with Pat to keep her and myself company. We lay on their king-sized bed, propped up with pillows and a fluffy pink comforter pulled up to our necks, eating chocolate-covered candies from a huge heart shaped box Peter had sent her for Valentine's day. As we lay there Pat gave me some insight into her family life.

In the Kennedy clan, the men were brought up as gods – they had to be "the best," but as a reward they didn't have to play by the rules of mortals. The father, Joe, set an example that infidelity was the best way. His wife, Rose, took the expected back seat in the family, while Joe screwed as many women as possible. The daughters, on the other hand, were brought up like little nuns...with their mother, Rose, the saint, being their example. In the Kennedy household the girls weren't anywhere near as important as the boys. Everything in their upbringing was geared towards having a president in the family, so the girls took a lesser role. The family was filled with privilege and love, but the utmost importance was the presidency.

Pat told me a horrifying story about how far the family would go to protect the possibility of having a Kennedy son in the White House.

The oldest Kennedy daughter, Rosemary, was born slightly retarded. In those days it took them awhile to figure it out. Meaning that Rosemary was a beautiful little girl and she didn't look like anything was wrong with her so at first they thought she was just a slow learner, as "some girls" …ahem…are assumed to be…but as the years went on it became more and more difficult for her to keep up with the other children. She was put in special classes and given extra consideration.

As she got older, Rosemary became more and more difficult to control. They tried to keep her locked up in a convent but she would escape and they would find her wandering the streets late at night, with no idea what she had been up to. She was the most beautiful of all the Kennedy sisters and being a beautiful young woman with a beautiful young woman's needs, and mental problems on top of that, she became something very dangerous in their eyes. Joe, Sr. became very concerned that Rosemary would do something to scandalize the family, maybe even something as terrible as becoming pregnant.

Joe became adamant that Rosemary had to be – well – let's just say that he had to get her under control. Trying to keep her locked up with the nuns didn't work. In those days there was a new experimental operation called a lobotomy. There wasn't that much known about it except that it was used mostly as a last resort in mental patients. But Joe had this new operation performed on Rosemary, even though it had been designed for unresponsive schizophrenics, not for people with a slight mental condition. I choose to believe he thought it was for the best and that he was actually helping her. I need to believe that fathers are that way.

The way the operation works is that they go into your brain with an ice pick. They keep the patient wide awake, by the way. They ask the patient to sing and count backwards while they keep on destroying more and more of the brain with the sharp ice pick. When the patient can no longer count backwards or remember the words to the song the procedure is over. They figure they've destroyed enough of the person's personality to render them safe.

The operation was not a success. It was botched. Actually poor Rosemary lost most of her personality, her fiery, mischievous nature, the very attributes that made her "Rosemary" – which reminds me of the movie *Suddenly Last Summer*, where Katherine Hepburn wants to get Elizabeth Taylor lobotomized, except there was no Montgomery Clift to step in at the last minute to save poor "Rosemary." She's still living today, tucked away somewhere being cared for by the nuns. Rendered helpless but safe.

It terrified Pat and her sisters to realize that they were in such a vulnerable position – get a little out of control and there's always the ol' ice pick procedure awaiting. I always thought that I had the worst childhood imaginable in this country but Pat's story made me think that even people with families, even people with rich families, have their own special brand of nightmares to deal with.

Yet Rose, the female head of the "house of Kennedy," did nothing to stop Joe from having the lobotomy done on her oldest daughter, nor did she do anything to stop her husband's affairs. She turned her cheek again and again at all the emotional slaps Joe gave her. While he was carrying on a long term affair with Gloria Swanson, the sex star of the 1920s, Rose was out praying and shopping.

Pat says that it was awful for her and I believe it. With all those brothers and sisters, each one brilliant in their own way, it was impossible to feel special. Her older sister Eunice was the father's favorite. She had a mind like a man, he used to say. Pat felt like a failure. Like a misfit. And I'm the world's biggest misfit, soon to be making a movie of the same name in which, I guess, I'll be playing the title role. So I understand.

Pat grew up a in a religious family. Saying the rosary every night and all of that. I'm pretty sure she was a virgin when she married Peter and

I'm also sure she was totally unprepared for sex in general—but sex with Peter to be more specific.

Poor Pat, going into a marriage bed like the one Peter had waiting for her, coming from a family where a woman's role in sex was to have babies. When Peter has a few drinks in him, he's fond of telling everyone within earshot how Pat crosses herself before and after sex.

But coming from such a strict background and all, Pat was sort of drawn to the show business scene. It was like being let out of the convent at last and into the world of lust and greed and sex—a little razzle dazzle. The Hollywood set holds a strange fascination for her which repels her and attracts her at the same time. Peter was the epitome of that attraction and repulsion, so what else was there for her to do but marry him?

I guess I am the epitome of the image that Hollywood offers of a woman. Pat was attracted to that. In many ways I am the opposite of her – but I do hold that peculiar mix of fascination and…is "repellent" a word?

She thinks I'm the most beautiful woman in the world. She says she envies my beauty so.

I like Pat's looks. She has an open and friendly face, a face that loves to laugh. When I first met her, I thought she was sort of plain but I grew to like her so much that each time I saw her she became more and more attractive until one day I arrived at her house and I couldn't get over how beautiful she was. Because I love her, I love looking at her the way you love looking at someone you're genuinely fond of. She feels the same way about me. Soon after we met she was saying, "Marilyn you're so gorgeous, you're so sexy."

So with all of our screwed up feelings about sex and family (although for very different reasons) Pat and I were sort of drawn together. Somewhere in this world, Florida to be precise, I have a half-sister. My mother had a daughter before me, Bernice is her name, but she was long gone, living with her father, before I was born. I hardly know her. Pat is more my sister than my sister. My spiritual sister, if you will.

Pat seems to really approve of me being with Jack. She says we're good together. I couldn't help but ask her about her sister in law. One...uh... Jacqueline Bouvier Kennedy. Pat calls her "The Statue."

"I can't feel close to her," Pat told me. "Everything she does is so perfect and pristine."

Sometimes you tell yourself the things you want to hear: I get the feeling that Jack's marriage to Jacqueline was an arrangement. He probably looked around and found the woman who would look and sound and feel the best on his arm at society dinners and political functions. The woman who would make him look the most appealing.

That makes me feel less guilty about being with him.

I also get the feeling that Jack's never been in love. Why should he be? He comes from a large, loving family of great wealth – and all the power that goes with that. Why should he fall under the weakening influence of something like love?

Pat says, "You and Jack belong together. Leave everything to me," and she sets up our little meetings at her place.

When Jack arrived at the beach house he said he didn't have much time. He wanted to get right down to business.

I didn't exactly object.

We went straight to the guest bedroom, I with little cartoon hearts popping out from over my blonde head. Jack sat on the bed and announced he had a backache.

"How about a bubble bath?" I suggested.

We took a bubble bath in the black onyx bathroom. I poured champagne over his shoulders and gave him a massage. "That'll make your back feel better," I said.

"I can think of something else that would make me feel even better," he said and, in the warm water, he pulled me on top of him. Then he said, "We fit well together."

Just then Peter barged into the bathroom with his camera and made out like he was going to take a picture of the two of us in the tub. "Freeze!" he shouted merrily. But just before he was about to snap I screamed for him to stop and he burst out laughing.

To my surprise Jack, who was also laughing, said he <u>wanted</u> Peter to take our picture. He liked the idea of two "immortals" immortalized on film. For him it was like a frolic of the gods in a pond on Mount Olympus and before I knew it – "SNAP!" "FLASH!" – Peter was taking pictures. Jack, hamming it up. Me, covered by bubbles, Jack trying to blow the bubbles away. "Oh what the hell," I thought, "It's not as if I have to worry about THESE photos ever getting out."

Finally Jack yelled, "Okay Peter, enough is enough. OUT!" And Peter scampered out like an obedient little pet.

Later, as Jack and I lay in bed I wanted to show Jack my serious side again and I asked him what made him want to be in politics.

"Some people have a hunger in them," he said. "A hunger to matter. To touch people. To make a difference. To affect the world in some way."

All that night I couldn't sleep. How could I explain to him that I had a hunger in me too? I lay in the darkness and watched Jack. His snores were music to me. "I would never get tired of being next to Jack," I thought. And I envied Jacqueline for having him. She probably isn't passionate about him the way I am. She probably never was. The Statue! He deserves someone to be *really* passionate about him. Pat is right! I am better for Jack. (At least that's what I tell myself.)

The next day Jack and I went sailing alone on a borrowed boat. He said, "After I become president, we won't be able to have this kind of privacy." That he was so sure that he'd win the presidency made me admire him all the more. I wish I could have that kind of confidence in myself. If that kind of self-pride came in an injection form I'd give myself a double dose. I'd say, "After I give a brilliant performance in *The Misfits* and win an Academy Award I won't be able to be photographed with you in a bubble bath." But I couldn't be so sure, so I didn't say anything.

We sailed around all afternoon. We drank champagne and ate pate´ from a basket Pat had prepared for us. We swam naked in the sea.

Later, when we were sailing back, the sun was going down and it was getting chilly and Jack put his arm around me and asked, "What are you thinking about?"

The way he looked at me, with such concern and tenderness made me think that, gee, maybe he could love me someday.

"Darling," I said, "all night last night I lay awake watching you and thinking about what you said about having a hunger in you to affect the world in some way. I've known this kind of hunger—and other kinds of hunger too! Do you think people are born with it? This hunger? Or is it something they develop because of the kind of lives they've led?"

Jack mulled it over and replied "A combination, I think."

Jack told me that he had an older brother who died in the war, Joe, Jr. He was good – looking, brilliant, charismatic, etc. It was he, the older brother, who Joe Kennedy, Sr. was grooming to be president. It was Joe, Sr.'s lifelong obsession to have his son rule the nation. But when Joe, Jr. died, all the father's attention was turned full force onto Jack.

"I was terrified," Jack told me. "Terrified that I wouldn't be able to live up to my brother's image in my father's eyes. That's when the hunger started to grow in me. A hunger to do better. Be better. Every time I achieved something I couldn't enjoy it, all I could do was look to the next level, the higher level.

"Oh my God," I thought. "In so many was he's just like me!"

When I was a child and no one loved me or wanted me or even paid the slightest bit of attention to me, I used to think that I was invisible. Literally. I thought no one could see me and that's why I was so ignored. That's when the hunger in me developed. The hunger to make myself so beautiful and so wonderful that people HAD to see me and hear me!

Yet every time I achieved some success in Hollywood, I really couldn't enjoy it for very long. Instead I started thinking about the next thing, rising to the next level, becoming more beautiful and more successful, lest I become invisible again.

I'm always afraid someone will take success away from me.

When I became popular for being a sex symbol, I knew that it couldn't last forever. So it became important for me to improve everything I could about myself—so that people would see other sides of me—I would especially like to be thought of as a real actress.

I was looking at Jack and I thought "I will never want anyone or anything as much as I want Jack Kennedy." And suddenly it occurred to me that no one really knows who I am. Who the real Marilyn Monroe or Norma Jeane – is.

I've never told anyone. I've never even confronted myself with who I am. Now, for the first time, it became important to me for someone to know who I was and who I am. The real me. Not the woman I present to my friends or my lovers or my public. Me! After all, there is a real person in here somewhere.

I often think that I can't be the only person in the world who feels this way, who longs to connect, who wants to believe in tenderness. But then I think that something in me makes me view everyone in the world as my enemy, as someone who is looking to see what they can get out of me. It destroys everything in my life, this feeling does. Whether it's true or not.

My good friend, Monty Clift, once told me that we all develop our masks early on in life, to cover up the weakest parts of ourselves, and that we realize that we really love someone when we want to lift the mask and reveal to the other person what lies underneath. The true un-masked self.

I know what he means now. I think that if you truly love someone you have to reveal yourself to them completely. You want them to know you inside and out and you want to know them. Everything about them. Everything! It's, like, if you can just connect with one person...one true connection where you both are the purest form of yourself...then you can let down all your guards and give over all your control to him and just truly live.

I've told so many lies in my life in the course of creating Marilyn Monroe. Sometimes I forget who I am myself.

And so as we sailed with the sunset shadowing our faces with a romantic, flattering light, I gave up all my resistance to Jack. I let down all my fences and peeled away the masks. I said, "Let me move closer to you and slowly and softly tell you what happened to a scared and lonely little girl." And Jack moved in closer and held me tightly and I told him my story.

Here it is:

I've been involved with so many men in my life.

I remember when I was shooting my first cover for *LIFE* magazine the photographer, while he was taking my picture, asked me how old I had been the first time I loved a man. He was trying to get me in what I call an "oozier mood."

"Seven," I whispered.

He was in shock. "Marilyn," he exclaimed, "Seven? – How old was the man?"

I lowered my lids and licked my lips and purred, "Younger."

He got the shot he was looking for.

But if I was to seriously consider the question, "How old were you, Marilyn, when you lost your virginity?" the truth is, I can't remember ever having it.

My real name is Norma Jeane Baker.

I know there's been a lot written about me being sexually abused as a child. Some journalists, the ones who hate me, have said that I made it all up to make people feel sorry for me. But it is true. Sure I may have made up specific incidents or exaggerated others and also left some things out. But part of the truth is always there. Yes, I may have called it rape when someone didn't do anything but…uh…touch me "there"…but when a little girl is taken advantage of for sex, in any way, isn't it rape?

You must understand that I never belonged to anyone. I don't know if you can imagine what that feels like. To never have protection. Maybe you can. I don't know.

I've never truly known who my father is. I'm not sure my mother knew. After I was born my mother became mentally ill and there were times when she was in an institution. One of my earliest memories is my mother trying to smother me in my crib. What I remember is a woman with red hair holding a pillow over my face—and soon there was no air and I was gasping and choking. Years later, as an older child, I confronted my mother with this memory. She told me that it wasn't her but my grandmother who had tried to smother me with a pillow – but I didn't believe her then and I don't believe her now.

Growing up, I spent very little time with my mother. During her sick periods I was sent to live with a lot of different foster families. Some of them were nice enough, but I didn't belong to them and they never let me forget it.

When I was a little girl, going from foster home to foster home, in between orphanages, some of the men, some of the "fathers," did molest me. They don't fit the profile of what you would expect of a molester though. These were respectable men. Upright and moral. Some of them were even fanatically religious.

I remember the first song I ever learned was called, *Jesus Loves Me, This I know.* So at least I knew something.

These men who I was sent to, to take care of me, had wives and daughters of their own. When I came along from nowhere and they were paid their twenty-five dollars a month to care for me, they regarded me as an interesting new toy that had invaded their home, or some exotic pet to be studied and played with. I don't remember the first time it happened – but I remember it always happening – as far back as I can remember. But then, I didn't know it was wrong because it was always there as a part of life.

I grew up knowing nothing of love. Nothing except that somewhere, some man named Jesus – a man out of my reach and untouchable – loved me. It was all I knew.

One of the times I do specifically remember being molested – but it wasn't the first – was when I was living with a woman who I called Aunt Grace and her husband who was called "Doc," although he certainly was no doctor. Grace was my mother's best friend. She never had any children of her own and, after my mother was institutionalized, Grace sort of took it upon herself to take care of me. But I didn't really belong to her. She was kind to me but when I got in the way of her life, or money got low, that's when I was shipped off to another foster home or orphanage.

When she was going through a sort of "up" period, she'd haul me out and bring me back to live with her, wherever that might be at the time. After Grace married Doc, her life became much more settled so she took me in to live with them. Doc liked to drink his alcohol quite a bit, and in most of my foster homes I was taught this was the quickest road to Hell. But I didn't let it bother me as long as he left me alone. Which wasn't often.

I was about nine-years-old now and Aunt Grace and I became girl-friends, in a sense. We'd go to the movies together. Aunt Grace loved the movies. "Norma Jeane," she'd say, "someday you're gonna be a famous actress. Even more famous than Jean Harlow." Jean Harlow was known as the "Platinum Blonde." She was beautiful and funny and all the men always wanted her. She was our favorite movie star. It was too late for Aunt Grace to become famous, so she wanted it for me.

If life is in blazing, glorious Technicolor, when I think back on those days I remember everything in black and white. Dreary. Grim. That's when I started wanting to become an actress. It seemed to me that every-one loved the movies. Everyone loved the movie stars. I know I did.

Once, when Aunt Grace was out shopping with a girlfriend, Doc asked me if I'd like to go to the movies with him. Well, I never said "no" to the movies. Never. So we went to the theater and, on this day, he was extra nice to me. He even bought me candy and popcorn. That was something that never happened.

When we got home, Aunt Grace still wasn't there and I was afraid. We had gone to see the movie *Dracula* and that's the main reason why I was frightened. But there was something else. Something that felt dangerous hovering in the air. Something I couldn't explain and couldn't name. I was alone in the house with Doc and it just didn't feel right.

We sat down on the sofa. An old, faded floral-print couch. I can see it now. Doc was teasing me, scaring me about the vampires in Los Angeles.

I was telling him: "There is NO such thing as vampires."

And Doc was saying, "There *is* such things as vampires and they live right here in Van Nuys."

I kept repeating, "There is no such thing! There is no such thing!" He got up to turn the lights down and when he sat down again, closer to me this time, he said that there was one, a vampire, living right here on this property. He said the vampire slept in the garage during the day in that big, old suitcase and roamed the neighborhood at night looking for blood.

I imagined the vampire curled up in the suitcase in the garage with his pasty, white face and horrible red mouth, waiting to break free. I was terrified.

My heart was pounding. I moved closer to Doc and he put an arm around me. He said, "Don't be afraid, Norma. He's a very friendly vampire. If you close your eyes he'll just take a tiny bit of your blood and then he'll leave you alone.

I only half-believed Doc but the movie was fresh enough in my mind for me to play along with him. I closed my eyes and lay down on the worn couch. Suddenly I felt Doc, or the vampire, very close to me. I could feel his breath, very hot on my face. I could smell his hair tonic, the cigarettes he had smoked, the alcohol on his breath – smells that in later years I'd come to associate with sex. But at the moment they smelled curious. Vaguely sinful, but new and a little thrilling. I felt his mouth, open, press down on my neck. Somewhere in me I knew it wasn't Dracula. I knew it was Doc, touching and sucking on me, but just in case, just in case…I went along with it.

When he sucked in on my skin, I felt a violent feeling rush from the pit of my stomach – shooting a million shockwaves through my entire body – as if I was being electrocuted. First on my neck and then he moved, not to my mouth but to the place just on the corner of my mouth. He sucked in on the skin there. He held the skin in his mouth for a long time and I felt the thrilling sensation in my…um…unmentionable place, and I knew I should stop him but I felt curious and horrified and aroused and scared and I was unable to move.

Then he touched me "there" and probed his finger, slipping it into my underpants, still kissing the side of my mouth. But it wasn't a kiss. It was something I didn't have a word for yet. Something astonishingly new. His finger went gently in me, and I tensed up! I guess, I gasped or something because he got afraid and withdrew his finger from me and left the room in a hurry. Leaving me there in the dark.

I lay on the couch for a very long time. The feelings he had aroused in me, which stopped abruptly, had left me drained of all feeling. Where is everybody? I pretended the vampire had sucked me dry. I was a corpse, cold and unable to move and absolutely unfeeling.

Later, when my body finally came back to me, I went to my bedroom and looked in the mirror. I was flushed and wasn't able to really see myself at first but after a moment I became horrified. There was a round purple mark on the side of my mouth. Deep, dark purple. Was it a death mark? Were there really vampires in Van Nuys? Was this their mark? Would I become one now? Or was it a stain of the sin I committed with Doc? The mysterious kiss, indelibly marked on my face. Would the mark ever go away? I scrubbed at it and scrubbed at it with my toothbrush, but that only made the purple deeper and the skin around the mark red – calling even more attention to the stain.

Later, when Aunt Grace saw the mark she was as horrified as I was. "Who did that to you? Who did that to you!?" she screamed. I don't know what scared me more, Aunt Grace finding out that there were vampires in Van Nuys and I was one of them now, or the fact that Doc has sucked on my face. I made up a story that it was only a bruise because I had been hit in the face with a baseball that the boys in the playground were tossing around. How ludicrous that sounds now! Aunt Grace wasn't fooled. That woman knew a hickey when she saw one.

That night I heard her shrieking at Doc. I could hear their voices rising and then hushing. I couldn't make out all the words but I knew the argument was about me. Of course, a few days later I was shipped off to another orphanage.

I stopped telling Jack my childhood story after the encounter with Doc. It was enough for him to understand how deeply I understood his hunger. I had a hunger in me too. A hunger to become so marvelous, so important, so loved that no one could touch me when I didn't want to be touched. A hunger to be the kind of person no one could violate.

Later on, back at the beach house on our last night together before I had to fly back to New York and he headed back to Washington, we kissed with a new tenderness. Later on that night, he poured himself into me with thunder and lightning and things that were frightening (forgive me for my slippery poetry).

"I could get used to this," he said.

Undated Letter Taped Above the Following Entry

Dear Marilyn,

It's impossible for anyone to spend even the briefest amount of time with you without being moved. I look forward to more.

Jack

Undated July 1960 Entry

Jack sent me a note saying how moved he is when he spends time with me. That's how men respond to me—they are touched by the part in me that has been hurt so often. The little girl part. It's like they want to protect me.

I remember one foster father who was very kind to me. The way a real father, I imagine, would be with his daughter. He looked just like the handsome movie star Clark Gable, with black shiny hair and a thin mustache. He always smelled like sweet soap. I don't remember what he did for a living but sometimes when he came home he would bring me a special treat—a piece of candy or a small toy.

Sometimes when I was scampering past him he'd swoop me up in his arms and say, "Who are you? Where are you going? What's your destination, little girl?"

Even then my young mind took the questions to heart: I didn't know the answer.

It became a sort of game we played. Oh, how I wanted this man to be my real Daddy! But his wife, a pretty petite lady, didn't like it when he gave me attention. They had three young children of their own. She didn't appreciate him favoring me. "Now, Hank," she'd say, "Leave the child alone." And he would wink at me conspiratorially.

My child's mind told me that he was Clark Gable! And I was living with him for a time while he wasn't busy making a movie.

I was only with this family for a short time. Yet I never forgot him. His gentle voice. His playful, kind nature. I would go see Clark Gable in the movies and I imagined it was him. I always pretended he was my real father and that I would be reunited with him someday. I'd be walking down the street and he would pass by and ask, "What's your destination, little girl?"

All my adult life most people have looked at me like I'm a beautiful invalid. Everyone thinks I'm vulnerable. I _am_ vulnerable! But vulnerability can also be a power.

Men like to play the savior (although they never truly are one.) This is something that I discovered and used early in my career. It was not manipulation on my part. It was survival.

I've told different things to different writers and after a while the lie becomes the truth and vice versa. I've decided from now on I'm going to write things as they happened to set the record straight, as they say. Telling Jack my story last week started me thinking: I'm sure they'll be writing books about me after I'm dead and someone should know what really happened. I've always written things down but I've been scattered. I'm going to try to be more disciplined in my journal keeping.

Not that I think I'm so important to history or anything like that, but people do seem to enjoy reading about me so they might as well know the truth. Well, not my generation – they wouldn't understand – but other generations, if they care to.

July 19, 1960

Why am I so afraid? I don't want to be afraid. I want to move forward. I want to act. I want to keep improving. And yet there is this fear, this unbearable fear. Actually, it's more like a strangulation.

What most people don't understand about me is that I'm the perfect prototype of a perfectionist. I always want to get it right. Whatever it is I'm doing I pour my whole self into it. It's not just in the way I look, although people like to say that that's all I care about. It's about everything I do. If I am sweeping a floor or washing a dish I'm going to do the best job I can, you know?

But I especially want to be at my best when I step in front of a camera. The most important thing in the world to me is to be wonderful. That's what frightens me most about shooting this new movie. I just feel it's nearly impossible to be any good in it.

I have to leave Los Angeles tomorrow and then on to Reno for the start of filming. I've been nervous before I began filming every movie of my career but I've never been more afraid than now—of making this film. *The Misfits.*

You know it's almost sort of funny, Arthur is telling everyone he wrote the screenplay as a valentine for me. He wants to be the hero in my history. He comes across as the wonderful, loving husband and brilliant playwright who used his sacred talent to write his sexy-comedic-star wife a dramatic script so she could prove to the world that she is a talented, serious actress.

Meanwhile, the truth is, I'm making the movie as a valentine for *him*! Not that I feel like giving him valentines at this point in our relationship – I can't wait to announce our plan to divorce after filming – but I did love him once and I feel I owe him something for loving me at one time.

And the reason I say I'm doing the movie for him is because, if I didn't agree to appear in *The Misfits* no one would have put up the money to get it made and all of Arthur's hard work would go down the drain. So you see? Subtext! There is a subtext to the story the media is putting out there.

Even when someone seems to be doing something for me out of love, I'm the one who's being used. Even by my own husband.

Arthur's trick, and he is quite masterful at it, is to make everyone think that bit by bit he's given up his writing career to take care of me. That he gave up his genius for love of me.

Unknown to everyone is that Arthur was dried up as a writer long before he met me. He admitted it to me early on in our relationship when there was still trust and hope between us. He was blocked. He had triumphed early on as a young man with his play *Death of a Salesman,* but all of his plays since then have been considered lesser works. He felt he might not ever write another play again. But with Marilyn Monroe as his wife he is assured to get a movie made.

Maybe I should leave this diary out in the open for him to read my true feelings, the way he left his journal out in plain sight so I'd be sure to understand what he truly felt about me.

Someone recently said to me, and I'm going to paraphrase here because it was such a marvelous insight from a very brilliant writer and it really hit the target: "I find it difficult to believe that having a beautiful young wife with a fantastic career and who is famous around the world would cause a writer to stop writing. It seems to me it would be the other way around. I think his writing had dried up and he sought you out, Marilyn, because his own career had hit a dead end."

My whole body filled with relief. Someone sees! Someone understands what I now know to be the truth. But, still, I didn't want to bad mouth Arthur so all I said was, "No comment."

Let's not leave me out of this. I'll take my share of blame. I wanted to be taken seriously. He was a way towards that. He wanted to write for the movies. My dream was to act on the stage.

Even so, Arthur offered his script to my own studio, Fox and they turned it down. It's my name, my box-office reputation, that allowed such a strange, non-commercial movie get financed by United Artists.

I don't want to be mean about it and I don't know much about a lot of things, but I did learn to be shrewd about scripts. And I think *The Misfits* is talky, pedantic, static and pretentious. Is that mean? What could I say? I could lie and praise it and say it's a great work and that I am flattered that he wrote it for me. But I'll say that to the press. Here in my private writings I'll say, I don't want to do it. True, the girl I'm going to play is obviously based on me but, as far as I'm concerned, she's just a cardboard character. You might even say she's a caricature of me—even though it's attempting to be a flattering caricature. I don't see it that way.

What's the movie about? *The Misfits*? Where do I begin?

Actually some of the themes of the story are quite wonderful. It is Arthur's execution of much of the story I have problems with. It's about a very sensitive, lonely women, Roslyn, (me!) who travels to Reno for a divorce and gets mixed up with three cowboys: Clark Gable, Montgomery

Clift and Eli Wallach. Every character is misplaced. Every character is longing to connect but doesn't seem to know how to change in order to fit in.

My character starts an affair with the Clark Gable character but the two other men also want Roslyn. They see her as a life preserver they can hang on to. She herself has been looking for a savior—as I once was looking for a savior.

Through this script I can see that Arthur is trying to portray my character as a sinned-against angel, adored by men—but since the character is based on me I know the truth about her even more than Arthur does.

She is desirable prey hunted all her life by ravenous men—like the men who had nothing but contempt and scorn for me in my starlet days but wanted to screw me for the sexual excitement I elicited in them. Had I not become a movie star I wouldn't be so adored—actually the number one feeling they had for me after the sex was over was contempt. The character in the movie, Roslyn, is not a movie star. In reality she wouldn't be so revered by the men she encounters in Reno. They would have a certain amount of scorn for her and, perhaps, she could do something to earn their respect. But that doesn't happen in this script.

Arthur Miller is ashamed of my past.

He never said that to me. At least not to my face.

But that's where his diary comes in. He did write his negative feelings about me in his diary just a few weeks after we were married. And let me tell you, because it is monumental to what happened to us, they were harsh words. It was obvious. He's embarrassed by my past reputation in Hollywood, he knows of my past as a "party girl" on the brutal Hollywood circuit, but he tries to be "big" about it in public. Singing praises about me that he doesn't truly believe. He wanted me to know that without coming out and telling me. So leaving the diary out was a coward's ploy.

Now, in *The Misfits* he's trying to justify the fact that he loved me once—even married me—in spite of my "sordid" past. But even he can't explain why he loved me—and there! I just put my finger on the major flaw in the script.

What bothers me most about the script is, well, I once read the quote, "There's no there there," by Gertrude Stein and I immediately jotted it down. It best describes what I feel about my character in *The Misfits*. The three cowboys are always telling her how wonderful she is, how beautiful, how inspiring, but there is nothing in the script that justifies their worship, other than the fact that they find her physically attractive. She doesn't say anything particularly interesting.

As a matter of fact, I find her rather dim-witted. She never really does anything to inspire their adoration. Arthur simply has them all immediately struck by some unseen quality. (It's almost as if Arthur is exploring through his writing why he fell in love with me in the first place. And he isn't coming up with reasons.)

She does not have a substantial identity. In simple terms, as an actress, there is nothing in the character of Roslyn for me to really dig into. It's up to me, in my performance, to identify this "quality" that makes them all view her as more than just a sexual attraction. It's difficult.

What I'm trying to say is that all three cowboys love Roslyn at first sight but the only thing she is, mostly, is neurotic and naive. The only explanation for their admiration is that she's supposed to be beautiful. Sexy and desirable. Is this the main reason Arthur fell in love with me?

As far as the rest of the script, although there is no action, there's plenty of talk, talk, talk. None of it—in my humble but experienced opinion—very interesting.

Eventually, in the story, the three cowboys take Roslyn up to the mountains so they could round up some wild horses to sell. When Roslyn discovers that these "misfit" horses are going to be hunted down and sold to be turned into dog food she relates to the animals, has a hissy fit and... oh, forget it... you'll just have to go see it for yourself. If it ever gets made!

I'm also worried because so much of this will be shot outdoors, in the desert, in the midst of summer! I hear it's over 100 degrees there now.

When Arthur finally gave me that early draft of the screenplay to look at, after working on it for many months, he sat in a chair opposite me watching me as I began reading. He lit his pipe and sat there puffing. I felt his eyes on me as I read, puffing, watching. Waiting for a reaction.

I liked the cowboy characters a lot. They seemed real to me—alive and believable. But when it came to the female lead, that's when I became apprehensive.

I saw that he had used actual lines I had said to him—but they were taken out of context. They weren't given any backstory—the reasons why I said these things. Perhaps if you were there when I said them they would seem charming. But the way the lines are incorporated in the script, they come out of the blue and don't make sense and make the character seem dumb. I, well, I have to say, I hated it.

"Excuse me," I said, "but what is this?"

"What's wrong?" he said.

"Is this what you think of me?" I asked him.

He scowled at me. "They all want her," he said gravely.

"For what?" I truly wanted to know. "Why do they want her?"

"I think, maybe, you're not understanding all the underlying themes," he said.

There was a stony silence for a moment while I worked up the courage to say something I have been wanting to say for a long time.

"You know, Arthur, the time for that is over."

"The time for what?"

"For making me feel like I'm so inferior to you."

"If you feel inferior to me, Marilyn, it's nothing that I'm doing. Look to your own past. You're used to reading a certain kind of story. Mostly lightweight…"

"I think I've earned the right to have an opinion on a script," I said. "And maybe, just now, I'm finding the confidence to say what I feel. Like when we first met, with your lectures and your reprimands and your criticism on the things I said…"

"You wanted me to educate you, Marilyn. You practically begged me. And I tried. You were screaming for help."

"The way you criticized me after we'd been with your friends. As if I wasn't good enough for them to like me for who I was..."

He cut me off, showing anger at last. "When we first got engaged you were considered a joke, being used by a group of men who were only trying to further their careers."

"And now I'm..." I stopped. I wanted to let it go.

"And now you're what?" he practically sneered.

My voice became a whisper. I could hardly speak the horrible truth: "Now I'm married to a man who is using me to further his career."

When I met him I had even less confidence than I have today. I knew that he was considered brilliant and I felt honored that he would want me. Especially since no one else seemed to take me seriously. What I learned since then is that knowing all the intellectual words doesn't make you any better (or smarter) than anyone else.

"Marilyn, you're so used to playing in fluff, you don't even recognize a good script. I wrote this for you."

"No," I said sadly. "You wrote it for yourself."

(Later)

Once again I was condescended to.

He told me I'd grow to understand the story, as if I was too stupid to get it on a first reading. He said it was a draft. He'd be revising some of it. The wall that was up between us grew stronger and higher.

"I had an affair," I blurted out. I was talking about Yves Montand. He knew I had an affair with Yves. And I knew he knew. I didn't bring it up now to hurt him. I wanted to force him to confront the fact that I am a real person, with flaws and complexities. He always knew this about me. But he refuses to acknowledge it because it would uncover his shame. I wanted him to put some flaws and complexities into the character or Roslyn. They didn't have to be *my* issues. Just something that makes her real.

"I know about the affair," he said. "Everyone knows. Do you really think that I was surprised? It only confirmed what everyone always thought of you."

Actually it confirmed what *he* always thought of me. But I didn't say that. How do you defend adultery?

I had the affair with Yves when we were in the middle of making *Let's Make Love*, which had a screenplay even more awful than Arthur's. A Fox studio film. I had to do it. I owed it in my contract. A big splashy musical without any splash. Not a single funny line or situation.

Arthur and I were already not getting along and at the time I still had hopes for a savior. The joke to be inserted here is that I took the title of the film too seriously. I had made love with my leading man in that movie. Big mistake. I thought I was in love.

The only reason I mention it here is because I want to let you know I'm not blameless. Not that I deserve any awards for this fact but that was the first time I committed adultery during our marriage. I don't know, maybe the affair was partially a revenge on Arthur for disappointing me so much.

To be fair to Arthur there are a few scenes in *The Misfits* that are absolutely lovely. If these vignettes had to stand on their own they would be very interesting. But when strung together, along with the long, dull scenes, as an entire story, it doesn't work. I could tell from reading the script that there's not enough action and there's not enough conflict and in the long run the story just comes across as boring and preachy.

But then my personality divides again and the other half of me says to myself, "What do you know, Miss Marilyn Monroe? After all, it's good enough for Clark Gable to want to do it. It's good enough for Monty Clift to do it. And it's good enough for John Huston to direct it. So there must be something in it that I don't see."

And another thing I must say. Maybe all my opinions are just my fear manifesting itself. Maybe buried in my subconscious is the fear that the script is beautiful, better than I am. That I can't do it justice. That's just another perspective I must explore and admit to myself.

And what <u>do</u> I know? Maybe John Huston will pull off a miracle and make the whole thing work. Maybe I'll surprise myself and give a good performance and really end up being respected. Stranger things have happened in my life, that's for sure.

July 19, 1960

It's starting to get around a little bit that Jack and I had been seeing each other in Los Angeles and that something might be developing between us. It's a very select group of people in politics and show business, the "high ups" who are saying, "Well, Jack is young and sexy and handsome, that's part of his appeal, and the American public is obsessed with celebrities, so maybe a fling with Marilyn Monroe will add glamour to his image, make him more popular and be good for his campaign." And other people are saying, "Well, no one wants a philanderer in the White House and his affair with Monroe will destroy his chances at the Presidency."

Me? I'm torn.

Sometimes I don't want to think "in the scheme of things." I'd rather live in the "right now." I want Jack to become the president. I believe in him. The country needs him and he will do wonderful things...

But another part of me, the selfish part, realizes that although I will be involved with the most important man in the world, as president, Jack will become almost impossible to get next to. Yet I need him, too. It's difficult enough to see him now; there's constantly an air of great secrecy and importance surrounding him. And there's always the stiff-lipped, stone-faced bodyguards, or whatever they are, protecting him and frowning on my relationship with him, but loving him and devoted to him nevertheless.

The main thing is I must not put unrealistic hopes in him. I've idealized most of the men who I've loved and who have loved me. That's the phase, I guess, I'm in now. My mind is turning him into some kind of god. I must, must, must keep my expectations down and let things develop with a foundation in reality, rather than what I need (or hope for.)

People have said to me I have become their fantasy. Maybe that's what Jack is to me—just a fantasy that gives me something to look forward to, to dream about.

Keep in mind: Every time I am frightened I allow my emotions to get out of control. And I have been frightened every day of my life.

July 20, 1960

Just a note: I have my period- very bad – and I spent the entire night writhing about in agony. No sleep. No sleep again. From physical pain and mental fear. Bags under my eyes. The massive amounts of blood and the agony seem to be physical manifestations of my fears. I look awful and I'm on my way to film the most important film of my career. The movie, the movie, *The Misfits*. The entire crew is waiting. The cast is waiting. Clark Gable is waiting.

August 3, 1960 (Reno Nevada)

I was in the hotel bedroom going over my lines. Saying them out loud. Trying to get them to sink in. Arthur was in the living room area typing. He called out using his annoyed voice, "Marilyn, could you make an attempt to learn your lines quietly? I'm trying to write."

We were in our suite at The Mapes Hotel where the entire cast and crew of *The Misfits* is staying.

I walked into the living room. "When you have to get in front of the cameras and perform a scene, then you can tell me how I should learn my lines."

He continued typing without a reply.

"What are you writing, anyway," I asked.

"I'm rewriting the scene between you and Gable for tomorrow."

I was astonished. "You're re-writing *that* scene? Then why am I in there trying to learn these lines if you're changing them?"

"What difference does it make," he said. "You won't have them memorized either way."

It was a low blow but I didn't want to respond to it. I've been feeling so sick and weak and every argument only robs me of more energy.

Instead I said, "Arthur, there's a scene in the script I've been looking at."

No response. He just kept right on typing.

"Arthur, I wanted to ask you about this scene." I couldn't let it go. Acting in this script. Saying these lines. All the while knowing he based it on me is bringing up things in me that are confusing, hurtful.

Still, he refused to acknowledge me.

I went on, "Roslyn's lover says to her, 'I could have looked down my nose at you too—showing yourself off in a nightclub for so much a night. But I didn't."

In the scene, her lover, Gay, is talking about her past. Once she had ambitions to be a dancer but ended up dancing in nightclubs. The inference is she was a stripper. 'Roslyn' is me. 'Gay' is Arthur. He's talking to me through the script. See, I had started out wanting to be an actress and I ended up being a sex symbol. The subtext is saying that he had the right to be embarrassed by me because he (and others) thought the things I had to do in order to become a success were dirty—and that people viewed my career lewdly—but he married me anyway. He made a big public show of not looking down his nose at me.

I wanted him to acknowledge this.

"Arthur," I said. "Gay looked down on Roslyn because of her past, right? I need to know because it depends on how I play the scene. When he says, 'I took my hat off to you anyway.' He means he accepted her in spite of the things he thinks she did. Right? I mean, for once, be honest."

There was a knock at the door.

"Come in," Arthur shouted.

It was a bellboy wheeling in a tray. I guess Arthur had ordered room service.

"Your lunch, Mr. Miller," the boy said

Arthur just kept right on typing. He still didn't look up. The boy waited, confused.

"One moment, please." I said. I went into the bedroom and found my purse. I took out several bills.

"Here you go," I said to the boy, handing him his tip.

He beamed. "Thank you, Miss Monroe." He floated out on a cloud. That's the nice part, you know? I can always depend on the public loving me a little.

Arthur said, "That doesn't make them respect you anymore, you know. You can't buy respect."

"Arthur," I said, "when someone does a service for you, you tip them. You can't buy good manners or kindness either."

He stopped typing. He was ready to strike. He said, "Huston saw you wandering around the hotel corridors nude last night."

I said, "What has that got to do with what I'm asking you about the script?"

"It means you're taking too many pills. It means you're wandering around the hotel naked. It means a journalist can see you like that. I didn't hear you get up."

"No," I said. "You didn't hear me. You never do."

That night we went to bed without talking. The answer to the question was "Yes." He did consider my character soiled. He did look down on me. He did think he was superior to me. He had been embarrassed to be associated with me.

The next night he slept on the couch.

We didn't talk on the set at all except angry sarcastic comments. Mostly by me. He wants to come across as the saint. Yet…

I know monsters, having dealt with them all my life.

He is, shall I say, a particular brand. He is a passive monster. He does his little malicious maneuvers quietly.

For instance, he keeps trying to communicate things to me through the script. I noticed that in the latest version of the ending he has one of the cowboys say about my character, "She's crazy. They're all crazy. You try not to believe that because you need them. She's crazy! You struggle. You build. You try. You turn yourself inside out for them. But it's never enough. So they put the spurs to you."

He also wants the movie finished no matter what so he stays as passive and in control as possible in front of the others. The same reason why he never confronted me about my affair with Yves Montand. He sees me as a loose cannon. If I go off, or breakdown, the production closes down with me.

They don't know how, when I loved and trusted him most, he got rid of all the people around me who really were trying to help me. All the people who really had my best interests at heart. He got rid of them so he would have complete control of my career. Leading up to this movie.

He knew how I worshipped him. He knew how I had been, sort of like, a small craft adrift without any kind of sail. I longed to have someone to navigate me to safety. Now, well, here I am! In the most dangerous waters of my life.

Last night, without discussing it, he began packing his things to move to another room in the hotel.

He said: "You want honest. Okay. Here's my truth: All you've been for your entire life is a sexy 'piece' trying to take yourself seriously. You were a joke. Your name—Marilyn—floating from one leering man to the next in the stink of sweaty locker rooms and through fogs of cheap cigar smoke. They were chewing you up and spitting you out. And you allowed it! You are a willing participant in some sick way! They laughed and you laughed with them. And I…I joined in the laughter. But then I thought, by God! I'll play God. What man wouldn't grab at that opportunity? What I've been trying to do is to mold you into something more, to prove to them, and to you, and even to myself, that you're not just a sexy 'piece.' You're not just a joke. I've written you *this* script so you have a chance to prove it to yourself and to everyone else. But you know what, I have no power to recreate you. You are what you are."

It hurt me! It did hurt me! It hurt me at a time in my life when my body was too defenseless to take on a new hurt.

So there it was. Finally the truth. The simple reality of his anger towards me and my fury towards him. I guess we both always felt it but refused to confront it. His phantom guilt for loving me from the day he left his first wife to be with me. Because I was in his eyes always a joke he couldn't resist.

"Did you ever *really* love me?" I whispered as he was heading for the door.

He paused for a long time, measuring how he was going to let down the hatchet.

"I always sensed that it was doomed. But I deluded myself. I was helpless by the pull of you. But I can't save you. I don't have the key to you, Marilyn. I never did."

I said, "You might have saved us both a lot of pain if you didn't delude yourself....and me."

"Try to be on time tomorrow," he said. Then he closed the door on our marriage.

August ? 1960

It's bad. Much worse than I thought.

When I finally am able to get myself on the set, everyone has been waiting for hours and hours. "She's here," you can hear them call out to each other. They're mad. They've been there, ready to start shooting, for a long time.

Yes, yes. I'm late. But there are reasons outside of my own fears. I guess John Huston realizes the script isn't working and he has Arthur re-writing the scenes every day.

I've already started learning my lines for tomorrow. There's a knock on the door. A delivery of a re-write. Everything in the scene has been changed. I have to start all over, memorizing new lines—and, really, they're not any better than the ones in the previous version. I take a pill. I start memorizing and it's getting later and later. I'm so nervous. I'm due on the set, in the desert, in the early morning.

Of course I am expected to be beautiful.

The anxiety! I can't sleep. But I must sleep. And I must memorize. What's more important, to get some sleep so I'm fresh for work or to make sure I know every line before the morning?

I take another pill.

I still feel wide awake. I don't dare look at the clock. I'm thinking about the next day's scene. I'm thinking about my marriage to Arthur being over – another hope dead. I think about Jack in Washington and wonder if he's thinking about me. And I take another pill because now I <u>must</u> get to sleep.

I ask, "Why is my mind so alive at night?"

They ask: "Why are her eyes so dead in the morning?"

I'm in bed with my eye shades on, waiting for the medication to do its job and knock me out. I say to myself: "If I can fall asleep now, right now, right this very minute, I can get enough sleep to function tomorrow." But that only puts the pressure on me and wakes me up all the more. So I take another pill and by this time I don't remember how many I've taken. I get up to go to the bathroom.

The sun is already rising.

It seems like there has been no night. No time of rest. Instead all the days and nights bleed together resulting in one endlessly long, hot, troubling day.

Before I know it, it's 6 am. Time for me to begin again. And, suddenly, miraculously, cruelly, what I have been waiting for all night happens: I'm tired! I want to sleep. I'm just starting to close my eyes. I don't want to work. I want oblivion. I feel dead in the morning.

I don't have the energy to get out of bed, and they're calling for me and I don't answer the phone. It keeps ringing and ringing—begging for an answer like a nagging hag.

It's time to drive out to the desert and start filming. But I'm not ready. I can't shake off the pills. It's all foggy. My eyes are swollen. They couldn't possibly be made up in their current state of puffiness.

I don't come out of my room for hours. My makeup man, my acting coach, Paula Strasberg, the rest of my entourage are waiting to drive with me to the location. They know, as I know, that everyone else from the cast and crew are already there. I order up coffee. I splash cold water on my face. I sit in front of the mirror. A long time passes.

Then the time comes when I can't put it off any longer. I don't even know what time it is. The afternoon? I must go. I walk out to my waiting—paid—team. We silently start driving to the location. We arrive at the spot in the desert where the scene for the day is set up. I'm hurried into the makeup trailer.

My makeup man, my old friend, Whitey, does my makeup while I'm flat on my back—trying to get in a little more sleep. As I lay dozing, being made up, I dream that I am on the set and I don't know my new lines—a dream that will come true in an hour when I am in front of the cameras.

Then I am standing. The costume is put on. They are adjusting the wig. I am drinking coffee and more coffee. I step out into the blaring sunlight.

Everyone comes alive. They snap to attention. They all have been waiting for me since the morning. By now the morning is long gone. Hours have been wasted. I am mortified.

Vultures have been sent: the photographers and journalists who swarm the set sending out any scrap of news about the production to the media outlets. Once they were friendly. Now they want me to collapse. They want me to overdose. Anything that will give them a worldwide scoop.

Oh my paranoia!

I'm still in a haze. The pills from last night remain in my bloodstream blurring everything, making me feel very slow, very deliberate. I'm trying to concentrate but I don't even know what's holding me up.

And the blazing hot sun. And the pressure! The pressure of all this set up, all these people, depending on me. The camera angles are so complicated, and we have to get this shot quickly because the light is fading, and all the new lines are jumbled in my head. We begin...long complicated unrealistic speeches...if I miss just one line everyone has to start all over. It is 110 degrees. The tempers and the temperatures are boiling.

So many witnesses. So many people on this jury. They all say I'm guilty of treating Arthur terribly. But they don't know. They don't know what has gone on behind the scenes. Behind closed doors. Or behind every situation that led us to this moment. They say I'm horrible to my husband. "Is it true Marilyn threw Arthur out of their hotel room and they're living separately?"

Yes, it is true. We are in different rooms.

They say I'm being disrespectful. "How can she do this to Clark Gable? He's been here since 7 am. Ready to shoot!"

Now the cameras are rolling. I have been given some unrealistic lines to act.

I say, "Birds must be brave to live out here. At night especially whereas they're so small, you know?"

I say, "I never saw anything grow before. How tiny those seeds were and yet they knew they were supposed to be lettuces."

Sometimes it takes me a long time, a lot of takes, to get it right.

People say that I'm late or that I don't come to the set at all or that I can't remember my lines because I don't care. I say, nothing could be further from the truth. I care! I care too much about the quality of the work. I become physically ill. If the scene or the lines aren't as good as they can be—my body reacts. That's another reason why I've been missing so many days.

August 26, 1960

Everything is black.

Suddenly I hear someone in the room. My tomb. I can't open my eyes. They have been sealed shut.

Why are they here? What do they want from me? I only want to be still and think of nothing.

My body is being shook. I hear Paula's voice calling me over and over. I guess it is very late in the day and I am still in bed. At times I had been aware of the phone ringing but I wouldn't have been able to answer it even if I wanted to. I can barely move. Even unconscious I am angry. I hate them all. Paula, my overpaid acting coach, is here to collect her pound of flesh.

I am stuck between life and darkness.

Paula calls for help and he arrives. They lift me out of the bed and start walking me around the room. The pills, my anchors, won't allow me to move. There is a hushed conversation between the two.

My death would be dangerous to all of them.

Each of them labeled a murderer. Each would suffer their own little death in some way. But I would sink deeper and deeper into darkness, peace—away from this hysteria.

"Stop trying to awaken me," I want to shout. "Can't you see what I am seeking?"

But my mouth feels as if it has been sealed too.

They are trying to walk me around the room again. They are splashing cold water on my face. More people are called in. My eyes slit-open for a split second and I see Arthur trying to put his arms around me. A demon face! *Don't touch! Don't touch! Your hands hurt me! They burn!*

I let out a scream. It is so raw and primal it scares even me.

They all step back. Concerned. Frightened.

A doctor is called.

He pumps my stomach.

A female Lazarus brought back to life by her crucifiers.

Once again I'm brought back to the panic and chaos that surrounds me.

One by one they all leave my room. I lay in bed in in darkness. I am in and out of consciousness for two days. Once in a while I hear them all in the other room whispering to each other urgently. What to do? What to do?

I guess the movie had stopped shooting. John Huston, the director comes into my darkened bedroom.

"Marilyn," he says, not unkindly, "Darlin', we're going to shut down the production."

I instantly sprung up in bed. Red hot fury searing through my veins, cutting through my lethargy. Now I am all white hot energy. "Oh no we're not! I'm fine! I'll be on the set tomorrow!"

"You need to rest, honey" he says. "We'll shut down for a few weeks. You get some rest. Then we'll see if you're in condition to shoot."

"Goddammit John! You know if the picture shuts down I'll be ruined. I'll never get insurance to do another movie again. My career will be over."

He looks at me. Hard. Sad. Inscrutable. But I know he knows it's the truth.

"I'll be on the set in the morning. On time. Ready to shoot. Okay?... Okay, John?"

"Okay," he says.

Once I am alone I start taking the Nembutal again.

When I stepped foot on the set the next morning in full makeup, wanting to continue, everyone was surprised. I was shooting a scene with Gable. He began. When I tried to say my line in response it was definitely slurred. We began again. I missed my cue. This wasn't unusual. I'll get it eventually. We were ready to try again when the cameraman approached

John. I heard him say, "I can't shoot her anymore, John. Her eyes won't focus. We'll never get a usable shot."

John sent everyone back to the hotel for the day. It was decided I'd be sent to a hospital in Los Angeles to try and get me off the pills. I had held up things long enough. The movie was very much over budget. It will never be completed at the rate we're going.

I said, "Okay. I'll go."

They used words like detox. But I knew the reality. This was a nervous breakdown.

August 30, 1960

(Carbon Copy of a letter drafted by Monroe to her New York psychiatrist)

Dear Dr. Kris,

I'm in the hospital!

I've made a fool out of myself and can barely stand to be in my own skin. The filming of *The Misfits* has been shut down—because of me. I'm sure you've heard.

They say I'm an addict. They say I need to get off sleeping pills before we can continue shooting. I've even heard them say it's the end of my career.

I can hardly stand to think about what Clark Gable or Montgomery Clift or my other costars are saying. All those brilliant people waiting around that horrible, hot, dry desert because of me. And, yet, the way I feel right now I don't care if the movie never gets finished.

Gable doesn't complain at all, which makes me feel worse. I know in his mind he's saying, "Where the fuck is she?" It tears me apart inside.

When I was growing up I used to fantasize that Clark Gable was my father. I'd see him in the movies all though those horrible "I don't belong to anyone" years, and I'd secretly pretend that I belonged to Clark Gable.

So you can just imagine what it's like for me to be there in the desert making a movie with him. MY CLARK GABLE in a movie with me, playing my lover.

To the press Gable says, "Marilyn is the ultimate woman. She makes a man proud to be a man." To me he says, "Marilyn, you're doing a wonderful job in this picture. Let's work extra hard to get it done." I know he likes me, but he can't help but get mad – waiting around in that heat when all he really wants to do is go home and be with his wife who is expecting their first child.

I'm not even going to write about what I think of Arthur, because I despise him so much at this moment that every good thing I ever felt for him would be crushed.

They don't understand. No one understands what it's like to be me. The pressure I have to live up to this...monster inside of me...who tells me I must succeed. I never wanted to do this picture. I never totally believed in it. How could I be any good in it? Meanwhile, the eyes of the world are on me constantly, waiting for me to fail so they could write it up and make jokes.

Did I mention we're filming outdoors? Did I mention that it's over 110 degrees in the desert? Did I mention that the entire movie company has divided into two camps: those that are for me and those that are against me? Marilyn's team versus Arthur's team.

Oh, Dr. Kris, if I ever make it through this it will be a miracle.

But don't worry too much about me (funny to say that after pouring out all my misery, I know). I know you've got a million things on your mind. I just keep telling myself that soon this whole mess will be over and I can see you and maybe even laugh about it all. Give my love to your family. And give my love to you too.

xoxo,

Marilyn

September 5, 1960

I'm still in the hospital, although the doctors are saying I'm (remarkably) well enough to go back to finish the picture. I'm feeling much better. My Los Angeles psychiatrist, Dr. Greenson, says, "You're very much addicted to sleeping pill but you don't show signs of the typical addict's withdrawal." He's slowly weaning me off and trying to teach me how to sleep. He thinks I am afraid of sleep.

I didn't try to call Jack Kennedy because I fear I'm feeling too desperate. A man will pick up desperation in a woman's voice and that can be a big turn off. Men seem to want a woman more when she's projecting a secure, confident, sensual aura—with maybe just a tad of vulnerability. Well, at least that's a recipe I've discovered works for me.

I didn't try to reach Yves Montand. He didn't return any of my calls after we completed *Let's Make Love* and I suspect the affair with me was part affection and part trying to get the movie done! I don't feel any ill will towards him. If he is happy with his wife, Simone, than I am happy for them both. It's rare to be happy. And I have wonderful memories to look back on. Not now though. My mind is still on THIS movie.

The scene I'm supposed to start filming when I go back to the set, if I ever go back to the set, involves me and Monty Clift. The only true friend I have from the cast is Monty. He's a soul-mate, a spiritual brother and I'm not just saying that because he's the only person I've ever met who makes me seem normal in the head. He's so thin and frail. He lives on pills and cigarettes and vodka.

In the scene we'll be filming, if we ever film it, he lays his head on my lap and tells me about his unhappy life. Both of our characters are strangers to each other, yet we're drawn to each other, each relating to the other's sadness and sensitivity. I'm looking forward to playing it because there's so much of our history, Monty's and mine, that I can bring to the scene. I know more about him, I think, than most people.

Once, a few years ago, he decided that if we were going to be soul-mates, I should know everything about him. Monty's thing is that he feels everyone dislikes him because of his homosexuality. You might say that he wears the stigma of being gay the way I wear the stigma of being a sexual object. It's difficult for him to feel anyone's love. His inferiority complex makes him feel that no one could truly love him unless they know him from the inside out. If they can stand what he calls his "dark side," then he knows that they're truly his friend.

So there we were one night, sitting around my New York apartment. Arthur was out of town and Monty had come over to keep me company. I had just poured us a couple of vodkas when he decided he wanted me to see it.

"See what, Monty?" I asked him. He was so out of it on liquor and pills – he had arrived at the apartment that way – and I hadn't been drinking so it was like two people trying to signal each other from different planets.

"My dark side," he replied.

I told him I would like to see it. He had a great deal of fun preparing me for our journey to his dark side. First we had to choose an outfit for me. For some reason Monty wanted me to wear Arthur's clothes. A tweed suit, a tie and a fedora. He tried to button the shirt for me, giggling all the while. "Your breasts will be a problem," he laughed. Of course Arthur's clothes hung on me but Monty said no-one where we were going would notice. The suit jacket covered up the breast problem. I knew what he was doing: he was turning me into a man. He was making me into one of them!

It was nearly two o'clock in the morning. Where could we possible be going?

I knew a thing or two about poor Monty's dark side already. He's always talking about orgies – one of his French boyfriends introduced him to European decadence – and once Monty asked me if I'd ever been to a group sex party. I quickly said "no" because I got the idea he was fishing around to find out if I'd be interested in attending one. Any orgy he initiated, I'm sure, would probably be "men only" anyways and I'd be there strictly as a curiosity piece.

We spend a lot of time together. His brownstone apartment is not far from my own apartment and I've seen what goes on there when I've visited. His place is always overrun with male hustlers, male models, male dancers—all wandering in and out of rooms, eating his food and drinking his liquor. Most of the time he seems oblivious to it all.

This night we took a cab to an old movie theater in Times Square.

The hag at the box office didn't even look up from her knitting when we paid our admission. It was not one of the nicer movie theaters that New York has to offer, although it must have once been very lavish and beautiful in the 1920s and 30s. Now, though, it stood there in splendid ruin. The movie screen was tremendous. I remember the soiled red velvet seats, the elaborate chandelier hanging high up in the center of the theater. Filthy bordello-red velvet material with gold trim was draped around the screen and on some of the walls.

The place made me feel terribly sad and the decay brought up horrible feelings of beauty gone bad. A place that was once grand and popular but now had become forgotten and unknown, overrun with the unwanted.

This was an "all night" movie-house that was now mostly used as a place to sleep for the homeless, the drug-addicted and the perverted. It was very dark.

"Follow me," Monty said.

I stayed very close behind him. I was afraid, but the fact that we were movie stars acted as a shield that protected me from the reality of any possible danger that lurked in the shadows. We were walking up stairs and I realized he was taking me to the balcony.

This balcony – smoky and dark and filled with a sharp odor I recognized as the smell that comes out of the body when it's being explored during sex – was a sexual hunting ground. I had never been in an atmosphere so intensely sexual.

Men were roaming up and down the aisles, peering into rows of seats. Occasionally one of them would make a connection with another and they'd disappear into the darkness of the rows and their silhouettes would form unusual shapes, one sitting, one crouched down. Or the two of them twisted in passion in the seats.

"Did you ever see anything like this," Monty asked me.

I had to admit I hadn't.

"Wait here," he said, and then he disappeared into one of the rows of darkness. He was swept up in the atmosphere of sexual frenzy and left me to my own devices. It was obvious he was familiar with these hunting grounds and he knew the rules. I didn't. I sat on an aisle seat, where it was the lightest and safest, for the deeper I looked into the rows of seats, the darker it seemed until there was only blackness. That's the blackness Monty soon faded into.

I tried to watch the movie – a black and white Western thing I did not recognize.

Being in such a situation without being drunk was a sobering experience. What kind of loneliness drives a person to such a place? For a moment I almost burst into tears. Poor Monty. He had everything in the world anyone could possibly dream of and yet he degrades himself this way. Was it his way of punishing himself?

At first it was easy to feel disgust towards these men, gluttons eating sex without any regard for what or who they were doing. But then I thought of them as little boys, knowing they were different, scared and alone, complete misfits, and I realized that this filthy world was the only place where they could feel comfortable expressing their sex.

Suddenly I had tremendous respect for these fellows who had to find love in the shadows. They weren't even allowed the fleeting dignity of a quick pick-up in sleazy bars. I understood them and, actually, felt a sort of closeness with them.

I saw so many things I've never seen before including a tall thin man with his hair carefully set with curlers. He was approaching everyone… sitting next to them and staring hard for several seconds and then tentatively reaching out and grabbing a crotch…but his hand was always contemptuously brushed away. No one wanted him. Even amongst these misfits he was a misfit.

Watching strangers have sex with each other in such a public place was weird and ghastly but I forced myself to look. "Remember this experience, Marilyn," I said to myself. "Someday you will be able to use this in your acting." This is what I felt: loneliness, fear, desperation.

We're all born sexual beings—and if the kind of sex that we like to have is considered sick or wrong, I guess we have to create places and situations where we can have it freely. The balcony of the movie theater allowed men to have sex, the way we all need to, but they have to strip it down to the rawest level of sex. No conversation, no tenderness, no intimacy — just pure sex.

At the same time they're enjoying degrading themselves because they've been taught all their lives that what they feel is wrong.

I was thinking of these things and sort of floating in my own dream world when I became aware that there was an emaciated black boy standing in the aisle next to my seat, his pants and underwear were pulled down below his knees and his penis was eye level with me. I looked up at his face.

"Hello," he said casually. "How are you?"

I shook my head rapidly to show I wasn't interested in whatever he had in mind, but I didn't want to hurt his feelings by not responding at all.

How could he possibly have been attracted to me? I had Arthur's hat pulled low over my face and with the baggy tweed suit, in the darkness, I'm sure he had no idea that I was a woman. I must have come across as some sort of freakish hermaphrodite but, to him, even that was desirable. I guess it wasn't so much who they were having sex with, just the fact of making some sort of connection with another human being.

I needn't have worried. He was soon sitting in the row across the aisle from me, getting a blowjob from the man in curlers, who was kneeling in front of him on the horribly sticky floor. I watched his roller-ed head in silhouette, moving very quickly up and down with jack-hammer movements. I thought it was strange. If you were going out specifically to do something as intimate as having sex in public, why not take the time to give yourself a comb-out? But, then again, who am I to judge?

After a while Monty reappeared, to my great relief, and we stumbled out into the night and into a cab. I couldn't think of anything to say and neither could he. Apparently he had sobered up during his hunting session in the theater and I could feel his embarrassment forming a thick barrier between us, a wall that both of us wanted to break down, but neither knew what to say to reach across and break through the wall to touch the other. And this excursion was supposed to have made us closer. Perhaps it did, ultimately.

"Sleep with me tonight, honey," I said.

There was no misunderstanding about what I meant. We were brother and sister, not lovers, and Monty quickly agreed. In my bed, we clung to each other into the morning. I couldn't stop myself from crying. Monty was crying too—and bitterly.

I'm thinking about all this gloomy and dark stuff as I lie here in my hospital bed, being weaned off (so they tell me) from sleeping pills, so I can use all these feelings in the scene with Monty if and when we film it next week.

November 12, 1960 (New York City)

The damned movie is at last completed and, here I am, FINALLY, in New York City, in MY apartment, in MY bed.

But alone. Empty. Sad. Once again.

Note: The feeling of loneliness. Use it in an acting exercise.

Have you seen the headline in today's newspaper? I don't see how you could have missed it. It seems to be screaming out from every newsstand on every corner. And I was only out for a very brief time this afternoon. But the collective screaming from the headlines on the newsstands is still ringing in my ears. "Miller Walks Out on Marilyn." Not exactly true but it makes for a better story if he walked out on me. What difference does it make who walked out on who? Emotionally we both walked out on each other a few months into the marriage.

Now the reporters are camped out in front of my building waiting for me to appear again. Today they won't get another scrap from me.

I don't know why I feel so sad.

It's not like it's something unexpected—it has been a "pretend" marriage for a long time. In reality it started ending in the first months that it became official. So the fact that our upcoming divorce was announced in the press today should not have had such an effect on me. But I did have great hope for us once and I do hate to see things ending.

I guess it's the death of hope. There was a time, please believe me, perhaps a too brief time, that I really did feel that we were meant for each other and that our marriage would be a beautiful thing.

I think, maybe, many of us go through a period when we feel that real love just isn't in the cards for us. In the first year of our love, Arthur's and mine, I said to myself, "Oh yes! He is a teacher. I am a pupil. He is a father figure. It's blissful. Comfortable. Safe. I want to be his wife. I want to have his babies."

But hope can skew reality. It can send you down a doomed path. Look where my hope in Arthur lead me.

Discovering that, for the most part, he married me because he could no longer write. Inspiration for him had flown the coop. That must be a terrible place to be for an artist.

So, in marrying me perhaps I could become his muse at the same time. That's the way I think he felt, anyway. His reputation was beginning to decline. So he wrote *The Misfits* and the eyes of the world are on him again.

I would never say this to a reporter, or even a friend. To a certain extent, he was using me as much as everybody else. He told everyone I was drowning. Meanwhile, I was *his* lifeline.

My career was flourishing but my life felt like I was stomping on thin ice at best. He was *my* lifeline. Two drowning people clinging to each other for all the wrong reasons and today we finally let go.

If I my feelings are wrong about *The Misfits*, and it is hailed as a great work at least we can always have that together. We collaborated in making something great. That would be something!

November 21, 1960

"Clark Gable has died," the stranger shouted to me over the phone. I had been sleeping, a deep drugged sleep, and as always I had to wait a few moments for orientation to set in...to know if this was happening in reality or still in a fragment of a dream.

I don't think I wrote that shortly after we finished filming Clark Gable had a heart attack.

I know I didn't write it.

I didn't write it because I couldn't face it and I thought ignoring it was the best way to handle it in my current condition, which is "tatters." While he was in the hospital everyone was whispering, "It's Marilyn's fault. She drove the poor guy up a wall, making him wait around in that blistering heat until she was ready to film."

I decided to ignore all the talk. I figured when the movie opened they'd stop talking about how badly I behaved on the set and Clark and I could walk splendidly arm and arm into the premiere of the movie and everyone would focus on the fantastic teaming of Gable and Monroe.

It was the middle of the night and I was foggy with the phone in my hand and a reporter was asking, "Miss Monroe, how do you feel about Gable's death?"

"What?" I whispered. "I don't understand..."

"Clark Gable has died," he said louder. "Do you feel responsible at all, Miss Monroe?"

It wasn't a dream after all...and I...you know...just died a little bit myself on the inside. Clark was dead? How could it be? His wife is having a baby. And I didn't get a chance to apologize for my behavior on the set.

I babbled to the reporter. Something about how much I admired Clark Gable, how great working with him was and I hung up. It was the blackest part of the night.

Arthur was gone. For the first time in a long time I missed him. I couldn't ask him to hold me. He was seeing another woman anyway. A photographer who was sent to the set to photograph me. Arthur is holding her now. Yves is with his wife, probably in France. Jack is with Jacqueline in Washington preparing to rule the world.

I had to be gentle with myself. I got out of bed and walked around the apartment carefully watching out for land mines. I don't remember tears. I kept my mind on reality and tried to strip away emotions. Emotions come in waves and then there is the danger of an explosion.

I just thought of a phrase for a poem: Explosions of emotions.

In the future there would be explosions of emotions regarding this death. My co-star. My friend. My childhood fantasy father. That couldn't be dealt with on this night. Just focus on the fact. Clark is gone. Clark is gone. I had to believe that it was simply his time.

Mr. Death had him earmarked for November 16th. That was the day. His day to go. Nothing could have changed it. Even if he hadn't made *The Misfits*. Even if he had skipped making movies for a few years and just rested and raised a family. He was fifty-nine years old and November 16th was his time. Those are the facts. I have nothing to do with the arrangements of Mr. Death.

But then, of course, everyone was saying, "Well you know, working with Marilyn killed him." And I stepped on a land mine. The explosions started.

Now I hear the studio is rushing *The Misfits* into movie theaters, hoping to make an extra buck on the fact that this is the public's last chance to see Clark Gable on the screen. It's ghoulish. It's another dark cloud over a production already smothered in darkness. I'm smothered in that dark cloud too.

Undated

Jack was elected! I am on the winning team (for a change.)

1961

January 19, 1961

Tomorrow Jack in inaugurated as president of the United States. In some weird twist of fate I'm flying to Mexico to get my divorce from Arthur on the same day. Actually it was not a twist, my press agent, Tricia, told me it was the best time to do it, since coverage of the inauguration will overshadow any negative press about my divorce.

February 1, 1961

Went to the premiere of *The Misfits*. I knew Arthur would be there. I didn't want to face him. I thought maybe I wouldn't go at all. Monty called. "Hell, Marilyn, I'll be your date," he said. "We have to support the movie." Finally I decided, "I'll do it for Clark."

The people who saw early pre-screenings of the film were saying, "It's wonderful! It's the ultimate motion picture!" And shortly before he died Clark Gable called me and said he had seen a rough cut of the film. "I'm proud to be a part of *The Misfits*," he had said. "I will always be remembered for *Gone with the Wind* and *The Misfits*. That is my legacy."

And all of that pre-premier hoopla sort of got my hopes up and I started thinking "Everything's going to be okay. Perhaps I was wrong. Maybe this picture will make them take me seriously after all. Maybe I'll even get an Academy Award nomination."

Why do I believe myself?

Sitting in the audience, when the credits started I got the peculiar feeling of unreality. It's not easy to express what I felt. Here I was sitting in a movie theater. Yes, it was a real movie theater in New York City. Plus a huge movie star, Montgomery Clift, was sitting next to me, and the name on the screen was my own. Clark Gable's name. Then mine. Then Monty. It felt as if it was happening to someone else. It couldn't be me starring in a movie with my name up there above the title along with Clark Gable and Monty. But there I was. Here I am.

It's like when I first started to get noticed in Hollywood and they were just beginning to put my name up on theater marquis. Usually it was just a very small supporting part I had done in the picture. I still wasn't making any money and I was living in little, one bedroom apartments here and there and borrowing clothes from the studio to wear to events. The studio executives were still dubious of my acting ability. But the newspapers were always using my photographs and the letters had started pouring into the studio so they were getting canny and began exploiting my name.

I'd be driving along Santa Monica Boulevard and I'd see "MARILYN MONROE" up there in lights. I'd pull over and stare at it. That name was still new to me and I kept having to remind myself, "That's you!" And I would call myself by my birth name. "Norma Jeane, YOU are Marilyn Monroe and that is your name up there in lights." It was right there in front of me and I still had a hard time believing it.

When I was a kid the movies were such a big part of my life. I try not to dwell on who I was and what my life was like back then, but I do hold on to the past a lot. Sometimes there's just no getting past the past.

Whatever foster parents I was living with at the time didn't give me much thought. I really didn't exist as far as they were concerned or even as far as the rest of the world was concerned. I didn't really have any friends. So what could I do?

The movies! I would spend hours in the movies. I'd go to the early matinee, watch a film and then when it started for the next showing I'd stay and watch it again. The story on the screen filled me with purpose. Sometimes I'd see the same movie three or four times in one day. Then I'd go back to the house I was staying in, no one even seemed to notice I'd been gone, and I'd lock myself in my room and I'd act out the movie I had just seen. I would play all the parts and say the lines. Sometimes adding my own spin on the story. I didn't really know at the time I was acting. To me I was playing! This was my idea of play.

Sometimes when I was lumped in with a group of kids I'd get them to play with me. That's when my imagination would kick in. I wasn't shy or afraid in that moment. I was like a director. I'd say things like, "Well, let's make believe this is a castle. I'll be the princess locked away and you can be the prince and you can be the mean stepmother who tries to kill the prince." And we'd all become very involved.

But sitting in the theater with myself really up there on the screen was really not a pleasant experience at all last night. *The Misfits* is not a movie I would have liked back then and it is, for the most part, not one I like now. Everything I suspected that was wrong with the script was right there being played out in front of a large audience.

There is a moment of beauty, perhaps a good line, and then it becomes dull. It becomes talky. In the first hour so little happens.

Plus, I feel the black and white photography, although expert, takes away some of the vibrancy it might have had in color. The desert. The skies. Everything is muted in shades of gray.

I heard people in the audience starting to cough. I'm very good at "feeling" what an audience is feeling. They were bored. Every time I heard another cough it felt like a dart being thrown at me. I took it personally. I feel as if someone is going to pay to see Marilyn Monroe in a movie they should enjoy it. I very much want them to be entertained.

But it felt as if they wanted to get up in the middle of the movie and go to the bathroom. Some members of the audience actually did. It wasn't holding their attention. I hadn't noticed that I had begun to involuntarily wring my hands until Monty grabbed ahold of one hand and petted it like it was a kitten.

My performance is—let me be honest: I have seen myself enough on the screen by now to know when I am really hitting the mark, when I'm really in the character. I felt it so few times in *The Misfits*. There are a few scenes here and there that I think are quite good. I loved the scene when I tipsily dance outside and end up hugging a tree. It shows how I relate to the bareness, the strangeness of trees. I can feel proud of my work in a scene like that.

But too many times, because of my insecurity, I slipped into the persona that the public expects from me. My voice gets a little too breathy. A little too little-girlish. It's wrong for the character of Roslyn. It's not the way I had prepared to play her. But, I guess, because I had doubts about the script I resorted to what was tried and true and hadn't failed me yet.

Yet, it fails me here.

I was in tears. All my life I've been playing Marilyn Monroe and now I really wanted to change the image and show something else. And there she was up there. Including close-ups of my ass as it bounces up and down on a horse during a ride.

In one brutally cruel scene one of the cowboys opens a closet door and sees cheesecake pinups from my past. Not pinups of Roslyn! Famous photos of Marilyn Monroe from years ago. Just so the audience will make no mistake of who I am supposed to be playing. And to really get the last squeeze of humiliation out of me they have my character say, "Oh don't look at those. Gay just hung them up as a joke."

Seeing it on the movie screen, I could have died right there. I thought, "If this is a valentine to me I can imagine what he'll write about me when I'm dead—his slut muse."

As soon as the lights in the theater came up, Monty and I bolted out of there. We rushed to the limo. There was a party but neither of us wanted to go. We had done our part to support the movie by attending the premier and posing and smiling for the photographers. Monty was proud of his performance. And I might add he is quite excellent in his role. But I think he felt the overall failure of the movie too. We both felt the audience didn't care for it.

At this point he also needs a hit. We didn't talk in the car. There didn't seem to be anything to say. There was the heavy weight of disappointment sitting between us. When we got to my building he asked if I wanted him to come up. "No," I said, "I'm really tired." He seemed relieved. We both wanted to be alone with our demons.

February 15, 1961

And the reviews were bad and the box-office is bad.

People just don't want to see *The Misfits*. I thought it was interesting that the *New York Times* said, that the characters are shallow and inconsequential and even singled out the part I play saying that the whole movie revolves around her even though there is nothing very exciting or interesting about her.

Another critic said the premise is like a man becoming infatuated with a pretty girl but who doesn't have much else going for her except her looks so he invents all these qualities in her that aren't there. Things I've been saying to myself all along about the character. Maybe I'm not so dumb after all. Maybe I should start respecting my instincts a little more, huh?

March 6, 1961

Well, let's see...where do I begin? It's been a long time since I've been able to write. I'll try to make up for the lost time now. I'll write it all down. I have a good memory when it comes to the miserable.

I've been in the hospital again but this time it was a nuthouse,

With *The Misfits* now flopping, on top of *Let's Make Love* flopping, the press is starting to ask, "What's going to happen to Marilyn's career?" They mention my age. They mention my weight. They are like a pack of wolves eyeing a rabbit in a trap. They made jokes about my marriage ending. Some are vicious! Blaming me for Clark's death. I couldn't sleep without massive doses of Nembutal. I stayed in my bed for days at a time. It was all enough to push a normal person over the ledge. And I've never been normal.

I was telling my psychiatrist, Dr. Kris, I couldn't bear it much longer. Life was closing in on me. I was feeling suicidal. Knowing my history, she became alarmed.

Dr. Kris, suggested I go into the hospital to "rest" and get off the sleeping pills again. She agreed I've been through an awful lot of tough times in the past year. I felt like I was trying to climb out of my own skin all the time, just to get away from myself, so I said, "Well, maybe going into the hospital won't be so bad."

I was thinking: Quiet. Rest. Sleep. The Payne Whitney Clinic.

But when I got there, I didn't find myself in a nice, clean hospital room for a little pampering and a lot of rest. This was a mental institution. A sanatorium. They had put me in an institution for the mentally disturbed!

My heart is beating so hard as I'm writing this.

I cannot, cannot, cannot convey to you the terror of having everything taken away from you. My clothes, my belongings, my very identity, all were stripped from me. And last but not least, my dignity. I was locked in a room, and even the bathroom didn't have a door. Worst of all there was a huge glass door looking out to the hall so that anyone and everyone could look in. Luckily word hadn't gotten around just yet that it was me who had been committed. So I just had to deal with an occasional nurse or doctor, who had discovered who I was and came to stare at me.

They already had their minds made up that I was insane. It became the utmost importance that I remain calm. That I convey to them my sanity. I tried to communicate to them. They seemed to ignore everything I said—as if it was useless information. They were hardened by constantly dealing with insanity. They had been trained to disregard whatever an "insane" patient said.

It was a horror show.

I heard women screaming. Loud, agonizing screams conveying absolute pain. I thought that maybe one of the doctors or nurses could go talk to these women. Perhaps hold a hand or try to convey some understanding of the torture that they lived with. But, no. They saw the patients only as medical statistics to deal with. They were interested, perhaps, in diagnosing what was wrong with them—maybe someday write a medical paper on it—but they ignored that these were living, breathing humans with agonized feelings.

Perhaps they would be able to learn from actual suffering rather than read about it but they weren't interested.

I realized I would need help from outside. They wouldn't let me make a phone call. "No" I was told. Very sternly. That's when the panic set in.

You see, my mother is in an institution now and has been for years and my grandmother died in one. My worst nightmare has always been ending up like them and here I was. Just like them. No one would listen to me. It was like being put in a dark box with the lid shut tightly and dirt being shoveled on top of it.

I started screaming and screaming. I was screaming because Clark was dead and I was screaming because *The Misfits* was a bomb. I was screaming because Arthur was gone. And I was screaming because I was in my mid-30s and I was screaming because Jack was married to Jacqueline and I was screaming because I was locked up. I started pounding on the glass door, "Please, please open the door," I cried, "I won't make any trouble! Just please let me out!"

They didn't let me out. But a crowd of hospital employees had formed. They stared at me with something that looked like alarm. "Okay," I said to myself, "if they're going to treat me like I'm crazy, I'm going to act like I'm crazy." I picked up a chair and hurled it through the glass door. I whipped off my hospital gown, to really give them something to talk about.

I stood there naked with a piece of broken glass in my hand. Of course I wouldn't do anything to harm myself. I'm an actress! I'll admit it, I have my vanities. Did they really think I would scar my skin? I simply thought that it would get them to allow me to make a phone call. How wrong I was! It just confirmed their suspicions about me: I was a danger to myself and to others. The glass shattering brought a bunch of doctors and nurses into my room. One of them was holding a straightjacket.

"Please, just listen," I gasped. "I'll be rational. I'll make sense. Give me a chance to explain…" But…they weren't listening to what I was saying. Instead, what they did do was give me a huge sedative injection. It was strong, but not strong enough to give me delicious oblivion. I couldn't speak, but I still knew what was going on.

And they put me in the straightjacket and they transferred me from the merely "crazy" ward to the "crazy and violent" ward. You have no idea, or then again, maybe you do since I have no idea who, if anyone, is ever going to read this, what it's like to be so utterly and completely helpless and at the mercy of others. By now I was too drugged to try to explain myself and prove my sanity. I needed to come across as sane in order to get them to listen, yet I was so upset and doped up that I'm sure I was babbling, just confirming their diagnosis.

I remember simply muttering, "I'll be good. I'll be good. I'll be good…."

By now the word was out in the hospital. Marilyn Monroe was the nut in the straightjacket who broke the glass window. And this you won't believe: all night, there was a steady procession of doctors, nurses, interns, janitors, hospital staff and God knows who else, coming into my room to look at me. Just look at me!

My arms and hands were bound. My voice was gone from screaming. I couldn't put words together anyway.

"My God," I thought, "I'm going to be raped here!"

I've long discovered that my fame surpasses anything I can understand. They can't believe I'm real!

They were thinking, "Is it really Marilyn Monroe? She looks beautiful," or they were thinking, "That's Marilyn Monroe!!!! She looks ruined," or they were thinking….God knows what!

I was thinking, "I'm a person! I'm a person! I'm a person!"

As time passed my mind started to say, "Okay, I will lie quietly until my voice comes back. I will reason with them. I will say, 'Look at me. I'm a human being! I'm not an object that was created for the movies! I'm flesh and I'm blood and I'm in pain. Please help me." But hours later my mouth could still only say gibberish.

The following morning, when I was a little more coherent, a nurse, a fan, promised to let me make one phone call. I called Joe (DiMaggio). He flew out to New York immediately and had me transferred out of there, to another hospital, which was a real hospital, where I was able to get the rest I needed.

Joe saved me. I must never forget that he is the one person in the world who has proven he loves me unconditionally.

(Later)

Now? I'm out of the hospital…off of the pills…and refreshed and rested… BUT…I am so uncertain about what to do. What to do next.

Joe comes around. He wants to take me away to Florida to rest. He's still in love with me. Dear Joe! Even after the disaster that was our marriage. Still, I love him. Very much. But I'm not in love with him anymore. He's a dear friend. I treasure him. I want him to be happy. I must also add that our, um, physical relationship has never diminished. We very much have this exciting chemistry thing going on.

Aside from that, in many ways he's the only family I have. But there is simply no way we can ever live together again.

Joe says, "I'm the only one who sees that your career is killing you."

I say, "I can't live without my career."

I sink further into gloom.

Frank Sinatra has been visiting me. Wooing me. And I must say he's my most realistic chance for romance. He understands my career. He LIKES the fact that I have a career. He wants to work with me. He cares for me. He bought me a little Maltese poodle. A little white bundle of love. I named him Mafia Honey. I call him Maf. I tease Frank, "You're mixed up with the mafia but to me you're a honey." I tell people that Maf is our baby.

Then of course, there's Jack. He calls. He flirts. He keeps me hanging by a thread. But he is a slave to his ambitions.

I don't want to fall in love with Frank to act as some sort of life preserver to keep me from going completely under. And I don't want to fall in love with Jack so he can become a safety net while I do my high wire routine.

I don't want to think of men in terms of "Who is the best option?"

Rather…I would like to think that at long last, I have found the man who I have been waiting for all these years.

Things that made me happy while I was in the hospital recuperating:

Joe DiMaggio's visits.

The telegram from Marlon Brando.

Long telephone conversations with Frank Sinatra.

Flowers from Jack.

And yes, it worries me that all the things that made me happy during my darkest time had to do with men who loved me, love me now, and may love me in the future.

Has it always been that way? And if so, what have I been looking for in a man?

(Dare I write it?)

….my father?

March 7, 1961

There are thoughts of mine that are too private for me to put on paper. There are things that I remember that are mine alone. I compartmentalize areas of my life. I think it's important for an artist to keep some secrets. Maybe I let some of them slip out for a brief moment when I'm acting. But some memories are only for me. I will never tell anyone everything. Let them figure it out.

March 8, 1961

The first time I was married it was because it was the only viable option I had. By the time I was fifteen I had spent years being shuffled from foster homes to friends of my mother's to orphanages. Living with whoever would take me for a while. I wasn't rooted anywhere. I never had a home.

At that time, I was sometimes living with a very loving elderly woman who I called "Aunt Ana." I truly felt she loved me and I loved her but, as she was getting on in years, she decided she couldn't have me live with her anymore. So I had a choice: back to an orphanage or get married. Well, I had felt I had done the orphanage routine enough by this point. I opted for marriage. I didn't know what to expect but at least it was something different. There was a very nice young man, a kid really, named Jim who lived a few houses away. He was twenty-one and he sort of liked me and for no other reason, other than to give me some roots, we decided to get married. However, he insisted we wait until I turned sixteen.

But, although he was kind and perfectly fine looking, I knew from the start it wasn't right. I never had that "gushy" feeling that I had seen in the movies. This wasn't *that* wonderful kind of "love." For the first few months it was sort of nice. I had never belonged to anyone so I felt, well, gee, a wife belongs to her husband and he belongs to me. Being held at night—I liked that. But I didn't feel like I finally had been rooted somewhere. I didn't feel "home."

Soon, I was restless and bored. I think I've always had too much ambition and too many fantasies to be a woman who only took care of her husband—cooking and housekeeping and making love and so forth. So when he went away with the Merchant Marines, it gave me the excuse to get back into the world and find what I was looking for.

What little I did know about myself I didn't like very much. I thought a good alternative would be to become somebody else. I guess that's why I started seriously thinking that I wanted to be an actress.

While Jim was away I started modeling. I was surprised at how quickly I was accepted by a top modeling agency. Don't forget I was still a teenager. The only way I could judge my looks was by the reaction of the men around me. Sure they would whistle when I walked by—but didn't they do that to every pretty girl? I knew guys considered me pretty but I didn't have the confidence to think I could make a living out of it. But right away the owner of the modeling agency, Miss Snively, took a real interest in me. She taught me how to smile. I had a tendency, she said, to show too much of my gums when I smiled and she trained me to lower my lip to cover them a bit. She taught me how to carry myself and what kind of clothes I should wear when I was going to be interviewed for a potential booking. Eventually she even convinced me to lighten my hair.

It's amazing how quickly I felt completely at home in front of the camera. With each booking I felt more alive, more free, more delighted with being photographed. I fell in love with the camera and—so the photographers told me—the camera fell in love with me. A mutual love affair at last.

I must admit that in front of a still camera is one of my favorite places to be.

It was encouraging to me how quickly I started getting booked into very good modeling jobs. Sometimes it was advertising fashion or beauty products and other time it was for what was called "men's magazines." Not like what *Playboy* is today. These magazines dealt in "cheesecake" pictures. Like girls in bikinis or shorts. I was very popular in those magazines and appeared on the cover quite often. It was good exposure, if you will pardon the pun. Each time I stepped in front of the cameras my confidence grew. I started to think that the next step was, naturally, the movies.

I filed for divorce from Jim. When he returned from overseas, where he had been serving, he tried to talk me out of it. But I knew we could never make each other happy. I wished him well and I wished myself well and I went out into the world for the first time without any supervision at all. I was alone.

Here I was, just out of my teens and already a divorced woman.

But as a result of my photographs appearing on lots of magazine covers I got a screen test at a major studio, 20th Century Fox. Darryl F. Zanuck, who was the head of the studio, saw the test and said something like, "Sure, she looks okay. Give her a one year contract to try her out."

I don't think I have ever been so happy.

In Hollywood beautiful young girls came from all over the world in search of stardom in the movies. I was born here. I felt I belonged in the movies. I felt that this was all part of the scheme of things. I thought, "Now my life will begin." To make it official they gave me a new name. I went from being Norma Jeane Baker to "Marilyn Monroe." It really was a chance to start over. It was my symbolic new birth.

The studio started giving me acting, singing and dancing lessons. I was willing to work hard but I had no idea what it would take to climb the Hollywood ladder. Although I would soon find out.

March 9, 1961

For years I've asked myself the same thing my favorite foster father used to say to me when I was a little kid, "Who are you? Where are you going? What's your destination, little girl?"

I find myself saying that again. And my mind turns back to Jack. They say that there's someone for everyone. Maybe he's the one for me. Certainly I've been with my share of men, sometimes it makes me feel unworthy of him…and then I think of all the women he's been with – and continues to sleep with. I always thought it was unfair, this double standard thing. Men can sleep with as many women as they want, and it does nothing to lessen their value; if anything it only makes them more desirable in their own eyes. Yet a woman—a woman is supposed to be with only one man, and anything more than that makes her a whore.

But that reminds me that I want to continue writing down my story and I want to go further into all of that and I'm too tired now so I will write more tomorrow.

March 10, 1961

Well, here I am writing my "life story." I'm not quite sure if I will have the guts to publish it while I'm alive, or save it for a posthumous revelation. Or maybe just let it come out when I retire—to correct all the lies that have been spread about me during my career. Certainly it's not possible to publish it now. It would destroy my career—but I do feel that somehow in the scheme of things I'd like to get things straight. Even if just for myself. Of course, there is always the possibility I will destroy it. I never know with me.

After a year under contract at Fox the studio decided not to renew it.

I had only been given two bit parts, not exactly a chance to prove myself, but Darryl F. Zanuck said that he saw no star quality in me whatsoever. He said that I was unattractive. He let me go without fanfare.

I must admit that I was devastated. I had invested my entire existence into the movie industry, all my hopes were wrapped up in it, and now it was rejecting me too. I was very low, very down. Fox's studio head, Zanuck, decided I had no future in films. For me, no future in films meant no future.

Dreams, hard work, and determination had led me nowhere. I had to find a different path.

I want to give my early years in the business some context. A little back story. What writers call "atmosphere." And also, of course, the subtext.

There are no women who run the movie studios or who are key players in the production of motion pictures. It's true today and it was true when I was just starting my career in the late 1940s. Perhaps someday this will change and someday women will be just as powerful in the areas of producing and casting. But for now having men exclusively in total control puts young actresses at a terrible disadvantage.

And it brings out the most disgusting aspects in the character of certain men. These weren't attractive men. Most of them were horrible. They were the kind of men who, in high school, could never get a date. Now that they have power and influence, they hate women. They see us as meat to sniff and taste and eat and pass around.

Drunk with power they become extremely cold and exceptionally cruel. Although these men have wives and daughters and mothers whom they love and respect very much, they view the ambitious girls trying to get into show business as invaluable objects.

Entertainment executives know all too well that beautiful young girls want nothing more than to be in pictures. I know how these very young, very desperate girls feel. I was one myself not too long ago, you know. You can be young and beautiful, but there is always someone younger and more beautiful right around the corner. Neither youth nor beauty is really valued, it's merely used. You can have all the talent in the world, but talent doesn't mean all that much to these men either. The amazing amount of available girls makes them dehumanize them all.

They say things like "I want to get in there," when they are talking about a new girl just starting out. I know. I've heard them say it. I've heard them say it about me.

These girls know what they have to do in order to have a chance in the movies. Before a studio executive, or agent, or producer "gets into" the girl, she is at her most powerful. It is then she has to try to somehow distinguish herself from all the other actresses willing to do anything too. Sexual favors are really their only hope. But once these men in power have a girl in bed, the girl loses some of her own power. She is considered a tramp, a chump, a nothing. She can pull herself together, slap on some makeup and move on to another man and hope he will see something in her. Before you know it two men becomes twenty and then you have the reputation of being all used up.

The men have scorn for you in the beginning. But after you've hit your twentieth man the contempt is complete. You don't have a chance. You're considered soiled goods. Finished. A woman who has sexual partners is the vilest thing to them. But in the eyes of men towards other men, the more women they sleep with the more they hold each other in esteem.

Oh it is maddening that these men—and most of them are married—can sleep with as many women as they want. A different girl every night and that only makes them respect each other more. The only woman they respect are their own wives. But the way they show their respect is by sleeping with any other woman who will have them.

Early on I had to be with men. This was around 1947. Already dropped from one studio, I was once again a *nobody*. I was considered a loser. I felt it was true. There were thousands, if not millions, of girls out there who wanted to be a movie star. These men understood this and they could use it as power. This power corrupted them but they never viewed it as morally wrong. Instead, they viewed the woman as corrupt. They took all the guilt and hatred and self-loathing they felt for themselves and projected it on the poor, helpless girl who wanted to "make it."

I was a poor helpless girl who wanted to make it. I didn't find a "self" in the orphanages or in foster care or a marriage or with my first studio contract. I so very much wanted to be a *somebody*.

I was one of those women willing to be used. Don't judge me on this, please. If you were in my position, you very well might do the same thing.

There quite simply was no other way to get a chance in the movies. When you were coming from nowhere, as I was, the most you could hope for was to catch some powerful man's eye and pray he'd help you get a role.

I guess it's always been the case. Hollywood didn't invent the casting couch but it certainly perfected it. Before movies I guess women slept with theater producers for parts and before that they probably had to sleep with men for whatever other necessary positions that were available at the time.

All the young actresses knew it was tough—everyone said it was nearly impossible to make it in the film industry, but we all thought we knew something that the others didn't. Each of us felt (about ourselves): "I am different. I am special—I'll be the one to make it to the top."

Some of these women were sweet and trusting at first, but it was hard to remain girlfriends with them because of how quickly the jealousies and mistrust would spring up. One of us would get a bit part or a modeling job and the others would try to find out just who it was that she was sleeping with in order to get it or what quality she had that they didn't.

Every time I needed to get to the next level, it seems, I needed to find some man to give me a boost there.

There was such a thing at the time in Hollywood that was called the "party circuit." This circuit was gatherings that these executives would put together at the home of one of the men who was currently single. The guest list consisted of men in the movie industry: casting heads, directors, producers, agents.

I guess they told their wives they had a late night business meeting.

Sometimes they would play cards, sometimes they would just sit around and drink and talk. I remember the smell of hair oil and expensive colognes intermingling with their greedy desires. Cigar smoke always fogged the room. The other part of the guest list was the girls: The "chumps." The "whores." The nicest thing they called us was "party girls." These were the starlets who wanted to break in the business. I became a part of this group. Although we knew for the most part we were interchangeable, our hopes always were that one of the men would take enough of a liking to us that he'd call in a favor and get us a small part in a picture.

We'd be there to empty ash trays, refill drinks, and laugh at jokes that weren't funny. The most important thing to be was gay and happy. If you became moody or stand-offish you would not be invited to another party again. Which, of course, meant your chances of breaking in were over.

As the men became more and more intoxicated it was expected that… how do I say this? It was expected that they could choose any girl he took a liking to and take her to one of the private rooms in the house.

It was brutally degrading. It was the stuff of nightmares.

But, when we were realistic about our dreams, we knew it was the only way available to get a foot in the door.

The fact that we were all in the same boat – being used and passed around, being treated like shit – didn't cause us girls to unite and combine power (because after all, sex is the most powerful kind of power.) Instead the girls turned against each other and kept their claws sharpened, always sizing you up, always jealous, always ready to put the knife in your back. No. Women weren't my friends either.

In this sordid world, I learned to not allow myself to fall too low. I would be as charming and complimentary as possible with any of the men who talked to me, but I would also often find a way out of going to one of those private rooms with them. If I was nice enough, it was difficult for them to become too insulted if I said "no." But sometimes they did become angry if they didn't get their way.

I specifically remember one incident (and how can I ever forget?) when I was at a party talking to a group of men. All of them were interested in me and vying for my attention. Suddenly a man I had rejected at a different party approached me, reached over and ripped the top of my dress exposing my breast.

I was horrified. OK, I will be the first to admit I have no problem with nudity. I have posed nude on more than a few occasions and I think the human body is a beautiful thing.

However.

One does want control over one's own body! This was a deliberate act of degradation.

The entire room of cigar chomping men and their "dates," gawked at me, watching and waiting. And what do you think I did?

I laughed.

I laughed with all the rest of them. On the inside I was screaming. I was violated. But I was required to remain the most important thing a girl had to be at these parties—the sexy, cheerful, dumb girl.

And then I would see the same men at the next party and they would smile at me because I was a good sport, a good kid. A cheerful toy. They had zero respect or empathy for me but I was fun.

It was just disgusting that people would treat other people this way, when all we were trying to do was get ahead.

We always secretly despise what we envy. And especially what we desire. I could almost see them thinking, "We must destroy beautiful women."

Don't get me wrong, I had to go with some of the men. But, for the most part, I instinctively knew which ones to avoid. The guys who would never help me. Who would use me for ten minutes and then discard me. Who would talk especially degrading about me to the others.

And, with the ones I did agree to "entertain," I would only go so far. Otherwise your reputation could become even further ruined and that might be another reason they'd stop inviting you.

I became expert at pleasing while doing as little as possible. It didn't take much really. Let's just say I spent some time on my knees. But still, it was dirty business however you look at it.

You have to understand that all I wanted was to be a famous actress. That was all that mattered to me. I didn't long to belong to anyone anymore. I had passed that point (or at least I thought I did) but oh, how I longed for respect. The only way I knew how to get it was to become a movie star. All I had to work with, all God had given me, was my looks. But being born in Los Angeles, well, that might be enough of a gift.

If one thing is all you have, believe me, that one thing becomes very important to you. I set out to develop and polish the looks God had given me. I needed to survive.

March 14, 1961

All this reflection about what I had to do to become a star—the indignities I endured in order to endure—has made me start thinking about what I should do next. All these years later, I'm in an equally insecure position—although in a different way. I'm not quite ready to be finished. I feel as if I have a lot more to accomplish...prove? No! Accomplish.

Look, an actress only has a certain number of years before they stop offering the good roles. I really don't have the luxury to put off my career for too long.

Now that my last two films have officially been unsuccessful my next project is of utmost importance. If I don't prove to the studios that my name can still bring in audiences...the offers may stop coming. Even after all my spectacular successes, even after all the money I made the studios, I can almost hear them saying, "Three strikes, she's out!"

Under my studio contract with 20ᵗʰ Century Fox I owe them one more film. As one of their most important stars you would think that they'd try to find good vehicles for me. Yet the last piece of garbage they put me in was *Let's Make Love*. They figured, "Oh, it's Marilyn Monroe. She'll dance. She'll sing. She'll show cleavage. She'll wiggle. It will be a success." It had always worked in the past. But this time it didn't work. I guess even a faithful public has its limits.

Now they offered me a script called *Goodbye, Charlie*. "Oh no!" I don't want to do it.

I saw it when it was a play on Broadway starring Lauren Bacall, who was in *How to Marry a Millionaire* with me. *Goodbye, Charlie* is the story of an unlikable man, a real womanizer, Charlie, who is killed and mysteriously comes back to life as a woman several days later. Well, Lauren could pull that off—she's very in touch with her masculine side. But even with her in the role the play was not a success on Broadway.

I don't understand why the studio bought the property, a known flop, with *me* in mind for the lead. I can't see myself playing a man inside a woman's body. It's not feminine. All my movements and gestures would have to be that of a man's man.

It could be a challenge as an actress, certainly, but, first of all I don't think the script is funny. It's a one joke concept. And second, I don't think my fans would accept me acting masculine. But legally I'd have to do it. I don't have script approval with my studio. Thank God that, when I was at my most powerful, I had the studio give me director approval in my contract. As of now, none of the directors on my list are available for this particular project. So although I legally have to make one more movie for Fox, they have to live up to their end of the bargain and give me a director I approve of.

There's lots of telegrams going back and forth between my lawyers and the studio as they try to force me into making *Goodbye, Charlie*. Most of the time I feel too sick and disgusted to even read the correspondence. I just want out of it.

To think of, all those years ago, the things I would have endured to be offered a role, any role, even some of the dreck that Fox has tried to force me to make through the years.

Back in 1947, a minute of screen time was worth more than a million dollars to me. It would have been a dream to be offered a lead in something like *Goodbye, Charlie*. Back then I didn't care about the quality of scripts. I didn't even totally know what quality was.

Now, almost fifteen years later, a script that flimsy could bring on the end to all my hard work. For too long now I've had to carry movies that have little else going for them other than my presence. My shoulders are weak from carrying so many bad scripts. So as of now I'm saying "goodbye" to *Goodbye, Charlie*.

March 18, 1961

In my early career, any time I got even the smallest role in a movie, it was because I was having relations with some guy who had the pull to do me a favor. The movie industry is run by men who have two things on their minds: how to make money and how to get more sex.

Sometimes they would become my friend and maybe even show me some kindness, but underneath the friendship there was always the feeling that I was beneath them. Like if I had to describe their attitude as an expression on a face, I would say it had on a sarcastic half-smile. That's why behind our backs they called us "chumps" and "tramps." "Pushovers," was another favorite description.

The first one of these guys of any importance in my life, and who was a bit different from the rest, was Joe Schenk. He used me too but he's one of the few who I don't feel anger towards.

Joe Schenk was one of the true giants in the industry. He actually helped create the entire studio system. Now he was a studio executive with enormous power at 20th Century Fox. The studio that had just recently dropped me.

Joe was close to seventy and I was all of twenty-two. I had been "seeing" a businessman named Patrick who invited me to Joe Schenk's Saturday night poker party. These parties were legendary. If you were on the party circuit, getting an invitation to one of Joe Schenk's poker games was like winning the grand prize. It was a party where many of the major men in the business would be. Only the most beautiful and desirable girls were invited. I was filled with excitement to be going to one.

Often when I am excited I appear the opposite. Sort of unconcerned or apathetic. I sat at the poker table beside Patrick with a poker face. But all night I could see Joe Schenk trying to catch my eye. He would wink at me. He would smile at me. I demurely pretended not to notice. It wasn't as if I was Patrick's girlfriend or anything like that. We most certainly were not dating. As a matter of fact, I was sure he would be out with another girl the following weekend. But to be brought to a party with one man and flirt with another is something I would not consider.

But the next day Joe called me. He had gotten my number from Patrick, he explained. As I mentioned, starlets were often considered delicacies to be passed around. But I must admit that being noticed by this powerful man in a room filled with so many beautiful women flattered me and gave me that boost of confidence I was always craving in order to move on.

I accepted the dinner invitation. He sent a limousine to pick me up.

By nature, I think, I'm a shy person. I realized this was something I'd have to overcome. But in those early years the way I looked was the major hook. They didn't seem to care whether or not I could put two sentences together. Although I always managed to. Joe liked what I had to say. He thought I was an interesting, clever girl. Plus I had that "hook."

Before long that limo was picking me up almost every night.

Now this troubled me a bit. There was always the probability that once one of these men had you a few times, your value goes down. And any new girl passing through town becomes more valuable, no matter what you've presented.

So I tried to become more intriguing to him. I started developing my mind. I liked literature and art. At first I was embarrassed foe thinking that I actually could improve my mind. But I enjoyed teaching myself. I had no idea where to start. But since I knew nothing, everything seemed interesting.

Joe Schenk actually admired my hunger to improve myself. It kept him interested. He encouraged me to grow.

He wasn't a bad man. As a matter of fact to this day I consider him kind. Joe appreciated beautiful young girls, the way some men appreciate possessions. Some men collect cars, some paintings, some race horses. Joe collected models and starlets.

But before long he only wanted to see me. He had a guest house on the property and sometimes he asked me to spend the night there. That way I could be on hand whenever he was "ready."

Soon it was going around that I was Joe Schenk's girl. That was quite a distinction. Here was a man who was constantly surrounded by youth and beauty and he wanted to be with me. He was one of the first really high-powered individuals to sense that "certain something" in me. He recognized it. He wanted it.

I could tell that Joe liked his friends to think that he and I were having a very hot and passionate love affair. But our relationship really wasn't about sex. After all he was nearly fifty years older than me. Yes, he certainly still had the desire but he simply just wasn't always able to perform. He liked to run his hand up and down my body. It meant so much to him, it felt rather nice to be so important to someone. On occasion he would kiss my breasts for what seemed like hours. But we only had what would be considered "sexual relations" a handful of times, if you can excuse the pun.

But Joe loved to talk to me. He was, like me, not very formally educated—which made him relate to my desire for self-improvement. He was incredibly smart and intuitive. He had a wonderful instinct about the film business. I would sit at his feet, late at night, and just listen to his tales of the early days of Hollywood. He was warm and comfortable. When you looked into his craggy face you could see the whole history of the motion picture industry written on it.

Aside from him being pleasant company – I won't try to kid you – there was the possibility that some movie project would come along that he would think I was right for. That was never far from my mind. In those days it was all that mattered. Getting a part in a film was more important to me than eating or having a place to live. And, before I met him, there were many days, when I went without eating.

I don't want to come across as if I was using him because I was extremely fond of him and I did enjoy his company. I don't want to say that he was using me, because I truly believe he admired me as a person. But let's just say that if he wasn't a big time Hollywood producer at a major studio I wouldn't have spent as much time with him as I did. And if I didn't open my mouth when he kissed me, he wouldn't have spent as much time with me.

Still, I truly think we became good friends.

But then something happened that sort of defined our roles.

I had been waiting for him to offer to help me in my career in some way. He never made an offer. Finally I asked him if he could help me get a second chance, another contract, at his studio.

Joe was an executive with Fox. He knew that his studio had recently dropped me. He was well aware that I needed weekly checks to survive. He realized how ambitious I was.

He knew everyone in the business! All he had to do was put in one good word for me at any studio and I would have been given a contract! But instead he didn't do a thing on my behalf. I had to ask myself, "Is this really someone who cares?" I don't know. Maybe he was afraid of helping me because he feared I'd become successful and not need him anymore. I don't think a relationship should be based on need.

I did the only thing that I could do. I removed myself from him. I had no money, no power, and no fame. The only thing I could do to let him know how hurt and angry I felt, was to stop seeing him. If my absence wasn't a loss to him, then he never was my friend anyway. It really came down to that. "If you don't value me enough to give me something that would be so easy for you, so inconsequential, something that you've done for dozens of other girls, than I must go."

So I stopped returning his telephone messages. I didn't go to see him. It was difficult, but I knew I couldn't waste any more of my valuable time on him. I needed to move on before it was too late for me.

Ultimately, I guess he did feel my absence in some way. One afternoon Joe called and said he wanted to see me and it was very important. Well, I figured one hour of my time wouldn't hurt me so I drove over to his place. Without discussing anything he picked up the telephone right in front of me and called Columbia Pictures to speak to the head of casting. He said "I'm sitting here with a beautiful young actress, name of Marilyn Monroe. I am indebted to her and I would appreciate it if you would give her a six month contract."

Well, as a result of that phone call I signed a six-month contract with Columbia Pictures. Now, at the time I didn't understand why Joe did not lift a finger to help me at his studio, Fox, yet he went out of his way to get me six months at a rival studio, Columbia. But six months of paychecks is six months of food and shelter! Besides, who was I to question him?

Much later, though, I found out that he tried to get me back with Fox but his colleague, one Darryl F. Zanuck, told him, "Don't come to me with requests involving your girlfriends. We've already had her under contract. She's nothing." Joe didn't think I was a nothing. So he used his power to get me something at a different studio. But after he got me the contract at Columbia our friendship changed for reasons I will describe another time.

March 19, 1961

Fox is still trying to get me to make *Goodbye, Charlie*. I'm thinking I would rather do a serious role and prove once and for all I'm a serious actress. As far as the public and most of the critics are concerned *The*

Misfits didn't prove anything at all.

I would like to try to breathe new life into the role of Sadie Thompson in *Rain* by Somerset Maugham. Yes, I am aware it's been done by Joan Crawford and Rita Hayworth but I think I can bring new things to the character.

My teacher, Lee Strasberg thinks I should do it because it's a volatile role. He thinks it wouldn't be healthy for me to do a lightweight comedy. Lee senses that I have a lot of hostility that needs to be unleashed and this can be the character that allows me to do that.

We've approached NBC about doing it for television in a big, high quality production. They've been very interested. The problem is, they don't want Lee to direct it. They say, of course he is an important acting teacher but he doesn't have experience as a director.

Well, I feel I owe him some loyalty. So I won't do the project without Lee.

But I must decide on something. The clock is ticking.

March 21, 1961

Before I forget where I am in my re-telling, I want to continue writing where I left off regarding those earlier years when I was trying to break into the business. I had been writing about how I had just been signed to Columbia Studios because of my friend Joe Schenk's phone call.

At the time, at the age of twenty-two, I had been aware of the magic of "first love" for years. I had seen this kind of this starry-eyed love in movies. That's all I knew of it—except maybe in dreams.

I didn't believe love existed in real life.

Oh sure, I had my experiences with men but I had little faith that it would happen for me. I felt I was unlovable. Well, no one had really loved me before so it was sort of a natural conclusion. As a result of being unlovable I thought I was unable to love a man. Experiences with men,

I thought, would just be a series of, you know, interactions, exchanges of favors. Transactions. For instance, when I was sixteen my fist marriage happened because I didn't want to go back to an orphanage and he wanted a pretty teenage bride. Another instance, in my early twenties I wanted a role in a movie and some executive wanted a pleasurable experience he couldn't get with his wife.

Then I met Fred and I discovered what all the fuss was about. What I learned is that first love always leaves a mark, sets a certain standard in which all subsequent loves are compared to, and is just generally unforgettable. I also learned that love, while being capable of bringing great comfort and pleasure, can also bring excruciating pain.

As a result of being cast in the lead of the picture at Columbia called *Ladies of the Chorus*, I was told to report for acting lessons to a woman who worked at the studio named Natasha Lytess. That would take care of my acting for the role. For my singing I was told to report to a man name Fred Karger. Soon my life was to take an interesting twist, although at the time my life had more interesting twists than Chubby Checker has today. In practically no time at all Natasha was passionately in love with me and I, in return, was passionately in love with Fred Karger.

While I'm on the subject of love, first let me tell you about Natasha; she was important in my life for a time too. She was an older woman, with grayish hair and the way her face was lined suggested she had led an interesting, if somewhat troubled, life. I never knew her exact age, but certainly she was old enough to look middle-aged but young enough to have a three year old daughter. She could have been thirty-five. She could have been fifty. It was impossible to tell. Natasha was Russian and she had escaped from Nazi Europe. She herself had been an actress and was now making her living as a drama coach. She didn't make much money, but then again, as an acting coach, she wasn't very good – although it took me years to figure that out.

But Natasha did give me something I was desperate for. I won't deny it. She gave me faith in myself. See, the thing is, in those days I was going from relationship to relationship looking for some validation in my value as a person, but only a couple of people made me feel that I had any worth outside of my body.

I believe that it's true of all of us, we need certain people at different times in our life to give us something to move forward to the next phase. I believe God, or whoever arranges these things, puts people in our path as we need them. Of course it's up to us to recognize them.

Somewhere deep inside of me, some tiny voice, some far away instinct had been telling me that there was something special in me. But I felt much more self-conscious and shy than I felt any semblance of confidence. I needed people to see this "thing" in me so that I could begin to explore and develop it.

I craved to hear people tell me I was good. Or more than "good." I needed to hear I was special. In the rare cases when someone who really believed in me, like Natasha, came along it fed this small quivering feeling in me that made me believe that maybe there was something worth developing about me, and maybe I could be wonderful someday.

Oh yes, Natasha wanted my body, just like all the men did, but there was more to it than that. She really did see a talent in me. The mistake I made was that I let her get a little physical with me once. I had never had sex with a woman before and I was a little curious, so I went with it. Starved for affection, I took what crumbs were thrown. I guess there were a few moments of real passion during that first time—or perhaps it was just an intense curiosity—and I actually kissed her back for a few seconds, but after it was over, I never felt anything near passion again for her.

But the more I didn't want her, the more she wanted me! She devoted herself to me in the hopes that those tiny moments of curiosity I had demonstrated would somehow ignite into passion.

She recognized my insecurity and that, when performing, I was inhibited and cramped. As a teacher, the most important thing Natasha ever said to me was "relaxation brings authority." I knew she was right.

As long as I appeared tense, no one would ever believe me when I was performing. My main goal was to feel relaxed and comfortable in the character before doing a scene.

I still have not been able to accomplish relaxation before performing. But I have developed a way to present the illusion of being relaxed. Through my teacher, Lee Strasberg, I learned that nervousness means sensitivity and that I could learn to channel this sensitivity into my performances.

As for Natasha, I suppose I used as much as she used me. I needed her devotion. Back then, so few people were willing to help me. And I needed help. *Ladies of the Chorus* would be the first time I was on screen in a movie for more than one minute. It was some very low-budget trifle about a girl, to be played by me, whose mother had been a burlesque queen and my character had grown up in the seedy world of burlesque. I'd fallen in love with a wealthy respectable man, and I have to prove to his family I'm worthy.

The script was lousy, the dialogue amateurish and fake, but it was a chance for me to be seen on the screen. I was the lead in it. Natasha and I worked very hard to try and bring some realism to that character.

Natasha was not a mother figure.

I knew she was in love with me. Once after we rehearsed a scene for the movie she blurted out, "Marilyn, you're wonderful! I love you!"

She had the kind of love that was devouring, and it frightened me. Before I could stop myself I said to her, "Don't love me, Natasha. Help me to be better." I realized that I hurt her, but I had to keep her at bay. The funny thing is she didn't realize that I understood exactly what she was going through. Life has a way of making things end up fair and square.

While Natasha was experiencing unrequited love for me, I was experiencing it for Fred Karger.

In this film I was going to sing two songs and to prepare me for my numbers the studio sent me to a singing coach who also worked for the studio, Fred Karger. I first saw him when I walked into the rehearsal studio and there he was sitting at the piano. My heart began skipping several beats. I looked into his eyes for the first time and I panicked. Looking back on it now I realize that that panic, that fear, was the fact that, although I had been wanted by men, I had never really wanted a man before. But, oh gosh, I wanted this one! It was a fear of being rejected. I retreated into myself.

"Shall we begin?" he asked.

I didn't say anything.

"Miss Monroe." He said, "Are you all right?" I just stood there trembling. I guess he thought I was nervous about singing in front of him. "Why don't you sing any song your feel comfortable with," he said. "And we'll see what we need to work on regarding your voice."

I said, "Love Me or Leave Me."

"Fine," he said, "That's fine." He started to play that tune on the piano.

"Oh," I thought, "he meant the song."

Before long, I was romantically involved with Fred. Up to that time, Freddy was the first man that I was with who was what would be considered traditionally handsome—with movie star looks and lots of sex appeal. He had dark hair which I loved to touch. And his eyes! Blue and deep and as changing as the sea, outlined with thick lashes on top and bottom. His eyes were the kind that made me feel, when I looked into them, I not only saw his soul but also *felt* my own.

Another plus was that Fred had a family. He talked about them often with a real devotion. He was divorced and had an eight-year-old boy. They lived with his mother who everyone called Nana. Also living in the house was Fred's sister, who was a widow, and she had two children – they all lived as one big happy family.

After our fourth singing lesson I knew I was really in love.

We went out to dinner, and then for a long drive. I didn't talk much. I was afraid I'd say something dumb. But I asked lots of questions and he seemed to enjoy explaining things to me. I enjoyed hearing his masculine, assured voice and breathing in his woody cologne. I could tell he was the type of man who liked to feel superior over women. Nothing new there. But he enjoyed taking on a teacher role. With me he found the perfect student. He enjoyed my lack of knowledge. In retrospect I understand it made him feel superior to explain to me...who Moliere was, for example. Sometimes he was very kind to me and I wasn't terribly used to that.

Late that night he took me back to his place while his family was sleeping. We crept very quietly into his bedroom. I loved being in his bed. Did you ever notice that when you love someone everything about them becomes a treasure? I found a hair of his on the sheets and placed it in my mouth. I wanted us to be one. One body, one love...I remember I saw a half-eaten cookie on his nightstand and I filled up with adoration for him. Fred. The man I loved! I could hardly believe it! Everything that he touched once, even in the most mundane way, overwhelmed me with love. We made love that night and it was very tender and for me, for the first time, it was wonderful.

The next morning, I could hear his family in the kitchen talking over breakfast. There was no way out of the house except by walking through the kitchen.

Now how was I going to handle this? I know that a girl who spends the night in bed with a man she just recently met in his family's house could be looked on with bemused scorn. I didn't want them to look down on me.

I decided that all I could offer this family was myself, so I chose not to pretend to be anyone else. I spotted his sister amongst the family.

"Hi," I said, walking into the kitchen dressed in the clothes I had been wearing the night before. "Can I have some juice?" I could see the family was startled to have this disheveled stranger in their midst, but I figured if I acted casual and comfortable it would put her at ease too. After a moment, I could see that bemused smile I had been expecting creep on his sister's face.

"Sure," she replied. "Orange or pineapple?" They made room for me at the table. I had played that scene right.

After that we were friends and his family became my family. It was a family as I always imagined a family should be. I fell in love with Fred, but I fell in love with his family too.

His mother encouraged me to call her Nana. That day she first met me she blurted out, "My! What a lovely, sweet, innocent, girl!" It wasn't exactly true, as the circumstances in which we met proved, and if these things are judged by actual deeds she wouldn't have thought that. But much of me did feel unspoiled and she treated me like a daughter—or at least a favorite niece.

I grew to love her very much. I still do to this day and we have remained in touch—even as my image has become more eroticized and my life more jaded. She doesn't judge me. I'm sill that sweet innocent girl who stumbled into her kitchen asking for juice. She became a mother figure to me, even more real than my real mother.

And so, at the age of twenty-two, a divorcee, a girl familiar with the Hollywood "party scene," I had my first love affair. I had been lonely. Not to be touched, but to have someone whom I wanted to touch.

I was crazy mad in love with Fred the way that only young girls can be. How lucky I am to have experienced that.

With Freddy, I would wake up in the middle of the night and watch him sleeping. It was such a relief to know I wasn't numbed to love and it was something I could feel. I would look over at him, snoring or grunting! Even that endeared him to me. I would say to myself, "Yes, yes… this is why people get married! This is why people love each other so much and they feel they can make a life-long commitment. This is what "forever" means."

"Perhaps, Fred has been your destination, little girl," I told myself.

Maybe that feeling I had inside of me, that I was destined for a special life, was a fraud. I was tired of being a "party girl" on the "party circuit." I still saw Joe Schenk from time to time, but only as a friend. I wouldn't let him touch me. He was angry at first but after a while he seemed to accept it. The entire party scene had left me soiled and depleted. It was always raining. With Fred I saw a life of shelter.

If I was to get married this time, it wouldn't be for a reason to stay out of an orphanage or to feel secure or to not be lonely anymore. It would be because, when I looked at him, my heart filled with joy and I'd say to myself, "I will never get tired of looking at this man. There will never be a day that I don't want to be near him."

Yes, I was happy with Fred.

I was almost ready to give up trying for a movie career. When he held me in his arms, it was better than any standing ovation or rave review could ever be. I so wanted to make him happy.

But my happiness comes with conditions. I had a feeling – an annoying feeling that kept cutting through my joy. It wasn't just my mind telling me I wasn't good enough for Freddy. It was an instinct telling me that he thought I wasn't good enough for him as well.

Fred was not a father figure.

But I knew I was in love with him. Still, I was canny enough to realize that it wasn't mutual. While he always seemed happy to see me and he enjoyed being with me, his feelings for me weren't anywhere near as strong as what I felt for him. If I had my way I would never be away from him. But he wanted time away from me. There were some nights when he wouldn't call. He was out with some other woman. I felt it. I knew I didn't consume his thoughts the way he consumed me.

I loved him too much. Too fast. Sometimes it happens for both lovers that way. Not this time. For him, he needed more time than I did. I should have kept a little distant—aloof—before I gave myself so completely. He needed time to get to know me, not what he thought he knew about me because of my circumstances.

Like many men I've known he displayed a certain resentment towards me because I had been with others and for sexually desiring me like those others—and he could be quite cruel about it at times. Just as he was very tender and nurturing sometimes, there were other occasions he would turn on me. He'd call me stupid and say things like, "You're not good for anything but fucking."

He had a way of making me feel obscene. He knew my past, from foster homes to a marriage bed to the party circuit to this. No wonder there was a layer of contempt in his feelings for me. I felt it in myself. And I would spend the rest of my life, up to this writing, trying to erase it.

When we were together he would sometimes ask, "What's the most important thing in your life, Marilyn?"

I would say (passionately, sincerely) "You are!"

He would just smile and say, "But what about after I'm gone?"

I would cry sometimes, which made him uneasy. He didn't want to be around me unless I was happy and witty and gay. He would say, "You cry too easily. That's because your mind hasn't been developed. Next to your body, it's like an embryo."

My body again.

Without it where would I be? Sometimes, when he was in his darkest moods, he would say again that I was only good for "fucking." That's when I began to realize it wouldn't last.

I'm probably making him sound more terrible than he was. Actually he wasn't terrible at all. He helped me. The way he brought me into his family is something I could never forget. But there was something... something in him...preventing him from loving me. He resisted it. And I couldn't...I could not break through his resistance.

What I hope I am conveying here is Fred's, well, sort of...schizophrenic feelings for me. On the one hand he liked me very much and wanted to help me. As a matter of fact he worked very hard on improving my singing voice and I think he helped me a great deal. On the other hand he couldn't stop himself from trying to make me see myself as a person of lesser value. Maybe as a way of making himself seem more valuable to me? I don't know.

Fred's mother, Nana, wanted him to marry me. But he didn't think highly enough of me to marry me. It didn't surprise me – that's the way I felt about myself – but it hurt all the same. Once he even said, "I couldn't marry you, Marilyn. I couldn't."

I knew I didn't want to know his reason why, but I asked him anyway.

He said, "Don't you see? If anything should happen to me, if I should die suddenly, it wouldn't be fair that a woman like you would be the mother of my little boy."

Gulp!

To this day, I wish I never asked him. That was a knife. After all, if nothing else I think I'm a good person. I have a decent heart! But almost without fail every man I've been with has made me feel the same way at one time or another. "A woman like you." As opposed to other kinds of women. The right kind. The problem for me is, I agree with them. Unlovable. Soiled. That's the child that I was. That's the woman I am.

That was near the end of our relationship. That Christmas I bought him a watch – I couldn't afford it – as a matter of fact I spent the next few years paying it off. But I wanted him to know how much he meant to me. I didn't have anything inscribed on it, though, except for the date. 12-25-48. He asked me about that. He wanted to know why I hadn't inscribed it with something more personal.

I said, "Soon you'll have some other woman to love. She wouldn't want you to wear a present with a different girl's name on it and I want you to always be able to wear this watch, Fred. And maybe think of me, from time to time."

I had tried love. It didn't work for me. Love didn't swoop me up in its arms, tight, tight, and take care of me. Love wouldn't be my salvation. Instead it had been momentary. A detour.

My heart was broken. I was crushed. But I'd get by. I always had. I was starting to get good at it.

I started thinking again about fame. Unfortunately, that meant going back on the party circuit and trying to catch the eye of men, or the man, who could help me get a toe in the door.

When that person came along, Fred's attitude about me changed completely. He didn't think I was so beneath him anymore. As a matter of fact he was frantic to have me back. But by then it was too late. I was back on destiny's pathway.

April 2, 1961

You can try to keep your mind off Mr. Death but when you're least expecting it he walks right up and says, "Hello!" Even at a small park on a clear day at the end of your street.

Feeling the blues close in, obviously.

Spent most of the afternoon just gazing dreamily into the mirror, sipping a Bloody Mary and letting my records play the soundtrack of my life. Sinatra singing "Only the Lonely." Suddenly I bolted out. Not sure where I'd go but just being outdoors I felt better at once. The notion that some kind of unspeakable peril awaits me outside my bedroom disappeared the moment I was out in the fresh air. I decided to take a walk to the little park that overlooks the East River at the end of my street.

Sometimes it still comes to me as a surprise. This is my street. I live here. At least for now I've certainly traveled a long way.

As you get older it's harder to be alone. I always feel the need to lean on someone. My doctors tell me that's wrong. But if I lean on myself I'll topple over. Yet, I guess, I'd rather be by myself than with someone who makes me feel alone. I won't write the next sentence that comes to mind. I want to avoid self-pity. No one likes that, least of all me...

Gentle wind. Warm sun. A few people on the street on their way home from their jobs or walking their dogs. I didn't even bother to put a scarf on. No one stopped me on the short walk down to where the park benches overlook the water. There are so many blondes now, with hair the same length and color as my own—which is almost white. I can't get it blonde enough. Maybe they were thinking "Who does she think she is? Marilyn Monroe?"

Some people go through their entire life meeting Mr. Death only once. And that's on their last day. Other people, like myself, come in contact with him on and off throughout our lives. I wouldn't say we're friends, but we do keep an eye out for each other. This is what I was thinking as I strolled along.

Back in the early days of my romance with Arthur Miller, when I truly thought we had a chance and he, I guess, genuinely thought he was in love with me, we were hiding out in this little apartment in Brooklyn. We weren't married yet. Arthur was waiting for his divorce to go through. The press was on to the relationship and were swarming like bees looking for us, hoping for a scrap to print about our affair.

It was a mixed up time for me. I finally felt like, maybe. I really was a star and that, perhaps I even had some power. I had fled Los Angeles and the studio and all those awful scripts they were trying to get me to act in. I was in the process of attempting, and I emphasize "attempting," to improve myself. I had already started studying at the Actor's Studio with Lee Strasberg and everyone there was telling me how good my work was. How great I could be. But the newspapers and such were saying the cruelest things. You know, it was as if, "We liked her the way she was. Dizzy and delicious. How dare she take herself so seriously—this little *actress*." And, then, because I was involved with Arthur they were writing things like "The Owl and the Hourglass," and saying I was out of my league intellectually.

I didn't need to read that. I already felt like I was out of my league. I always feel, somewhere deep inside of me, that I'm a little out of my league.

Arthur was constantly saying how happy our life would be. I didn't totally believe it but I wanted to believe it so badly it almost felt real

One night, when he was out for a walk, a panic set in. Sometimes life seems like it's too big for me and it seems ridiculous to try to cope. I took one sleeping pill. And then another. Then....I was looking for that oblivion and I guess. I found it for a while. Mr. Death brings it quietly

Well, when Arthur came home, he told me later, I was comatose.

He couldn't call an ambulance. The swarms would descend. It would be headline news for weeks. He used the phone book and found a doctor whose office was nearby. Arthur explained the situation. He was in a panic while I continued in my obliviousness. The doctor didn't believe him. Didn't believe Marilyn Monroe was dying in Brooklyn a few blocks away. Arthur said he would meet him out front.

The doctor recognized Arthur immediately. Arthur brought him up to where I lay dying and he saved my life.

After he saved me, the doctor went into the room where Arthur was waiting and he told him I'd be alright. Arthur thanked him. The doctor said, "Look, I won't tell anyone that you are here or that any of this happened but could you get me her autograph?"

Arthur came in and crouched near the bed. He had a prescription pad and a pen. He held my hand and helped me scrawl my name. Somewhere in the world, Brooklyn to be precise, is a prescription pad with my signature on it. Ironic in many ways.

Mr. Death was asked to leave that day. He didn't get me. But we had most definitely met before and we've seen each other several times since.

Three little boys in the park. Two of them were about eleven-years-old and one much younger, maybe five. The older boys had been catching pigeons in a trap. It was startling to see them carrying a bunch of cooing pigeons in a wire cage. I started to feel trapped. I didn't want the boys to think I was going to scold them so I pretended to be interested instead.

"How did you catch the pigeons," I asked brightly.

The older dark-haired boy was most eager to explain. "You set up the cage and you start leaving the bait a few days before."

"What kind of bait?"

"Just some dried bread or corn. They like that. Then the pigeons feel safe going in there. And after about three days they feel so safe in the cage that they're easy to catch. You just shut the door."

"Oh," I said. "What are you going to do with them?"

The other boy said, "They pay us fifty cents apiece for them at the market."

I was confused in the moment. What kind of market was he talking about? I'm not aware of anyone eating pigeons in New York City. Or did they? Is it squab? What else would the pigeons be used for? Killed for? Something horrible, I'm sure. Obviously I didn't want to say any of this to the boys. I simply said, "How about this, I'll buy all the pigeons you caught today. I'll pay you the fifty cents. How many do you have? Six?"

"What will you do with them?"

"I think I'd like to see them fly away. This way you'll have your money and the pigeons can go home."

"You don't want them to go to the market?"

"Well, I think I'd rather them go free."

"Okay, lady. As long as you pay up."

I reached in my purse and found three dollar bills. I gave it to the boys. They opened the trap door on the cage. Surprisingly the pigeons didn't seem too eager to leave the metal contraption. I guess they liked the idea of steady food, a regular home, and the illusion of being in a safe place. They didn't realize it's only an illusion.

The boys took the birds out one by one. When all the pigeons were free (and they didn't fly away they just walked on the sidewalk piddling around for more food) the boys started to walk away.

"Hey," I said, trying to make it sound like I just came up with an idea, "how often do you trap the pigeons?"

They said once a week. I made a deal with them to meet them there every week, same time, same place, whenever I'm in town, and I will pay them for however many pigeons they catch. I suspect it will often be the same pigeons over and over. They said "deal!" and shook my hand as if we were signing a million dollar contract. The littlest boy hadn't spoken. But I could see he knew what I was up to. I was in the saving game.

"I catch ants." he declared suddenly. "My name is, Ralph."

"You do, Ralphie?" I said. "What do you do with the ants?"

"I see them walking on the ground. And then...and then...my big foot comes down and I crush them. He pronounced the word "crush" like "prush." I wasn't sure if he was a shrewd little thing trying to get some money out of me or just a talkative little fellow.

"Now, that's not very nice, Ralphie. Is it?"

He looked down, embarrassed.

"Do you have a mommy and daddy," I asked.

And this little boy, Ralphie, said, "Yes," and I could see his eyes fill up very quickly with many emotions. Love was the main ingredient he radiated it—but there was also pride and a little fear in that little boy's eyes. It was like he was afraid that I was threatening his parents in some way. I am not his mother. I am not even an aunt (or an ant) or distant relative and yet my heart filled up for this little boy with a love so intense I thought I would burst. I didn't only want to teach him. I wanted to comfort him and love him.

"Well," I said, "those ants might have a mommy and daddy too. And maybe all they're trying to do, all they want, is to get home to their family. Maybe one of the ant's mommy and daddy are waiting for him at home."

The older boys had grown bored with the story, my little analogy, and they picked up their pigeon trap and started walking away. But I could see I had reached Ralphie.

"I'm not going to 'prush' ants anymore," he said. "I'm gonna let them go home."

"Good, Ralphie! That's so good!" He's a smart kid and willing to learn. Maybe I taught him that being kind is always an option. Next we were laughing, hugging each other, loving the moment and life itself.

He ran off to catch up to the two other boys.

I'm not going to make fun or belittle myself for this small afternoon adventure. I'm not so naive that I don't realize that I can't save everything in the world. Still, I don't think it's so unusual to not want to see something suffer. Although Arthur seemed to think that it's the most fascinating thing in the world for a woman not to want to watch something die, and he revolved the plot of *The Misfits* around it. The whole thought of that movie still leaves this bitter aftertaste.

Still, it does make you feel better about life in general if you save one.

Even if the life you save is a pigeon. Because, after all, a single pigeon's life is just as important to them as ours is to us.

April 15, 1961

I feel it's time to move back to Los Angeles, for a while at least. I'm feeling stagnate and there are too many bad memories here for the time being. My relationship with Arthur. My nightmare at the Payne Whitney Clinic. I simply feel I can't trust Dr. Kris anymore. And, facing the facts, I do feel I still have a long way to go in psychiatric therapy.

And just the general feeling that things are moving too slow right now in both my life and career.

I'll keep my apartment here of course. New York will always be a home to me. I mean I'll go back and forth, coast to coast, a lot. But for the time being I need to move on with things and that means being based in LA. The clock certainly isn't slowing down for me. Thirty-five is just around the corner.

Frank Sinatra is there. Let's give that a real chance!

Plus my Los Angeles psychiatrist, Dr. Greenson, is there. He's a good replacement for Dr. Kris. I think some serious, steady time with him might help me grow in confidence and independence. I mean, I don't like to put too much hope in doctors. Well, let's say I don't like to put too much hope in anyone. Yet, the truth is, I'm not strong enough or confident enough yet to stand alone. I guess I don't have enough hope in myself.

I need people, even if they are paid people, to give me guidance. I need to believe their main interest is to help me.

May 11, 1961

Now that the word is out I'm settling in Los Angeles for the time being my show business friends are determined to get me involved in the lifestyle (which I never really fit in, in the first place.)

I've decided to rent an apartment. I think I must have lived in a hundred apartments in the last 15 years! A place I lived in a few years ago on Doheny was available again so I snatched it up. At least it will be familiar surroundings.

Frank (Sinatra) sent me a telegram from his concert tour (he invited me to live at his house while he was gone.) It said: "Marilyn, remember the time you tried to cook a turkey for me in my kitchen and the bird you bought was so big it wouldn't fit in my oven? Why don't we try again?"

When he came back from his tour we started seeing each other again. He is so dynamic. We have such a good time together. I can't cross him off of my list of possibilities. We've been seeing each other a lot since I've been here.

I have so little confidence in my decision making that even the smallest things become disasters that I can't begin to handle. Frank can smooth out anything. He exists in a world—which is his state of mind—where there are no disasters. Any problem can be fixed. As a matter of facts, disasters are his specialty—he takes them in his stride. If he can't fix it he has someone or something that could. "Marilyn, you have a contract that's a financial disaster? Let me have my lawyer look at it." "You have no place to live? Here's the keys to my estate in Bel-Air." "You have a meeting in San Francisco? I'll have my private jet fly you." He's chivalrous. He loves a damsel in distress. Lord knows I'm distressed. So I not only love him, I'm grateful for him.

Although I never did try to cook him a turkey again.

June 1, 1961

Trying to stay hopeful even though today I am thirty-five.

Doing my best to feel good about myself: dieting and exercising daily. Part of me, the hopeful part, is optimistic and looking forward to another year. But the other part of me, the smart part, knows what's coming.

Undated Fragment

...sometimes a loneliness wells up in me. An isolation. Or a strangulation. And I wonder if there is anyone in the world who could take away this loneliness. I guess most of my life I've been searching for someone. I guess everything I've done has been motivated by the desire to free myself of this lonesomeness—even just for a short while.

June 8, 1961

Sometimes when my days feel too empty, or I take one sleeping pill too many, and perhaps some champagne gets mixed in, people from my past get confused with some current dilemma.

Often my mind goes back.

Being in Los Angeles again brings up all kinds of scenes from the past. They meld in with the present and it's like one moment I'm here in 1961 thinking about what movie project at Fox might help put me back on top and the next I'm a starlet talking to Harry Cohn at Columbia pictures hoping he'll give me a chance in the movies.

By late 1948 things were not going well. The ship was sinking. I was the only person on board.

After my first movie at Columbia opened—and let me tell you it was a very modest opening—I once again felt my destiny was being fulfilled. Even though this was a small B-picture with no known actors and a teeny tiny budget. It did what it intended to do—and that is give an undemanding audience some light entertainment for an hour.

It was hardly noticed at all in the press, but one critic did say "Miss Monroe shows promise." That was something to hold on to.

The movie was fine. I wasn't going to set the world on fire in this one, I knew, but it was a step up. I most certainly felt it would lead to other roles. I thought I looked nice, my acting was okay (although no one understood better than myself that I had a lot of improving to do) and thanks to Fred Karger my voice was pleasant.

I sang a song called "Every Baby Needs a Da-da Daddy." I thought it was ironic when, a few years later, I was playing the lead in a big budget, glitzy movie named *Gentlemen Prefer Blondes*, and I sang a song called, "Diamonds are a Girl's Best Friend." My mind couldn't help but go back to that song in the little B-picture. The songs were remarkably similar in themes. About how women need rich men to take care of them. In "Every Baby Needs a Da-da Daddy," the lyric went, "It was cold, outside of Tiffany's I was trembling in the storm..." The two songs have a message that snagging a rich man is a woman's ultimate success. "To keep her worry-free."

Of course, it wasn't true for me, I wanted to make my own way. But it seemed impossible without some man to help me.

Some executives at Columbia Studio saw genuine potential in me when they after viewing the movie. I mean, there was talk of grooming me for a bigger budget picture with a better part. But, really, the only opinion that mattered was the studio head, Harry Cohn. After he saw a screening of *Ladies of the Chorus* he summoned me to his office.

"Not bad, Marjorie" he said, lighting a cigar. (No matter what Freud said—a cigar, for some men, really becomes their penis. They're always pulling it out and waving it around when they start a conversation with a girl.) "We might be able to do something with you. You have to lose some weight, of course, and we need to give you some more training, but I'm thinking of signing you for another year."

Oh joy! Another year filled with chances of proving myself. I was in heaven

But I soon found out what Mr. Cohn's real interest in me was. He brought the term "casting couch" to new highs...or should I say new "lows." While I was there in the office with him, he invited me to spend the weekend with him on his yacht.

Now, mind you. I was not at this point in my life, nor any other point I can remember, a prude. I had been with men for advancement before, and it was likely I'd have to do it again. But in the case of Harry, my instincts told me, "Don't do it."

Even if he was the head of a prominent movie studio. There was something dishonest about him. My intuition told me he took great pleasure in degrading girls. The way he blew cigar smoke in my face. The way he refused to look me in the eyes, instead letting his eyes run lewdly up and down my body. I got the feeling that H. Cohn would fuck me and then discard me.

And that, my dears, is something I wasn't willing to allow to happen.

So I said, "Oh, Mr. Cohn, I would love to spend the weekend on your boat with you. And I am so looking forward to meeting your lovely wife who, no doubt, will be spending the weekend with us." Of course that was my way of saying "no."

That's when the ship started sinking. As a result of me turning him down, Cohn turned truly vicious.

As a matter of fact, an important director at Columbia had seen my appearance in *Ladies of the Chorus*. This director was just about to cast a picture called *Born Yesterday*, which had been a huge success as a Broadway play. It was the kind of role that could create a star. He thought I had so much potential that he asked me to make a screen test for the part.

I studied hard with Natasha for the screen test, and I thought I did a pretty good job in it. This could be my breakthrough!

But Harry Cohn wouldn't even walk the short distance from his office to the screening room to view my test for *Born Yesterday*. No actress dared say "no" to him sexually. After I did, everything about me became one giant "no." Of course the director of *Born Yesterday* couldn't seriously consider me without the approval of the head of the studio.

Next I heard my contract with the studio had lapsed and would not be renewed so that I was no longer employed at Columbia Pictures—all my chances of being groomed, being given better roles, and rising and becoming a star there were also over.

As a matter of fact, to make matters worse, Harry Cohn said about my appearance in *Ladies of the Chorus*, "Why did we put that fat pig in a movie?"

A statement like that, from an influential and respected studio head, could destroy a girl's chances forever. Plus, I'm sure it got a lot of snickers on the party circuit where, by this time, I was well known

Harry Cohn was the one who was truly a pig. But word got around Hollywood that Cohn called me a pig and after that it was unlikely anyone would seriously consider me for any role again.

So as a "fat pig," who two major studios had signed and fired, and the studio heads themselves said was unattractive and without star quality, I started to question myself. I started questioning the few people who had ever expressed a certain belief in me.

I was still getting modeling jobs. I mean, it seemed photographers wanted to take my picture all the time. Still, I began to question my path in life.

I was only twenty-two but I felt like some people must feel at the very end of their lives. My own life had gone down so many complicated roads which I tried to maneuver the best I could—backing up, moving forward, being thrown into reverse—but somehow I was always crashing at a dead end. I was very weary by now.

That was when Mr. Death started hanging around me most of the time.

I was starting to see myself as the kind of girl they find dead of an overdose in a lonely hotel room. That's where I was heading. I thought about it an awful lot.

June 10, 1961

CARBON COPY OF A LETTER TO PAT KENNEDY LAWFORD

Dear Pat,

I'm high as a kite but I had to write – if you'll excuse the poetry. No, dear, I'm not going to talk about your famous and powerful brother. Guess who I'm thinking about right now? Hint, hint: He's playing in the background on the phonograph.

Out of all the men I ever dated, one of the most fascinating is Frank Sinatra.

Now that I'm free from Arthur, Frank has been coming around again.

Since your brother is so busy in Washington, I figured that I'd allow myself to get involved with Frank. I mean, men can whiff it out in you when you're pining away for them, and that sends them running for the hills. Meanwhile, if you're occupied, happy and in-demand, they come sniffing around. So if I'm going to be happy I might as well be happy with Frank.

When Frank invited me to watch him perform at the Sands in Las Vegas, I couldn't say no. Oh Pat, I wish you could have been there. I know you wanted to!

Frank Sinatra is so charismatic and fun and interesting and talented. He loves me, no doubt, and he makes me feel safe. Yet, with men like Frankie you're always pushed a little in the background. The Italian machismo thing (or is "machismo" Spanish? Who cares? Frank's got it!). To him, a woman is just a woman – the woman in his life comes after his career and his buddies. Although he probably felt differently about

Ava Gardner. But there's only room for one Ava Gardner kind of love in anyone's life.

Just like there's only room for one Jack Kennedy kind of love. Now even the way Frank makes me feel is a little dimmer after falling for Jack…your brother has ruined me for other guys! But I don't dare tell Frank I'm involved with Jack.

Sitting at my table at The Sands was Miss Elizabeth Taylor with her new husband Eddie Fisher. Yes, yes…she is beautiful, with her jet black hair and unnaturally blue eyes – already she is wearing the kind of makeup she will wear in *Cleopatra*, heavily lined in black Kohl, which makes her eyes stand out even more. And yes, she was alluring dressed in white to set off her dark beauty.

A scandal like the one she created by stealing Eddie from his wife (poor Debbie Reynolds) and kids while her own husband was not yet cold in his grave, would have destroyed a star twenty years ago. Today that kind of press only makes a star more desirable—and in her case, a much bigger box office draw.

She glared at me, austere and beautiful. She knew I was awed by her beauty. I looked back at her unflinching. "That's okay," I told myself. "I have my own beauty." I wrapped it around me like a blanket for protection. I also have the horrible ability to read people's minds and I could hear that Elizabeth was thinking: "You may think you're something special Marilyn Monroe, but *YOUR* studio is paying me one million dollars to play Cleopatra. They didn't pick you – they picked me!"

I couldn't answer her with my eyes because it's true: 20th Century Fox is paying her a million to play Cleopatra, taking her away from MGM, even though Fox has ME under contract. Yet they keep offering me the same garbage to appear in and at the cheapest bargain-basement salary. I am Cleopatra! And even though I brought them in millions, they're still treating me like shit and paying me a fraction of what I'm worth to them.

Is it because I don't value myself that no one else does?

So what I did was turn up the "Marilyn Monroe" and when Marilyn Monroe is turned on it's like an electric light switched on "high." I was dressed in sheer black to set off my whiteness. Low cut, lace top.

When Frankie sings he makes me feel amazingly oozy and gooey and beautiful. I mean, I melt. And he was singing most of the songs directly to me. I swayed sensuously to Frank's music, pounding my hands in rhythm on the table. I have this ability to call up the MM persona and it never fails me. This is the character that people become fascinated with.

I could feel that all eyes were on me—not her! I could sense her burning up.

I tried to be nice to her but she was having none of it. Answering all my comments with a demure, mumble. "Yes." "No." "Excuse me?" She was acting very grand. When she got up to excuse herself to go to the ladies room I heard her say to Eddie, "Keep that trampy dyke away from me." For the first time that evening her voice was loud and clear.

Well, Pat, it hurt, that's all. I didn't do or say anything to make her think I am a lesbian. And if I was one I wouldn't be interested in *her*. Why did she feel the need to be kept away from me?

Surely, I think, she was just jealous because I was getting more attention. But I also believe she didn't like me. After all we were both drinking and I think the truth comes out when you're drunk. She was about to get a mountain of truth.

I'm sick and tired of trying to be nice to people only to have them hate me in return—and for no good reason. I was tipsy enough to feel confident and so I followed Elizabeth into the powder room to confront her.

When I got to the ladies room, Elizabeth was looking at herself in the mirror adjusting her skin-tight, white satin dress – bursting at every seam. For the first time, I noticed how short she is—and the weight she has recently gained makes her more than "pleasingly plump." Meanwhile, I am very proud of the fact that I recently lost fifteen pounds and I'm in better shape than I have been in years.

I heard that Elizabeth hates being called "Liz," preferring the more dignified "Elizabeth."

"Hi'ya, Liz," I said.

She caught my eye icily in the mirror.

She stuck out her ass in my face and said, "I'm just making sure my panties don't ride up, honey. I don't want to ruin the lines in my dress."

"Oh, don't worry about that, dear," I replied, "Your body already does that."

I tell you no lie: Smoke came out of that woman's ears!

"Well, I'll admit I may have gained a few pounds," she replied, bitch-ily, "but I'll knock off the weight before I start filming *Cleopatra* at Fox. After all, they're paying me a cool million to do it."

"I'm starting a new picture at Fox too," I said, "and when I'm finished with it, my contract with them is over and I'll be free to accept the eleven million dollar picture deal in Europe I've just been offered."

She looked at me skeptically. She knew that contract would make *me* the highest-paid actress in the world. Not her!

"Well," she said at last, "Maybe you can give me your diet tips. You seem to have lost a bit of weight yourself since your last picture. What was it called? *Let's Make Lunch*?

"It was *Let's Make Love*," I said, my eyes narrowing.

"What a picture that was!" she said with a laugh. Then she did a little imitation of me, in complete caricature of my image singing, "My heart belongs to Da-dee…"

"Well, of course it wasn't in the league of the aptly-titled *Elephant Walk* you starred in several years back," I said, not to be outdone by her sarcasm. "Maybe it's time for a remake?"

Obviously scanning the names of my movies in her head, and not coming up with anything she could make fun of, she changed the subject by saying, "I'm delighted you're with Frank Sinatra, honey. I'm sure you could use a *real* man after Arthur Miller."

That did it. "At least I divorced him," I fired back. "I didn't wait for him to die in a plane crash and then hop into bed with his best friend."

"You bitch!" she screamed.

"That's rather an extreme case of the pot calling the kettle black," I said.

"Are you looking for a fight?" she asked.

"Me???? You called me a tramp," I said.

"It takes one to know one," she hissed.

"You've been hostile and jealous towards me all night," I said. For some reason this comment irked her more than anything else I had said, although I personally thought the "Plane-crash-and -then-hopping-into-bed-with-his-best-friend" line was much more insulting—in my opinion anyway.

"You take that back!" she screamed.

"I will not!" I screamed right back at her and stamped my stiletto-heeled foot down for emphasis.

And then she reached out with her plump little arm and grabbed at the top of my dress before I could stop her the spaghetti strap broke and a breast plopped out.

Now it was turning physical. Someone was going to get hurt, either her or me. I opted for her.

And so, with all my might, I punched her good and square in the stomach (how could I miss with that as a target) – and she let out a little yelp and lunged at me and before I even knew what was happening we were both rolling on the tile floor pulling hair and slapping and punching away like a couple of cats with our tails tied together.

My goodness, I had never been in a fistfight before but, being a perfectionist, I was certainly willing to give it my all. Just as I was removing the wig-let that was interwoven in Liz's hairdo, the lady who is the powder room attendant, a dignified Hattie McDaniel type, screamed out, "Miss Monroe! Miss Taylor! C'mon now! That ain't no way for no sex goddesses to be actin'!"

And being scolded by Mammy from *Gone With the Wind* got me giggling and then Liz was giggling and she sat up and, seeing her sitting there with her legs spread out, sprawled on the ladies room floor, made me start laughing even harder and she clutched her stomach and we were both hooting and cackling and then the powder room attendant was laughing too and Liz couldn't catch her breath and she was waving her hairy little arms (oh yes, she is quite hairy) in distress and glee.

I helped her up and said, "Let's go get a drink."

The attendant helped me repair the strap of my dress with a safety pin and then Liz and I walked unsteadily back to the table arm in arm: her wig-let askew on her head, my dress strap holding on for dear life with a safety pin, both a little less perfect for the wear and tear.

"You know, maybe we should make a picture together," she suggested.

"Now that we're both at Fox, I don't see why not," I replied.

When the concert was over, there was a party in Frankie's suite. Much to my chagrin, Frankie did not want to have his picture taken with me! He's got this thing about not wanting Joe DiMaggio to see pictures of us together 'cause he doesn't want to upset Joe – even though they are bitter enemies right now (mostly because of me). But I wanted my picture taken with Frankie, and I motioned for a photographer to come snap us.

"Oh Frankie," I sighed tipsily, "I love you, I want the world to know."

The photographer came over and snapped.

Actually, I'm not sure if I'm *in love* with Frank. When I'm with him I think I'm more in love with Jack. But to be fair, when I'm with Jack I feel that Frank is the better man to spend the rest of my life with

But Frankie grabbed a photographer and, just like the gangster that he swears he's not, he said, "You try that again and I'll crack open your skull."

The big bully.

Then he turned to his bodyguard and said, "Keep an eye on Marilyn," as if I couldn't hear, "I don't like the way she's wobblin' – let me know if she faints or something." And with that, he took off to be a mobster with his mobster-type cronies.

He was just acting tough because he was out in public. I knew very well in a couple of hours he'd burst into the hotel room we were sharing, climb into bed with me and hold me all night, singing to me, whispering love lyrics—and doing other passionate things too!

All of a sudden the alcohol, the fight with Liz, the music, and my confusion of Frank versus Jack, all came rushing towards me and hit me in the gut with the same "give-it-your-all" impact as the punch I had given Liz in the ladies room. I felt sick. I went over to Frank and said, "Frank, I'm going to throw up."

He said, "Oh for god's sake, Marilyn…when?"

"Right now," I said, "I mean it, Frankie."

"Jesus Christ, Marilyn" he said. "Not again." Then he had his bodyguard come escort me back to Frank's suite.

But, as I was being led out, I saw Liz saunter over to the photographer who had been watching the entire scene. I motioned for Frank's body guard to wait. With Liz's back to me I elbowed my way over towards her till I was within earshot. I instinctively knew she was going to say something to that photojournalist about me and, although I had a feeling it would hurt my feelings, I eavesdropped anyway.

"Oh my God," Liz said to the photojournalist, "that Marilyn Monroe is a mess, isn't she? How she keeps her beauty I'll never know. She simply shouldn't drink if she can't hold her liquor. Now *me*, for instance. I for one can drink like a fish. And hold it!"

And with that she downed her martini in one huge gulp, laughed giddily—and slumped to the floor. Out cold! Much to my delight.

I scurried out of there in a hurry whilst they carried my new friend, Liz, out. Now, Pat…not a word about any of this to anyone! It's TOP SECRET! After all, I want to be the one to tell it at your next dinner party.

Kisses,

Marilyn

Undated

Frank Sinatra. John F. Kennedy. I know I'm playing with danger – but that's the only way I know how to play. If I played by the rules, I never would have gotten this far in the game.

July 2, 1961 (New York)

I have been in so much pain lately I don't even know where emotional pain ends and physical pain begins. Back to New York for more tests.

Well, as it turns out, some of the pain at least has been caused by a discernable problem. My doctor discovered that I need to have my gallbladder removed. That was the reason for the severe stomach pains and indigestion. Not just "nervousness" as some doctors have suggested.

The first thing I thought about was the scar. I mentioned this to the doctor.

"There will be a scar," he said, definitely.

"Will it be bad," I asked.

"It will be...significant," he replied.

"Oh," I said. I let the subject drop. There's nothing I could do about it.

So here I am in the hospital again. This time Polyclinic. I had the operation on Thursday. Right now I'm foggy. Groggy. In pain.

Maybe it's a sign. Maybe it's my body telling me to stop relying so much on my body. I mean, the appearance of my body. I've relied on it for, well let's be truthful, just about everything.

The idea of being sick is frightening.

The idea of a scar is frightening.

It's kind of depressing on top of everything I've been dealing with. Is my body failing too?

When I woke up from surgery who was there for me? Joe. Joe DiMaggio. The one person who loves me without question. And the one person I know, without question, I can't be married to. I would only end up hurting him. He would only end up hating me. I love him too much for that.

I haven't seen the scar yet. It's heavily bandaged. I brace myself for it. As I brace myself for life at 35.

July 3, 1961

Finally got the guts to look at the scar when they were changing my bandages. An angry red slash across my belly that made me gasp,

The doctor says it will not always be so prominent but it will never go away. It will make wearing bikinis a problem that's for sure. I'm learning to deal with it. I have scars on the inside that don't show. I hide them well. I'll learn how to hide the one on the outside just as well.

Fragment in Monroe's Notebook for Dr. Ralph Greenson (Undated)

Well, Doctor, you told me to write down some things that cause me pain and then bring the list with me to my next appointment when I'm back in LA. So I figured I'd write some of my memories down while I'm recuperating in the hospital.

Back in the days when I was climbing I did a lot of things I don't like. I can't say I regret them. I'm canny enough to know that if I didn't do them I wouldn't have been able to become an actress. I just wish there had been alternate routes. What causes me pain? Primarily when I think about the people I've hurt. And the ones who hurt me.

July 4, 1961

I've been thinking about what I wrote regarding someone in every relationship loving the other more. Johnny Hyde is the one instance when the man's love for me was so strong that it changed everything for me.

You know when you think about it, there's always one major event, or person, or opportunity that can change the course of an entire life.

A lot of successful people don't like to give others credit. It's sort of like they want the world too think that they are so talented, so beautiful, so special that their success was inevitable. But I have to say with all honesty, and all the gratitude I have in my heart, that if there was no Johnny Hyde there would never have been a "Marilyn Monroe."

As 1949 approached, I thought about giving up on everything every single day. I came close. Still there was this unnamable "something" living deep within me that kept pushing. I wanted to be an actress so badly and somewhere inside me there was still that nagging feeling telling me that I had something special to offer that needed to be nurtured and released.

I was tired of hearing studio heads say, "You are not pretty enough." "You are not photogenic." "You're not star material." All the while trying to fuck me—literally and figuratively.

But there was always that one person that would come along and say, "Hmm. You know, I can't seem to put my finger on it but there *is* something special in you." I always opted to put my trust in those compliments, but now I was beginning to believe the insults more.

Even the modeling jobs weren't coming in as often as before. When you don't have money you're always at the mercy of people. Especially if you're young and ambitious. To make extra money I started posing for nude photographs. At one point I was really low on cash and a photographer called me. He said, "Marilyn we're looking for a golden girl to pose nude for a calendar."

I sighed. "How much, Tom?"

He said, "Fifty dollars."

I took that as a sign from God because fifty dollars was exactly what I needed to get my car out of the mechanic's garage. Before you could say,

"January," I was sprawled out on a piece of red velvet backdrop without a stitch of clothing on.

I did the photos. Collected my check. Got the car out of the garage. And forgot about it. Not a big deal. Although a few years later it would become a very big deal.

Whenever I doubt that there is a God, I remember Johnny Hyde.

I had been desperately praying for something to happen. I think of 1948 and then I believe that there has to be a God, because he sent Johnny directly to me at a time when I needed him. See, I had smashed into that dead end for the last time. I had nothing left in me. I felt no one loved me and no one ever had. All I was, was a receptacle for sexual desire.

It may be hard for people to believe today, because of the publicity and legend surrounding "Marilyn Monroe," but the truth is, there was a time, right before Johnny Hyde, when it really was the end. I truly had nowhere else to turn and no one else to call for any favors.

And then just as the year was ending:

Sam Spiegel was a Hollywood producer who, every year, gave a New Year's Eve party that everyone in the business dreamed of being invited to. It was a major event in the industry. I guess the girl Harry Cohn had called a "pig" was still a novelty act. I received an invitation. I said to myself: "Big deal." "I don't want to go." "I'm tired of parties."

Tired of the men with a hand on my thigh, pawing at my clothes, and their promises, and the hopes that were ultimately smashed.

I knew what to expect.

But it was New Year's Eve and I was one of the chosen few who had been invited and I had nowhere else to go. So I rallied myself: "Put on your makeup." "Pick out a gown." "One more time." "You never know."

The party was different than the others because most of the executives had their wives with them but there were more than enough beautiful starlets for them to flirt with and give their business cards to with the promise of a fling in the future. Every major director in town was there, along with every influential producer and quite a lot of big stars.

Among them I saw Johnny Hyde staring at me from across the room. I knew he was one of the top talent agents in the business. He was the kind of agent I would never have been able to get an appointment with. Had I just called his office and said I was a new actress with a lot of potential they would have laughed, "Sure, come in, like, two weeks from never."

The fact that this top agent was staring at me with such intensity gave me a glimmer of hope, but I was too jaded to put too much faith in it. I had been stared at before by powerful tycoons and all I had gotten out of it in the long run was humiliation and disappointment. I smiled at him but turned away. I wasn't going to be obvious. I wasn't going to appear as desperate as I was.

I said hello to a few of the girls I knew. I saw Johnny staring at me. I walked over to the bar and got another glass of champagne. Again I spotted Johnny across the room, staring at me. I smiled and turned away. I forgot about him for a while but when I looked up, I saw he was still watching.

Suddenly, he elbowed his way across the room very quickly. He approached me with purpose. He put his hands on my shoulders and looked into my eyes so deeply and so intensely that I felt more naked than when I am naked. He got right down to business.

He said, "Honey, excuse me for staring but I must tell you: You really have 'it.' I'm never wrong. I work with them all. Lana Turner. Esther Williams. Rita Hayworth. They don't have what you have."

The way he continued to look at me I didn't doubt that he sincerely believed what he was saying for a moment. It wasn't lust talking. It wasn't champagne talking. He was passionate and excited and crystal clear.

"Y-you think I have something more than Rita Hayworth?" I asked. "And Lana Turner?"

"Honey…" he said, "…what's your name?"

"Marilyn."

"Marilyn," he went on, talking very quickly, a little spit flying out here and there. "I'm Johnny Hyde. Have you heard of me? I don't know if you know this, I'm an agent. I'm with The William Morris Agency. Actually, I'm the vice president there. I see a hundred girls a week. I've been seeing a hundred girls a week for longer than you've been alive. And none of them have what you have!"

Johnny and I spent the rest of the evening talking. What surprised me was that it wasn't a conversation filled with sexual innuendo and snide derogatory compliments about body parts and what kind of "talents" I might have. He was curious about my career. What studios had I been signed to? What small parts had I played? Why didn't the studios renew my contracts? What direction did I see my career going in?

New Year's Eve was going on all around us in full force but we might as well have been alone in a cabin in the woods.

When the evening was over he knew more about my career than anyone else. He saw this special "somethingness" in me, which I have always felt but was unable to identify or name. And there was something I knew for sure: He wanted a career for me as much as I wanted it for myself.

Of course sex did come into play. The next week he invited me to Palm Springs.

He was fifty-three, I was twenty-two. Over the weekend, I learned that he was married and had four sons. I learned that he was in poor physical health—he had a bad heart.

It was in Palm Springs that he found out about my past. Born a bastard. A mother in a mental institution. The foster homes. The orphanages. The sexual abuse. The teenage marriage. My years of ups and downs on the party circuit. He saw that I was broken. His passion was to fix me.

He wanted to help me expand my horizons too. He didn't look down on the fact that I had no formal education, was a high school dropout. He encouraged me to read the classics. To write poetry. To listen to great music. He made suggestions.

One day Johnny was studying some new photographs of me.

"You know, Marilyn," he said, in a very gentle voice, "I've been thinking that maybe you should have just the slightest, tiny bit shaved off the tip of your nose."

"A nose job?" I asked, surprised.

"Well, not exactly," he said. "Just a minor alteration."

I informed him that I had been a successful model for years, had been on many magazine covers, and had already appeared in several minor movies. No one had ever suggested I needed any modifying.

He spoke directly. "Listen, honey, in this business everyone has something done at one time or another. Things we don't see in real life show up magnified on the movie screen. You can never be too careful. The camera will catch you from every angle."

I trusted him. I let him make an appointment to have the procedure done.

Afterwards, there wasn't much of a difference. I mean, no one I knew mentioned anything. But knowing that Johnny was satisfied gave me a little more confidence.

First he was infatuated, then he was obsessed, then he was deeply and obsessively in love with me.

He left his wife. He left his family. I became his family. He rented a beautiful house in Beverly Hills for us to live in. Although I kept my tiny apartment, too, so I could have a place to escape to just in case I needed to....escape. I never learned to trust any situation.

Johnny became my agent. He was my advisor. He was a friend. We became lovers. Soon he was asking me to marry him. I couldn't. Although I appreciated him. God, how I appreciated him! And I did grow to love him very dearly. I simply wasn't *in love* with him. I knew the difference after being with Fred.

I wanted to please him. I wanted his happiness. I *was* his happiness. But I had too much respect for him to marry him if I wasn't in love.

But he continued to work for me.

He would call all the important directors and say, "I have this new girl. Marilyn Monroe. You must see her! She is a knockout."

They'd say, "We've seen her."

And Johnny would implore, "See her again!"

Johnny wasn't a physically strong man. God, you could feel that just being with him. He was frail. His bad heart left him gasping for breath many times. Before we went to bed he would take a pill and I would say, "Johnny, maybe it would be better if we didn't have sex," and he would very quickly say, "No, no…it's alright, Marilyn. It's all right." But I know his doctors had warned him that sex with me was dangerous.

I had never experienced anything so total, so complete, so all-encompassing as Johnny's love for me.

Each evening Johnny would escort me to all the important restaurants and clubs, and introduce me to Hollywood's elite. Being "Johnny's girl," as I was dubbed, gave me a faux respectability in this ice cold town.

Oh how I wished I could feel about him the way he felt about me. It would have made things so much easier if I could fall in love with him. We'd be a perfect match. But I was still in love with Fred. If there was some magic potion to swallow or injection to take or some mountain to climb that would make you fall in love with a person, I would have done it for Johnny. I felt Johnny deserved my love. After all, he loved me.

What was it that made him love me, being that I was so unlovable? Or was it the very fact that so many men, although they used me sexually, found me unlovable that made him love me so?

Still, I could only look at him as a very loving friend and mentor. When he kissed me, there wasn't a strong passion on my part. When he touched me, there wasn't that incredible tingling. I'd close my eyes and pretend it was Fred and sometimes, like that, I could reach orgasm. Other times I could fake it well enough—by this time I'd become an expert at becoming what men wanted me to be.

But I wouldn't cheat Johnny by becoming his wife.

That's the way things are set up in life, I guess. Everyone has to love the other a little more or a little less. God did that, I think, just to keep things interesting for Himself.

Because I couldn't love him in the same way, his anger and resentment came to the surface sometimes. At times Johnny Hyde treated me the way the others did. He'd call me a "chump" in public. He'd pinch my ass. He ridiculed me in front of his friends. But underneath it all I knew he felt differently and was just doing it to save face. It was, I guess, considered degrading in his circles for one of them to actually fall in love with a "tramp." Yet in private, he never gave me anything but kindness and love. He was the first man in my life who understood me. Or tried to.

Because of my intense <u>need</u> to make it, most men and women saw me as two-faced and scheming. No matter how truthfully I treated them or how sincerely I behaved they always thought I was trying to put one over on them.

Johnny had a strategy for my career. All through 1949 he worked very hard to make people see in me what he saw – he constantly recommended me for parts. He urged directors to let me audition for them. At first it was "No, no, no." But eventually all of his hard work paid off—he had the kind of power that people in this town respected so some smart cookies said, "Hmm, well maybe we're missing something. Maybe I better give this girl a second look."

It was because of him I got to audition for the director John Huston for an important film called *The Asphalt Jungle*. I think just about every young actress in town wanted to be in this movie—and tested for it.

I got the part.

People in the industry started talking about this sensational new blonde. It was because of my role in that film I got another small but influential part in *All About Eve* directed by Joseph L. Mankiewicz. These were two wonderful roles that didn't have a lot of screen time. But the parts were in compelling scripts with top notch directors and huge

Hollywood stars. And my role in both films was intricate to the plot. They were "stand out" roles.

In late 1949, Johnny got me a new contract with Fox, the studio which had dropped me like a hot (or cold) tamale only two years before. Oh Darryl F. Zanuck still despised me. Still thought I had zero charisma. But he couldn't deny that my roles in those two films were causing a quite a buzz in the industry.

This time Johnny fought for a long-term contract for me at Fox, the studio that had dropped me after one year. The new contract, however, guaranteed me a very good income for seven years—I couldn't be dropped after six months or a year. I didn't know at the time he was ensuring security for me for when he wasn't around to take care of me. He was dying.

Johnny continued to beg me to marry him. I just couldn't. I had too much respect for the man.

He kept stressing the fact that when he died, which he was sure wasn't far off in the future, as his wife I would inherit everything that was his. Nearly a million dollars.

I said Johnny, "'I love you,' and 'I'm in love with you,' are two different feelings." He winced a bit but he recovered. He shrugged his shoulders. He said it didn't matter. He had already left his wife for me. His children were ashamed and angry at him. They saw me as a home wrecker. "None of that matters," he said. "I love you more than any soul on earth. I want you more than I've ever wanted anything."

And I, of course, was the only thing he couldn't have. I knew I was hurting him but I felt I didn't have a choice.

It was at about this time, right on cue you might say, that Fred Karger started coming around again! Now that I was no longer available to him, my value shot up 100% in his eyes. Also, the fact that a rich, powerful, successful man wanted me, made Fred appraise me anew and say, "Well, maybe she *is* quite a catch."

I still loved him but I saw his game. I would sleep with him from time to time (please don't judge me) I was a young, healthy woman and I needed to get the sexual fulfillment from Fred that I wasn't getting from Johnny. But the difference was that, this time, I wouldn't give Fred a commitment. I wouldn't spend nights with him. I wouldn't say "I love you." I could feel movie stardom closer to my grasp than ever before and it made me realize it was more important to me than the love of one man. This made him want me all the more.

He'd come banging on my door late at night screaming, "I love you! I love you!" The drama of it all, starring me, was sort of interesting. But I would just pull the covers over my head and try to ignore him. Finally I had to stop seeing him altogether, lest he ruin things for me and Johnny.

But that didn't stop Fred. He sent his mother, whom I loved and still love to this day, to my apartment to beg me to marry her son. It was amazing. Months before this man couldn't care less if I came or went and I would have gotten down on my hands and knees and crawled that way clear across the country if it would have made him feel the way about me I had felt about him. Now he was lowering himself to have his mother come do his begging for him! I told her I couldn't.

Meanwhile I would go to the movie theaters in the afternoon to watch, again and again, the few minutes of myself on screen in the two movies I had recently completed. I'd watch myself up there and I simply would burst with joy. I mean, there I was standing next to Bette Davis or Louis Calhern or Anne Baxter. And I was pretty good, even if I do have to say so myself.

Johnny died.

Just as I was entering the happiest and most thrilling time of my life he died.

We all know that pain of loss. That terrible goodbye. It was the first time I had experienced such a death. Johnny was an agent and a lover and the best friend I ever had. No one ever believed in me and loved me as much as that man. And all of that was snatched away from me so quickly.

When Johnny lay dying in the hospital his family kept me out. They wouldn't let me see him. They wouldn't let me in the room. To them I was the "blonde tramp." I had to linger in the hospital hall where I could hear him calling for me. Did he know that I was there and that they were keeping me out? I never knew.

I should have ran down the hall into his room, pushed them aside, and said, "I'm here Johnny! I'm here! Don't die afraid. Die knowing I love you!" But back then I was even more timid and fearful than I am now. And I fear he might have died without knowing I was there for him, just a few yards away.

The more I thought about that the more unbearable it became. I relived his last moments over and over in my head. Thinking of all the things I wished I could say. Death is just so…so final. The door is closed. The phone is unplugged. No one is home anymore.

I needed to at least see his body one last time but I was also strictly forbidden by his family to go to his funeral. But I was so devastated at not being at his bedside when he died that I screwed up all my courage and went to the funeral anyway. I had to take some pills and have a few drinks before the ceremony so I could get up my courage to go…but during the ceremony I could feel the stares and the whispering and the hatred.

The powerful combination of liquor and pills didn't calm me. Instead they unleashed the anguish in me and I threw myself on Johnny's coffin sobbing and sobbing.

Won't anyone put their arms around me? I needed Johnny to console me about his own death. I wanted to crawl in and join him in his cold, cold slumber.

In his will he left me not one thin penny. I was fine with that. All I ever wanted from anybody was love and respect. He gave me that. Still, he could never forgive me for not marrying him—I understood. But what he gave me no amount of money could buy. Some belief in myself. The feeling of being loved.

Again I thought of killing myself. Mr. Death, again. Nearby, again. Hello, again, Mr. Death.

Johnny had been my life preserver on the violent sea of Hollywood. Now he was dead and my choices were to stay afloat or let myself go down with him. I was tired, but the contract that he had arranged for me gave me some fight. Because of him there were two hit movies playing in theaters which I had been a part of.

I decided to survive.

Now that Johnny was dead I wasn't as hot a property for films as I had been with him alive and in my corner. His plan was for me to only do important roles with the best of the best. But in this town, in the beginning, you are only as important as the man you are associated with.

September 2, 1961 (Los Angeles)

Well, if anything good came out of having the gallbladder surgery it's that I've lost more weight since July. Because I already started dieting and working out with dumbbells before the operation my body is better than it has ever been.

If I can't say I'm completely happy I can at least say I'm slim!

And although the scar is still nasty I have hope it will fade. I'm feeling good about myself again.

Frank Sinatra has been the main man in my life these past few months. And there are times when I am with him it feels so right. Like we're meant to be.

He's been hurt in love. His career has had many ups and downs. He understands the artistic temperament. He's reached a level of power and success in the entertainment business now that I think will last for the rest of his life. Don't get me wrong, I think it's well deserved. He's one of the most amazing performers of our time.

We'll take off in his private jet. Or spend a weekend on his yacht. He'll say, "Marilyn."

I'll say, "Yes, Frankie."

And he'll say, "Nothing. Just 'Marilyn.' I like saying your name. I like knowing you're with me."

I melt.

He flies me to the moon. I've got him under my skin.

Then, though, without explanation, I won't hear a word from him for a week or two. No phone calls. Nothing. I don't even have any idea where he is. But I read in the gossip columns that he is with some other woman. "A different dame," as he would say.

I start to wonder, "Am I wasting my time? Is he just using me?"

Then he shows up with a pair of exquisite emerald earrings.

"Oh Frank, these are gorgeous. They must have cost a fortune!"

"Chump change, compared to what you're worth to me, baby."

I know that he recognizes the darkness in me. It's there.

I think there is a sickness that lives in me—buried and hard to reach. I can't get rid of it and I can't deny it. I think it scares Frank to death. No one wants to always be around someone who can get lost in a fog of depression and despair as deep as I can. I try not to show my sadness when I'm with him. But sometimes it just comes through. As a result I over-medicate. I can tell he gets uptight.

I heard that one of his advisors advised him to dump me. Someone else who was present during the conversation told me Frank shrugged and said, "By now I would have cut any other broad loose. But, Marilyn—I just can't do it. I can't get her out of my system."

We went on a four day cruise to Catalina on his yacht last weekend with Dean Martin, his wife Jeanne and Mike and Gloria Romanoff.

We played cards, sunned, and drank an awful lot. It was fun.

But then, sometimes in the night, that familiar darkness would fill up in me. I'd be lying next to Frank, who was sound asleep. I took some sleeping pills because I'd want to be asleep too—to be with him in his dreams. But sleep stayed away and I could literally feel a gloominess creeping through my body. My body was tired but my mind wouldn't shut up. I couldn't lay there any longer.

I'd stumble out to the deck and look at the sea. I was always careful to crawl back into bed next to Frank so I'd be there when he woke up. He'd want to make love again.

When we docked they had all planned a get-together ashore. But I couldn't bear it. I had put all my energy during the cruise into being the happy, witty hostess. I just called a limo service and went back home thinking, "They won't miss me anyway."

September 10, 1961

A few days after I got back from the weekend with Sinatra, Jack called me. It's as if these guys have some inner bugging device that lets them know when someone else is after their property. Every man wants what another man has. It seems to me when you are off the market, your value goes up! They want you more than ever!

Jacqueline was going to be out of town and he asked me to come and visit him at the White House! How can I refuse? The house that I've seen in history books and on money and that will be talked about for as long as there is America. Me! Invited! And as a guest—not as part of the gawking, popcorn chomping public.

Part of me said, "No, Marilyn. You're involved with Frank. But then I replied, "Hey Marilyn, why don't you live like a man?"

I had just seen a picture of Frank in the papers with a young and very pretty dancer named Juliet Prowse. The item said that they were very chummy. It stung. I hope I'm worth more to him than a pair of emerald earrings.

The old story. They are in love with you while you're with them. But they're able to go off into a private adventure for a week or a month. When they get back they expect you to pick up where it was left off like nothing happened. They love you again.

I think Frank needs a break from the disarray of me from time to time.

It's true! I want to love more like a man. I said to myself, "Okay, Frank. Have fun with your dancer. I'm off to spend some time with the president."

Peter made the arrangements (of course.) He had me flown in – it's all in great secrecy and intrigue and urgency. Which made it all the more fun! I put on my black wig and horn-rimmed glasses. Peter, the clown, told everyone on the plane that I was a secretary. He gets on my nerves, Peter does, sometimes. I don't have that kind of sense of humor. I don't think a clown is funny. And I know that deep in Peter's seamy little heart, he likes to humiliate me. He resents the fact that I am with Jack. He wants me for himself.

Or, perhaps, I just thought of this, he wants Jack for himself. Sometimes I get the feeling that Peter is....oh, how do you describe it? It's as if he's a woman inside the body of a man. Oh, he has affairs with women, I know, but his sexual activities are so weird that it's almost like he's trying to punish himself for some reason. Well, let's just say I've heard rumors which some of his behavior confirms.

But when I got to the White House Jack and I spent a glorious three days together.

Have I ever been in love like this before? With Fred, my first true taste of love? With Joe? With Arthur? With Yves?

With Frank?

I think I have been in love with all of them.

With Jack, though, I feel a mixture of complex emotions of elation and hope and, well, power. It's intoxicating. As a matter of fact it's so overwhelming it's difficult to figure out if it's love in its purest form or just some sort of forceful infatuation with lust and power.

Then there is the reality that my last two films didn't do well. That I'm getting older. That I need to get on with my career before there is no career to get back to. But…still…Now that I have Jack in my life, all my career problems seem less important. And I feel like an ingénue again. More than that, I feel his strength. I feel protected.

While I was in Washington, he took me on his boat called "The Honey Fitz." And we went sailing and the sun was new and the wind was new and the sea was new. I've never experienced any of them before. I had been blind to the beauty around me and now I could see—and I could feel. He took me all the way down the Potomac and went all the way down to Cyanic Cove and we didn't come back until it was very late at night.

We spent an entire day on the boat. We sailed at high speeds. We swam naked in the sea. We made love, and for me, it was the first time. Well, not really – obviously – but even "that" felt like something absolutely new and special.

While I had the run of the White House. I pretended I was the First Lady. I made it a point to make friends with a woman on the White House staff. She is one of Mrs. Kennedy's (AKA JACQUELINE) many assistants. Her name is Irene Chatterton, but everyone calls her "Mrs. Chatterbox" behind her back. Irene said to me, "This is probably totally inappropriate, but I'm a big fan of yours."

She could come in handy. I saw the value of her as an ally in a situation that could run amok with enemies, so I turned the Monroe charm on high for her. She said, "May I ask you for a big favor Miss Monroe?"

"Of course, Irene," I said.

"Would you sign something for me?"

"I'd be delighted," I said and I started fishing around for a piece of paper and a pen.

"Actually," she said, "it's something I want to give my husband. I'm almost embarrassed to ask…"

"Oh you don't have to be shy with me Irene," I laughed. "By now I've heard it all."

"Well," she blushed, "I was wondering if you'd sign me a pair of your panties." And then she added hastily…"For my husband, of course."

"Oh well I…you know, I'm not wearing panties," I replied. "I never do."

Irene was crestfallen. Then she said: "I have an idea," and she scurried upstairs. A few minutes later she returned with a white lacy pair of undies.

"These are actually Mrs. Kennedy's," she said mater-of-factly. "But she hasn't worn them yet. They are brand new."

The idea of signing a pair of Jacqueline Kennedy's panties was pretty appalling, even if they were unworn, but what could I do? Mrs. Chatterbox was an important link and I didn't want to offend her. So I took the panties and started signing.

"No," she said, and blushed once more. "I mean, you have to put them on first. Otherwise it wouldn't be the same."

The idea of putting on a pair of Jacqueline Kennedy's panties was equivalent to me as the notion of swallowing a live goldfish. But, (I kept telling myself) back in the 1920's, swallowing live goldfish was a college hobby and many people went through with it, so I guessed I could stand to put on Jacqueline's unmentionables for a few, short seconds. I pulled them on under my dress, while Mrs. Chatterbox ogled me wide-eyed, and I shook my fanny a little to break them in. Then I rolled them down and signed the back of the silky material, "Some like it HOT! Marilyn Monroe."

It was a mission accomplished – and well worth it. Now Mrs. Chatterbox calls me regularly now with the latest in White House news. If you ever want to find out any gossip out about a couple, befriend the help.

September 12, 1961

I've been with more than a fair share of married men. It's not something I'm proud of. It's not something I set out to do. And it's not that I'm not sympathetic with the wives knowing their man is out with someone else. I know how horrible I feel when I hear that Jack is with some other woman or Frank is linked to someone else.

The way I look at it, and perhaps this might only be a way to justify it to myself, is that you can't break up a happy marriage. If a couple is happy neither one is looking for someone else. And they'll fight every temptation that comes their way in order to be true and loyal to each other.

I think the basic instinct of human nature is to look for happiness. An awful lot of couples I've known aren't happy and they're sticking together because, well, maybe moral conventions, or children, or even career reasons. Yet both of them would rather be anywhere else.

I know this to be true because from my earliest years, back in my days on the party circuit, most of the men I became involved with were married and they told me unhappy stories about their marriages. I can only hope that their wives were finding fulfillment, as well, outside of the marriage.

I'm also speaking from experience. I've been in marriages after they have gone sour. Life is too short to live that way.

September 13, 1961

"Why are you crying? A girl like you! A young, beautiful girl. You have your whole life ahead of you." These were the first words the great director Elia Kazan said to me back in 1951.

I was lost and I was afraid.

With Johnny Hyde's death there was quite a lot of talk about me in a sexual way floating around Hollywood. Men would say, "Gee, Johnny Hyde's dead, his girl is adrift, and she's a knockout." Sympathetic things like that.

But, you know, I didn't want fear to be the dominating force in my persona at the time. Later I learned (and used) the power in being the little girl lost. But at this stage in my life the men in control wanted the starlets to be the happy, gay girl.

However, it was fine to be sad and cry if it left them an opening to seduce you. Then it was okay

All the cigar-puffing, gum chewing, studio executives in Hollywood started smelling around me as if my sexual relations with Johnny had left a strong scent which intoxicated them and summoned them to sniff and slobber in my direction. They all wanted to get "in' where Johnny had been, to see what was the reason for his obsession.

"If a great and talented guy like Johnny Hyde was fucking her she must be some great lay – I want to get me a piece of that."

So my phone was ringing off the hook with show business tycoons, agents, up-and-coming movie stars and any other man with a penis that pointed in my direction. I despised them.

I talked to no one. I saw no one. My grief was real.

But more than that, I knew these men and their tactics by now. They still didn't believe in me as an actress. It was only an erotic curiosity. I wasn't about to give into that now. Johnny had convinced me I had something to offer the industry. I mean, I wasn't about to throw myself away on just anybody.

Darryl F. Zanuck conveyed to them all that he still considered me a talentless party girl, Johnny had been wrong about my potential, Zanuck liked to say. In spite of my two good performances—and I do think they were good—he intended to play out the seven years left in my contract by just putting me in bit parts in forgettable pictures, hoping that I would then just quietly skulk away into a dark corner of the world and leave him alone—never to darken the entrance to his studio again.

Oh how I was hated! You have no idea.

I was in the middle of making one of those forgettable movies, playing the bit part of a secretary. But mostly I was mourning Johnny. I would do my scenes and then go hide in some corner of the soundstage and collapse in tears.

I was actually hiding in a dark corner weeping (I wasn't important enough to have a dressing room) when Elia Kazan, who everyone called "Gadge," came over to me in the darkness – his dick leading the way.

Gadge was a friend of the director of this movie and was visiting the set. He had watched me shoot the scene. The talk around town had reached him. He knew who I was. He followed the scent.

He said that he was very sorry about Johnny. He said, "If there's anything I could do," I should let him know. He said that he knows how difficult it is for "a little girl like you" to be alone in a town like this.

Basically he was saying to me everything that the tycoons, agents, and actors with the pointed penises had been saying to me since Johnny died. But then he just fell silent and sat beside me breathing softly, not saying a word. I thought that was kind of strange. We sat like that for over a half an hour, until they called me to the set again for the next take. When I got up to go, Gadge grabbed my hand and said something that pierced me in a way that cut through my fog of despair.

Gadge said, "I'd like to take you out to dinner. We don't have to talk or anything. I would just be with you. You wouldn't have to say a word."

I was so naïve back then. I thought, "Well, gee, here is a really nice guy. Here's someone who can see that I'm in pain and he just cares about my well-being." So I accepted his offer.

Okay, wait a minute.

I think it would only be fair to add that I knew who he was too. Elia Kazan was and is a very in-demand film director. He came from the prestigious New York stage, and had done several very well-received films. But his latest movie was *A Streetcar Named Desire* starring Marlon Brando and Vivien Leigh. The word was out: It was electric! It was clear to everyone that he had a great future in the movie business.

If the question was put to me, asking if I would have accepted his offer to go out to dinner if I didn't know of his high ranking position, I must quite honestly say I would have. After all, other important men had called inviting me out and I had refused them. But Gadge was patient. I thought he had a kind face. He seemed good-hearted. He made me feel safe.

After that first dinner we saw each other quite a bit for the next year or so.

Yet, even in my torment in those days, I...uh...well...was thinking about my career in movies. I was well aware he had a new movie in development called *Viva Zapata*, which was also to star Marlon Brando. I could only hope that there might be some part in it I could play and that Gadge would come to recognize the talent that Johnny had seen in me.

Now I know, of course, that Elia Kazan was all about his cock.

And so it came to pass that we did have an affair. With the greatest trepidation I entered his bed.

Survival mode at the time: A girl needed a bed.

Afterwards, Gadge ever so sweetly said, "No night will ever be the same."

Gadge Kazan: What can I say? He was like so many of the older men I dated during the late 1940s and early 50s. You just knew he had been the shy, unpopular, not terribly attractive, book-worm kid in school. The kind of guy that looks at the pretty cheerleaders in their lipstick and heels and longs for them but could never get them—and a burning, lasting resentment towards them grows. But a fascination grows as well. In his climbing years, he married a plain but devoted and intellectual woman who became the mother of his children.

But with his talent now recognized and his success on the New York stage and in Hollywood assured, his prominent nose, small, compact body and uncanny instinct for talent took on the form of charisma. And he now became coveted by the very type of women that spurned him in his youth, and although he was nice to us, I think he secretly scorned us.

He was the type of man, not exactly rare, that looked down on young women who weren't married and had affairs—particularly girls in show business. At the same time he jumped into bed with a new girl at every opportunity, but that only raised himself up in his own estimation.

With the overpowering power of power, and his wife back in New York while he was on movie business in Los Angeles, Gadge was all about making up for what he missed out on in his earlier years. His mind was dirty. He couldn't help but experience as many young, sexy girls as possible. I was one of them.

Most of his technique was simple. What he didn't have in facial good looks and bodily brawn he made up for with his brilliant ideas for stage and cinema. He had artistic vision. He made us girls feel that the big, handsome, muscular males were the undesirables—and the little giants like himself were the most attractive males of the species. And, with fluttering eyes and beating hearts—and the hopes of being discovered—we fell for it.

But, still, at night, I found myself waking up crying, "Oh Johnny! Help me! Help me!"

He mastered the art of seduction: When talking, Gadge whispered in your ear to make what he was saying seem more urgent. He ran his hand up and down your back for emphasis. He swaggered about and flirted and teased.

He often commented on my loveliness.

I do think he was truly fascinated by beautiful women. He was one of the best listeners I ever came in contact with. He liked to listen to the stories I told him about growing up as a child and coming up in show business.

His theory, and it made sense to me, was that "girls like me," who grew up without a stable family, and particularly without a father, have no self-esteem and we seek out men who will give us a sense of self-worth. It was obvious he believed this theory and sought out "girls like me," so he could assist in giving us a sense of worthiness.

He said, "Marilyn, your great tragedy is that the men you seek your self-worth from are the ones who treat you with the most scorn because deep down inside you share their opinion of yourself." He added, "Don't throw yourself away on those jerks." What he didn't even admit to himself, though, was that he was one of those men.

But I also think, and this just came to me (it's very exciting when a revelation comes as I'm writing), that he found the worth of a woman based on the men she had been with. For example, I'm not sure he would have had as much interest in me as he did if he hadn't known of my relationship with Johnny Hyde.

Mixed in with his passion, Gadge felt a certain amount of disdain for me even as he was being kind. And maybe even he didn't realize it. See, rather than feel scorn for himself for wanting me so much, he turned that feeling vaguely towards me. This was common among all the men of his ilk.

And, in me, a tiny seed of rage was planted.

When we first started seeing each other I tried to put Johnny out of my mind when we went on dates. After spending the night together Gadge would drive me home, as the sun was rising, in his convertible. In the unrelenting sunlight, we'd be screaming, laughing, and singing at the top of our longs. He called us, "two mad monks."

During this time, I often wore white, partially because I think it suits me. It compliments my blondness. But I also wore a lot of white, I think now, because wearing white was a way of purifying myself.

It was after one of these madcap car rides that Gadge said I was the happiest girl he ever knew. I was a better actress then he gave me credit for. I was in great distress during most of the time we were together. I kept hoping he'd offer me a role or at least a screen test for *Viva Zapata* but that never came about.

Still, he's not easy to write about. He was filled with contradictions. Our entire relationship was filled with contradictions.

Gadge could be kind.

We would lie in bed for hours while he counted the freckles on my breast.

Being kissed up and down the arch of my back was a comfort.

He never sent me home in a cab—he always made sure he drove me home and escorted me to my door. Maybe that sounds like a small thing, but the way girls were treated: *Oh my God!* That seemed like a huge sign of respect back in the day. Only now can I look back and see what a tiny dignity it was.

He was the type of friend who you could call at any hour with a problem and, if he was alone, he would try to help you. Note: If he was alone.

He was very wise about art and theater and literature and always filled with ideas. He shared his wisdom and his advice without hesitation.

Once when the loss of Johnny and the feeling of loss and hopelessness overwhelmed me, he held me very tenderly all night and rocked me in his arms. That kind of kindness I could never forget.

I could be wrong, but I think he fell in love with me a little bit that night. He told me he did. He was such a strange dichotomy, Gadge was. As long as he was in the dominant role and I was submissive, and in awe of him, he was completely infatuated.

Actually, I think he loved me in earnest for a year.

He often told me "Be proud of yourself!"

But his feelings were certainly a mixture of love, hate and obsession. He disliked being in the thrall of a "girl like me."

My damaged self, allowed him to show me his sensitivity. On certain nights we cried together holding each other.

Years later, after I became a star, I heard that he had said about me, "I never thought a girl like Marilyn was star material." He downplayed our relationship. Whatever it was he truly thought of me, he certainly seemed as if he couldn't get enough of me at the time.

What kind of girl was I?

It made me wonder. It was something to consider.

There were many kinds of girls in the world. This much I knew. I didn't understand my place.

I had known quite a few "girls" in my day. The world allowed us certain roles in life.

Girls who were born into wealthy families, had wonderful educations, married young into the kind of family that was expected of them, and spent their lives sexually dissatisfied—blind—while their husbands played around.

There were girls who were born with ambitions and had the means to follow their dreams. They worked hard at their careers, achieved marvelous things, but were spurned by men because they were accomplished—so they spent their lives as successful, lonely, divorcees or spinsters.

There were also girls I had known whose only gift was beauty. Girls who hoped that a successful man would marry them so they would have a life of protection and comfort—if not fulfillment.

Don't let me leave out the girls who grew up in poor backgrounds who had no direction but had a sexual attractiveness and slept around in hopes of finding some "thing" to fill them up.

These were the "kind of girls" who I knew during my journey through Hollywood. I didn't fit into any of these categories. Nor did I judge them. Instead, I admired them for trying to find a place in a world that did everything it could to exclude them.

I must admit I didn't like being judged or compared—especially by men who had no standards by which they were judged. It made me feel helpless and angry.

The truth is, I came from nowhere. I had no resources. When it came to survival, I found what I could that worked for the moment. Something that might move me further in my ambitions. I longed for a place where this ambition and conviction might be admired by some. Instead it was always met with extreme distaste. I was a woman!

SHE HAS GOALS THAT REACHED BEYOND WHAT A MAN COULD DO FOR HER! HOW DARE SHE!

There came a time that I knew my relationship with Gadge was a dead end. After all, he had a wife and family and many other women to explore. Although he enjoyed being with me—he enjoyed teaching me things, giving me advice, and steering me in the right direction when I was lost—we would never have a life together.

When it comes to moving on, I could be ruthless.

The main reason I broke off the relationship was he gave absolutely no encouragement for me as an actress. His assessment of my career was brutal. He thought it was something I should give up. Although he at times gave me advice on the direction of my career, his ultimate opinion was that the price was too high. That the only parts I'd be given were cheap floozies in low budget programmers. He said there was no future in the movies for me—but that he cared for me—and if I wanted us to continue seeing each other he wanted me to give up acting altogether. This was very damaging for me to hear, being as he was so talented.

His lack of belief in me as an actress left me bruised. I knew I had to cut it off completely. I thought if I continued to see him I'd lose all my hard-earned confidence. What little of it there was.

The hunger in me to make it was greater than anything else.

It really sort of came down to the level of self-preservation. I was struggling to develop in my work. I told him if he couldn't support me in that, I didn't want to see him anymore.

Gadge was surprised I chose to continue with my career rather than be with him (part-time.) He was furious. I think he was really shocked that a girl like me would cut him loose. He wrote me an angry letter saying that he wanted to see me and talk it over face to face, adding "Don't you think I'm worth that much?" (Was that the ignored school boy in him imploring a cheerleader to acknowledge him?)

Of course, I replied to his letter. I said, I knew his worth. I appreciated the time we spent together, and that I realized life is a series of compromises, but I wasn't willing to compromise my career. Not that! I said I would cherish some of the times we shared and that I was willing to bury all the negative times. I ended it by saying that I knew he would respect my wishes for him not to call or write me again.

Eventually we became friends again. After all he had introduced me to Arthur Miller who I did fall in love with. Arthur treated me very different than Gadge, outwardly anyway, but I would come to realize that on the inside he felt the exact same way about me.

But I want to finish writing what I know about Elia Kazan while I'm on the subject.

He enjoyed girls like me while he was the powerful one. While he could be the mentor and feel superior. Although sexual desire brings everyone down to the same level, he still had the power to help a career along. He liked that he could lord his influence over us.

Once I became more famous and, in my way, more powerful than him, his scorn really came to the surface. A few years after I was with him, I was one of the top box office attractions in the world and I had just negotiated a new contract with Fox that gave me approval of any directors on all of my projects. I included Elia Kazan on the list of directors I would work with. No matter what I will always respect his talent.

After I made a sexy comedy called *The Seven Year Itch* I very much wanted to star in a dramatic picture that would show my range. Tennessee Williams had written a script called *Baby Doll* and it was to be directed by Elia Kazan. It was one of Tennessee's steamy character studies that took place in the deep south and focused on a character, "Baby Doll," who is a sexy, backwards, thumb-sucking woman who sleeps in a crib— and the men vying for her affections.

Yes, it was another dumb, sexy role, but "Baby Doll" was a real character infused with Tennessee's poetic dialogue. It would provide the chance I had been waiting for to prove myself as a serious actress. I desperately wanted to play the role. It was exactly the kind of prestigious, artistic venture that would have given me a higher profile in Hollywood and would have encouraged them to consider me for a wider variety of roles.

The studio thought I would be good in the film. Tennessee Williams certainly wanted me to play the part. But for reasons I couldn't understand at the time, Gadge refused to cast me.

This was a message he was sending me. I see very clearly now that he could not stand that the balance of power had shifted. I was a bigger star than he was. How could he work with a girl like me?

Even, now, in the past few months the studio wanted him to direct me in a drama that they had been thinking of casting me in. Again Elia

Kazan refused to work with me. He cast Lee Remick in the part instead.

See, the thing is, I had rejected him as the girls in high school had rejected him. And now I have risen to a level that no "girl like me" should rise to—especially without his help and blessing.

He'd be damned if he'd squander his talent on "a girl like me."

That's how he demonstrates his low opinion of me—by refusing to work with me. But somehow I get the feeling he really wants revenge on me—and somehow, someway, he will find a way to get it.

This would happen over and over again during my career with many people.

October 3, 1961

Jack called.

He announced that Jacqueline was going out of town again. He asked if I'd like to fly out to Washington to see him. He was confident that it would be a "kick."

"More fun than last time."

It's kind of hard for me to take this roller coaster ride. I wonder if he's thinking about me when I don't hear from him for weeks at a time. Is he busy? Is he seeing someone else? Is he afraid of the gossip?

And then, just when I'm trying to forget about him and getting on with my life, I hear from him. He has some incredible hold on me and I can't say "no." Every ounce of blood in my body, every fiber of my being, tells me that he's using me, that he doesn't feel anything for me except maybe lust and the satisfaction of being with the most desirable woman in the world. But then all he has to do is throw me a little bone…a crumb of flattery…and I go running after him like a dog.

Is it the challenge, I wonder, that keeps me tied to him? The challenge of making him love me? Every single time I'm with him I think that this is the breakthrough. This is the time that I actually got him to feel something for me. I leave him, thinking that he loves me.

And then he disappears out of my life once more.

Yet, when I'm with him, I can't show him how hurt I am. I can't be sad. Jack wouldn't relate to sadness at this point. He knows of my tortured past. Depression, fear, sadness, pain: these qualities would spell "trouble" for him in his current position. Now he likes me beautiful and sharp and sexy and witty. I pull myself together. I try to be all of those things for him.

I know, I know what you're thinking: Just stay away from him.

How can I, when everything reminds me of him? He's the president! He's discussed everywhere! I know that I should stay away. Yet here I am, skyrocketing towards a crash on a planet called "Hurt."

I flew to Washington to be with him.

I was sneaked into the White House as a secretary again. Brother Bobby Kennedy was nowhere in sight. However, the youngest Kennedy brother, Ted, approached me – just for comedy relief. He is as bad as the others! A real grabber. He's the most classically handsome of the three, but the dullest. Actually, he struck me as a bit of a buffoon.

It doesn't seem to matter to any of them that they're all married. For them, life is a free-for-all at the buffet table and women are the lobster salad.

To my surprise, Teddy asked me out to dinner. He seemed sincere. I didn't want to hurt his feelings so I flirted a little, "Now, now little boy," I teased, "Maybe when you grow up."

He said, "Oh, but let me show you, Miss Monroe, how grown up I am."

I let that be his exit line. Only I was the one who did the exiting.

Jack and I didn't have time to go out on "The Honey Fitz" this time, but we did take a late afternoon skinny-dip in the White House pool. You can't imagine what it felt like, me, Norma Jeane the orphan, the waif, the starlet no studio wanted to put under contract…the woman the press refers to as a joke…me, Marilyn Monroe, at the White House, in the pool, completely naked with the most important man in the world!

Teddy sort of made excuses to be out by the pool so he could watch.

And, the ol' exhibitionist in me couldn't help but give him an eyeful. I played and squealed and hopped up and down in the water, knowing that the setting sun had me back lit and he really couldn't see all that much. But enough to, shall we say, "hook him."

Now he's been calling me up. Ted! I don't know how he got my number. What do the Kennedys' think I am? A silver plate filled with caviar to be passed around for each one of them to put on a cracker and nibble on. I mean I have to laugh but it's really not funny. "Why, Master Kennedy," I said. "What a surprise."

I immediately called Jack at the White House to tell him about his baby brother's phone call. I really couldn't care less, I mean, if there's one thing I've learned in life, it's how to get rid of an overly-zealous suitor. But I hadn't heard from Jack since I got back from Washington (not even to thank me for coming out there while being very busy with pre-production for my picture, no less) or even just to say hello. So it gave me an excuse to telephone him.

Well at least he took my call right away, without giving me the runaround. I told him his baby brother is trying to play like the big boys.

"He's been after you, has he?" Jack asked.

Then he laughed and laughed as if it were the funniest thing in the world.

Later that day, Mrs. Chatterbox called me and said that she heard Jack tell Teddy, "Listen little brother, hands off where Marilyn is concerned. She's mine."

If I'm his, why aren't I living in the White House?

October 17, 1961

News today from 20th Century Fox.

I've been fighting for so long and so hard to make movies where the script is good and the director is good and the other actors are good. Unfortunately I could count the number of times that all of those things came together on a movie set on one finger.

I want to tell you about this movie I'm being forced to make for Fox. I was informed of the assignment this past week. It's a remake of a classic old movie from the 1940s called *My Favorite Wife* and it originally starred Cary Grant and Irene Dunne.

I DO NOT want to make this movie for a number of reasons. The main reason is, I've seen the original movie. I think it is perfectly good, and there's absolutely no reason to remake it. It is a very light romantic comedy. I wouldn't mind doing a remake if I thought there was something new I could bring to it. But *My Favorite Wife* is fine just the way it is. And it's very much a movie of its era. Why try to compete with it in 1961?

The problem is I owe Fox one more picture on that contract I signed in 1955. It pays me $100,000 per movie, which is peanuts compared to what film stars get these days. I mean they really have absolutely no respect for me and look at me as a money making machine for them and want to give me as little as possible in return.

But I already turned down *Goodbye, Charlie*. If I give them any trouble about making this movie they could, maybe, sue me and keep me from making another movie for a year or two. I've already been off the screen for too long. And there's always new stars coming up.

Once I get this picture out of the way, I'll be a free agent and I can (perhaps) make the kind of movies I want to make and get paid the money I deserve. I figure I'll make this picture and flush Fox out of my system once and for all. The problem is I need my next picture to be a success.

My last two movies, which I didn't want to make in the first place, were not successful on any level.

So if I have to remake *My Favorite Wife*, which the studio has renamed *Something's Got to Give*, I at least want to make it as good as possible and try to bring some new life to the tired, old story.

I don't understand why it always falls on my shoulders! How about a little loyalty from a corporation I made millions for? I don't understand why they're not buying me the best properties around, tailored just for me! It's infuriating! Don't I ever get a moment to stop fighting?

The plot is about this woman – me – who is shipwrecked on a desert island. She has been missing for five years and is considered dead, when her husband decides to remarry. On the day of the wedding I get rescued and come home to reclaim my husband and two small children and of course the usual complication arise.

I asked them if they could at least have it rewritten so that it is tailored specifically for "Monroe" and so it has some sharp lines and funny situations. It's light but let's at least make it entertaining. Let's get the audiences into the theaters.

I don't know if anyone is listening. I often wonder if they really care what I feel about a new project. Or if they just say, "Yes, yes, yes." With the intention of doing exactly what they please.

October 18, 1961

Frank (Sinatra) called late last night. Just as I was finishing my writing.

He said, "You know, Marilyn, we are going to end up together. The chemistry is right between us."

He said, "The timing isn't right at the moment. But the right time will come and we will be together."

He ended the call by saying, "You know I love, ya."

It's nice to know Frank Sinatra is out there loving me somewhere. He can be a very loving and sympathetic guy, but he doesn't have the patience for my disarray.

And, obviously, it's not going to be enough to sit around and wait until he's ready—while, in the meantime, he dates dancers and showgirls.

October 19, 1961

If I ever marry again I will always want the other person to be in love with me a little bit more than I love him.

About Arthur Miller. Now that the divorce has settled in and some time has passed, I feel as if I can be more rational about analyzing our relationship. I can look at it through clear eyes and see it for what it really was.

So let me write some of it down before all the anger returns.

I think we were more in love with each other before we were married. Perhaps we were more in love with the idea of each other. I fell in love with Arthur because he was one of the first men to make me feel as if he was interested in me for more than my beauty. I first met him back in 1951. I wasn't a star yet I was just beginning to be known in Hollywood.

Here's the story:

I was introduced to Arthur Miller through Elia Kazan in early 1951. The two of them were good friends at the time. "Gadge," wanted to take me to a Hollywood party at the producer Charlie Feldman's house, but he had a commitment in the early evening so he said that he would meet me there. He suggested his friend, Arthur Miller, the playwright, pick me up and take me to the party and we could meet there later.

I said, "Hmm. No. I'll get there myself."

He said, "But you will stick close to Arthur at the party, won't you?"

"Yes, Gadge. He's a friend of yours. Of course I'll be nice to him."

At the party, Arthur and I sort of hit it off. He was so nice it was easy to like him.

On the surface, Arthur wasn't all that different from his friend, Gadge Kazan. They both were already powers in the New York theater scene. Arthur's play *Death of a Salesman* was considered a masterpiece (which Kazan had directed, by the way). Arthur was the bookworm type. A

Jewish, intellectual. Probably not popular with the glamorous girls back in his youthful days. And, like Gadge, he was married with children and he certainly was in awe and in lust with the pretty young girls Hollywood had to offer. But I thought I recognized a shyness regarding sex in him that the others lacked.

Yes. I remember clearly, he was as intimidated by me as I was of him.

Gadge hadn't arrived at the party yet so Arthur and I plopped down on a couch, away from the other guests, and we began talking…about my career, about his career, about Johnny Hyde and how I missed him, about his marriage and how he was terribly unhappy in it.

At one point he said: "I'm sorry if I seem a little awkward. It's just that, well, you're so beautiful it almost hurts to look at you."

Then he looked away.

I said, "Being a little shy isn't anything to be embarrassed about. It's refreshing, actually."

The way he looked at me was really, how can I say this—remarkable! I mean, I had grown used to men looking at me with lust or even admiration but Arthur looked at me, like, outside of himself. As if just being in my physical presence made him feel like a better man.

Obviously I was flattered. But, then, maybe I was misreading what he was feeling. Maybe it was just a mixture of lust and anxiety. Or even indigestion. Who knows?

If Gadge showed up that night, I didn't see him. He didn't make his presence known.

And while Arthur and I sat there on the couch, talking, I kicked off my shoes and tucked my legs under me, and Arthur, very gently, very discreetly, reached out and took hold of my big toe and held it while we talked. It was one of the tenderest things anyone had ever done to me physically. It was as if he had grabbed hold of my heart. I think that night we both fell a little in love.

But he was married, and he would soon go back to New York to his wife and children. Yet on that night at the Party at Charlie Feldman's we both touched each other in areas that we needed to be touched. Not literally…but emotionally…and that stayed with us. Our fantasies of each other started that night.

After the party Arthur drove me to my apartment and, even though I certainly would have been available to him, he didn't try to take me to bed. He said, "I wish you'd learn to have more respect for yourself."

He kissed me tenderly and left. He didn't even try for anything else.

I thought I had earned his respect. That was the main reason I fell a little in love with him so quickly – even more than the toe-holding.

In the following days, I went back to my semi-relationship with Gadge and Arthur went back to his family in New York. We didn't see each other again for about four years. Even though so much would happen to me in those years, we never lost touch.

We would write to each other occasionally and try to keep those feelings we brought out in each other that night alive.

Now let me say a few words about misconceptions. Because I do feel that a single misconception can change the whole direction of a person's life. I know. It happened to me.

That night I first met Arthur Miller I was simply another girl trying to succeed. We revealed intimate things to each other and he didn't grab at me. He didn't make a play at all. The only thing he did was talk to me. A real conversation with a man! At a Hollywood party.

I took it as a tribute.

It wasn't.

When I married him, over five years later, one of the main reasons for me loving him so much was that I thought he had respect for me from the very beginning. The seeds for that respect were planted at that party. He seemed to be interested in me as a person.

After we were married, during one of our many arguments when we angrily made revelations to each other, he told me that the only reason he didn't make a pass at me that night, why he didn't try to get me in bed, was that he was merely intimidated.

"It wasn't out of any sense of respect for you," he said. "I was simply afraid. Fearful that I wouldn't be able to compete with all the other men you've had."

Oh!

He was afraid he wouldn't be able to satisfy a "woman like me." He figured I had lots of experience and he wouldn't measure up. It had nothing, nothing at all, to do with honor. So there you have it.

The foundation of our entire relationship was built on a misconception.

During our last miserable year together our masks came completely off. We no longer needed to try to make it work. Nor did we need to justify why we loved each other. Our arguments were more about explaining why we ever ended up together in the first place.

Arthur said: The main reason I was so attracted to you that first night we met was because it had been a very long time since a girl, especially a lovely girl, had talked to me in a long time.

Arthur said: I was flattered at the high esteem you held me in. Even though you were a girl I laughed at with all the others.

Arthur said: It meant a lot to me to have such a sexy, desirable girl give me praise. But, even after we were married, in my quiet moments, all I could see you as was a tart, out of her league, trying to take herself seriously. Even though I tried very hard to convince myself otherwise.

These comments sound cruel. And they are. They were said at a time when it became important for us to hurt each other. What I said to him in response to these remarks was probably equally as vicious (and true!) But I never lied to him.

In the beginning, I did enjoy talking to him. I did value his opinions. I did hold him in high esteem. And I did love him.

October 22, 1961

Putting all the drama with Arthur and Gadge aside, I had started to become successful by late 1951.

Johnny Hyde's hard work had paid off and my own hard work was paying off. Once fame started it was like a snowball effect. I was getting a lot of fan mail and my photographs were constantly in the papers. The public—both men and women—started having a passionate curiosity regarding me and, well, almost a fixation on my physical image and my personal story.

She doesn't know who her father is! A childhood of foster homes! Orphanages! Her mother is in an institution—Marilyn is helping her!

See how beautiful she is now!

Yes. It was something to do with a Cinderella story. A fairytale about a tragic girl who triumphantly rose from the ashes.

But there was something faintly dirty mixed in with the story of my life. They could smell it and the odor intrigued them. Maybe they were tired of sanitized versions of other actresses' rise to stardom. I offered something new and to them my story was raw and real. The aloneness of orphanages. Poverty. Sex. The public was intoxicated.

All of these little bits and pieces from my past—which had always seemed to me to be simple survival—came together now to help build my success.

For example. Someone recognized that it was me, naked on the calendar. The one I had posed for a few years earlier. The person who discovered that the naked "Golden Dreams" model was indeed the new star Marilyn Monroe, got the idea in his head to blackmail the studio.

Fox was getting ready to pay him. They threw up their hands. "If the public finds out that Marilyn posed nude she will be finished in the movie industry. Her career is over."

But I knew my public better than they did. I said to myself, "Hmm.

This can do me more good than harm."

I told the studio executives to let the truth come out.

They said, "This is career suicide! You are finished, young lady!"

And then the news that I had posed in the buff came out. Again the public took it with that peculiar mixture of disgust, admiration, and curiosity.

"Is it really you?" a journalist asked. "Did you really pose naked?"

"Sure I posed nude," I said. "My refrigerator was empty. I was hungry."

The people loved that. They realized I was being sincere. I mean, how many people in the world have found themselves in a jam, when they needed cash and would be willing to do almost anything? The story fit in with the narrative of me. It made them love me more. It wasn't career suicide. Actually it was a huge boost in my popularity.

Everyone wanted to know more and more about my history. An interview with me was very much in demand.

The men who ran the industry, the men at the very top of the studios, did not like the idea that I was becoming successful. For the most part, they handpicked the actresses they wanted to succeed. They nurtured and guided their careers, picking out her look, her image, and then choosing the scripts, directors, and publicity she would receive. If audiences did indeed identify with the actress, she became a possession of the studio. She has to make every picture they choose for her. They run her life entirely, who she dates, when she marries, etc.

Movie executives were furious with me. I had no studio-head grooming me for stardom. As a matter of fact, they were doing everything in their power to make me go away.

It was all well and good when I was young and available and powerless. When they viewed me as a puppy they could pick up, hold, play with for a moment, and then put down and scat away. Girls like me weren't supposed to become powerful. You see, when my stardom began to build so did their hatred.

But my career started having a life of its own. Even without a continuous stream of good movies, my photographs were appearing in the newspapers almost every day. Magazines were putting me on the cover and reporters were constantly quoting me. The public wanted me and that was that. The studio executives had no say whatsoever in the matter. And this enraged them. If I was a silly joke to them before, now they were forced to deal with me.

I was still under the contract Johnny had gotten me with Darryl F. Zanuck at Fox. The fact that he had dropped me after my first contract only made him despise me all the more. How dare I become successful without his stamp of approval?

He took it personally and he fought me at every turn. He saw himself as a pimp and me as the prostitute. His outlook became, "Well, if she's going to be a star, then I'm going to make as much money off of her as I can and give her as little as possible in return."

Zanuck had to put aside his personal feelings for me—his unwavering contempt—and put on the hat of a Fox studio head. He saw that he had a potential money maker under contract and suddenly he was saying: "Put Marilyn Monroe in every picture that has a part for a sexy blonde."

Oh yes, they started viewing me as a money making machine very early in my career.

They wanted to squeeze out every penny they could get. They didn't care if the movie was good, they just wanted me to show as much sexuality as possible. I played along with them—and I even enjoyed it. My body is the one thing, up to that time, that had always brought me attention. Why not show it off on a bigger scale? My plan was to use it to bring me greater success which would mean more control in the long run.

No matter how small the role was in the movie, if my name was on the poster and the marquee, the public would show up to see it. The studio was forced, and let me say that again, forced to acknowledge that I was of value to them and that it would be a smart move to start putting me in higher profile movies.

I was given the third lead in a film called *Monkey Business* and it was a thrill to be co-starring with Cary Grant and Ginger Rogers. My role again was that of a secretary but she had funny lines and the character was central to the movie. It was directed by Howard Hawks who was a legend in the business and, may I add, one of the men I often saw on the party circuit only a couple of years before. At one of those parties he once told me he saw nothing special about me—that I was indistinguishable from hundreds of other blondes. If he remembered that I was the same girl he said that to, he never told me.

They were all changing their opinion. Fame does that. It forces them to look at you through new eyes and many of them say, "Gosh, I saw it in her all the time. I always knew that girl had something special." They want to take a piece of your fame away and keep it for themselves.

But even becoming well-known didn't completely bring me the power I craved. I had looked to fame as a shield that would protect me and make people respect me, but instead it made some people view me as a monster of sex or as a dirty joke.

For example the way I walk. I've always had a strange walk. Sort of a half gallop. Half strut. With a lot of wiggle. People accused me of walking this way for attention, but believe me, in earlier years it was a great source of pain and embarrassment. One more thing to feel "different" and self-conscious about.

When I was in school, the other kids used to make fun of the way I walked. It got to the point where I couldn't walk down the halls without feeling stiff and awkward and this only exaggerated "the walk," making my hips sway back and forth more forcefully.

When I started to become well known the press picked up on "the walk" and they would write things like "no one could wiggle like Monroe," although I never considered it a wiggle before that.

Now, suddenly the entire world's attention was on the way I walk! Then the studio wanted me to walk in a movie entitled *Niagara.* It was one of the first pictures that they were allowing me be the main star, the main attraction, and they had written in the script for my character, a long walk in high heels down a cobble stone street. The camera would be stationary and I would walk away from the movie camera and it would document every painstaking step.

In those days I was eager to please the studio. And they proved to be right. Whenever I snuck into a movie theater to watch that film, *Niagara,* when the walk scene came on the audience would go wild, cheering and whistling. That was one kind of power. I mean, once I was ridiculed for something, now I was reveled for the very same thing.

But then the bad things started happening. Fame stirs up all kinds of anger and jealousies and as a result there was a fair amount of people ready to attack. People started making fun of me again.

Once I was walking down a lane on the Fox Lot and I was just, you know, sort of lost in my own thoughts, not paying attention. I passed a group of extras. I didn't even notice them but then, after I had passed them and was some distance away, I became aware when they burst out laughing—and continued laughing. And I stopped and turned around and there was a middle-aged "extra," a bit player, a woman, walking behind me, imitating my walk in an exaggerated way.

She brazenly looked directly into my eyes and continued imitating me, pleased that I saw what she was doing and proud that she had all the others laughing at my expense. It had always been very important to me that people like me, but in the moment I was able to feel real hate for someone. I couldn't think of anything to say so I just said, "Hi," idiotically. And I continued walking, hating her and hating myself for not standing up for myself and defending my walk.

But then when I thought about this "extra" I started to feel a strange pity. I remembered the way she looked – bloated, aging, drunk. I had accomplished everything she had ever dreamed of accomplishing when she was younger and here she was – a nothing. Standing around on movie sets all day as an extra in, maybe, a restaurant scene or some other crowd scene, for many hours a day, hoping that a glimpse of her might end up in the finished picture. All her years of taking classes. All the "parties," she had to attend. All the horrible men she had to be with. And this is where life led her.

I still don't like her for trying to hurt me for no reason other than her own jealousy. But at least I can have some empathy.

But her cruelty, my dears, is why she never made it to my level of success, I believe. Simple as it seems, you can't be mean to people for no reason and expect God, or whoever it is that takes care of these things, to reward you. So instead He allowed her to remain a minor player. While He recognized that I have a pretty good heart, and He rewarded me for it. I like to think of it that way, anyway.

Now, after all these years, what can I say about my walk? It's become a part of who I am. And I accept it. Sure I would have liked to go through life with a more normal walk, or at least one that I could control, but what can I do? It's the walk that God gave me and I do need to get around.

November 7, 1961

I haven't heard from Jack in weeks.

I suppose I don't have as much power over him as I thought I did. I guess he doesn't feel about me as strongly as I do for him. Actually, I feel Jack's feelings for me are cooling. There's all those tell-tale signs and, being as horribly sensitive as I am, I've become an expert at reading people's feelings.

And when we are together he doesn't reach for me as often as he used to. His caresses aren't as lingering. In the beginning he would always take my calls, even when he was in an important meeting—or if the meeting was too important—he would return my call almost immediately after. Now sometimes he doesn't call me back for several days. Of course that's a message in itself. And the message is: "Gee, baby, you're getting too close."

What did I do wrong? I didn't ask him to leave Jacqueline. To marry me. To make me First Lady. I didn't even say "I love you." So why is he backing off?

It could be that, now that he's had me, the thrill of the conquest is over. It could be that he suspects I'm in love with him and he's panicking and pulling away. It could be that now that he knows the person behind Marilyn, Monroe, he found that I didn't live up to the fantasy, the fancy façade.

It's funny I read somewhere that Rita Hayworth once said that men went to bed with "Gilda," her most thrilling character in a movie, but they always woke up with Rita. Oh, how I relate to that! It's difficult to live up to someone's fantasy. The fantasy is always different. Sometimes it's better. Sometimes it's a disappointment. Sometimes it's just not what you expected.

But reality is always different than the way you imagined it.

Certainly I know that Jack uses people. Frank (Sinatra) told me as much. When Jack was campaigning for the Presidency, he used Frank to entertain at all the fund raisers. People paid thousands of dollars. He was Frank's best pal. Frank even recorded a special version of "High Hopes" as a campaign song for Kennedy.

When Jack won the election, it was Frank who put together the inauguration ball, booking all the entertainment and making sure that the Kennedy White House years were starting off with a glorious, glamorous, swinging bang. But as soon as he was safely encased in the White House, Jack distanced himself from Frank.

The rumor going around is that he was afraid of being linked with Frank's mob connections. So it was good-bye Mr. Sinatra.

November 10, 1961

It's more than a little ironic. For a while there in the summer I was juggling both Jack Kennedy and Frank Sinatra, sort of wondering who I'd end up with.

Now Frank has distanced himself too and is still dating that dancer, Juliet Prowse. Suddenly they are very close. I've even heard rumors that they are engaged.

I don't feel anger towards Frank. He's been nothing but kind to me. I made myself available to him and if he loved me he'd be with me. It's as simple as that. So I'm grateful for what we had. I treasure our friendship. I wish him well. (And I'll try hard not to choke on that if I ever have to say it out loud.) But I mean it.

Frank still calls me. He says, "I miss you, baby. Do you need anything?" He always hangs up by saying, "…love you, baby."

As for Jack, I still haven't heard a word.

I can't say it doesn't hurt me.

In the movie, *The Misfits*, the film that Arthur Miller wrote for me, he had me say a line. "Maybe all there is, is the next thing. The next thing that happens. Maybe you're not supposed to remember anyone's promises." I don't recall saying that exact line to him, but I'm pretty sure I did at one time. It sounds like me. And he probably wrote it down in his damn diary to use somewhere. Yet, I have to admit, that line does sort of represent the way I feel most of the time.

It terrifies me to think that maybe true erotic love lasts only a year or two. That desperate frantic, yearning yearning yearning! The feeling of loving someone so much you feel as if you will never have enough of him. Of being near him. Of hearing him talk. Of making love with him.

But after a few years, or just a few months, the same doubts, the same deceptions, the same boredoms take over and they crawl into bed between the two of you. I'm guilty of it too. And having something new often looks better than what you've got.

I'm hoping that, even though a person may go through their entire life having many lovers, and even a lot of marriages, that when you meet the right one you just know it right off the bat. *This is what I've been waiting for!* And when you compare it to all the other loves of your life, you realize that they were flawed from the very beginning.

I truly loved Arthur Miller once, for example, but now, in retrospect, I can see that it was a very damaged relationship from the start.

It was about 1952 that I went from being a tremendously successful blonde in pictures to becoming the biggest star in the world. Which was hard for me to believe. It still is hard for me to believe sometimes.

I would go out to a movie premiere or some big Hollywood event and these huge crowds would be screaming for me, trying to touch me, attempting to rip something off of me, snapping photos—and the photographers would be going crazy trying to get a picture of me and the reporters were shouting questions.

"Marilyn! Marilyn! Marilyn!"

It was pandemonium! It was all I ever dreamed of—to be wanted by so many and with such intensity—but it often felt like it wasn't really happening to me. Like, it was all for some weird double I could see her—sort of like a stand-in for me—but she wasn't me.

A couple of years earlier I often couldn't get an appointment with an average casting director. It was nearly impossible to get a decent audition. Now it was like I was the only star. The photographers would actually say that to me, "Oh, Marilyn, you're the *only* star!"

I guess the thing that really made me feel as if I wasn't an ordinary movie star was the way *everyone* treated me. See, it wasn't just the fans. I mean to say that when I walked into a restaurant in Beverly Hills, with some of the most famous people in the world sitting there having dinner, I would see them turning around and craning their necks to look at me. I'd feel the room ripple with excitement. It was electric and I was the source of the electricity. I'd hear the urgent whispers "Marilyn's hear!" They would stare and stare and stare. It wasn't just famous actors and actresses who were staring either. It was the esteemed writers, famous artists, even the politicians!

I had to develop a way of continuing on with my dinner companion without acknowledging these stares—which never stopped, by the way—otherwise I wouldn't be able to function during the course of the evening. I had to kind of "blank" them out. This is when the pressure of being, "me," first started to swell to terrifying proportions.

I'm a normal, mortal woman but at this point people stopped viewing me that way. They called me a goddess and that's the way the public treated me.

And even with all my fame and all the fascination that the mystique of Marilyn Monroe represented, I still didn't feel valued by the studio.

The studio (had but no choice) but to offer me the lead role in the picture *Gentlemen Prefer Blondes*. It was an important movie. It had been a big success on Broadway. I was co-starring in the film with my friend, Jane Russell, and she was making many thousands of dollars more than I was, because I was still under that contract Johnny Hyde had negotiated when I was a starlet, grateful for anything. But I didn't know how to stand up for myself and I let everyone take advantage.

The studio executives never could get it out of their heads that I became a star without their help. It infuriated them. It really sort of killed them that a girl from the party circuit who they had scorned, had become so valuable. "How could Marilyn be so adored," they asked themselves.

They tried to degrade me every chance they got. They wouldn't even give me my own dressing room. Really! I was being made up and dressed in a shared dressing room with the supporting and minor actresses in the film. Even they couldn't believe the star of the picture was sitting in a lineup of makeup chairs with the chorus girls.

Finally I had to take matters into my own hands. I had to develop a little confidence (which wasn't easy because it doesn't come naturally to me) or they'd always be slapping me down, treating me like the starlet at their stupid parties. I went to the executives and I said, "Well, gentlemen, you keep telling me I'm not a star. And maybe I'm not. But whatever it is you think I am, I'm the blonde in the picture. The name of the picture is *Gentlemen Prefer Blondes* and, well, maybe you should give the blonde her own dressing room."

They were incensed when I asked for anything at all. Their feelings were that I was a tramp and I should feel grateful for any scrap that was given to me.

Now, I don't mean to sound arrogant in saying this, but the ultimate power was mine. If they wanted a "Marilyn Monroe" movie, Marilyn Monroe had to show up to be filmed. Sometimes the only way I could wield my power was to not show up. After all, no one deigned to listen to my requests.

I started to become viewed as what they termed, "difficult." But my pictures were making them a fortune so they started throwing me little crumbs here and there. Giving me a little more money and my own dressing room, for god's sake!

I realized, though, how disposable they thought I would be to them some day. And just how cruel they could be.

After *Gentlemen Prefer Blondes*, they took me to the great star, Miss Betty Grable's, dressing room to meet her. I thought they were introducing me to her as a courtesy. She had been the queen of the 20th Century Fox lot and I had been enjoying her film for years.

No one EVER had a bad word to say about Betty Grable. Anyone on the Fox lot who you talked to said she was terribly sweet and always down to earth. All through the war years her movies brought so much happiness to the country—all the while she was making tons of money for the studio.

But when we arrived at her dressing room I realized from their attitude that they had brought me there to show Betty what they really thought of her. They saw her as being used up and they were telling her that I was the new queen of the lot. As if they were saying, "Here's the new blonde star. We're finished with you."

I was mortified. I sensed that she was humiliated but she only showed me warmth and kindness.

When I was leaving her room she took me aside and whispered to me, "Honey, I've had a great run! I made a lot of movies and I made a lot of money. I'm finished now. It's your turn. Go get what you can from them."

Soon after that they did give me her dressing room—which was the best one on the Fox lot.

Betty and I were slated to make one picture together before they were totally through with her, *How to Marry a Millionaire*. But everyone at the studio knew after that film, they were planning on getting rid of her. I guess they were trying to squeeze out every last bit of juice they could get out of her by pairing (what they considered) the aging queen of Fox with the new queen.

See, the thing is that Miss Grable had been very popular during the 1940s playing the pretty-girl-next-door-type in gaudy Technicolor musicals. They were fun and entertaining but after a while it was like they were using her in the same movie over and over again. But Betty never said, "No," to a script. She didn't care what the picture was. She just finished shooting one picture on Friday and showed up on Monday morning to start a new one.

They never developed her or let her try other kinds of roles. So, I mean, it was inevitable that the public would grow tired of her playing the same part for years. And besides that, she had grown too mature to play the ingénue next door. Instead of changing her image, though, and trying to help her continue with her career in a new direction, the studio simply made plans to discard and replace her.

All my life I've been at the mercy of people who have no mercy.

All my life I had been used and then abandoned so I recognized that's what was happening to Miss Grable. I was their new star, but I was smart enough to realize that in ten years or less they'd do the same thing to me—with some new girl (who was probably just starting on the party circuit) if I let them.

The studio was already coming up with replacements for me for when I became "difficult" and didn't want to do as they told me. They would bring in a new young actress now and again. They dyed her hair my shade of blonde, styled it like me, and copied my makeup and they wiggled around in a costume from my last film. She would try to be me.

But "Marilyn Monroe" comes from my soul. She's real—and a part of me. For them it's a fantasy – like putting on a Halloween costume. That's why it doesn't work for them.

Some people are looking for an identity. Surprisingly, some people find theirs in me!

Planning ahead, I told the studio that I wanted to try different kinds of roles. I didn't just want to be thought of as a sex freak. Of course I used sexuality to climb the ladder. Certainly it was a big part of my persona. But you have to keep growing and changing and expanding your scope if you want to survive in this business. On top of that, it's not interesting to me personally to keep repeating the same thing again and again.

I certainly didn't want to keep making the big splashy Technicolor movies over and over. But every time they sent me a script it was the same old, tired story: the sexy blonde in tight clothes, wiggling around – sometimes singing sometimes just wiggling—oblivious to her charms. Often the character was dumb. The studio didn't realize that when I played "dumb" in *Gentlemen Prefer Blondes* and *How to Marry a Millionaire*, I was acting! It's not easy to make people believe a girl is that naïve and yet charming and kind of smart at the same time. It's certainly not easy to make people laugh! It takes some comedy chops, if I must say so myself. That was a character I created. But I could do other kinds of roles too! At least I wanted to try.

I had just "made it," and I was already worrying about the future.

November 15, 1961

My suspicions are right! There is something going on in Jack's life that's making him step back. It's not that he's getting tired of me at all. It's all because of Jacqueline Kennedy. "The Statue!" has spoken.

Jacqueline Kennedy's ever loyal (to me!) assistant, Irene (aka Mrs. Chatterbox), called me today. She said that she happened to be passing by a room in the White House (dusting, no doubt) where Jack and Jacqueline were having (a rather loud) argument.

Irene, of course, couldn't help to pause at the door for a few moments. I guess the door knob needed polishing. It seems I was the subject of their...um...discussion.

Jacqueline said, "Listen to me, Jack, if you are fucking Marilyn Monroe, as I believe you are, I want it to end and I want it to end now."

And Jack told her, "I don't know what you're talking about, Jackie. Marilyn and I are just friends."

"Jack, everyone from Washington to Hollywood is talking about the two of you and I think..."

"Aw, come on Jackie. You were never one to listen to gossip."

"Look," Jackie raged on, "I'm not a fool—so please don't treat me like one! This isn't like your other little flings. This one is different, Jack. Yes, I know: She's beautiful. She's sexy. She's magnificent. But underneath it, she's extremely fragile. She's trouble, John."

"She's just very vulnerable and lonely," Jack said to his wife. "It makes her feel important to have the president to talk to from time to time."

"She's a suicide waiting to happen," Jacqueline said, according to Irene. "What would happen if someone in the press got wind of you carrying on with her? Don't you understand even the slightest little hint of a scandal with her would ruin your chances at reelection."

Jack said, "I already told you Jackie, Marilyn is nothing more than a very casual friend who I see from time to time when I'm in L.A. But, sure, if you want me to stop being friends with her then I'll stop seeing her altogether."

Imagine! The nerve. Calling me a suicide waiting to happen!

I mean, I can understand Jack telling that ice princess that we're just friends but eventually I would hope that he would own up to the fact that he loves me. That's my goal with him. To make him want me so much that he would leave his wife for me. Although I wouldn't expect him to do it until his presidency is over.

November 17, 1961

In therapy with Dr. Greenson I'm trying to learn independence. How to rely on myself and trust my own decisions instead of always looking to some agent, or some friend, or some lover for affirmation.

My therapy sessions have become almost daily. There are times when he acts like a psychiatrist but he has become more, a father-figure, a friend…and something else I can't yet name. He invites me to stay over for dinner with his family. His wife and daughter and son. He takes my calls no matter what time it is. And he always comes right over when I am in real distress.

He has become like an extended family. Which is nice.

And now the part comes where I must push away that tiny bit of mistrust that creeps up on me and says to myself, "Marilyn, dear, this is not proper doctor patient relationship. He should know better. You should know better."

I push that doubting voice away. I have to have trust in SOME people. And it is nice to have a family—even if it is a surrogate family. Someone looking out for me.

November 18, 1961

The studio still refuses to let me see the script for *Something's Got to Give*, which is supposedly my next and last movie for them under my old contract.

Well, I felt I had to assert a little power. I mean, they still want to treat me as if I were a starlet in 1951

They wanted my husband to be played by James Garner. He's a good actor. Handsome. But I asked them for Dean Martin instead. He's a good friend and I think we'll be able to ignite a few sparks on screen (I seem to have good chemistry with Italians).

They wanted one of the other characters to be played by Don Knotts, but I knew Wally Cox would be perfect for the role. Sure, he is also a friends, and if I have to make this lousy movie, why shouldn't I be surrounded by people I like so that maybe we can bring some spontaneity and fun to the situations in the script—whatever they might be.

Also, I insisted the director come from my list of "approved" directors, so I got George Cukor again! He's the only one available (or willing.)

I would rather not work with George, my experience with him on *Let's Make Love* was not a happy one and the movie is a dud. But I couldn't exactly complain since he is on my list of the only directors I would work with. It was one of the few concessions of control the studio gave me when we made up a new contract.

I also asked for the cameraman who shot *Some Like it Hot*. It is, after all, a Marilyn Monroe movie, so why not give me the professionals who showcase me at my best? I wish they could understand, I'm not asking for these things to pull a spoiled little movie star routine.

I simply want to be seen at my best so the movie will be a success. But they don't see it that way.

I hear them say, "She's too demanding! She's too much! She's off her rocker!" They call me a bitch. They call me a cunt. All because I simply want to make good pictures!

It seems ridiculous that at this stage in my career, after all I've accomplished, all the money I brought them, I still have to fight fight fight for anything decent. They throw me into any old script they fish out of the trash can. "Oh will give her a few musical numbers and let her shake her ass and the audiences will come."

I want to make films that are artistic and enjoyable. In the long run, it's me that people are paying to see. I've reached that enviable position in any actresses' career where any movie I appear in will be considered, "The new Marilyn Monroe movie." As far as I'm concerned, this comes at an emotional cost and a huge responsibility. It's up to me to make sure that the people want to see the movie. It's up to me to make sure that the people get their money's worth.

They tell my lawyer: "Just make sure she shows up for filming on November 15th." And my lawyer says to them: "Send her the script. Marilyn wants to see the script."

They say, "Fuck her! Just tell her to be there. Marilyn doesn't have script approval! But we will give her a big bonus when she completes *Something's Got to Give.*"

What kind of shit are they pulling? The studio knows I've never cared about money! If I did I could have been making a hell of a lot more at Fox. That could pay me all the money in the world and it wouldn't give me a feeling of self-satisfaction on the inside. Instead I asked for certain conditions.

The most important thing to me has always been if the picture is any good and if I'm any good in it.

All these years I've been fighting for respect—and still they treat me like some sort of a "thing!" What am I? A performing puppet? A mugging chimpanzee?

(Later)

Why doesn't my own studio respect my talent? I mean there are enough people who seem to believe I have it. I just don't understand why they don't utilize what I have to offer properly.

You'd think they would trust me a little by now. *Let's Make Love*, the last picture that Fox <u>forced</u> me to make, is the worst film I've ever been in. When I read that script I couldn't believe that they would put me, supposedly an important star, in such garbage. I begged the studio—I literally begged them—to buy me *Breakfast at Tiffany's* so I could play the lead. Even Truman Capote said that I was his choice to play Holly Golightly. When I saw it with Audrey Hepburn I sat there and cried throughout. I hate to lose. Oh how wonderful I could have been in that! But they didn't buy it for me and Audrey Hepburn got to make it for a different studio.

"Okay," I said. "Let me do *Pillow Talk*. That script is crisp and funny – and I'm dying to make a film with Rock Hudson. Plus, I truly think it's the kind of movie that can help me transition into other kinds of roles.

But once again they ignored me and the part went to Doris Day. The studio said, *"Let's Make Love* will be your next picture."*

Even at this stage, I had no say in the decision. I didn't have approval of the script. They picked it for me. I couldn't say this is not good for me. That's not part of my contract. I thought, at the time of negotiations, having director approval was more important. I should have held out for script approval too.

After all the revenue my pictures brought to them they gave me a flat story with nothing interesting about it. Even my character was just a big blank. No funny lines. No good original songs. I hate everything about that movie. Even the way I look in it. Fat! Liz Taylor was right on target when she called it *Let's Make Lunch*!

I think my feelings of self-disgust were part of the reason I had an affair with Yves Montand. Arthur was making me feel bad about myself. The movie I was filming was making me feel bad about myself. And the weight I had gained was making me feel bad about myself.

Nothing like a love affair with a charming Frenchman to—what can I say—make you feel a little *better* about yourself?

About being overweight: I think I got carried away with my own image for a while there. Thinking "Well, I'm Marilyn Monroe, I'll look good on the screen no matter what." Well, guess what? I learned my lesson the hard way. Even with all the people I had working on me just to make me look beautiful, I looked awful! One of the critics wrote: "Marilyn Monroe is a little on the fleshy side. Diet anyone?" Oh how I regret that movie! And it's there for eternity, for all to see.

Now that I'm thin again and looking pretty good I want to do something special – but I guess I'll just have to wait until I get *Something's Got To Give* out of the way to do a really great film.

I know that George Cukor has come to hate me. Some of my biggest fans are gay men, but not George. He's persnickety and snooty and he prefers "Ladies of the Screen." Some of his biggest successes have been with Greta Garbo, Joan Crawford and Norma Shearer.

In his mind he's more of a lady than I'll ever be.

I know a guy who is part of Cukor's homosexual circle and he's told me that at Cukor's pool parties he keeps all of his friends in stitches by doing imitations of me, speaking in a mock baby-doll voice, and telling them all that Marilyn Monroe is not "all that pretty," and that she's "totally nuts and destined for a straitjacket, like her mother."

Imagine having to work with someone who you know feels this way about you! And yet, on the set, it's all smiles and fake respect. Oh well. I guess that's what life is all about. Putting on your different masks for different situations in order to get through them.

Besides, he is a hell of a talented man, and all I really want is to make a good movie. So I could put up with him, I guess. If he could put up with me.

November 21, 1961

With all the disagreements and contentious feelings going on right now between myself and Fox, it reminds me that, since I became a star, there has never been a time when I felt that the studio, or anyone in the business, was looking out for me, cared about me other than what I could do for them. Or tried to help me without a fight. Everything that's happening with *Something's Got to Give* is just business as usual for me.

By 1953, everyone wanted a piece of me. Everyone was trying to make a deal with me. Everyone wanted me for this project or that business opportunity. These were the same people that had spurned me a couple of years before. Now they told me, with sickly fake smiles, how wonderful I was.

I met Joe DiMaggio on a blind date and we just hit it off right away. For me he represented a good, decent man. I hadn't known many. He wasn't "Hollywood." He wasn't show business-y. He was already a legend in the sports world. He didn't want anything from me except <u>me</u>—the person I was. He didn't care at all about my past. Joe DiMaggio's love was uncomplicated. It was pure love. He didn't want me to become something I wasn't. He didn't try to mold me into anything. He didn't want to teach me things. He didn't want me to change my personality.

I longed for a love with no strings attached,

It was my first experience of dating a man just for the fun and enjoyment of each other. It was true companionship mixed in with a strong physical attraction. How wonderful it was to be involved with a man who I was attracted to and who I liked—and who accepted me and loved me exactly as I was. He came to represent a certain kind of life I wanted. A comfortable home life, a family life, possibly children. But I also wanted a career in the movies—that was the only thing Joe didn't like about me. Those were his strings! I understood that juggling making movies and having a family life wouldn't be easy, but I don't see why it should be impossible.

I really felt that I couldn't trust anyone in Hollywood and ultimately that is what led me to my marriage to Joe DiMaggio. He was so strong, and confident and sure of himself. I knew that he loved me completely and I needed to be protected. He wasn't going to let anyone push me around.

So when he asked me to marry him for the one hundredth time I finally said, "Let's do it."

It was my second try at married life. We rented a lovely cottage in Beverly Hills and I gave being a housewife another go, but as soon as I started making plans to continue with my career Joe started complaining.

He saw the Hollywood monsters that surrounded me. He didn't approve of show business and didn't want me to be a part of it, didn't want me making pictures. I tried my hand at being a housewife. I cooked meals (and I was pretty good!) I cleaned. We made love (and it was *very* good!) I watched television with him. But every time a new script arrived or there was talk of a new movie he grew cold and distant. In a very short time it got to the point where we wouldn't even talk to each other for days. I began living in one part of the house and Joe in the other.

As it turned out, it was another example of someone loving only a part of me. Not the total package of me. He couldn't stand "Marilyn Monroe," the most publicized woman in the universe and all of that. But I think it was unfair of him to want me to give up my career and be only his wife. After all, he had already done everything he wanted to do in his profession – he had made his mark in baseball—which was *his* passion—and he filled his hunger to be great. I think that, gee, if anyone should have respected my ambition, it should have been him.

Our marriage lasted for only nine months. We could have had a baby in that amount of time. But that never happened. Although we had planned to at one point.

It was during the time I was filming a comedy called *The Seven Year Itch* that we broke up for good. I was in New York shooting the scene where my sheer white dress flies up over a subway grating, exposing my legs, my thighs, and even my panties. Well, it is never actually shown in the movie but we certainly shot it that way and there were thousands of photographs taken of it.

A mob had gathered, even though it was three in the morning, and the crowd consisted of mostly men and Joe was among the onlookers. He was there with his friend Walter Winchell, the famous newspaper columnist. Every time we did a take, and the fan under the subway grating would be turned on, and my skirt would fly up, the men in the crowd would scream out, "More! More! Show more, Marilyn." And the director's camera would move in, focusing on my crotch area. I had on two pairs of panties but I still wasn't sure how much showed through with the lights and all. Joe became extremely upset. I really can't blame him.

It was a sensation. By this point everything I did was a sensation. I know it couldn't have been easy for him to be married to that.

Through the crowd and the production equipment I saw Joe walk away. His face was a horrible combination of anger and sadness. I did feel for him. He's a proud man. It had to be difficult for him to be watching his wife being displayed like that in front of so many dirty minded men. It would be too much to ask him to try to separate the "public" Marilyn from my private self. He would have to accept both if he really wanted me.

I said to the director of the movie, Billy Wilder, "I hope you're not filming this for your Hollywood friends to enjoy at a stag party." I couldn't imagine how the censors would allow a scene of a close-up of my private area in a Hollywood comedy, made for a family audience. And I was right. Later we re-filmed the scene in a more dignified, controlled manner back in Hollywood at the studio. But the night we filmed on the street brought the movie millions of dollars of free publicity. The photos were all over the place.

But that scene was the camel that broke the straws back, as far as Joe was concerned. By the time the skirt blowing scene was finished shooting on the Manhattan street, it was early morning. Joe was waiting for me at the hotel and we had a dreadful argument. He grabbed me forcefully by my arms and said passionately, "Can't you see how they are using you?

They will destroy you!" Joe really loathed the Hollywood crowd. He truly wanted to protect me from them. I wanted his protection. But his way of protecting me was to take me away from my career. I wouldn't allow that. So we couldn't agree on how we could have a happy married life together.

Yes there were bruises on my arms from the forcefulness of his passion. But I had bruised him in a much worse way.

Ultimately, after we stopped screaming at each other, Joe said he would always love me but he just couldn't take me being a movie star.

After that the only thing left for us to do was get divorced.

I guess I should comment on the skirt blowing scene, since it has become the most famous screen moment of my career thus far. Well, I can't say I didn't enjoy the attention. I mean, don't get me wrong, when I say I want to do dramatic roles and be taken seriously, that doesn't mean I object to being sexual and feminine. But I don't see why I should have to choose one or the other.

I'm most definitely a woman, and I love everything that comes with that. I'm also an artist who wants to grow. I'm happy and flattered to be thought of as beautiful. I enjoy being sexual. That was a fun night. It was playful. I was happy to offer up the goddess. It was wonderful to be worshipped. When I complain about all that "sex publicity," I only mean that I don't want that to be the ONLY thing I'm known for. It's only a part of who I am. But there's so much more of me dying to get out.

After a series of roles that relied on sex appeal I was ready to try something new.

Meanwhile the studio kept sending me any old script that played up the sex symbol image. At one point they sent me a trashy script called *The Revolt of Mamie Stover* and, as far as I can recall, it was about a prostitute who is run out of town and tries to start a new life in Hawaii

Now, mind you, I would not mind playing a prostitute if the script was good and the character was interesting. Something like *Rain*, the story by Somerset Maugham which I'm interested in making and I'm still trying to get off the ground! But the script for *Mamie Stover* was so inane and false. Really it was just an excuse to put me in heavy make-up and fishnet stockings as they had done in *River of No Return*. (That unremarkable Western in which I as cast as a saloon singer.) Ugh!

I had my eye on the future. I didn't want them bringing in some young blonde in a few years, telling me that this was the new queen and I was all used up: "Clear out of this dressing room, Marilyn." I had worked so hard to get where I was. I wanted to be respected and loved for the rest of my life, however long that may last.

I made suggestions of roles that I wanted to play. They paid no attention. Every time I asked for something that might broaden my range they turned a deaf ear. They felt they had found a money making formula with me and they intended to stick with it until the last penny had been eked out of me.

To hold the public's interest I needed to be in good movies. It was all I thought about. It worried me sick. It was very difficult to get good material.

There were many roles I asked them for—always they refused. For example, when Marlon Brando expressed interest in *The Egyptian*, I requested to be considered for the character of Nefer. At that point I wanted to act with Marlon Brando as much as I wanted anything. Okay the role I would play was a prostitute. But it was a different kind of role in a historical epic—it certainly couldn't be compared to anything I had done before. Instead, Darryl F. Zanuck gave the role to his mistress of the day. My only consolation of not getting it was when Marlon Brando dropped out.

I begged them to buy the rights to the Tennessee Williams plays *Cat on a Hot Tin Roof* and *Suddenly Last Summer* for me. Both of those marvelous roles, complex and compelling, would have allowed me to be sensual, but also given me the opportunity to show different aspects of a many-layered character. But, I guess, my studio didn't think enough of my talent to seek out those highbrow properties for me. Elizabeth Taylor's studio bought them for her and they were terrific successes for her. I might add she was nominated for an Academy Award for both of them.

There were other roles I asked for. I felt I had proven myself and my worth as an actress and deserved some considerations. But this you won't believe, they would often give me the title of my next movie, and a date to report to the studio for rehearsals, without even letting me see the script!

Instead of finding me a screenplay that was fresh and exciting, the studio had the idea of putting me in something they were calling *The Girl in the Pink Tights*. A musical I suppose they pasted together in a few hours. I think it was a quick reworking of one of Betty Grable's old films. I had been given the date shooting would start, but they didn't send me a script. I kept having my agent ask for it. I had my lawyer ask for it. I even telephoned. "May I see a script, please?" Darryl F. Zanuck didn't think I deserved that particular courtesy. Finally, when I made it clear I wouldn't show up unless I saw a script, they sent it over. Trash. I sent them a telegram: "I READ THE SCRIPT AND I DO NOT LIKE IT."

Hollywood's image of me was becoming all wrong. And I knew it. And I felt as if I couldn't do anything about it. They would have liked me to make one picture right after the other. The scripts were almost all the same story. I knew it would continue until the public grew bored and I stopped bringing in the money.

It was perfectly clear that they were never going to give me any say at all in the movies I made. I would like to think I should have some control over artistic decisions. After all, I am not a puppet. So instead of arguing with the studio I simply left Hollywood. I took off.

I flew to New York and hid out and started studying acting at the Actor's Studio with Lee Strasberg who had been a teacher for such actors as Marlon Brando and Shelley Winters. It was an honor to be accepted as his student.

It was there, in New York, that along with my acting skill I decided to continue to develop myself as a person. I started reading good books again and meeting intellectual people. I often went to Broadway shows and browsed the museums. It was during this time that I began having an affair with Arthur who I hadn't seen since he left Los Angeles a few years before. He was there. It was easy.

November 29, 1961

Pat told me that Jack was going to be in town, so I called him at the White House to see if he planned on seeing me while he was in Los Angeles. I've been feeling sort of melancholy for days because I haven't heard from him in such a long time. I've been snapping at people and not showing up at the studio for meetings regarding the new movie, etc. And I've been worrying that Jack has taken Jacqueline's threat seriously and I would never hear from him again.

Not that it should matter. I should just move on, I know. But the heart doesn't always do what the head advises.

When I got through to him at last he confirmed that he was going to be here in Los Angeles. "But," he said, "I don't know if I'll be able to see you. I have a lot of conferences and meetings and I won't be staying with Peter and Pat—so there's a privacy issue."

He was cold and distant and I could tell that he was thinking of the threats Jacqueline had made to him. I pressed him to see me and finally he said, "Well, okay," he'd squeeze in a dinner with me on Saturday night.

Then I said, "I miss you, Jack" and there was a long pause and he didn't respond with "I miss you too," the way he used to. Instead he said, "Good, I like to be missed," And by the time I hung up the phone my body had blushed red and there were welts on my neck. I was burning up with humiliation. I began to cry.

But still I felt that it was all because of Jacqueline. That in his heart he still had feelings for me but that he was afraid of her fury...so when Saturday arrived...

It had been such a long time since we had seen each other I was pretty sure he was looking forward to having dinner with me. He said he would call me as soon as he was done with his meetings and conferences. By 5 he still hadn't called me.

So I called the hotel and left a message. I was angry by then and I very brazenly said to a desk, "This is Marilyn Monroe and I would like President Kennedy to call me back as soon as possible. He has the number,"

I waited and waited and waited or him to call me back. I worked out with my dumbbells so my breast would be firm and high.

In *Something's Got to Give* I will wear a bikini – a tiny one – because I want the world to see that I'm still in good shape. I worked and worked for an hour. He didn't call. I took a bath and brought the phone into the bathroom.

He didn't call.

Whitey came over and did my make-up; I chatted and gossiped with Whitey, trying to keep my real feelings at bay, and I kept the phone by my side.

He didn't call.

Whitey left and I closed myself in the bedroom and tried on different dresses. I wanted to be more beautiful than he's ever seen me. I always want to be more beautiful than he's ever seen me. I want to make myself better for him. More clever. More witty. Especially more beautiful. But what more can I do? I already have the very best artists in the beauty business working on me. And I can't stop time.

I finally chose a black dress with a filmy lace top that looks like a slip. It's a dress I wear a lot. It never fails me.

He didn't call.

I put on a stack of Sinatra records. Sinatra's singing always makes me feel more sexually appealing. Did I ever write about the time I was living in foster care with a family that was religious to the extreme and they taught me to sing "Jesus Loves Me This I know." Well, now, as a grown woman, I can put on Sinatra records and say, "Frank Sinatra loves me this I know."

I started drinking champagne.

He didn't call.

I took off my dress and lay down on my bed. If only I could get my mind off of him – I knew the phone would ring if I stopped thinking about him, but I couldn't stop.

I had just finished an entire bottle of champagne when he called me, finally. It was about 11 at night. I imagined him sitting importantly in his hotel room.

He charged right into conversation without any endearments: "Can we do dinner the next time I'm in town?" he asked. "I've had meetings all day and I'm really exhausted."

I was flabbergasted and crushed but I, of course, didn't want him to know that. I tried to make my voice as regular-sounding as possible.

"Of course we can," I said.

"Great," he said. "I'll call you next week."

He would have hung up at this point if I would have let him and then I knew I'd be up on the tightrope again all week, waiting, wondering whether he was even thinking about me at all.

"But…" I started hesitantly. He waited. "But, if you really missed me and wanted to see me, it wouldn't matter how tired you are. You'd make it a point to see me. You'd find the energy."

He paused. "I don't know…" he said. And it felt like there was a torrent of words waiting to break free from him. Words I didn't want to hear but knew I had to hear. There was an awful silence and then I asked:

"You don't' know what?"

"I don't know how to tell you this." (Pause) "I never wanted to hurt you," he said.

Ah. So I was going to be hurt. "Well, Marilyn," I thought, "you might as well get it over with. Take the blows as quickly as possible and let the healing process begin."

"Hurt me how?" I asked.

"I can't see you anymore," he blurted, letting down the damn of words. "Jackie has been ranting about us for weeks. She doesn't believe that we're just friends. We've been fighting about it all week. And actually...frankly, it's not just Jackie. People are talking, Marilyn. About us. It's gotten to the point where it could really jeopardize my position. And my campaign for re-election in '64. We have to stop seeing each other."

"And you're telling me this over the phone?" I asked incredulously. He knew what I felt for him, and yet he was willing to dismiss me on the phone? I found this notion absolutely impossible. After all, aren't I somewhat important in my own right? It was like a throwback to the old days when I was some movie executive's plaything.

"I thought it would be easier if we just broke off cleanly and easily. Aw, you know how I feel about you, honey. It's just that, well, right now it's impossible. I never meant to hurt you."

That was the second time he said he never meant to hurt me. But he didn't go out of his way NOT to hurt me either.

"Jack," I said, trying to keep the hysterics that were running rampant through my body from erupting in my voice, "I would really rather you say goodbye to me – if you really are going to say good-bye – in person. It would make me feel more...dignified, somehow."

"Well, I...are you alone?"

"Yes," I said.

"I'll come over. But only for a little while, Marilyn."

I put the sexy, black dress back on.

It's a very short drive from his hotel to my place. I didn't know why I wanted to see him. There was a finality in his voice that made me feel like, well...like it was over for sure. I guess I always knew that I couldn't have him. I wanted him too much. Happiness is not something that I ever had much of so I don't take it for granted. And I never expect it to last very long.

But I decided that I'd try to make it last a little longer with Jack. I knew it would be difficult for him to say goodbye to me in person, and maybe I expected him to see me and forget about everything and everyone else and shout, "I LOVE YOU MARILYN! FUCK JACKIE! FUCK THE PRESIDENCY! I WANT YOU!"

But when I looked in the mirror to touch up my makeup, I saw how ugly I am and I realized that would never happen.

I always think I'm beautiful until I see myself in the mirror. I guess you might say I'm beautiful through other peoples' eyes. They are always saying to me, "Marilyn you're so gorgeous! You're so *this*. You're so *that*," and I read in the magazines about how beautiful I am. And I listen. And it sinks in. As a result, in my imagination I always look better than in my reality.

Some people do see the ugliness in me, the ugliness I see in the mirror. They are in the minority at the moment – thank God.

The idea of losing him hit me. I threw up in the bathroom sink.

Every day I feel a little bit more of my power, my relevance slipping away.

I didn't want him to see me distressed or out of control. That would only panic him and send him running for the hills faster. "Gotta get away from the crazy lady." I brushed my teeth. I took a handful of Nembutal. I drank more champagne. I adjusted the dress. I fixed my hair. I put on a fresh coat of lipstick.

The doorbell rang.

He didn't want anything to drink.

He couldn't stay long, he said again. The secret service men were out in the car, he said.

He paced around looking over my new house. Making benign comments. He seemed nervous, furtive. But, when we got to the bedroom, almost by rote, he undressed immediately – and I did too. Because he was always in such a hurry our habit has become taking all our clothes off and making love first – ready or not – as soon as we were alone together and the bedroom door was closed—and then doing our talking afterwards.

I only wanted to kiss him. I only wanted him to hold me. I didn't want his hands roaming my body, feeling where I was most vulnerable. I didn't want to fuck him. After sex is over, most of my power I have over him is gone. Kisses on the other hand, are just as enjoyable as an orgasm, yet they leave everyone wanting more.

But he wanted to have sex and I have no control in me to say no to him. He was very passionate this night. His kiss almost hurting me. I could feel his teeth on my lips and on my neck, as if he suspected that this would be our last time and he wanted the taste of me to linger. He drank from me as if I were a soda. I put my all into it, too. If anything I had was going to make him keep on seeing me, I knew it was sex.

After we make love he usually likes to lie still and hold me, but I sensed he wasn't enjoying it the way he once had. It was if I had said, "I love you." Which I did not. But the feelings in the air was as if I did. What I mean is that it was as if he felt my feelings were too strong and he reeled back as if from the cave of a witch. For someone who just ate out my ass and drank from me like a soda, he was pretty damn cold.

I was silent for a very long time, hoping that the experience for me was making a mark on his heart and making him reconsider leaving me.

Finally I got out of bed and started putting on my bra. I never wear a bra during the day, and sometimes to compensate for that, I wear one at night. I have one that is a knockout. A little black lace number called a "no-no bra." I sat next to where he lie on the bed and lifted the straps over my shoulders.

I said, "I don't see why we can't keep seeing each other – casually. I mean, it could be casual, right? It doesn't have to be anything serious. I've been thinking about it, and I realize I've been sort of pressuring you into a more serious relationship. But to be honest, I'm at a point in my career where I really have to focus on my movie-making. The truth is, we *are* friends, and we do have a good time together. So I don't know why we can't keep seeing each other…from time to time."

He cupped a hand on my breast through the filmy, black nylon material of the bra, as if testing for firmness. It is very firm indeed, and I was glad I'd worked out earlier. He seemed to be considering what I had suggested.

Or, perhaps, he was considering what he'd be losing.

"Of course we can see each other," he said finally. "As long as you understand the situation between Jackie and me—and how discreet we have to be about our relationship, Marilyn."

"Of course, Jack," I said. "I would never do anything to hurt you, or ruin your chances for a second term. And, believe it or not, I don't want to hurt Jacqueline either."

"That means no talking to your friends."

"I wouldn't," I said.

He didn't say anything more but I could tell it was a done deal. He liked the idea of being able to come back to the buffet table now and again for a little nibble when he was feeling hungry.

Degrading to me?

Sure thing – but at least it would give me time to think. Time to think of what to do next. Time to make him fall in love with me—or time for something else to come along and ease my pain. A new plan. A new direction. Something.

If all these stupid hurts, all these broken relationships, all these nights of game-playing and ridiculousness didn't add something to me, build character and make me a better actress or something, then so much of my life has been an incredible waste.

Jack had said he wouldn't stay long but I saw that he was falling asleep. No doubt his agents were getting impatient.

I wanted to take more pills. Should I die next to him? An overdose in his arms – drifting off to sleep while I'm at my most happiest – whenever I'm near him. I would die next to him. Alone. Not dying with him as I once hoped. He would wake up next to my corpse – blue and cold- and I would become an object. Not of desire but of horror. Horror.

November 30, 1961

So now I'm in a kind of limbo. I set myself up for this torture though. It probably would have been better for all concerned if I let him walk away. If I severed all ties and started the horrible healing process.

I wish I had been stronger.

Now he can have the best of both worlds and I'm stuck here, longing for him, pining away for him, dying for him a little each day, while he goes about the business of ruling the world and sleeping with whoever he wants, whenever he wants, and when he wants me—well, I have to be available.

Sometimes I think it's not worth it to love anyone. You put all this investment into it, you cut yourself open to reveal yourself, for a very short time of happiness. In the long run you end up alone anyway, so maybe you were better off by yourself. I've never been one of the believers in that old sentiment, "It's better to have loved and lost than to never have loved at all."

It probably is better to go through life being happily blind, than to have a brief opportunity to see bright colors and then have to go back to complete darkness.

Is there something more, I wonder? Is there the kind of love that lasts forever, those strange, strong feelings never dulling, never ending?

December 8, 1961

After I left the studio in 1954, during the first year of living in New York, when the possibilities of every dream coming true still felt real and I was studying at The Actors Studio.

Arthur Miller and I had never forgotten that strange, sensual, stimulating, night we spent talking with my toe in his hand. We started seeing a lot of each other and it became serious fairly quickly.

See, we were still relating to our fantasies of each other.

I know I have spent my entire life looking for a father.

I was sitting in a shabby little diner with Arthur one winter afternoon. This was before we were married and in fact, he was still married to his first wife. But we were in the first exciting stages of love. And we were out on a date like two normal, average people. We went to see a picture call *Marty*. I had on a white knit hat covering my hair, dark sunglasses, a bulky sweater, and a long wool skirt. The waitress didn't recognize me as Marilyn Monroe, but she liked me anyway, and she kept coming to the table to fill my coffee cup and smile. She called me "Sweetie." I called her "Honey." And she'd smile.

I was chattering away with Arthur when he stopped me suddenly, took my hand, and out of nowhere he blurted, "I keep trying to lose you but I don't know how." I was dumbfounded for a moment, I took off my sunglasses holding back the tears that were begging to fall and I looked at him with all my might and asked "Why must you lose me?"

If I wasn't so desperate to find my next savior I may have been able to see the signs. When you love someone you keep looking for ways to be together—not to lose them. If I had been looking at the subtext then, as I do now, I would have been able to see that what he was saying, quite clearly, was: "What is a distinguished and respected man like me doing with a 'girl like you?"

He didn't say that but I *felt* it. And my face turned red and the tears came to my eyes.

The waitress, who liked me, a middle-aged woman, with heavy legs with lots of veins in them, and a smile that conveyed all the disappointments in her life, happened to be passing our table just then and she heard our exchange and she looked at me closely. At first she was looking at me because I was "Sweetie" and I had been hurt but I slowly saw the look of recognition come across her face. She lit up! She knew me! Well, that is to say, she knew Marilyn Monroe from the movies and fan magazines and she loved *that* Marilyn Monroe.

She was so astonished and delighted that Marilyn was sitting in her diner and I was just as nice as she had imagined. These are the people I could always trust to love me and defend me: the waitresses, the truck drivers, the postmen. The working people. They knew I came from them and they looked towards me with pride and adoration.

So she looked at Arthur with an expression of hate and disgust as if to say "How dare you make this enchanting child unhappy".

She came back to the table with a piece of paper for me to autograph. I signed it.

Before long the other diners caught on that it was "me" sitting there. They swarmed around the table. "Oh, Marilyn please sign this." "Oh my God, I can't believe it. Please wait here while I go get my friend." "I love all your movies!" "Hey Marilyn do a dance like the one you did in *There's No Business Like Show Business.*"

They weren't being rude. They recognized me as they would a friend. And yet they were astonished by me because I was also their goddess. I laughed and chatted with them.

Suddenly, though, Arthur rushed me out of the diner in a hurry before the small crowd started to grow.

Because before you know it a mob would form. I was used to that by now. Arthur wasn't. Sometimes it can get a little out of control. A little dangerous.

Arthur's mood was grim. "What's wrong," l asked him.

He said, "They act as if they own you."

"They don't mean any harm." I said softly.

He said, "They don't have any respect for you."

"You mean they think I'm a joke?" I asked him.

"Well, no. It's just that they see that you're not ashamed of what you are."

"W-what do you mean, 'what I am?'" I said. I was disoriented. Stung.

He tried to smooth things over. "They just see that you're in love with life and, well, you live life the way you want to."

I knew what he meant. But I wasn't ready to admit it to myself yet.

I said. "They just can't believe I'm real. It gives them the fantasy that anything can happen to them."

Still, I could see how much this little episode upset him. But secretly, on the inside, I felt that these strangers who loved me, were God's way of giving me a family that looked out for me. My people.

I have a lot of pain because I never belonged to anyone. I'm rootless in so many ways.

I belonged to the waitress and the kids in the diner and the rest. Not because they thought I was beautiful and paid to see me in the movies, but because I didn't belong to anyone else.

Arthur thought he was in love with me. But it wasn't that he was just in love with me, or thought that he was in love with me, he was by this time in awe of a public figure called "Marilyn Monroe." See the thing is, this persona I created, this Marilyn Monroe character, has somehow become a phenomenon.

I'm writing as honestly as I can. I'm not being arrogant here. I am at the center of this phenomenon. I am in awe of it as much as anyone else.

I mean sometimes I don't believe it. I can't feel that we are one and the same—their Marilyn Monroe and me. And I want to feel a part of it, too!

Everyone wants me. Everything I do is newsworthy. Every important person in the world wants to meet me. Me? When people see me on the street it's like they want to die right then and there. It's their dream come true, they can die happy. Normally people want to be part of a phenomenon. Arthur did. Even though he'd never admit that even to himself. I think he did love me a little, at least for a little while. But part of that love was the excitement of being part of the life of this incredible icon. He thought that I needed to be protected from that, he convinced himself that he needed to help me.

His love, though, wasn't completely genuine, at least I couldn't feel it completely. I remember the day we got married I felt so insecure, so unworthy, I guess these feelings were so strong they were coming out of my pores. He felt my fears. He put his arm around me and pulled me close. We started walking down the aisle and he felt me trembling. He whispered, "Oh, Marilyn, can't you see how everyone is adoring you, loving you? I love you, dear. Why are you so sad?"

See, my insecurities were saying: He's ashamed of you. He's thinking, "She's been with so many men. She beneath me. I'm doing her a favor by marrying her. I'm legitimizing her."

But I chose to believe what he said in that moment and I ignored my fears of what he might be thinking. Later I learned that my fears were what was true. He felt he was being so honorable, the famous respected intellectual playwright marrying the poor abused sexpot slut. He wanted to be a hero and I, fool that I am, allowed him to feel like he was one. He was the one who was using me worse than all the rest of them.

When we were first married, he tried to make me feel like he was the only one who truly cared about me and the only one who was trying to help me. He'd say, "This one is taking advantage of you," and "That one is using you." He made me get rid of a lot of people who, now that I think of it, maybe were on my side.

Sure I was being used by some of them, that is to be expected by someone who is bringing in the kind of money I was, but maybe they weren't all enemies. Yet, by now Arthur was in love with the idea of going down in history as my savior.

He felt that he "the genius writer" needed to justify being in love with me, so he told himself that I was this underappreciated genius of an actress. That I was an innocent angel being sinned against. That I was an orphan of the storm. But then he got to know me as the real-life, flawed, human being that I am. He was mortified. He didn't think I was good enough for him. And I wasn't sorry for it anymore.

What does he think I did in my past that was so terrible, I wonder? That he should feel so superior.

December 3, 1961

Yesterday I sat in the Polo Lounge of the Beverly Hills Hotel, drinking champagne with Nunnally.

Nunnally Johnson is the writer who wrote one of my biggest hits. *How to Marry a Millionaire.* I feel nostalgic about that movie now. As little as two years ago if someone asked me if I wanted to work with him again I would have said, "No!" Not that I didn't enjoy that movie, and it certainly advanced my career but, you know, I've been all about moving forward.

Now, after two unsuccessful movies, I feel I need someone who knows how to write good "Marilyn Monroe." My standing at the box office has, perhaps, slipped a bit because of my last two films, as the press keeps reminding me, and I need another blockbuster to bring me back.

It's Nunnally I want to do the re-write on *Something's Got to Give.*

Three bottles of champagne later, Nunnally had finished telling me his ideas for the story. They were good! For the first time I started to feel a little optimistic about the project.

He assured me he'd have a draft for me right away.

December 9, 1961

From the very beginning of my acting career I was most eager to improve my skills and to use those skills in great material. I always longed for wonderful scripts.

During the time I was with Arthur, I had been studying with Lee Strasberg in New York at the Actor's Studio and I was anxious to use all of my new knowledge of the art of acting in my screen rolls.

20th Century Fox was desperate to have me make more movies with them and they finally realized I was serious about wanting some control. It was at that time that they—and please let me say very begrudgingly— renegotiated my contract. I was to receive $100,000 per movie. Still much less than I was worth, but it was important for me to show them that I didn't care about the money.

What I wanted most from them was respect. I cannot repeat this enough: my main ambition was to be great. I forced them to give me approval of any director I would work with. I submitted a list, and under this new contract, if they couldn't get one of the directors on my list to direct the movie, I didn't have to make it.

The studio also finally realized I was serious about wanting good material to work in and they bought me a fine vehicle. It was a movie called *Bus Stop* and in that film I had the opportunity to use a lot of the things Strasberg taught me. *Bus Stop* is a tender comedy in which I play a bad night club performer with whom an unruly cowboy falls in love. The character I played is a hillbilly with big dreams, but underneath it all she's just a bruised and sensitive soul yearning to be loved. It was a good part and I got the best notices of my career up to that time.

I was approaching thirty, and I went into high gear to show the world that I was more than just a pair of boobs and a nice ass.

My production company, Marilyn Monroe Productions, was now a reality. I was incorporated for real. I bought a property I wanted to appear in that was eventually called *The Prince and the Showgirl.* I hired the greatest actor in the world, Laurence Olivier to direct the movie and also to be my co-star. I thought, who wouldn't respect an actress acting opposite Olivier?

Respect doesn't come easy though. To this day I'm still fighting for it.

I bought the rights to that script because everyone was saying I was perfect for it. My part was that of a chorus girl who on the surface seemed dumb and shallow but as it turns out she has a lot of character and smarts and is eventually able to make the prince feel real love for the first time in his life. Olivier had played his role on the stage in London with his wife, Vivien Leigh, in my part.

It was period piece with fancy costumes and a lot or respected British actors in the cast and of course Laurence Olivier was every actors' ideal. Well along with Marlon Brando. But did you ever meet someone who in reality turned out to be somebody totally different from what you imagined?

I had expected that working with Olivier would be the greatest artistic experience of my life. But early in the filming we were starting to shoot a scene in which my character is a little drunk on vodka and is admiring the Prince's face when Olivier gave me the following direction, "Okay Marilyn, just be sexy" and I, you know, fell apart. I mean, what does that mean? To be "sexy?" Sexy? It's not something you turn on with a switch. Imagine we all had a built-in "sexy" switch! We'd be flicking it on all the time.

I could understand if his direction was, "Marilyn your character is smelling the hair oil that the Prince is wearing and it arouses her so much that she wants him to kiss her" or something like that. At least I would know why she was feeling sexual! But to direct an actress to "be sexy," to me is offensive. It is the equivalent of Hollywood saying, "Stick out those tits young lady and wiggle that behind".

So you see what I'm saying, I had broken away from Hollywood, started my own corporation, bought a screenplay with my own money and hired the greatest actor in the world to work with me only to end up exactly where I started. "Be sexy."

I had no answer for that. I couldn't say "That is the dumbest thing I ever heard." It might be considered kind of disrespectful.

Instead I just walked away off the set, without saying a word, past the crew and into my dressing room.

Like I said, the only way I get them to acknowledge or respect me is to remove myself.

I cried and cried because of the mess I had gotten myself into and because this great artist viewed me the way everyone else did. Olivier of course was simply horrified that I had embarrassed him in front of the crew by walking off. He had no idea why I did. I guess he thought I was being temperamental.

After that I lost all respect for Olivier and he lost all patience with me, filming became a nightmare. I no longer had faith in my director, the script, and the whole project. I started to fear that I wouldn't be any good in the picture. My confidence was gone. I never showed up on time again. On top of that, I stopped showing up on the set on days that we had to film key scenes. I mean I missed an awful lot of days.

Okay, okay I admit it, I'm afraid of the camera. I feel I have to be absolutely, completely ready for a scene, before I feel comfortable enough to shoot it. I love to act more than anything and when I hit a line right on the mark, I can feel it. That is the greatest pleasure of my life. But being the self-conscious wreck that I am, I worry for days and days before I have to do an important scene. I have to sort of … how do I explain this? I have to find the inspiration within myself in order to make the character believable and if I'm not ready to do it, I simply don't show up. I owe a lot to my audiences, getting no help with performance from my director, of course, makes me feel not ready to give my best. Understandably the cast and crew grow furious with me.

But see the thing is I'm not the normal actress. If I may be so bold and arrogant to say my pictures don't get the average amount of attention. I've made them a lot of money, so can't they indulge me a little? I do feel that people who pay to see me in the movies ought to get their money's worth. I want to give them my best.

If a movie I'm in does flop, they don't blame the script or the director or the other actors—they blame me. Of course the flip side of the coin is that when everything works, like in *Bus Stop* I get all the credit. "She's Magic".

So much has been made of "Marilyn Monroe," with publicity and such, that much more is expected of me than the normal movie personality. Some days on my way to the studio, I see a certain cleaning woman leaving the gates. She had probably been working all night, alone and in peace, maybe humming to herself, and I envy her. She can go home and prepare her husband breakfast and no one expects anything more from her and I say to myself "I should have been a cleaning woman, that's my ambition in life." But of course, I don't really mean that.

But my mind has been digressing, and I wanted to tell you about what happened between Arthur and me, but I also wanted to explain why I have so much trouble on the set of my films.

I need to have an environment where I feel confident and appreciated in order to give my best. Very few directors have given me that. Most directors expect actors to be performing seals. That's fine for some actors. They can do it. But I have a lot of the pressure and nervousness that comes with extraordinary fame. It's almost like certain people are waiting for you to make a mistake or do something they can pick at. I'm working on trying to make that matter less. But for now, I take it upon myself to show up when I'm good and ready to perform. If that makes me an unprofessional bitch, well, I have to accept being guilty of that.

So everyone on the set was complaining about me. Arthur was hanging around the hotel room with me trying to get me to go to work. For him, the excitement of being Mr. Marilyn Monroe had died down already. Now he was stuck with Norma Jeane Baker Dougherty DiMaggio Miller, a real woman. Not only a real woman, but a difficult, erratic, demanding woman and a spoiled movie star, to boot. But instead of having the guts to tell me what he was feeling, he played a dirty little trick.

He told me what he thought of me on a piece of paper. Like a coward.

He wrote in his diary about what a disappointment I was to him. He wondered if marrying me had been a mistake. That I wasn't anything like the "sinned against angel" he thought worthy of saving before we were married. Instead I embarrassed him in front of his friends. He wrote about how Laurence Oliver thought that I was nothing more than a troublesome, ignorant bitch and he couldn't defend me against that because he agreed. He also wrote how disappointed he was in me. Worst of all he said that he was sometimes ashamed of me.

Then he left the diary out on his desk, opened to that exact page.

There was no doubt I would see it. That was his plan. He wanted me to read it. I read it alright. It felt like a smack across the face. A hard smack. The kind that leaves a mark. I only wish he had smacked me with his hand instead of his words. At least then he would have been behaving honestly—directly to me. Then we could have a real argument.

I fell to the floor in a dead faint.

I fainted because shortly before I read that, he was always saying, "Darling, you are so wonderful! I realize now that you need more love than I thought. But I've got it! You can't feel how much I love you yet, but I'm going to make you see, someday you'll feel it."

I wanted to feel it. I had been counting on feeling it. I bet my life I would feel it.

Now that was all over and done with.

I can put up with a lot—but a conniving, ass-kissing liar is a bit too much. Especially one who acts so superior.

Yes, you're damn right, I'm angry as I write this!

This was the man I had built up to be a White Knight. I guess we were both wrong about each other. We were still in our honeymoon months and we both knew—without speaking the words—that it was already over. Although we did try to make a go of it, for the most part, in the next four years, Arthur spent half of the time of our marriage trying to justify being in love with me and the other half looking for reasons to "lose me."

Long before we became seriously involved he couldn't write anymore. He was out of ideas. When he married me, he found the perfect excuse not to write. He didn't have to be brilliant because he was so busy playing nurse maid to the crazy, neurotic movie star, he was kind enough to marry.

He started accompanying me on the sets of all my movies. Don't get me wrong, I appreciated it at the time—although I never asked him to. But Arthur was clever, he made me feel as if he was making this great sacrifice, by helping "see me through" the filming. I'm always very unsure and vulnerable when I'm working, so it was great to have my husband there for me.

Underneath his noble front he was making me indebted to him.

While we were married our friends, or shall I say *his* friends, his intellectual friends from the theater world, they all said, "Look what she's done to him! He's carrying her makeup case! It's because of that bitch that he's stopped writing! He's become her secretary for chrissakes!"

But really he loved it! He adored being part of the Monroe sensation. He loved not having to write so he could be part of the spectacle that was created around me. All the while making himself come across as the long suffering martyr, taking care of the needy, drug addled, crazy bitch. I hate him for that. That is why I grew to despise him.

And may I add to the story of our marriage by adding, rather indelicately, that he wasn't making a dime. Please believe me, this is the truth: I didn't care at all at the time but he was living totally off of me. I paid for everything. Of course it wouldn't have mattered if he really wanted to be with me but now I see things differently.

I hear Arthur is writing an autobiographical play now. I can only wonder if there is a character based on me in it and, if so, what he will say about me.

Someday he will write about me, I'm sure. A play or a movie or a book. In it, he will make himself out to be the all-suffering, all-patient, all-loving saint. I, no doubt, will be the grasping, stupid, unstable, childish, destroyer. A modern day Lilith. Wanting to destroy myself and all those around me.

He needs me to be that to justify the end of our marriage. In the end of this play, or movie, or book, he will leave me, because it's the only way he can save himself. He won't talk about how he used me. He won't write about how I walked out on him because it was the only way I could find myself again. And try to find my self-respect.

He thinks he's so smart and I'm so dumb, but I can see all this. But, as usual, my realization came too late.

December 12, 1961

Nunnally Johnson delivered his rewrite of *Something's Got to Give*. It's pretty good. He changed the plot quite a lot so that I'm more suited to the female lead character. I could see the possibilities of this being a first class Marilyn Monroe movie. I said, "I think this is a good start. It needs some work but I think we really might be on the right track here! I would like to see some more jokes and a few funnier situations."

The studio was pleased to know there was a version of the script I was enthusiastic about. They assured me they would keep working on it until it was just right. But, you know, I'm not about to take their word for it. I'll believe it when I see it.

December 14, 1961

When I'm in an optimistic mood: Well, Jack is president now. Of course he doesn't have time to fall in love with me. Plus his life is under such scrutiny, he really can't risk anyone finding out about an affair. But maybe in a few years the time will be right for us to be together completely.

I have to laugh. Frank said that to me. About "the time being right." Maybe that's where I got the idea from.

Well! The time isn't right for me either. After all, there is still a few more films I want to make. For example, my biggest professional ambition right now is to work with Marlon Brando—as it has been for years. So maybe after I accomplish all of the in my career that I want to accomplish and Jack has accomplished all the things he wants to do in improving the world, maybe we can find each other and just enjoy each other for a few years. Maybe we can find comfort in each other and live for a while.

But then the old darkness creeps in reminding me how not all dreams come true and nothing lasts forever.

December 23, 1961

I heard some Christmas music on the radio this afternoon and it made me feel glum.

Well it doesn't feel like Christmas around here, I want to be with Jack but I can't and I feel very sad.

I'm just going through a bad spell, which I've gone through before, but the fear is always in me that maybe this time it won't pass.

Sometimes when things don't work out as you planned early on, I like to think that it's God stepping in and stopping it before it gets out of control and really causes emotional damage. But since I can't feel God most of the time anyway, I rarely heed his warning. So instead of just letting Jack go, I feel myself trying even harder to make something serious out of this relationship.

I see Jack in my dreams, wanting other women, having sex with other women. I've never really been the jealous type, but in these dreams I'm beside myself with sexual jealousy and rage.

Isn't it sad, we are always searching but rarely finding. So few of us ever end up with the right person.

1962

January 1, 1962

Jane Russell once told me, "If you turn to God, He will fill up your heart with his love and you won't feel so lonely. The need for romantic love, or sexual fulfillment, won't seem so important."

All night while I'm trying to find sleep, I pretend that God is lying next to me and that he is holding me, like a father would. He's strokes my hair and says "What's your destination little girl"

In rare moments I can actually feel Him. I try to summon that feeling during the day, but I feel nothing but vulnerable. When I was little, a foster parent taught me to sing "Jesus Loves Me This I Know." And even though I didn't have a real concept of who Jesus was, I at least felt certain that someone somewhere loved me. Now I try to feel that, but I'm not so sure, and I don't know anything.

But it's a new year. Let's get on with it!

Dr. Greenson, knowing how blue I feel, suggested that I start looking for a house of my own. He stresses the fact that I have never lived in a place that was truly mine. He seems to feel that it will fill some gap in me. A gap of not having a husband. Or children. I don't see how a house can take the place of a family. But I do like the idea of a comfortable place to live while I'm in Los Angeles. It will also give me a place where I can have friends stay with me when visiting.

Well at the very least it gives me something to think about while I sit around and pine for Jack. So I'll start house hunting.

It looks like *Something's Got to Give* will start shooting in the spring.

Dr. Greenson wants me to make the movie. He says that it will help me get out of my depression. He feels that I hate my studio, Fox, so much that it will be good to get this movie over with to fulfill the end of my contract and be free of them.

It seems that he gives me an awful lot of advice. Even if he is my psychiatrist. Advice about my business. Advice regarding my personal life (even when I don't ask.) For example he didn't like me dating Frank Sinatra. He certainly doesn't like me seeing Jack Kennedy. He describes these relationships as being with "men who will only hurt you."

I feel, well, no matter how many problems I have, I should at least be free to date who I want.

I know he's only looking out for me. I mean, I THINK he has my best interests at heart. Yet, I don't know. It seems like he is a bit controlling.

Dr. Greenson also suggested I hire a live-in companion and he found me a woman named Mrs. Murray. I actually think he knows her from somewhere in his past and I should make a note to ask him where he found her. She's supposed to drive me around, mostly to and from my appointments with Dr. Greenson. She's also supposed to do some cooking for me and light housework.

Mrs. Murray is an older, soft-spoken lady but I can't warm up to her the way I should. There is something creepy about her. I mean she speaks in whispers, like everything is this great covert conspiracy. She's odd. My friends have told me they don't feel comfortable around her. I feel she watches my every move. Listening to my phone conversations. Maybe even reporting back to Dr. Greenson.

But, I tell myself, I *am* a star and I shouldn't have to do my own dusting.

January 4, 1962

Mrs. Murray was helping me look for a house and we were just sort of driving around looking at different neighborhoods. I know I don't want to live in Beverly Hills. I want a quiet place. Near the beach. Near Dr. Greenson. Small. Not "Hollywood-ish." I always feel safer in small rooms.

I saw a house in Brentwood with a "For Sale" sign on the lawn. It looked promising, from the outside, anyway. I got out of the car to take a look at the property. I was only there for a few minutes when a man came out of the front door. He said, "Are you looking for a house?" I told him I was.

He said, "Well, if you'd like a tour I can…"

He stopped abruptly. Then he said, "Wait a minute! I um…Aren't you Marilyn Monroe?"

"Yes."

His face turned red. He was so excited! He said, "Oh my! Well, oh oh…please. Just wait here a moment. I want to get my wife. She'll never believe this."

And I waited on the pathway thinking the couple would come out and show me the inside of the house.

The wife came out. Red hair in curlers. Wearing a housedress. Scarlet lips. She very sternly said, "Will you please get off of this property right now."

It was so unexpected! I was stunned.

"I…I only wanted to…" I stammered.

"Get off my property!" she screamed.

Her husband looked stricken.

I felt that hot rush of humiliation and anger and hurt. The feeling of being judged without having a chance to explain yourself or reveal yourself. I know I should be used to attacks by now but it still affects me every time. In the press or in real life.

I went back to the car. "Marilyn, what happened?" Mrs. Murray murmured. I just shook my head. There weren't any words.

January 7, 1962

Jack rarely returns my calls anymore. I don't want to feel bitter about him, I still believe he is a great politician, a brilliant world leader. I still feel the Kennedys will do wonderful things for this country, they will go all the way for Civil Rights and such. But what I feel for him as a man in his interpersonal relationships is changing.

January 9, 1962

I've been thinking about that incident with the woman screaming at me to get off of her property. I guess I shouldn't be surprised. For the most part, women have never liked me. Ever since I was a teenager. It's been difficult for me to maintain friendships with women. In particular, wives loathe me. I suppose I should be flattered that they think of me as such a threat.

It's not that I'm prettier than them or have a better figure. I've been hated by some real glamour gals. But I would much rather have hundreds of women be jealous of me, than me be jealous of just one of them. I've felt jealousy and it's not a good feeling at all. I've practiced and kind of trained myself to avoid feeling any kind of jealousy whenever I can. I just try to look at everyone as an individual with good qualities and bad qualities. There's no need to make every encounter a competition.

One personality I remember really going at me, much like the woman on her pathway, is Zsa Zsa Gabor. Gee, she really is one nasty lady. She rarely has anything nice to say about any woman—except herself.

Early in my career, in one of my first important movies, *All About Eve*, I had all of my scenes with her then husband, the great actor, George Sanders. He would flirt with me and joke that if I was interested in running away with him, he'd be amendable to that. I just laughed it off. It was very innocent. There was certainly nothing going on between us.

Well, during this time, I went to a Hollywood party. I was alone. And, I've always been petrified when I first walk into any kind of party by myself. I still am. I was only a few steps into the living room. I heard a commotion. It was a screeching woman's voice but I couldn't understand a word she screeched. Then I saw them dragging a blonde into the kitchen, her arms were flailing and her hairdo was coming undone, and the shouting kept on going and then I heard glasses breaking and the clanging of pots and pans being thrown around.

Finally she was removed from the house.

The host of the party approached me with a bemused smile. He said, "My dear, what on earth did you ever do to make Zsa Zsa Gabor so upset? It must have been quite something to get such a reaction."

I had to reply, quite honestly, that I had no idea what I had done to create that kind of reaction. That can be something I can say about a lot of things that have happened in my life.

Undated Notes

I found a house that I like and impulsively decided I wanted to buy it right then and there. It's in Brentwood and hidden in a cul-de-sac. It's a small, two-bedroom, Mexican style house. It has a swimming pool and a garage that I plan to have renovated into a guest house.

When I was signing the papers I burst into tears. I always imagined picking out a house with a spouse and building our dreams on it.

Here I was buying my first home and I was doing it alone. But in essence I've always been alone so I don't know why it should have had such a gloomy effect on me. Now I'm a person alone who owns property.

Undated Note

I don't want to become one of those desperate, grasping women, but I have too much invested in Jack at the moment. I can't imagine what life would be like without him.

I can't go back to the darkness again, as when Fred left me, and Johnny died soon after. I'm not strong enough now, when I was twenty-three I still had things I felt I had to accomplish.

I thought that maybe a career would be my salvation, it was for a while, but now I know it's not enough, I need love too. Sometimes you just have to walk away and admit defeat, but in this case I can't. I can't let go till I give my last drop of blood.

January 12, 1962

What I have always dreaded has started to arrive. Some of the press is turning on me. I guess it's only natural that my age would become the story.

When you're just coming up, that's a good story. So the people in the press say, "Wow, this girl is really something. She's going places." And you play into it because you DO want to get ahead. Then when you finally make it they say, "She's the hottest thing in motion pictures. Everybody wants Monroe."

But after a few years that story isn't front page news anymore and they have to come up with other things to write about. Even though my name still sells papers they need a new hook. So now they're saying, "She's older. She's slipping. She's not as popular as she once was. She may be finished in the movies."

But it's totally up to me to change the narrative.

Some of them try to be, I guess, a bit chivalrous about it. They don't come right out and say, "She's getting older." But there are quite a lot of stories that talk about me being at a "turning point." The subtext is I can't go on having the same kind of career that I've had. They seem to see a bleak future for me.

Some of them are quite vicious, gleefully questioning what I'm going to do now that I'm thirty-five. Hinting that it's only a matter of time before my looks are gone and I will be finished.

"What will she do then?"

I don't know what I'll do, actually.

I don't understand it. I can't understand!

Why is it everywhere I go someone tells me how beautiful I look—and I see the look of astonishment in their eyes. In the meantime, I mean, simultaneously, some of the press is like a herd of cadaver dogs waiting to catch the scent of decay on me.

They write things like, "Her curves will soon turn into lines—on her face."

It's hateful. It's cruel.

Some other reporter could have rushed to my defense and called their attacks, "vicious."

I think they're vicious.

I guess they want me to look bad so they can feel better about themselves.

Yet, I do want to say that almost from the beginning most of the press has been very warm and friendly towards me. Some still write about me as if I'm a friend and they still say very kind and flattering things about me, my looks, my talent.

Of course it makes me feel good, but these aren't the articles that stick in my head. It's the mean things I can't get out of my mind.

I don't like to acknowledge these articles but once I, very fearfully, brought up the kind of publicity that was starting to crop up about me to one of my press agents. He laughed. He said an article about Marilyn Monroe's last movie not doing well at the box office gets more headlines than any new star in the biggest hit of the year.

He said, "Marilyn, if your career being in danger is front page news you have nothing to worry about. When they stop speculating about you in the headlines it will be time to worry."

But I worry.

January 14, 1962

Pat called me today, she is having a party for her brother Bobby Kennedy and his wife Ethel on February 1st. They will then be leaving for a world tour. Pat asked Bobby, "Who in Hollywood do you most want to meet" and he said he wanted to meet me.

So don't write me off as finished yet, as the newspaper columnists are trying to do. I still have a few tricks up my sleeve. I refuse to be just another Hollywood toy for the president to play with for a while and then discard.

I've decided I want to meet Bobby Kennedy. My plan, if you can call it that, is to flirt with him, get him interested. Sort of play brother against brother. It's all kind of scatterbrained and innocent—something a character in one of my movies might do—but who knows? It could work.

When Jack hears that his brother is making a play for me, he will want me again. Let's face the brutal facts, men always want another man's woman. After Bobby wants me, he'll have to have me for himself again. It's sounds simple and far-fetched, but I've seen similar schemes work.

January 19, 1962

My plan to seduce Bobby Kennedy is in high gear already. I've had a special gown designed, daring, even by my own standards, clingy black satin with a shear see-through, lace top.

Whitey will arrive early to give me a special makeup—the works—and then he will escort me to the party. Well, he will walk me to the door and then disappear. I want to be alone and appear totally available that night. That takes care of the physical side of things.

Next, to dazzle him with my intellect, I'm studying up on current events and politics. I plan to pull out all of the Monroe stops, mixing sex with wit and intelligence. I asked my doctor's son, Dan, to help me prepare. He's a college student and he knows all the current political language. I know what I want to talk to Bobby about, but I want to phrase everything in just the right way, so Dan helped me put together a list of questions that are on the minds of the youth of America.

It may sound terribly presumptuous, but I simply know that I have the power to make certain men fall in love with me. Bobby will be one of them.

February 2, 1962

The party

I was late. Again. It's not so much that I planned it that way, it's just that it takes me a little longer than most woman to get ready. And then, well, okay, maybe I do like making them wait for me. It's fun to be important after all those years of being a nobody. Part of me likes to think all those people waiting for me are the same people who ignored me when I was a little kid and if I had not grown up to be a movie star they'd still be ignoring me.

When I arrived at the Lawford beach house, the reporters camped out in front were in peak frenzy, oh yes this was a very important party. Bobby and Ethel were leaving the next day for their world tour and this party was their send off. The guest list mixed Hollywood glamour with Washington politics. It was a real who's who.

When I stepped out of the car, all of the reporters and photographers tried to get to me shouting their questions. They wanted to know who Whitey was. I didn't tell them that he was my makeup artist simply giving me a lift. I said "Oh, he's just some sailor I picked up" and they scribbled it down frantically. Flashbulbs were popping continuously and I could feel the importance of the night.

I'm good at talking and flirting with the reporters and photographers. It's what helped me during my climb. There is an unreality about it all. They only want the image, the "Marilyn" character that I created and can do by rote. But when I get inside the party, that's when the fear takes over. When I have to be the combination of the image "Monroe" and the real woman Marilyn. Instead I just become the orphan who is shy and terribly afraid.

As was part of my plan, Whitey was just dropping me off. I wanted to be at the party intriguingly alone. So Whitey beat a hasty retreat, leaving me at the party to fend for myself.

When I entered at the top of the stairs leading to the living room, the party sort of stopped. I have come to expect that reaction at my arrivals. The whispered chant, "Marilyn's here," drifted like wildfire through the room. And then that rush of excitement. That electricity! When it first started happening, when I had my first taste of fame, it made me shiver and cry to think just my appearance could cause such a stir. Now the expectation of it is one of my vanities. I don't know how I'll feel if it ever stops happening.

There I stood, frozen at the top of the stair. A pillar of white set off by my stark black dress.

And the entire party looking up at me.

First things first. I sized up the competition. Kim Novak dressed in a glitzy, red sequined gown. Thank goodness I didn't wear sequins! Janet Leigh in black velvet – okay, no threat from Janet. Natalie Wood (thank goodness not another blonde) was wearing a cocktail dress. These were the biggest female stars in the room and I more than held my own.

With every eye on me, I languidly walked down the stairs in my clinging black. My breasts tantalizingly displayed. I felt like Cleopatra offering herself to Marc Antony. I once read that she had dressed herself as Venus, the goddess of love, in their first meeting, and I sort of modeled myself on that incident tonight. Planning to offer myself, so to speak, to Bobby Kennedy.

When I got to the bottom of the stairs, I felt somewhat adrift and I looked for the hostess to come and rescue me. I spotted Pat wearing a flowing white evening gown. She made a bee-line towards me. I know that Monroe was the crowning achievement of her guest list. Sometimes I kind of expect my hosts, my friends, to protect me all night and stay at my side. Of course that's impossible…and they don't realize what's going on inside of me and how afraid I am.

"I didn't think you were going to come," Pat said. "I know how you hate this kind of crowd."

"Are you kidding," I told her, "I'm dying to meet Bobby."

"Well, we sat him between you and Kim at the dinner table," she said.

I had to laugh. "Thanks a lot,"

It's so like Peter to think it's funny to seat the Attorney General of the United States between what the world considers two bubble-headed sex pots.

Pat took me by the arm and started introducing me to all the people I didn't know, saying with pride "This is Marilyn Monroe," as if that name wields some magical force. Little do they know that the person bearing that name is more afraid than anyone.

Because I'm so incredibly frightened all the time, I've learned to cover up my fear with an air of complete ease, a mask of indifference. I make believe I'm in my own little world, although inside of me there's always hysterical chatter. Champagne and vodka, and sometimes pills, help lessen the fear…sometimes. And they add that languid, dreaminess that has become part of what they consider my "allure."

I was drinking but I didn't have any pills on me. I was glad. A few days before I had taken that new prescription and I slept the entire next day (forgetting most of the previous.) I wanted to feel at ease tonight, but alert all the same. I was on display and had to be ready for anything.

Finally Pat brought me over to Bobby. He was so shy and intimidated. Pat said to her brother, "Bobby, you remember Marilyn." Even though we had never met. She was playing it cool, being very casual about the whole thing.

But Bobby just stood there sort of agog.

I remember shortly before we were married Arthur said to me, "They all tremble in your presence. No matter how high or low up the ladder. No matter what they might have thought of you before, every son of a bitch trembles in your presence."

"Bobby, this is Marilyn Monroe!" Pat said.

Bobby finally snapped out of it and said: "Hello, Miss Marilyn Monroe."

Bobby looked like a watered-down version of his older brother. I didn't feel those electric currents I feel when I look at Jack. Which was kind of a relief, actually. It's horrible enough to feel that way about one man…it would be too much to feel that strongly about two men at the same time…brothers no less.

"A pleasure, Mr. Attorney General," I replied.

Just then Ethel Kennedy walked up and took her husband's arm. She certainly was not what I expected. Plain but pleasant-looking enough. She certainly didn't seem like someone who could snag a Kennedy. Actually she reminded me of a lesbian, a bit butch looking and sort of severe. And the way she stared at me didn't do anything to change my opinion. I'm not saying she's a lesbian, but let's just say I've known my share of those ladies and she gave off the lesbo-vibe. But then again, what do I know?

Ethel, with her frozen smile, had this specific look in her eye. It was part admiration, part fear. I've seen it in people when they meet Marilyn Monroe. It's as if some dream they've had has actually come to life, some vision that till that moment has only existed on film. This, too, I've come to expect.

I remember one time I was in front of my building in New York stepping into the limo on my way to some event. I was in my full Marilyn getup and there was a small crowd of people gathered around, as there usually is in front of my NYC place. One of the kids...he was kind of cute... stared and stared and finally said, "Wow! You're real!"

I said, "Gee, I hope so!" And we both laughed. It's times like that, when people connect with you, that it's so nice. I made a person's day just by being me.

When Ethel emerged out of her daze, she quickly whisked Bobby away, but I didn't care. I already knew that I would have him next to me at dinner and I could tell by his reaction to me that my mission for the evening, to bewitch him, would be accomplished. I had felt that familiar sexual current pass from him to me, as real and potent as if it had been an electrical charge sent through an invisible wire. I'm never wrong about these things.

The thing was that, now until dinner, I was on my own. I had to mingle through the crowd and there were a lot of Hollywood types, studio officials who hate me. All the executives at Fox hate me. They look at me as if they know shameful secrets about my past that make me way beneath them.

Now they are rushing me into this *Something's Got to Give* with an unfinished script, so they can make some quick money to rescue the studio, which is going bankrupt. They need me to save their careers and that makes them despise me even more.

"I can tell she wants to get fucked," I heard one of them say about me to his cigar chomping crony as I passed. He doesn't know how wrong he was, but that's the way they talk about me.

I know I shouldn't let things like that hurt me anymore, but they still do.

I found myself leaning against a wall alone, saying to myself, "I don't belong here. I don't know where I belong."

All the while guests staring at me and wondering.

Even the rich and famous: they adore me. They worship me. They rush to see me in the movies. They beg to be invited to events I'm scheduled to attend. So why do I always feel like they're the enemy? All of them plotting and waiting for a way to push the knife deeper into my back? I guess because I feel that under their admiration and adoration, is some envy.

Some of them stare and stare and if I catch them looking at me sometimes they do a head flick and look quickly away – as if they don't want me to think I'm worth looking at. It's like part of them admires me, but there's another part that makes them envy me and hate me. "Why does she deserve to have it all?" they ask themselves.

Which just goes to show how much they know about me. Nothing really.

It hit me again, how much I want Jack. Jack and only Jack. I imagined him at my side at this party. I imagined him completely in love with him and proudly escorting me around. I imagined him as my husband. In my imagination, Jack's protection, his love, allowed me to feel at ease and enjoy the party and view everyone, not as my enemies, but as my equals.

And I thought about how all men now, when I meet them, seem washed out next to Jack. Not just his brother. In the beginning when I thought Jack would surely fall in love with me and I felt secure in our relationship, I felt as if no one could hurt me. Now, unsure of his feelings, I feel like a turtle without a shell.

Sometimes I try to move through the crowd and make eye contact and, you know, just connect with people. But they see me as a thing. An entity named Marilyn Monroe, not a living, breathing person who needs to make a connection with others from time to time. No one at the Lawford's party seemed able to give me this connection. All I could do was give them what they wanted.

So I forced myself through the crowd, my beauty – my nakedness – my only defense.

Finally dinner was ready to be served and we all took our places at the set up tables. Kim was there, sitting on the other side of Bobby. Now what can I say about Kim Novak that hasn't been said a million times before? Hmm. Although she's one of the actresses another studio had groomed to compete with myself, I can't dislike her. She *is* beautiful. She's always very nice to me.

During dinner Kim was much more chatty and personable and "present" in the moment, while I was sort of vague, distant, and blurry, which can have its own mystery and charm. The sleepy-eyed vagueness and the moist parted lips are my own secret power. I could tell everyone at the table was fascinated, sneaking side glances at me, dying for me to snap out of it and say something clever or double entendre or unanswerable.

I saw Bobby, too, sneaking side glances at me, drinking rapidly, trying to build up the confidence to speak to me, while Kim chattered on in his ear. When Bobby talked I listened intently–all eyes. He was brilliant in his own right, but not nearly as sexy or brilliant or charismatic as his brother—and therefore not as dangerous to me (and ultimately less appealing.)

When I got my chance with him, the thing I wanted to talk to him about most was his position on civil rights. I had all these notes on things I wanted to ask him in my purse – the ones Danny had helped me phrase. I knew that I would be too nervous, or drunk or disoriented to remember all the subjects I wanted to talk to Bobby about, so I scribbled all my questions on tiny pieces of paper. In between courses, I peered into my purse, casually pretending to look for something, and when I looked up, I was filled with intelligently constructed political conversation.

Bobby was impressed, "Have you been taking some sort of political course or attending civil rights meetings?" he asked me.

I just laughed and said, "These are the questions on the mind of the American people."

Just before dessert, Bobby saw me peering into my purse and asked me what I was doing. "Oh, gee," I said breathlessly. "You caught me cheating." And I explained to him about my crib notes. He was delighted. "Ah, a women who comes prepared," he laughed. I was liking him more and more.

It was after dinner that I had my real chance with him. I sat down on the floor in a quiet corner and sprawled out on the carpet. It wasn't long before Bobby found me. I knew he would. He sat down next to me. He was sweet. Away from the table, just the two of us in the corner, Bobby became shy again. If I had to find a single word to describe him I would say "enamored." I took out my lipstick and wrote on a napkin "What exactly does an Attorney General do?" And I slid him the note like a school girl secretly passing notes during algebra class.

I guess he had had enough to drink because the note opened him up. He began a lengthy conversation about his duties as the Attorney General.

I noticed he carefully folded the napkin and put it in his pocket.

As we talked he became more and more comfortable with me. I got caught up in the moment. With the drinks, and the talk, and the eyes, and the flirting we were quickly heading towards the tingly, pleasant emotion called "infatuation." I hadn't noticed when they first started playing music. Now, suddenly, I heard the song, "The Peppermint Twist" come on the record player.

"Do you twist, Bobby?" I asked.

"Well I...I never had an occasion to," he said.

"Come on," I said. "Now you have an occasion. It's very easy," I led him to the middle of the room where people were dancing. We started dancing and the floor soon cleared and there I was, twisting the night away with the Attorney General of the United States. With everyone watching. Ethel stood watching too, with her frozen smile intact.

The way she was looking at us made me think of a story that Billy Wilder once told me – well, when he still liked me and was being nice to me. After I did a scene in *The Seven Year Itch*, a scene in which I played

"Chopsticks" on the piano, he was so delighted with me that that night he went home and told his wife, "The only woman I would ever leave you for is Marilyn Monroe." Instead of becoming angry, his wife looked him up and down and replied, "Me too."

After the dance, Bobby said shyly, "Marilyn would you do me a favor?"

"Sure," I said.

"I have a friend, a college chum, who has been in love with you for years," he said. "Would you mind saying hello to him if I called him up right now?"

"In love with me?" I said. "Well, then, the least I could do is say hello." And even though it must have been about two in the morning on the East Coast, Bobby called his friend and said, "Guess who I just danced with?" And he put me on the phone.

"He's not a bad twister," I said in my Marilyn-iest voice. The man couldn't speak at all and afterwards Bobby and I just laughed and laughed.

Then he asked me to call his father! The legendary Joe Kennedy! I had to wonder how much he knew about me and Jack – and if he thought that I was now making a play for his younger son. I also wondered if Joe thought he had a chance with me. After all, it's well known that years ago he had an affair with Gloria Swanson, who was the biggest sex goddess of her day. Ah, how history can repeat itself.

By the end of the night, I was pretty high. Bobby was too. I figured it was time to call for the limo but Bobby said, "I'll drive you home." Then he turned to Ed, the man who handles his press relations, and said, "Take a ride with us, Ed." I guess he couldn't explain driving a drunk Marilyn Monroe home to a wooden-faced Ethel unless he had Ed with him.

So Bobby and Ed and I left the party together. In the car, Bobby and I sat in front while Ed sat in the back. I thought Bobby might grab for my hand and I think he would have, had the ride been a longer one.

When we drove up to

my house I proudly announced, "This is my new home." It did feel good having my own place to be taken to.

Bobby walked me to the door. It felt like a first date. He made a move to kiss me but I made sure he just got my cheek. I didn't want to give too much too soon – a mistake I made often in the past, particularly with his brother. But I let him press his lips against my cheek for a long time. I wondered if Ed was watching from the car. Whether he was or not, I was sure that the story of "the kiss" would never make it to the press. But surely it would make it to his brother!

When I got to my bedroom everything was spinning. Usually my bed is like a womb but I tossed and turned and couldn't find my place between the sheets. Before long I was tangled in them. I should have felt triumphant but I felt sad and insane.

I tried to summon God for comfort. "Hold me Father. I'm lonely," I said. But there was no response and I remained in my bed alone.

Bobby had fallen for me – an honor, I suppose, being that his position in the world is so important. But if I was to be honest with myself, my feelings for him when I compared him to his brother as a man, were weak and wan. While Jack is the most important man in the world, which impresses me, I am also in love with him as a man. He is the one I want, not Bobby. Why is it so easy to reach and touch the one you don't care about while the one, the rare someone you want…backs away unaccepting and unreachable?

I put on a stack of Sinatra records and lay down on the floor. I thought of calling Frank. It was suddenly important to talk to someone who loves me, ("Lucky me," I thought, "when most people have the blues, all they can do is listen to Sinatra's records, while I have the man's number committed to memory and he loves me.") But it was late and if I woke Frank up he might be grouchy.

My snowball, my doggie, Maf, scurried up to me. He sniffed me tentatively. He knows when I'm blue and he wanted to comfort me.

Sometimes I put Maf in the guest house to sleep. I must have forgotten this night, but I was glad for the company. That's what Maf was for. Frank gave me Maf to make me feel less lonely after I divorced Arthur. I'm so lucky to have a dog who is not frantic and hyperactive! I'm so glad Maf is languid and moody, like me.

I got up and crawled into the bed bringing Maf with me.

I always say, when life gets to be too much, too complicated, I go to my bedroom. My bed is a safe place.

God has the power to make things right and, as Jane Russell says, He loves me unconditionally, but most of the time I just can't feel Him at all. Maf, although only a little dog with no power to do anything, is flesh and blood and I can feel his little body filled with pulsating life and love for me. I put my arm around him and he snuggled in. And that's how I fell asleep. Maf too.

March 3, 1962

I decided to fly to Mexico City for a couple of weeks.

At first I thought it would just be nice to be in new surroundings to rest up and come back refreshed and restored and ready to face the making of a new movie at Fox.

Then I thought, well, I just bought a new Mexican-style house. If I'm going to be in Mexico I might as well shop around for authentic furniture and art.

Frank (Sinatra) made all the arrangements for me. Frank, well, Frank likes to keep a string attached to me lest I stray too far away. And he likes to take care of me. And I'm not complaining. I mean, I like to be taken care of.

I planned to do it all quietly. As usual, things didn't turn out as I planned.

Flying off to another country felt like I was entering a new world. It seemed like I left my worries in Los Angeles and I could lose myself for days just exploring and being anonymous.

But, you know, when the word got out that I was staying at the Mexican Hilton Hotel, reporters and photographers started surrounding the place and security guards had to be hired. My press agent, who was traveling with me, thought it would be best to hold a press conference for the Mexican Press. Let them ask all the questions they want, photograph me to death, and then they might leave me in peace.

A press conference was scheduled. I haven't done a press conference in a very long time. Now was my chance. Now was the opportunity to show the media that I was not the haggard recluse that some of the newspapers have been trying to make me out to be.

I am sleek and thin. My hair freshly styled by my hairdresser who is traveling with me. I am wearing a body-hugging green silk Pucci dress. It is my favorite. I can wear it forever. Pucci is my new designer of choice. Almost everything in my closet is Pucci. And I'm holding a delicate, green, chiffon scarf to match.

I enter and there is a mob of reporters. At least two hundred, or more. They have been waiting for a couple of hours. The room is filled with cigarette smoke. I am escorted in. They clear a path for me.

I walk to the center of the room. I turn. I shrug. I want them to see me from every angle. Let their cameras record each moment. I am ready. I am in control. I throw the chiffon scarf over my shoulder. I pivot and spread my arms.

The photographers are going mad. I am composed. Loving it. I've been through this a thousand times before. The reaction is always the same. There is the frenzied mob and there is me. We feed off of each other.

I am handed a glass of champagne.

Imagine seventy-five snapshots of this press conference in Mexico.

In the first twenty-five photographs I am serene. Composed. The goddess as expected.

They fill my glass with champagne.

They ask, "Will you get married again?" I reply, "I'm keeping my options open."

They ask, "Will you get back together with Joe DiMaggio?" I respond, "No, we tried it once and it didn't work out. But we're still good friends."

They fill my glass again. The champagne is mixing in with tranquilizing pills I took earlier. I drain the glass and it is instantly filled again.

In the next twenty-five photos I'm the sex siren. Laughing. Flirting. On fire. A little bit out of control—but still in control.

They ask, "Would you pose again for a nude calendar?" I say, "I'm more particular now about who sees me in the nude."

They ask, "Is the dress you're wearing more clingy than usual?" I say, "You should see it on the hanger."

They laugh. They applaud. More champagne is poured.

In the last twenty-five pictures I'm sloppy. Tired. Trying too hard. Climbing up on a couch to pose. Almost parodying myself.

They ask, "Are your measurements still the same as from your calendar days?"

I say, "I never measure myself and I don't want to boast but I think I'm better now."

They ask, "Do you wear underwear?"

I tell them I do not.

They ask me if I can do the twist.

And I get up to demonstrate I can.

My better judgment has left me. I've lost control.

It's those last twenty-five photos I wish I could destroy.

March 4, 1962

Forgot to mention that while I was in Mexico I met a man. Sort of. Well, I mean, he *is* a man, but he's not a man I plan on getting involved with. I guess you could say he was part of the vacation package. He's a handsome Mexican filmmaker named Jose Bolanos. Now, if I were writing a story about a Mexican fling, I don't think I could invent a better name than that. He also looks the part.

I also actually did get to see the sights. And I bought a lot of things for the house. Carved chairs, mirrors, tiles for the bathrooms and the kitchen. And lots of odds and ends, which, I suppose, will be arriving over the course of the next few months as I bring this house to life with my Mexican themes.

Jose took a flight to Los Angeles to woo me some more. He's a nice guy but I can hardly understand a word he says. I haven't been encouraging him. I don't need another man thrown into my cocktail. But he is in town for the Golden Globe Award Ceremonies. His friends' movie is nominated for "Best Foreign Film."

Oh, did I mention. I will be there too. I've been tipped off that I am being awarded the "Female World Film Favorite." Even as the newspapers continue to write I'm "finished." Irony?

March 6, 1962 (Monday)

Earlier that day I stood statue-still on a chair for hours while two seamstresses sewed me into my gown. An emerald green sequined gown that plunged low in the back and fit me like skin. I gulped champagne as they sewed. I have infinite patience when it comes to presenting myself at my best.

"It won't be easy to walk," one of the seamstresses said.

"She's obsessed with showing off the crack in her ass," I heard my new hairstylist say from the other room.

Marilyn Monroe had been voted as the favorite female star in the world by The Golden Globe Awards and Marilyn Monroe they would get.

The newspapers want to say I'm "slipping." Allow me show them what slipping looks like.

I am blonder than ever. I am "pillowcase white." My body looks better than back in my modeling days.

Frank Sinatra's emeralds were dangling from my ears.

The green goddess.

I've been fairly reclusive this past year. Every star in Hollywood was scheduled to be there.

When I arrived at the Beverly Hilton Ballroom I was already a bit high. You can't expect me to do this without any help.

I am afraid but I will call in my gods. I need to be undeniable.

I chose Jose—dark, mysterious, handsome—to be my date. He flew in from Mexico for this event. No one will know who he is but they'll all wonder.

I walked into a riot of photographers. A chaos of onlookers. It's like they are being struck by lightning.

"Marilyn!" "Marilyn!" "Marilyn!" "Marilyn!"

I have been away from the Hollywood cameras for a long time. They've been waiting for me to appear again. "What will she be like now?"

I was switched on.

I heard what they were thinking: "God! She's thin! She's fresh! She's sensational!"

They shouted questions. Inevitably, "What does it feel like to soon be thirty-six?"

I will not answer.

They screamed for me to "Look this way, please." I just smiled and smiled and held Jose's hand. I took the tiniest steps but I turned my head this way and that way, my smile never wavering.

When we entered the banquet hall more pandemonium broke out. People were jostling to get a look at me.

My breath was small gasps. My mind introduced me: "Ladies and gentlemen, Miss Marilyn Monroe. Her breasts. Her rear. Her unblemished face. Is she blonde enough? Is she delicious enough? She turns. She smiles. She shoots off sparks. Giving goose bumps! That's her specialty." It was just in my head, my imagination, but the room seemed to be hearing it and reacted accordingly.

Even the biggest celebrities stood on their chairs, undignified and a bit crazed in formal dress, to gawk at me.

Slipping?

If I were an emotionally stronger person, oh the things I could do with my power and fame and talent and beauty!

We made it to the table. I was aware that every eye in the room never stopped staring.

I had made a vow to not get as drunk as I did at the press conference in Mexico. But I am known to not keep my word. And I didn't disappoint myself.

Boy, I really went overboard.

I don't remember the ceremony at all.

As the night went on, I kept drinking more and more wine. But even though I was drunk, I could still manipulate myself to perform in the way that was expected of me. Like driving very carefully at dusk through a translucent mist.

Rock Hudson and Charlton s announced, "Marilyn Monroe. The World's Favorite Female Movie Star!" That was me. I stood up. And the audience got up on their chairs again.

It took me a long time to get to the stage. The restrictions of the gown. Hands reached out to help me. They walked me to a microphone ever so slowly.

Shimmering. Shimmering!

I didn't have to make a speech. I was the speech.

"Thank you," I whispered. "I'm grateful to you all."

Afterwards I fell into Rock's arms. He was smashed too. We held on to each other. Holding each other up. "We must make a movie together," I thought. But I couldn't say another word. Charlton, who was the male film favorite winner, posed with us too, although he seemed distant. I do remember Judy Garland jumping out of her seat to rush up and congratulate me. And dear, sweet Judy made Rock and me look sober.

One thing that was undeniable: Everyone kept telling me how beautiful I looked. Obviously the reality of the way I look in person is very different to what the newspapers are implying.

The next day some of the claws came out.

She is still beautiful. Damn! We'll just have to wait.

Hedda Hopper wrote in her column, "Marilyn never looked better."
Yet she was sure to add, "But she needs a hit."

March 16, 1962

JACK CALLED!

March 28, 1962

Perhaps my little flirtation with Bobby is working. The rumor around
Hollywood is that I'm sleeping with him, which I am not. He is not the
Kennedy I want. It's Jack I want and he started calling me again.

Now I have had a taste of true power. Now that he's president, he is
tremendously protected and he feels confident in that. He's not afraid to
let certain people see us together because he's so sure they would never
let it get out in the papers. But he is terrified that Jacqueline might hear
about us. It doesn't stop him from seeing me though. I'm winning!

Last week he was staying in Palm Springs at Bing Crosby's sprawl-
ing estate. He invited me there to spend the week with him. The Crosby
compound was crawling with people – Secret Service men and staff and
such – but we were both sort of roped off like gods, surrounded by a wall
of protection. We stayed in a bungalow, as a man and wife would, and he
allowed select, important staff and friends to visit us there.

But it's the time we spend alone that I like best. Later, I gave Jack a
massage as we lay in bed talking about all the people we had spent time
with. He said he was surprised at my knowledge of issues and he called
me a "political animal." I have never felt more important, more beautiful,
more witty, more complete. That's the way he makes me feel when he's
really *with* me—at his most attentive.

And there we were gossiping about people and talking about politics, while I rubbed his bad back.

There was no hint of any trouble between us. No indication that we had to slow down or stop seeing each other. I couldn't hold the moment all to myself. I just had to share it with someone. I called one of the people who I trust most in the world, Ralph Roberts, who is my masseur and good friend.

I said, "Ralph, I'm sitting here with my 'friend'...he has a bad back and I'm giving him a massage. I told him you were the real pro and that you know everything there is to know about anatomy. Would you mind explaining to him how the (and I sang here) "the back bone's connected to the neck bone?"

Ralph knew I was with Jack, but—for Jack's sake—I made believe it was all mysterious and unknown. Then I put Ralph on the phone with him and they talked at length about remedies for a bad back.

When they hung up, I said to Jack: "You really should get a massage by Ralph. He's an expert."

Jack replied, "Somehow, Marilyn, I don't' think it would be the same."

In any case, I think I made his back feel better again.

April 10, 1962

I'm really furious. I just found out that they are bringing in a new screenwriter, someone by the name of Walter Bernstein (a writer I never heard of) to do a new version of *Something's Got to Give*. I finally felt that Nunnally Johnson had delivered a script that was a real "Marilyn Monroe" vehicle and all I wanted was a few minor changes and I was ready to go. I had already started memorizing much of that script and working on the character!

But it seems my wonderful (ahem) director, George Cukor, felt the script just wasn't right. He feels it strays too much from the original.

Of course it strays from the original! That's the whole point of doing a remake. To bring it up to date and make it feel new!

I feel Cukor wants to do anything just to act disagreeable with me.

I'm leaving for New York for few days. I want to talk to Lee Strasberg about my character and the story and see what he thinks.

April 13, 1962 (New York City)

What's the date? I don't even know....April something, I think. Suddenly it's April. I look out my bedroom window and spring is stamping its images of newness and of hope all over the city.

A lot of people seem to know about Jack and me. Even though I didn't mention his name at all in New York, it's obvious people are talking. Gossip springing out of semi-truths, turning into full-fledged rumors— traveling from person to person like an infectious virus. Well yes! If I was to be totally truthful with myself, a small piece of my ego is proud to be linked to him. But in the long run, I'm trying to have a life, not simply be fodder for juicy cocktail chatter or blind items in the gossip columns.

I had been drinking champagne and scrutinizing my body from every angle in the mirrors lining the bedroom walls—it was making me feel better than I've felt about my figure in a very long time. I hadn't realized how much my weight gain, starting in 1959 (when I was pregnant) and all through 1960, had been feeding into my gloominess.

I wasn't looking good and as a result I wasn't feeling good but people kept telling me, "You look wonderful." How can you know who to believe? A lot of their paychecks depend on me looking good. I should have believed myself when I saw the rushes of my last two films. Sloppy and past my prime in *The Misfits* and *Let's Make Love*. I think I was eating too much because I was so unhappy in my marriage and the eating became a sickness. It was partially a comfort but partially an anger. It felt good to gorge but I was also angry. I think I subconsciously blamed my body for some of the unhappiness. Without giving it much analysis I was destroying my body to punish myself.

But now.

How wonderful, how delicious to have my figure back!

The phone rang.

I wasn't really in the mood for picking it up but I was expecting a call from Pat, and hoping for a call from Jack, so I answered before the maid could get to the extension. To my surprise it was Jacqueline Kennedy.

I guess I shouldn't be surprised that the news of an affair reached the First Lady. But I was certainly taken off my guard to have her on the other end of the telephone line, to say the least.

Her voice is elegant, girlish, almost shy but with a determination that surprised me. She said she wanted to meet with me. Obviously word got back to her about my rendezvous with Jack at Bing Crosby's place. After all, he was openly affectionate with me in front of a number of people. We were a couple there—no mistaking it.

Had I been prepared for her call I would have matched her cool cucumber demeanor. I would have said "How lovely to hear from you. Thank you for the invitation but, 'no.' I couldn't possibly meet at this time."

I would have said my social calendar was absolutely filled up. I would have said that I was in preparations for a new movie. I was flying back to Los Angeles in a couple of days. I would have exerted my own self-worth and power (this has been a theme in my analysis.) But for the very reason that I *was* caught off my guard, I said "Of course. Would you like to come to my apartment for tea?" She paused and said, "I would prefer it if you would come to my hotel." By now I was gaining my balance and I thought, "Why should I meet her on her turf?"

Finally we agreed to meet the following day—today—at a nondescript restaurant in the East 70s. We decided that we would both wear disguises. We didn't dare being recognized out in public together, so at least I didn't have to worry about putting on my Marilyn-getup. She said she would make reservations under the name "Mrs. Hart." Or Heart?

I began wondering what her plan was. There's always a sneak plan of attack. Isn't there?

April 15, 1962 (Today)

I took a cab to the restaurant. I held my head high. I walked in.

Something was wrong.

I waited and waited for the host to acknowledge me. He took a long time looking through his reservation book. He picked up the phone and gave the restaurant's address to the caller. Finally he looked up with an insultingly bland expression. I asked for Mrs. Hart. He motioned to a waiter who languidly led me through the smoke filled room. What was wrong?

Then I realized: not a head turned to look at me as I walked past the tables. The host had taken his time before greeting me and the waiter treated me indifferently. Then the answer hit me! I was in disguise. In my brunette wig (with a little blue pillbox hat plopped on top of it, no less), an elegant, conservative blue suit, and modest strand of pearls, no one knew it was me. I was just like everybody else in the room. Just an Upper East Side lady out for lunch.

Celebrities always talk about the burden of being famous. The loss of their privacy, etc. Well, I agree. Sometimes it can be a burden! But, oh boy, just take that burden away from a "star" on any given day—the special treatment, the admiration. The fawning desire to please—and see how they react. The panic sets in. I felt the panic. I mean, I often roam around the streets of New York totally unnoticed, in a scarf and an old polo coat, and that's fine. I'm not going anywhere in particular and I don't want to talk to anyone. But here I was, all dressed up, in a very different way than usual, and going to a very important meeting, yet I couldn't possibly feel more stripped. I didn't have my persona for protection. Funny the things you notice when they're gone.

I saw Jacqueline Kennedy then. Sitting in a corner, smoking nervously. I almost laughed out loud. She was wearing a frowsy blonde wig, lots of cheap rhinestone jewelry and a low-cut, red dress that looked as if she bought it off of the mark-down rack. She smiled and gave me a little nod when she recognized me, in spite of my disguise. I approached her table.

The waiter pulled my chair out for me and I sat across from her. We ordered drinks and then sat silently studying each other for several long moments. Jacqueline in her disguise, I in mine.

Then—by God—I realized that we were both dressed in our own version of each other. She was in character as the cheap and vulgar movie star and I was the prim and icy First Lady.

The waiter brought our drink orders and set them down in front of us. The time had arrived. We had to talk.

"Jack is a wonderful man, isn't he?" she said. I was surprised this was the way she was opening up the conversation. If this was some kind of a contest she didn't project nervousness. Her tone, ever so soft but eerily confident, assured me that she already knew that she had won. "How long have you known him?"

"We've been friends for years but…" I let it go.

Why was I telling her this? I didn't have to make any guilt ridden confessions. There was actually more power in what I didn't say. I kept telling myself, "She isn't any better than me." I didn't have to give her any explanations.

"But…?" she asked, pressing to go on. And for some reason I felt compelled to go on. To let her know. But I chose my words very carefully.

"…but we've grown closer over the past year or so."

There. It was out. No more secrets. I felt relieved until…

She was telling me everything that I thought was a secret between Jack and me, in her girlish voice. I found out she already knew all about the affair. Every detail. Jack told her everything. Everything!

I sat there and listened as she repeated the entire history of my relationship with Jack. She didn't leave out a single detail—the "secret" meetings at Peter's beach house, me sneaking in and out of the Carlyle Hotel, even.

She is the wife of the man that I'd been sleeping with, yet I was the one who felt betrayed. I instinctively knew that Jack, in confessing all about our affair to Jacqueline, in "coming clean" to her, he was apologizing. It was his way of letting his wife know that what intimacies had happened between us—Jack and I—were over.

I couldn't believe he would tell her about what we shared in such clinical detail—things I said, things I wore, the way I looked. She knew everything. Jack did this to me! After the only thing I asked him, when I sensed we were coming to an end, was to please, please…don't talk about me to anyone, not even to his wife. Especially not his wife. I had thought what we shared was something special. Some dignity please! But in the end he passed on the details of our love affair as casually as some tawdry gossip about an unimportant, slutty neighbor.

I guess the shock and hurt showed on my face, for Jacqueline stopped her account and asked, "What's the matter, Miss Monroe?"

I felt dazed and small and my voice was the same. "I can't believe that Jack…told you all of this." I toyed with the glass in front of me. "W-what else did he say about me?"

I could feel her studying me, trying to decide how much more she should reveal. She, after all, had the upper hand now. She was the wife. I was merely the discarded mistress. "Well, he didn't tell me what you did in the bedroom, if that's what you mean."

That is exactly what I meant but all I could manage to say was "gulp" meaning I was just speechless at the thought of being discussed and dismissed by someone I sincerely loved and trusted.

Jacqueline said, "Don't worry, Miss Monroe. Jack is a gentleman. He doesn't kiss and tell. Just as I know that you are a lady and would never want to soil anyone's reputation."

But my gut instinct told me that even if he didn't tell Jacqueline about my bedroom performances, he surely told other people about them. The men in his life. His political cronies. I'm never wrong about such things.

It's in the nature of men like him to brag about their sexual conquests and Marilyn Monroe is the biggest trophy of them all.

In a flash moment of absolute clarity I remembered Jack saying to me in bed, "You're the sexiest women I ever met. The sexiest woman in the world." Even then I didn't take it as a compliment because I wanted him to see me as more than that. Maybe if he used the word "beautiful." But even that....would seem shallow. I wanted him to see all of me. I thought he might even love me someday.

Suddenly I questioned if everything I thought I knew about him was a lie.

Even as I write this the tears are falling on the page blotting some of the ink.

Had I really meant so little to him? That he could so easily and casually ignore the one thing...the one thing I asked him for?

"It's over between the two of you, you know," Jacqueline added. "Jack and I discussed it. He won't be seeing you anymore."

"I want to hear Jack tell me that," I said.

"He won't be contacting you either, Miss Monroe."

"I wouldn't be so sure of that, Mrs. Kennedy."

"Oh I am very sure. We have an agreement, Jack and I."

I was silent. Jacqueline continued, "Surely you don't think that you're the first? This sort of thing has happened in the past. More than a few times."

She is a formidable woman. Her presence was undeniable. Jacqueline sat there and chain smoked with an air of detachment. I so very much longed to be detached. She had a naturally beautifully constructed face. Bone structure! She talked in a baby doll whisper that sounded even faker than my own screen persona voice. But more than anything she had a stony charm, an elegant charisma all the while exuding an aura of superiority. She innately made me feel like I had to live up to her expectations. She effortlessly made me feel as if I was coming up short.

I thought of Angie Dickenson and all of the other women I heard Jack was sleeping with. I wondered if they all felt that they were special. I felt that old familiar jealousy rising up in me. I may have made myself into the *sexiest* woman in the world but I could never turn myself into the *only* woman in the world. And then I thought of something and asked, "And do you meet with all the others, Mrs. Kennedy?"

She blinked very rapidly and I was surprised to detect a noticeable nervousness seeping through her composure. She paused for a long time before answering. "You're the first one I felt it...necessary...to actually meet with face to face."

It was only a brief instant but for the first time during the meeting I felt she had removed her armor. Her face softened. It was open and vulnerable and receptive. She wanted to reveal something to me but she was unsure.

In that moment I tried to feel God. I sat very still, "Come to me, Father," I said in my head. "Help me. Give me peace." But I couldn't feel Him. I knew God was there but He wasn't ready to come to me yet. Or, maybe, I wasn't ready to receive him. And I felt so utterly alone.

Almost as soon as I felt that sensitive "opening up" in Jacqueline, she closed it down. She obviously thought better of it.

Without warning my inner rage got the best of me and the "digni-fied" Marilyn Monroe vanished in a moment, only to be replaced by the low-class, snarly, waif, Norma Jeane. I said, too loudly, "I'm not going to be crumpled up and thrown away like some used piece of trash! Not by you and certainly not by him! I want Jack to call me! I want to hear him tell me it's over! I want to hear it from his own mouth!"

She leaned forward. "And what do you think will be gained by that, Marilyn?" She spit out my first name as if it were the vilest word in the English language. The venom in her voice startled both of us and brought us back to the reality of where we were. And who we were.

"I'm sorry," she said.

She sat back in her chair and glanced demurely around the restaurant. "The Statue" again. Her face became serene, her demeanor sedate, and then she smiled. There was so much condescension in her voice, so much cruel superiority that I doubted I could have been imagining the false-ness in her smile, so full of cloying sympathy. And then she said:

"Don't worry, dear, someday you will meet someone who is right for you."

Meaning that Jack—with all his pedigree and charm and power—was the right man for her! But way out of my league.

I saw myself then as she probably saw me. A decorated whore who had been elevated to the level of a national freak show. A mediocre actress already given too much in life: a sensational infamy. Worthy of nothing more.

And her words snatched away my breath and cut into me deeply, like a surgeon's scalpel carving into my chest—working towards the heart. I waited for that familiar rush of despair to well up inside of me and, in a matter of seconds, it did. I could not speak.

Because I knew that, even with all that I've accomplished, all my films, all the adoration, all of my supposed beauty…I knew that even with all of that…I shared her opinion of me. I am a freak show. That's how I feel about myself.

Without another word, Jacqueline gathered up her handbag, her gloves, her cigarette lighter, and she stood up to leave. She must have felt triumphant. She looked down at me, turned around, and started to walk away. I was once again the chump. I felt as if I'd just been beaten up, knowing all the while that the scars that this meeting between Jacqueline and me would leave on my heart would ache for months or years to come. Maybe even forever.

And she, with all her wealth, her class, and life of privilege, was going to have the last word on the poor orphan girl who grew up to become a famous slut.

No!

In a matter or moments I saw hundreds of doors slamming in my face. I know that, as First Lady, Jacqueline Kennedy is tremendously influential. I saw all my contacts to the White House disappearing: tele-phone numbers being changed, secretaries being instructed to brush me off. "If Marilyn Monroe calls say, 'President Kennedy is not available,'" I could practically hear her instructing the entire White House staff the minute she got home. This may be my last chance with her. I could not let it end like this.

"No!" I heard myself say, although I had not intended to speak out loud. Jacqueline stopped and turned to me.

"I'm not a 'nobody,'" I said in a voice that had become little more than a whisper but the passion behind it caused her to raise her eyebrows in alarm. I held on with all my might to not let go of the floodgate of tears that were waiting to escape from my eyes.

"Excuse me," she said, keeping her voice even-toned. She didn't want a scene. She's the type that never wants a scene. But I could see she was trembling.

I lifted my gaze so that my watery eyes could look directly into hers. I'm sure my voice quivered only for a moment. "I am a 'somebody,'" I said. "This isn't anywhere near over Mrs. Kennedy." Our gazes locked for what seemed like an eternity. Then she turned on her heels and click-clacked away in that ridiculously insulting parody Monroe costume she was wearing—until she was out the front door.

"It's not so bad to be humiliated," I reasoned to myself. "There are people in the world who are dying! Don't you dare be unhappy over this!"

It was no use though. I couldn't fight the despair-attack off.

I stumbled out of the restaurant only to discover there was no limo waiting. I wasn't "Marilyn Monroe" today. Earlier in the day I had easily gotten a cab, but it was rush hour now and the sky was darkening. It had started to rain. I was blocks away from my apartment. I looked around helplessly. Manhattan traffic and people and crush were all around me. Well, there was the subway. I had taken it before and….well…what were my options?

But once I walked down the subway steps into the station I realized that I had made a terrible mistake. I was as trapped in the crowded, disorganized station just as surely as I was trapped in my own life. I gasped and gasped and gasped but there was no air forthcoming. I couldn't breathe.

After a lifetime of searching I thought I had finally known real love. The cup was held out in front of me just long enough for me to take a quick sip. Now, before having a chance to really taste it fully, to enjoy it, it was being taken away.

Every time I'm almost making it…every time happiness seems within my grasp…every time I'm almost safe…something comes along and snatches it all away! And I'm back at square one.

This is life as I know it. And there are no miracles. There are not knights in shining armor. There are no happily-ever-afters. There are only men who use you. There are trains that roar through subway tunnels—fast and hard and unfeeling. I might throw myself in front of one and become one, SPLAT! with the train. My blood and liver and guts and heart splattered all over the front, hot and red and running, as the train ROARED from station to station. And then, whatever was left of my body would grow cold. But unfeeling.

Unfeeling.

April 14, 1962

If I had any pride left—which I don't—I'd never want to see him again. But it's always so difficult when there is just some murky ending. Noting definite. No answers. I need that so desperately.

Meanwhile, we filmed the wardrobe and makeup tests for *Something's Got to Give* last week. I was annoyed when Cukor didn't show up to supervise the shooting of them, a deliberate snub. I decided my best revenge was to perform wonderfully for the cameras to show him how little he is needed.

And when we screened the footage a few days later there was a collective gasp in the projection room. Even I sighed a lovely sigh of relief. I have to admit I looked pretty damn good up there. Better than I've looked in any film since *Some Like it Hot*. Maybe even better than I've looked in any other film in my career. Oh, I can't wait for the world to see how I look on the big screen again.

Yes, there will still be a Marilyn Monroe.

The working out, the dieting, the focus—it all comes shining through for the movie camera. It shows up there! If we can only get a good script to work with we really might have a big hit on our hands. It gave me a temporary boost of confidence and I started thinking, "Stop pining away for unreachables. Get on with reality before your time has passed."

But my real reality is wrapped up equally with love as much as it is in my career. I want that one great love as much as I want that one great role. Frankly, I don't know how I'm going to make this picture with all I have on my mind.

Jacqueline is in the White House picking out elegant tableware and planning state dinners. She has no time to fret over a battle that she knows she will inevitably win. Actually I've been thinking so much up Jacqueline since our meeting. I don't hate her. I hope she doesn't hate me. I have no idea what she has gone through in her life.

Now that I can look back on our meeting, I realize she was just as nervous as I was. I could tell that she had talked herself into taking a hard stance with me. She probably even practiced in front of the mirror. Yet underneath her steely resolve to let me know it was finished between Jack and me, I could tell she wanted to be nice. I actually felt her sensitivity reach out to my own vulnerabilities and try to connect. That tiny thread of sweetness she was trying to send out to me was broken apart by the storm of other emotions battling between us. But I felt it. I did!

I want to say to her, "God Bless You, Jackie."

I know…I realize, she has her own pain. Different from my own, of course, but just as real to her. Maybe in different circumstances we could have been friends and learned things from each other. After all, who knows better than me that the mask we wear isn't the total picture—the total person. It's our many inner selves, the characteristics we keep hidden, that really makes up who we are.

Now the big question is, should I let the affair go? Can I? I'm not even sure it's possible for me to let it go without a fight. I feel I need him. I can't explain it any further. I just feel I need him. I have convinced myself they are not in love. It's a marriage of social standing. Of politics. At least that's the way I HAVE to look at it…or I wouldn't be able to stand myself. And the signs are there. Jacqueline would go on with her steely resolve. Maybe she'd even be happier.

When it comes to men, competition isn't something I'm normally afraid of. In the past, when put against other women, I've usually won. But I know that with Jacqueline Kennedy I met my match. As a matter of fact I burn up with jealousy when I think of her. I assess her assets over me. She has elegance and intelligence and class. I have my ass. She also has the advantage of being the mother of his children

"How can I seriously compete," I ask myself. What do I have over her? Well, I must keep in mind that I still have my sex appeal. A potent weapon, especially when dealing with Jack. And let's face it, Jacqueline is not sexy. Oh she is beautiful in a classical way but I can't imagine Jack putting his hand up her dress under the dinner table. That sense of sexual play is a big part of who Jack is. But on the other hand (pun intended) is that all I want to be to any man? After I spent all this time trying to develop all the other aspects I have in me?

And with all this on my mind, there is a movie that I must complete.

April 15, 1962

It's not over yet!

Bobby called me today and asked me if I would entertain at Jack's 45th

Birthday party at Madison Square Garden. He said that officially they are saying Peter suggested it but that in actuality Jack specifically made the request. It was practically an executive order, Bobby said. Marilyn Monroe singing "Happy Birthday" to the president.

I have to sit back and think about this. I have to catch my breath. Just in the scope of my life. When I think about, not so many years ago, when I was continuously being told, through people's words and deeds, that I was worth nothing. All those nights that I looked up at the sky, a sky without stars, wishing that I could release that something big in me. Something that would prove to them all that I am a "somebody." Here I am now. I would be performing in front of the most powerful man in the world in a crowd of the most important people in politics and show business. The main attraction. The main event. I can't believe it. I can't catch my breath. I can't help but remember the time no one wanted me.

But looking at it in a smaller context, the context of here and now, I can't believe my good fortune. Here is my chance for Jack to see me! To want me again. When he sees me in front of an audience…when he feels how many people want me…he won't be able to help himself. He will have to love me. This time everyone will see it.

I immediately called Jean-Louis and told him he must design me the most spectacular dress he ever created.

"I must, must, must, absolutely, look my very best. Better than I ever looked before." I pleaded to Jean-Louis, who is a creative genius and really works with you on his designs.

"And my dear Marilyn, how do you envision yourself at your very best?" asked the famous designer.

"Naked," I answered without hesitation. "I want a dress that only Marilyn Monroe could get away with wearing."

My enthusiasm is contagious, I guess. Even though it is Sunday, Jean-Louis came to my house this afternoon. He had a sheer, chiffon fabric with him which he appropriately called "nude." It was the exact color of my skin. When he held the material up over my face I could see him right through it. Clearly. It seemed incredibly daring.

"Ah, but Marilyn I will cover it with hundreds of strategically placed crystals. When you stand in the spotlight it will look as if you are naked and your body is covered only by a delicate morning mist." I imagined myself emerging from the darkness like that.

"Perfect," I said. "I will be perfect."

We started fittings for the dress right there and then.

April 16, 1962

Can't sleep.

My mind keeps going back to:

I am a little girl. No one really wants me living in their house. They do it for the money the state gives them.

Yes, that old story.

My mother never really wanted me. That's a hard thing to write. Imagine how difficult it is to say it, even to myself.

I know I have spent my entire life looking for my father. I think that is apparent in my relationship with men.

But right now I don't want to think about my missing father. I can't deal with the absence of both of them at the same time.

I want my mother.

It's funny in a way. I started reading about me growing up without a mother and a father in newspapers very early on in my career, during my climb. It was me who gave the information during interviews. I talked about the foster parents, the foster homes, the orphanage, the never belonging to anyone.

But it was as if I was reading about someone else. It's become part of the fable. I've learned never to ascribe one reason for a complex action. Part of the reason I talked to reporters so much about my early diffi-culties is because I felt I needed to make explanations for who I was. But at the same time I knew I could use it to my advantage. I've always understood the fact that everyone loves a Cinderella story. My childhood was undeniably grim. But by letting the public know about it, it sort of put them on my side. They were rooting for me.

Still, though, it's me that has to deal with the reality that dwells darkly in me. My mother didn't want me. And when I am alone with my thoughts and there are no cameras, no tape recorders, no journalist looking for a new angle, it's all very real to me. It's something I'd like to say someday, maybe, to someone who isn't looking for a headline. Someone who just might want to know. As a child I was always lost. And no one noticed.

I remember once when I was about five, living in one of my foster homes, I called the woman who was taking care of me, "Mama." She reacted immediately. "I'm not your mother!" she snapped. It was confusing because she was the older woman figure who took care of me and that, to me, meant "mother." Her husband was passing through the kitchen and I said, "But he's my father." She was quick to shoot that down too. "He's not your father. The lady who comes to see you sometimes, the one with the red hair, that's your mother."

I guess it was during a time when my mother would get weekend passes from the mental institution and she'd come and visit me. She was frightening in a way. A stranger, really. I remember watching her from the doorway, walking up the pathway to fetch me. I recognized her by her red, red hair and clouds of cigarette smoke that billowed from her as she approached.

Cloyingly sweet one moment and remote…almost cold…the next. I wanted to love her. She was strange and made me feel uncomfortable. Still, there was some bond, some unexplained connection that—even when we were strangers—conveyed that we were linked to each other.

Right now I want to go to my mother and say, "Mamma, I'm in love but I'm not sure he feels the same way. I'm losing him" I want to say, "Mom they're saying mean things about me in the press and it hurts my feelings." I want to say, "Mother, I'm afraid."

One of the things that I remember about living in the house of the lady who was not my mother is that going to the movies was considered a sin. It wasn't the only time I was told that. Another foster mother said to me, "If the end of the world were to come and you were in a movie house, you would go straight to hell." Then in the next foster home I'd be dropped off at the movies and left there all day. I was always being told this or that. Contradictory things. I began to believe the things that made sense to me. Or I began to believe only the things I wanted to believe were true.

It was while I was living in the house of the man who wasn't my father and the woman who wasn't my mother that I started having a dream. I was standing in church without any clothes on. All the people, in their Sunday best, were lying at my feet looking up at me. I was nude before the entire congregation and nude before God. I slowly walked up the aisle of the church, careful not to step on any of the people lying on the floor staring up at me. I would continue to have this dream though all of my childhood.

Undated Note 1962

Do I really think he would ever leave her for me? Do I dare to consider—even for a moment—that he would give up being a national hero and a world power? No! Not now. He wouldn't.

Realistically what I am hoping for is that he will fall so deeply in love with me that his feelings will last. He will hold on to his love for me after the presidency. Then, after he has changed the world, his children will be older and he will be free to leave Jacqueline and marry me. That's not so farfetched.

After all Wallis Simpson, who was divorced three times and had a rather plain appearance, was able bewitch Prince Edward and he gave up the thrown for her. Imagine giving up being a king for the love of a woman? Wallis was able to cast her spell on him and he gave up a kingdom. I'm only asking for a small piece of the kingdom…after the king has ruled.

April 20, 1962

I guess I drank too much champagne.

With all the pressure of going back to work and my mind working overtime about, well, not only Jack Kennedy but also his wife.

I don't know what I was thinking at the time, but I can write in all honesty I had good intentions. If it wasn't for the champagne I'm sure I would have never been able to rouse up the courage.

I called Jacqueline at the White House.

To whoever it was that answered I said, "May I please speak to Jacqueline Kennedy."

My heart was pounding.

"Who may I say is calling?"

"It's….er…um….well, I'm Marilyn Monroe."

Within an instant she was on the phone. I can't say I was exactly prepared for that. Actually I wasn't prepared for anything.

"Hello, Marilyn," she said in her breathy, little-girl tones.

Her voice was friendly. I mean, there wasn't any condescension or ice in it. It gave me courage.

I said, "Oh, Jackie. Ever since we met I've been thinking about you."

"I've been thinking about you too, Marilyn."

"I just want to say, I never got involved in this to cause any unhappiness or trouble. It's just that, well, I think when you're dealing with famous, well-known people you sort of forget that there are actually human beings involved. People who are more than what you…hear about them from others. Or even what you read about them in the newspapers."

"Yes! I'm sure you experience that yourself, Marilyn."

"Oh, that's my point. You know, Jackie. So often people hurt me because they think I'm this paper cutout or a publicity photograph rather than someone with a human, beating heart. I'm guilty of it too. I'm ashamed to admit, I didn't think of you as a real person."

"I guess the more mature we get the more we realize that every situation is more complex than it initially sounds."

"Jackie! That's exactly what I'm trying to say."

There was a pause. Then she added, "If you'll forgive me for saying so, Marilyn, I sensed your loneliness."

I forgave her. I said, "I sensed your strength."

"I can't say I dislike you. Or even blame you. I know how Jack can be. It's not your fault."

"Can you believe he was so persuasive with me I even had fantasies of what it would be like to be First Lady and to live in the White House?" I giggled, but it was a tentative giggle.

She laughed. "That's fine, Marilyn. You come live here and take on all my problems. And maybe you can get me a contract with your studio and I'll take a crack at being a movie star."

I said, "Oh, Jackie, if only you could live in my head for five minutes. But, believe me, I wouldn't wish that on you."

We both laughed. I like her.

After we hung up I was feeling better about everything. Although I made no mention of me breaking it off with Jack, in my favor, she didn't either. In some ways (I tell myself) she was giving me her blessing with Jack. Although, I'm pretty sure she wasn't.

April 23, 1962

Tired. Sick. Laryngitis. Dizzy. No sleep.

Today was the first day of shooting for *Something's Got to Give*. I called in sick very early this morning. I'm sure no one is happy about that.

The script isn't even finished yet. I have never been satisfied with the

Walter Bernstein script. But they are in such a rush to get a Monroe picture in theaters so they can make some money to finish *Cleopatra*. Maybe I shouldn't feel this way but it makes me more than a little angry to have to make a movie so they can afford to finish an Elizabeth Taylor film. I pleaded with them, "I want to go back to the earlier script. The one I liked."

They said, "George wasn't satisfied with that screenplay. We'll keep having it worked on until there's a script you both agree upon. The writer will continue working on the scenes you feel don't work. Meanwhile, Marilyn, we'll only be shooting the scenes that you approve."

Well, I don't approve.

I am sure no one believes me that I didn't work today because I'm not feeling well.

Even though I have been feeling ill all weekend and the studio doctor, Dr. Siegel, came by yesterday. He gave me a thorough examination. He informed the studio that the production of this movie should be delayed for one month while I recuperate. The studio denied this request.

I don't know, I mean, I don't understand, how they expect me to perform when I'm not well.

April 26, 1962 (Los Angeles)

"Please try to understand," I say to them (even if I'm only saying it in my mind) "There's a lot of responsibility that comes with being me."

Sometimes I can't believe how many people are thinking of me, waiting for me, depending on me.

Four days into filming and I still have been too sick to report to work. Oh, I am ill.

I have this damn respiratory infection that has been lingering on and off for months. Right now it is "on." My throat feels so sore that I would most certainly have difficulty reading lines and Dr. Siegel says I have something called "sinusitis" which makes my nose red and my eyes puffy and just gives me a generally miserable feeling. I've called in sick every day this week, and I know the studio bosses are getting more and more angry with me. But I'd like to see them try to act in a comedy with a temperature and a virus infection—and look pretty while doing it.

The studio heads say, "She's too much! She's not sick. She's faking."

They are implying it's all in my head. And I'm not denying that I am sick in the head. A certain amount of my illness just might start out as psychosomatic—but the imagined symptoms lower my resistance and soon they manifest as real and my doctor says, "You have a temperature. You have a virus. You are ill."

I'm terribly nervous about this movie. It's not funny. Which only makes me have to work harder to try to find the humor in a lackluster line. There is so much to prove. It has to be a hit. If audiences don't come it will mean three flops in a row and what will that do to my career?

I feel so weak. I feel so incapable of being in front of a camera. I say to my press agent, "Call the studio and tell them I won't be in today."

Word gets back to me in my bed. Everyone on the soundstage is fuming. They are waiting for me to come to work.

"Is she coming in tomorrow? What is her temperature?"

It's not just that I'm physically sick. I feel so horribly alone through it all.

Jack hasn't called me and that's making me feel worse. I wanted to talk to him about his birthday celebration next week.

I'm beginning to feel anxious about performing live in front of all those people. I've left several messages for him at the White House. Unreturned, all of them. Then I did something I totally regret now. I called his secretary and I was told the usual, "The president is not in at the moment." And I shouted, "This is Marilyn Monroe calling and I expect to speak to Jack!" As if my name held any power in the Oval Office. I'm sure word got back to him that I sounded like a shrew. Some deranged woman. Obsessed or even unhinged.

When I see him at Madison Square Garden I must be serene,

composed, and perhaps a bit aloof. Of course I must be super dazzling too.

I talked to my psychiatrist about all of this. He stressed that I have to start feeling worthy within myself and stop looking for my value through the men I am involved with. I say to myself over and over again, "I am a good person. I am worthy of love."

He also says, "You must complete this movie, Marilyn. It's very important that you don't sidetrack what's important to you (meaning my career) for people who will only hurt you."

But then my mind keeps on going further and I can't understand why Jack doesn't want me and I add to my list of qualitie, "I'm good in bed." After all this time I still feel that sex is all I'm good for, the only possible reason anyone would want me—and a million hours of therapy sessions go down the drain.

Being in love with Jack, my emotions swing from being enraged to just feeling very sad. With all of these things in my mind, and a virus infection on top of it, how can I concentrate on giving a performance in a film?

Okay, Okay. This is supposed to be honest so I will say…

….there is something else mixed in with all of these other feelings that make me terrified of facing the camera. It's hard for me…difficult for me to even write it down…so I will just scribble it very quickly and then not even read it back.

I'm afraid. I'm terrified. Soon I will be thirty-six-years-old.

April 27, 1962

I called in sick again today. This means I missed the entire first week of shooting.

Each time a movie of mine has been a success it didn't make me feel any more confident in the long run. It only made me feel that expectations were higher for the next film. In my earlier films, like *The Asphalt*

Jungle, and *All About Eve*, with my brief appearances, some critics said, I was a highlight in the movie. People walked out of the theater asking "Who is that blonde?"

Then my roles got bigger and more of the movie's success depended on me. They wanted me to be more beautiful, more entertaining, more "Marilyn."

With *Gentlemen Prefer Blondes* I reached a sort of pinnacle. I was at my freshest. My most dazzling. I sang. I danced. I acted deliciously dumb. People clamored to see it. But I couldn't keep doing the same type of role. I didn't want to always repeat myself. How long before the public got tired of me?

So I've been branching out. Trying to at least. Experimenting, when I can, with different kinds of performances.

They are always raising the bar for expectations of me. I'm always expected to be better, look better, and act better. More so than any other actress.

I can't live up to my own standards that I set for myself. Every time I reach the finish line, I have to start all over again. There is a new script, a new director, a new set of co-stars. Do I weigh too much? Do I weigh too little? Did I sleep enough last night? Am I reading the line right? Is the story good? What happens if I disappoint? I have to live up to this monster I created named Marilyn Monroe.

Every time I step in front of a camera I feel as if the love of the entire world is at stake.

April 30, 1962 (Monday)

Still not feeling completely well. But, then, I have to wonder if I ever will.

I reported for work today to shoot my first scenes in the movie. The press was there in full force and everyone was jubilant and excited. "She's here!" "Marilyn's going to work!" "God, doesn't she look great?"

Even George Cukor kissed on the cheek for the photographers. It has been such a long time since I've been in front of the cameras. Since *The Misfits* (but I mustn't let my mind go there.) I feel like I've been away for an eternity.

Ironically the first scenes that I was scheduled to shoot are the ones where my character returns home after being lost at sea for years. Most of what we shot was just me reacting emotionally to being home again. Deep within me I pulled up the emotions of being brought back to a safe place. I felt, in some takes, I was hitting the mark. Then my focus goes fuzzy—I lose concentration.

George says, "That was lovely, Marilyn. Let's do another one." But there is a condescending tone in his voice. He doesn't want to be there any more than I do. We begin again.

Not many lines to say today, thank goodness.

I left exhausted and disillusioned. They're still working on scenes in the screenplay which enrages me and makes me feel uncertain. They keep changing the dialogue. I still don't find very much of it witty or clever.

Oh don't let the rage in me come out! But why am I being forced to make such a drab and mechanical and unfunny comedy? Haven't I proven myself enough? Haven't they figured out how to use me properly? Don't I deserve a first-rate script?

I really am tired of this. At this stage in my career I think I deserve to start work on a script that is bright, polished and COMPLETE.

May 13, 1962

Jean-Louis came by the house to do the last fitting of the "Birthday Celebration" gown for me. I kept him waiting for a while (I woke up late) but there was plenty of champagne and caviar to keep him entertained while I pulled myself together. It's the pulling of myself together that's the main reason I'm usually late.

Soon as I appeared we went to work. The nude chiffon net has been fitted like another layer of skin over my body. It really does look as if I am wearing nothing and that some sparkling droplets of water have been splashed across my body—shimmering with every move.

"How's the movie going?" Jean-Louis asked, through the pins in his mouth.

"Let's just say the costumes you designed for me to wear in it look lovely," I replied. "And let's let it go at that."

But the shimmering gown made me feel like a hot property again. I felt so euphoric I wanted to work! I will show up on the set tomorrow no matter how I feel…or how much sleep I've had! I will give them what they expect of me.

Mrs. Murray, always lurking around some corner, was watching as Jean-Luis made his final adjustment.

"Let's see how you move in it," Jean-Louis said.

The gown is so tight I could only take the tiniest of steps. Mrs. Murray looked very prim. Mrs. Murray did not approve. "Maybe if it were looser and less revealing it would be more graceful," she volunteered.

Jean-Louis broke up laughing.

"Have faith in me, Mrs. Murray," I said. "Keep the faith."

But, come to think of it, maybe I was talking to myself.

May 14, 1962

What keeps going through my head tonight is: *Speak! Speak! Speak!*

Okay. Let me say this: I'm trying not to be paranoid or anything but I'm really starting to think that Mr. George Cukor, my director, is trying to make me look bad with the studio.

Okay, okay, I'm making *me* look bad with the studio by missing so many days of shooting, but he is certainly salting the wounds. Look, I know it's difficult for everyone when I miss work days. But when I'm there I'm there to work! Today I was feeling up to it.

I arrived at the soundstage on time—6:30 am for my makeup call—and that is not easy for me considering that I usually only fall into sleep a few hours before that. But I was there. I walked on the set and everyone sprang into action.

The scene I was to film first was a fairly simple one. The family dog sees me after an absence of five years and runs to greet me and barks as my children, who don't recognize me, look on. My line, after his bark, is: "I used to come here a long time ago." It should have taken a couple of hours to film. I'm talking full coverage. Longshot, mid-shot, 'over the shoulder,' and close-up.

The dog was sweet. His name is Jeff. God knows Jeff has the best trainer in the world. I mean, he trained Lassie. Need I say more? But for some reason the dog would not bark. He was hyper. Running all around. The trainer was yelling, "Speak! Speak! Speak, boy! Jeff! Speak!" And the dog said nothing—just kept panting away.

Okay, seriously, I was laughing. It was hilarious. We kept trying all different kinds of things to get the dog to cooperate but Jeff was out of it.

It's no secret that I'm in no hurry. So I wasn't concerned at first. I was enjoying it.

That being said, every day, several times a day, I'm getting calls....my agent is getting calls...my lawyers are getting calls...saying "The movie is behind schedule! We need Marilyn to start showing up! We're losing money. We need to pick up the pace!"

Well here I was! Working.

I was kneeling by the pool in high heels under those lights. It was getting uncomfortable. An hour went by. Then another. We weren't getting anything usable and we all knew it. I was feeling feverish again.

Sometimes at random moments the dog would let out a sort of half-hearted bark and I would start my line, "I used to come here..." and then he would run out of the shot. And George would call out, "Once more." I was being a sport. After all, the dog didn't know he was blowing his line. No one could blame the dog!

But after half the day was down the drain I started thinking, "Well, all they do is complain about how far behind we are in filming so why doesn't George just get another dog? What's going on? Why doesn't he shoot something else?" I mean this "dog reunion" moment will only last a few seconds in the final movie and we spent almost an entire work day shooting it. I was enthusiastic. I was in the moment. I wanted to work! There were so many other things we could have filmed.

So we're even further behind. Who do you think they'll blame?

George wants to paint me as more difficult than I am. He wants to call me temperamental. Meanwhile, the reality of it is that any other star would have walked off the set after an hour with that dog. I stayed there the whole time. Never said an annoyed word. I went along with it.

It's very hard to work with people who don't respect me.

My legs went numb. My smile stayed in place. "Speak! Speak! Speak!" the trainer called out.

I didn't dare show my growing anger.

After a while I felt like he was shouting at me.

May 17, 1962

Worked several days straight through shooting the movie. I haven't called in sick.

Still, everyone is in an uproar because I left the studio early to head to New York to perform at Jack's Birthday gala at Madison Square Garden.

We are making some small progress with the movie although my faith in the project still waivers. We're moving slow. But I feel I'm looking good. The clothes are lovely and my figure is back. And some of the scenes are fine. Although I still think the entire script could use an expert polish.

I'm absolutely sure now that Cukor hates me more with each passing day. He has me doing things over and over again even after I feel we "have it." Now I am the first one to admit that I want to do it again if it's not right. But once we get the best take possible, I don't feel the need to keep doing it.

It's his sort of punishment to me for missing so many days. And for always being late. I thought he got his revenge on me out of his system after shooting the scene with the dog.

After all, I'm not causing delays to be disrespectful to anyone. I only care about being the best I can.

When the helicopter arrived to take me to the airport for my trip to NYC for Jack's birthday celebration, everyone went crazy. They said, "You can't go!" "The picture is behind schedule!" "Marilyn, you must stay in town and work!"

Are they nuts? This is a command performance for the president of the United States. Do they think I would say 'no' to that? Besides, I asked the studio for permission weeks ago to take the time off and they said I could sing at the birthday.

Of course I'm very nervous about performing at the gala. But no more nervous than every time I have to face a movie camera.

May 20, 1962

On the plane back from New York, headed for Los Angeles. Here's how it went:

I was terrified. What if I tripped on my way to the podium? What if no sound came out of the microphone? What if I forgot the words?

Earlier that day, at my apartment, I had been sewn into my gown. Sewn into it like a layer of skin. Or like a shroud.

While I mingled a bit backstage with all of the other performers waiting for their moment, I was sipping champagne but I wasn't feeling it. I was in the kind of panic that champagne can't penetrate. I switched to vodka. That didn't help either. I could hear the other entertainers, Bobby

Darin, Ella Fitzgerald, and Maria Callas. One by one, going out there, knocking them dead, and a big applause.

Minutes before I was to go on, I found myself in my dressing room shaking violently. "I will never be able to get through this," I said softly to myself.

Then I remembered the children's book my psychiatrist's young daughter gave me. It's called *The Little Engine that Could*. The engine thought it would never be able to get over a steep hill but he kept repeating, "I think I can. I think I can." I decided to use this to get my own engine in gear. "I think I can," I started saying. "I think I can." And then I was repeating, "I know I can." I wrapped a white, ermine stole around my upper body. I wasn't ready, yet, for the unveiling. Two men came for me, ushers I guess, and they literally carried me to the wings.

I heard Peter Lawford starting to introduce me, I could see him from the darkness off-stage where I stood, but I was frozen with fear in spite of the champagne, the vodka—the fuel in my little engine that was terrified.

"Ladies and Gentlemen," Peter was saying as a way of introduction, "there's been no one female who has meant so much, who has done more for….."

Suddenly unseen hands, coming out of nowhere, gave me a shove, propelling me onto the stage. I was running over to Peter and I was overcome with fear. Teetering, really, in my high heels and skink tight gown that didn't allow me more than a tiny step at a time. The crowd was screaming.

Suddenly I was blind.

I gripped the white fur tightly around me as I made my way across the stage, yes, "teetering"—I think the most graceful woman in the world would find it difficult to move in the dress, which had been sewn to my body. Gliding was out of the question.

As soon as I arrived into the spotlight with Peter I felt waves of love ripple over the audience towards me. He introduced me, "Mr. President, the late Marilyn Monroe." Okay, okay. My recurring lateness on my current film set has made all the papers and has been on television and on the radio. Everyone was in on the joke. Peter had been introducing me all night and the spotlight would shine onto an empty spot. I wasn't there. It was a big joke. My actual arrival was the punch-line. Now was the time. The moment had arrived.

Peter was whispering, "Here, I'll take that," referring to my fur wrap which I still held tightly around my body. I was the package waiting to be unwrapped. I handed him the fur and there I stood.

Naked.

Naked, with some scattered crystals, before the throngs. First there was a loud collective gasp. And then a hush fell over the audience. I hadn't heard search quiet from backstage all evening. It was one of those moments that a lady might think her bra strap was showing. I was wearing no bra nor anything else under my transparent gown. Then I realized that under the white hot spotlights the gown evaporated and it was if I was standing before the crowd naked covered only with glistening crystals. They were stunned silent.

I remembered my dream again. The childhood dream of me standing totally nude in church in front of the audience. But this, perhaps, wasn't the time for remembering childhood dreams.

I flicked at the microphone. I shielded my eyes from the lights to look out at the audience. I spotted Jack in his seat. His feet propped up. Chomping on a cigar. Not Marc Antony but Caesar waiting for his Cleopatra.

"Here I am," I thought. "Now do you want me?"

A surreal montage of lights and noise and faces.

I sighed.

I realized quite a long time was passing. Tension was building. There was a heat emanating from my skin. It was almost unspeakably important for me to be the most desirable woman in the world at that moment, and so my personal gods came to my rescue again, surrounding me with that magic, and in instant, in that excitable moment, I was exactly what I wanted to be. I could feel myself transforming into something "other" as I took a few more moments for the sensuality to fill up in me, the sex and the beauty flowing through my veins like warm oil. Every part of my body screaming, "Love me! Love!"

I sighed deeply.

Then I began. "Happy Birthday to you…."

The audience went crazy cheering and screaming, "Marilyn! Marilyn!" I was invigorated by their good will and, dare I say it, their love!

After I finished singing I led the audience in a chorus while the gigantic cake was wheeled out. Everyone was cheering and clapping and… Ecstatic! My part was over. I made it.

I couldn't believe it. I pulled it off again. Undeniable.

The president then got up from his seat and made his way to the stage, to the podium, and announced to the world, "I could now retire from politics after having had Happy Birthday sung to me in such a sweet, wholesome way." Which started ideas in my head of him REALLY retiring from politics for me. "For him to say something like that in front of the entire world," my every-working mind reasoned, "he must really think about it somewhere deep inside."

Imagine? If he gave up everything for love…for me!

After the performance, my body was drenched in a cold sweat. It was as if in those few minutes on stage I had used every ounce of energy in me. No athlete running a one hundred yard dash in some Olympic game gives more than I give to every second that I am performing. It had been one simple song. I gave it everything I had in me. I was completely depleted.

Back in my dressing room, my beauty team, my little circle of experts, took over. They carefully slit me out of the dress (in the seams of course. I'd have to be sewn back into it.) There was still the after-party to go to. They hung the dress up to dry. I stood there naked and they covered my body with cold, wet towels to bring my body temperature down. They put ice cold rags behind my neck, and rubbed ice cubes on my writs. They rubbed down my arms and my back—the coolness bringing me back to earth.

Celebrities, politicians and prominent New Yorkers were trying to get into my dressing room to congratulate me. But I had Tricia stand by the door to make sure no one came in. "Miss Monroe is resting."

After my body temperature returned to something near normal the makeup had to be redone. The hair brushed out and re-styled. Then when the gown was almost dry I had to stand statue-still again as the seams were sewn up so that once again it became a second skin.

Marilyn Monroe was recreated once more.

Then there was the after-party. It was held at the penthouse of Mr. and Mrs. Krim. Passing me in the foyer, Bobby Kennedy said to me, "You are the most unforgettably beautiful woman I have ever seen. I haven't stopped thinking about you since February."

I didn't say a word. I just let him and his political cronies dodge around me like bees near nectar—basking in their ardor for me. Half-lidded. Open-mouthed.

Most of the important people, from both the stage and the audience, were there. The all seemed in awe as I languidly moved from group to group and once again I amazed myself at my ability to entice and captivate.

Later I slipped away from the party to meet Jack at the hotel. He had been ushered out a few minutes before me. We were meeting at a hotel where he was not checked in. I don't know how he got to the room unnoticed but I was flanked by Secret Service men and ushered up to his room using a service elevator. It was late. I was surrounded by dark suited men. We used a back entrance. No one seemed to know we were there.

The Secret Service men practically carried me by my elbows to my destination—the King. One of them said to me (and by the discreet way he whispered it to me I could tell he had been instructed to not say a word) "Miss Monroe, there were so many pretty women in attendance tonight but no one came close. You were by far the most fascinatingly beautiful."

"He thinks Marilyn Monroe is fascinating and beautiful," I thought. But at the moment the only one I wanted to hear that from was Jack.

Later, in the hotel room, Jack lay on top of me. He was with me but in a hurry. It wasn't exactly what I'd call romantic. Still, I tried to convince myself, "Now I am important to him. All day long he is flirting with women reporters, maybe even calling Angie...what's her name...Dickenson? His days are filled with equal parts lovely ladies and ordering around powerful heads of state. Having fun and making top secret decisions. But now he's with me. And I am the most important thing in this moment."

Again I thought how nice it would be to die with him here, in this moment, frozen in time. Our names linked in history forever. Without Jack life was starting to feel less and less important anyway.

I wanted to say to him, "Darling, when we are together like this I feel as if you are so much my own." But I thought better of it.

He said, "Oh baby I really enjoyed that." That's his idea of pillow talk.

I had come back to New York for his birthday celebration, sure in my heart that when he saw me again, saw me perform, he would want me in his life again. But it was a vain and stupid dream.

He got out of bed and put on a royal blue robe—his signal that it was time for me to evaporate. Our entire time alone together amounted to maybe fifteen minutes. The secret service men were waiting, I knew, to escort me out. I got out of bed and picked up my gown. The dress that was designed to transform his heart. The dress that was going to turn me into someone he would love. I would have to squeeze into it myself now, using the clear zipper that ran up the back. The seams that had to be opened in order to step out of it had to remain open for now. This is how I would return home. In tatters.

Of course I had the ermine wrap that would cover the top half of me but the idea of putting on the gown now seemed absurd. I placed it on the sofa.

I walked over to him at the mirror where he stood combing his hair. I pressed my face gently against his back and clasped my arms around his waist. He responded positively, as he always does to physical contact, and turned from his reflection in the mirror to kiss me. He kissed me with such force and passion. What did I care if movies got completed or careers were destroyed? I was with Jack! A hope for stability. My grasp at happiness.

I looked into his eyes and saw confidence and power and desire but not a single ounce of vulnerability.

Still, I had to reach him somehow. I didn't know when I'd have another chance. I wanted to pin his feelings down. I asked him when he would call. When would I see him again? But he would not give me a definite answer. He refused to commit. My hopes deflated. I turned my face away so he wouldn't see the tears.

"Other men want me," I said.

"Maybe one of them could make you happy," he replied.

That stung. This time he wasn't even going to throw me a crumb.

"I don't want anyone else," I managed.

"Look, Marilyn," he said, "You're a beautiful woman. You're intelligent. Talented. Funny. But I'm not that man for you."

I turned to him. I played my final card. "Your brother wants me," I whispered.

He looked at me for a long time. "The truth is, Marilyn," he said finally, "that there's too much talk going around Washington. Hollywood too. You have to stay away from both of us. For your own good. There's rumors that journalists are aware of your movements. I've even heard that your house is bugged. Staying involved with us can be…dangerous."

"I love you," I said simply. As if those words held some magic power.

"For god's sake Marilyn. What's gotten into you? We agreed we were going to keep this casual…"

Still naked I sat down on the bed. "I made a mistake…"

He cut me off. "It wasn't a mistake! What we had was lovely. But it has to come to an end. It's over." It was a statement. It was final.

The focus of my life had been my love affair with him. How could I have been so wrong about it? I was crying fully now. I lay down on the bed. I was so ashamed of myself to feel so much for someone who apparently felt so little for me. The champagne and the pills and the despair stripped me of any restraint I had left. Along with any dignity. I rolled around on the bed weeping. "I made a mistake…I wasn't paying attention…I wanted to feel…I fell in love with you….I made a mistake. I made a mistake…"

It's over.

It's over.

It's over.

May 21, 1962

Back in Los Angeles. Back to the movie set.

The studio is still furious with me for flying to New York. They made it known to me before I left that they were angry. Now they are livid. Their line of reasoning is I've been missing so many days of work on the movie how can I risk my health by flying across the country and exhausting myself?

But I think that, gee, maybe they should consider that my presence was requested as the top star in the world, the headliner amongst headliners, to entertain the president of the United States, and maybe, just maybe, it will be good publicity for the movie and the studio. I think they should perceive it as an honor. They should be proud of me. Instead the fools look at it as some kind of act of willful disrespect on my part towards them.

Yes, I have been too ill to show up for many days of shooting. And the truth is, I am sick! In many different ways. Oh let's face it! I am in no condition to be making a movie. I can pull myself together for one evening of being what's expected of me. But to do it day after day in front of a camera…it's just too much right now. I want to rest and reconsider where I'm headed.

I just want to get this damn movie done with and out of the way so I can move on. But at the same time I want it to be great because I need it to be great and because of that I only want to be in front of the cameras when I feel great and that's not too often these days. This script is not a winner. Yet I must make it a hit...because, well, there's no way of getting around it. I have to say it: I *am* slipping.

Really, at the moment, all I have is my career. I'm starting to feel as if I can't even trust my friends. There's always some hidden agenda in every friendship. Some unspoken "thing" that they hope to get out of me. So I must concentrate on getting my career back on track for myself.

And since the whole world loves me in movies and maybe Jack will see me in this one and it will bring memories of me back to him and he will want me again.

He's made me think that things were over between us before, yet in the long run he's always come back. I have to put my hopes in that.

So I'm trying to keep the studio bosses happy and enthusiastic about this movie by being wonderful. One scene I was scheduled to shoot on my return to Los Angeles was this: I want Dean Martin to tell his new wife, Cyd Charisse, that his first wife, ME! has returned from the deserted Island and is not dead as was presumed. I encourage him to inform her of my return by taking a noisy, late night skinny dip in the pool. "Now," I said to myself, "This can be a classic Monroe moment." And I decided to make it so.

When we first started filming I was wearing a flesh colored body stocking which, I was assured, in the dim lighting, would give the illusion of nudity in the water. Then I thought, "What the hell?" The script is lousy. The jokes aren't funny. Let me add a little, you know, spice to this tepid comedy. Let me add at least one really memorable scene to a mediocre movie. So I suggested to my director, George, "Wouldn't it be better if I really swam naked?"

He looked at me with surprise, "Really nude?" he asked.

"Oh, why the hell not?" I said.

I could see at once that he was excited by the idea. He is so angry with me all the time it made me feel good to please him. He went to confer with the crew and before you know it the news was spreading like a fire:

Marilyn Monroe is going to do a nude scene.

Immediately the entire set was a-buzz. People were running back and forth. There was a feeling that something very important was about to happen. George cleared the set except for the key crew members. I wanted the photographers to stay. By now I am very canny on the subject of publicity and let's just say I knew that what was about to happen would be worth millions of dollars of press coverage.

Of course I didn't want it to be pornographic! I said to Whitey, keep an eye on what is being photographed. A bit of nipple is okay. A glimpse of the behind, but absolutely NO frontal. Whitey understood.

So I dipped into the pool and slid off my body stocking. It was fun. I was splashing around. "All I can do is doggy paddle," I called to George. "That's fine, dear," he called back. Everyone was excited. My character was teasing Dean. Jumping in and out of the water. Exposing a leg here, a glimpse of "behind" there. I never felt more delicious. And the photographers were click, click, clicking away. Everyone in Hollywood has been saying I'm finished. Let's see how "finished" they think I am when these photos start to appear on magazine covers. Even Elizabeth Taylor will have to acknowledge who the real Queen is.

Through it all I kept thinking about the time I acted the same way for Jack at the White House pool. That was my motivation. See, Lee Strasberg? There is a method in my madness.

And the movie cameras rolled, and the still photographers clicked, and the director and the assistant director and the rest of the crew on the set were all noticeably giddy and delighted because at last, at last, *Something's Got to Give,* was coming gloriously alive and sexy and exciting.

But of course the other part of me had to step in and take some of the fun out of it. This part of me said, "Marilyn, they are using you. You are using you! How long do you think you will be able to pull off these antics? Your acting in this movie is good. Why not stand on the merits of your performance?"

I asked myself that, but I knew the answer. Whenever I've been afraid or insecure I could always fall back on my body. Well here I was falling back on it again. And see how far I've fallen!

But the exhibitionist part of me won out—as she usually does. As in that all too familiar childhood dream, I was nude before the masses again. How much longer can I be naked and tantalizing and delicious? Each time I do it, I feel the threat that this can be the last time. "Go with it, girl," my mind urged. "This is only one small moment in time. Get it on film and it will last forever."

Funny, I'm thinking of a legacy when there is still so much more to accomplish.

Funny, that it made me feel important. The studio didn't need spend the millions of dollars in sets and costumes and special effects that they are pouring into Elizabeth Taylor's *Cleopatra* for a Monroe picture. All I had to do is take my clothes off and my little bedroom comedy is as big an epic as hers.

I performed in the nude for hours. Afterwards, in my dressing room, one of the freelance photographers that had been allowed to snap during the filming came by to ask me what I wanted in return for the release of the photos. Some of the shots were what we would call semi-nude. It was clear that they wouldn't be able to publish any of them without my permission. I said, "Look, all I want from you is a guarantee that these photos will get Elizabeth Taylor and any news about the making of *Cleopatra* off the front covers. Put me there."

He assured me these photos would do just that. He was astonished that I asked for no money. The pictures, no doubt, would bring in hundreds of thousands of dollars by the time world-wide sales were negotiated. What he didn't understand about me...what no one has ever understood... which I wish I was on a roof top so I could shout from: I DON'T CARE ABOUT MONEY! I just want to be perfect so the world still loves me.

Undated Note 1962

Is this pain because of how very much I want him or because how much he doesn't want me?

I never expect it to last. In spite of all the love I've received I still feel unlovable. Men have adored me. Showered me, covered me, inundated me with what they swore was their undying, unending love. Yet I never completely felt it. I thought I could say something wrong. I could do something unappealing. I could look unlovely. And that would be it. I always…always had the feeling that it would go away in an instant.

Missed more days of work. The anger and resentment towards me grows. Every day that I don't show up it makes a newspaper headline. I promised them I'd be in for the next day of shooting. No matter how I feel.

June 1, 1962

Another birthday.

Spent the day filming.

Then, after the day's work, there was a birthday party on the set with the cast and crew. I drank some champagne. A nice cake (with a cartoon of me on it, semi-nude. "Happy Birthday, suit," it said.) Sparklers. Pictures were taken. But the overwhelming feeling was, "Will we ever get this movie finished?" Presents, flowers and telegrams arriving all day from Marlon (Brando) Frank (Sinatra,) Joe (DiMaggio.) So many others. And it does make me feel good to be remembered.

But…

Well, I guess it's true. Today I'm thirty-six. I've officially reached the age that Hollywood considers a has-been, and it scares me.

All I know how to be is Marilyn Monroe. It's the only thing I've ever really been successful at. Time is making it impossible to continue. And I don't know who I will be anymore.

God is not going to stop time. Not even for Marilyn Monroe. I thought He might give me a present. I thought He might feel as if I earned the right to remain young and beautiful for as long as I lived.

But God is no savior tonight. Where have you been all my life, Father? Daddy?

I'm going to pray to God. I am! I'm thinking about You and I'm thinking about my struggle. I want us to be close. Give me an award, Father, out of the blue. An unexpected, unasked for gift. Jack loving me back? Something wonderful that I don't have to work too hard for?

Surprise me.

Just any present from you, God, so I can feel you more.

June 2, 1962

Jack did not call for my birthday. No flowers. Nothing. It would have been a nice gesture if he sent a message or something. Particularly after the spectacle I brought to his special day.

I have to accept the fact that I am ugly and Jack will never call me again and it is over and with all this in my head I can't eat or sleep or concentrate.

June 6, 1962

I didn't go to work today or the day before or the day before that. If I don't pull myself together and show up tomorrow Darryl F. Zanuck himself will drive over to my house and fire me personally.

My psychiatrist has left for a vacation with his wife to Europe leaving me here floundering. It's not that I expect the world to stop for me but he knows I need support to get through this movie. He treats me very well but, I mean, the hourly bills do arrive regularly for his services— and they are substantial. Not that I care but I would like someone to do something for me without a price tag attached.

I'm trying to come to terms with my life but all I can think about is how I've always been alone, how I've never belonged to anyone, and how no one has ever belonged to me. Alone. So alone. No parents, no husband, no baby. No doctor, at the moment. No one.

Why does every intimacy become a betrayal? Why does everyone who I reach out to desert me? Why do I never find the power to change things?

While Dr. Greenson is away, perhaps, the time is right to write what I've been feeling about him lately.

"Now, Marilyn," I say to myself, "write truthfully. Don't let paranoia color the way you feel. But don't let sentimentality change your true feelings either!"

See, one of my biggest problems is, I instinctively know what's right for me but because I have little faith in myself I seek out others for advice and guidance. For their part, they see an opening to take control.

Maybe Dr. Greenson's initial motives were to simply help me.

But I think it's too tempting to *not* take control of the money, fame, and power I represent.

They could never get it for themselves. They see me as a conduit. That had been the case with Arthur, certainly, and other lovers, agents and friends. But also with doctors, drama coaches. You name it.

They get in. Seduce me into trusting them. Then they try to cut out everyone else so they are in complete control.

The most terrible thing is that I'm aware of this but seem helpless to stop myself.

I never trusted anyone—so in my weak moments I keep seeking people to be on my side—and the cycle of being used begins again.

I'm becoming aware that Dr. Greenson has been using me.

"I've got Marilyn Monroe under my thumb."

If not erotic love, I feel he has formed some weird obsession with me.

He has made me become more and more dependent on him. I see it so clearly now! Part of this is his prescribing the drugs I ask for and am, without a doubt, addicted to.

But also bringing me into his family. I often told him of my sadness of never knowing a true family life. It might be looked at as a kindness to share his family's dinner table. Now I see it as a manipulation.

How stupid have I been to let him take control of every aspect of my life?

He suggested I hire his friend, Mrs. Murray, as a driver and housekeeper. I know now she is a spy for him. Her soft demeanor, her whispery voice, covers up a duplicitous character who watches me and reports back my every move to Dr. Greenson.

He demanded I bring in his associate Harry Weinstein as a producer on this movie, even though he has little film experience. Like a fool I agreed. Now I have come to dislike Weinstein. I refuse to deal with him unless absolutely necessary.

Dr. Greenson tells me I must get rid of certain friends because I am too dependent on them. Meanwhile he makes me more and more dependent on him.

Oh, it is so apparent now!

The most frustrating thing is I'm aware of this but seem helpless to put an end to it.

Well, let me record it now: when this movie is over I'm cleaning house. I'm going to rid myself of the Dr. Greenson. I won't be able to do it overnight of course—I'm almost as addicted to him as I am to the Nembutal he prescribes—but I will cut down my visits with him little by little, day by day, phone call by phone call, until I can do without him.

It's true! I'm a grown woman. I have to stand on my own two feet.

Mrs. Murray will be dismissed as soon as I complete *Something's Got to Give*.

Oh please, dear God, help me to get through this movie. Then it will be like starting over. I won't make the same mistakes this time.

June 8, 1962

More days of calling in sick. Another Friday with missing an entire week of shooting. What makes me feel the angriest is when they say I'm not showing up because I just don't care. At night I'm plagued with my disillusionment of how the movie is coming along for the most part. I worry if audiences will show up. And I care! I care so much I became physically ill. In the morning I am violently ill. I get a temperature. Sinus headache. All kinds of physical things happen to me and I simply cannot perform.

June 9, 1962

The studio has fired me.

Excuse me if I don't make too much sense or if I write in a self-righteous way, but I've made them millions of dollars but they won't stand by me and see me through a hard time and have a little faith that I will come through for them if they are patient and give me just a little understanding. How do they pay me back? They sue me! I'm supposed to be an artist not just a money making machine. Fuck them. I told my lawyer, "Sue them back—for twice as much." And then Dean Martin said, "No Marilyn, no Dean Martin." Which made the headlines in the newspapers. He walked off the picture. Ah, a little loyalty feels so good.

I say to myself, "He's a real pal." Then I revise that thought with, "People are only nice to me because of what they can get out of me." That might be unfair to Dean but, I sigh as I write this, I just don't know who my friends are.

June 11, 1962

Have you seen the papers?

I try not to read newspapers but it's hard not to. The latest story of me is all over the place. "Monroe fired from *Something's Got Give*. Career in Crisis."

I have been committed of a crime. My crime is I am thirty-six years old.

Marilyn Monroe is not allowed to age.

They say I'm finished.

Why do they hate me so much?

Even Hedda Hopper, that wolf in hag's clothing, who always pretended to be so nice to me, who always said she was so fond of me, wrote in her column, "It's the end of the road for Marilyn. She has had it." Whereas, with her power, she can come to my defense and say something complimentary she cares only about writing the more sensationalistic headline. The scoop.

It's as if they have been lying in wait. They built me up when I seemed to have it all—but their predatory nature must have been waiting for the blood to spill out. Now they are on the attack. Reporters who once were on my side are gleeful reporting my ruination.

Once they all loved me. The headline was I was beautiful. I was sensational. I was lovable. Now it's, "She's finished."

Others simply can't stand the thought of a middle-aged Marilyn Monroe. Well, I can't stand the thought of it either but what am I supposed to do about it?

June 13, 1962

Dinner with the Lawford's last night. Bobby was there. Warning or no warning he hasn't stopped calling me since his brother's birthday celebration. Seeing him made me realize how much I don't really want him. But as is usually the way, the more I don't want someone the more they want me. And I can't help it: the attention from a Kennedy is hard to resist and I sort of play into it.

"If Bobby wants me so much then maybe there's still a chance with Jack," I tell myself.

And, also, I know that if I sever my ties with Bobby, that would end all ties with Jack and he will drift away. My only link to Jack right now is in Bobby. So I let him think that I am available…while I bide my time, waiting for Jack to come to me.

I didn't want to give Bobby too much of me. Yet I pulled out all of my tricks, using all the charm I had, with one eye on the clock. Just before midnight I lowered my eyes and said, "I guess I should be going home, lest I turn into a pumpkin."

Inevitably Bobby said, "I'll drive you home." But when we got to my place I didn't invite him in. I warned myself, "I mustn't go to bed with someone just because I'm desperate or I'll regret it later." And I was talking to myself from experience.

Instead I invited him over to the house for today, when I'll be fresh and sober and on my guard. He said he would come. He'll be here a little later.

June 14, 1962

Bobby showed up around noon. I showed him my house. We walked around the pool. Actually he looked very boyish and handsome. It made me think, "If Jack didn't come first maybe I would have fallen for Bobby." But there IS a Jack and all I can do when Bobby and I are together is compare him to Jack. That's all I can do with any man lately.

I wasn't sure if this visit was expected to be a "date." He's been calling me an awful lot lately and acting terribly flirtatious on the phone. I resisted sleeping with him. I thought if I did, word would surely get back to Jack and I don't know how he would interpret it. He might be filled with jealousy and longing and call me and ask to see me and try to win me back. But more likely he would think, "What kind of whore is she?" Or worse, "She is using my own brother to try to win me back! How desperate can she get?"

So I've just been playing that old game of making Bobby think that he has a chance with me and let the hint of sex linger in the air like a whiff of Chanel No. 5.

But as we were standing in the yard Bobby dropped a bombshell on me. He wasn't visiting for the sole reason of seeing me.

We were walking around the pool, casual and at ease, Bobby was playing with Maf, tossing him a stuffed toy tiger to fetch, as he chatted with me. We were like a couple of kids on a secret date while my parents were out of the house. Then his face grew serious and he said, "Marilyn, there's something serious I have to talk to you about."

"Uh oh," I thought. I assumed he was going to tell me he was in love with me.

He said, "There's been a lot of talk lately."

"Oh really? About what?" I asked. But I knew what was coming.

"About you and Jack. You have to understand this is a very serious matter."

"What is serious?" I wanted to know.

"Marilyn, if actual, reputable sources reported that you and Jack were seeing each other…er…romantically….it would be very, very…bad. Not only for Jack. Bad for you too. Both of you would be destroyed."

"Did Jack tell you this?" I asked.

"He didn't have to tell me. Isn't it obvious what would happen?

Everything that you both worked so hard for all your lives would be taken away in a blink of an eye. The media would destroy the both of you. You've got to stop calling, Marilyn."

His words hit me like a sucker punch. I felt a strange panic and queasiness spread throughout my body. I thought I might throw up. It was obvious that Jack sent Bobby to me. Sent his brother to do his dirty work. To break up with me. To end it. "We need to get rid of her," I could almost hear him demanding, "Bobby, you do it."

It felt like the world was crashing in all around me

What really bothered me, I mean in spite of my heart being broken, was how I was being made to be completely culpable in this. Like I was some unhinged woman who had been bothering the president of the United States. He seduced me. He led me to believe he had feelings for me. Now I was being treated like an out of control shrew,

This news. The hot sun. The nausea. The humiliation. I actually felt like I was going to faint. Bobby could at once see how distressed I was. He put an arm around my shoulder to steady me. "Marilyn," he said very gently, "if Jack were not married things would be different. He's very fond of you and who knows what would develop if he were...uh...available. Or even if he wasn't in such an important position. The timing is off. But the fact is he is the president of the United States and he has to take that responsibility seriously."

I could almost laugh at that. Sneaking in and out of hotel rooms, clandestine meetings with me and God knows who else. Seriously? My God what a joke!

I couldn't find my voice but my mind was screaming, "What about his responsibility to me?" I felt dizzy and tired and empty. And before I could fall limply to the ground, Bobby put his other arm around me. He was squeezing me very tight. At first he was holding me up but then I felt his hands probing me, the curve of my back, the firmness of my ass. I felt one hand slip under my blouse and I could almost feel his astonishment at the softness of my skin.

This has happened before with others.

He looked at me with disconcerting yearning. I looked away. I could see that he was hurt, crushed at the possibility that I might not want him. I recognized the look because I had felt it myself.

"Go," I said softly. "Go. Leave me alone. Just go."

He didn't.

Then, before I could react, push him away, start screaming, swoon, anything—he was kissing me, pressing me forcefully into him. I don't think (and this is saying a lot) I have ever felt such passionate longing from a man. He wanted me so! In my utter confusion I could feel tears streaming down my face and he was kissing my tears and licking my cheeks. Somewhere between a faint and a scream, I acquiesced. I opened my mouth and his tongue entered at once. He kissed me feverishly for a very long time. It felt like he wanted to devour me.

We separated.

"Darling," he gasped.

June 19, 1962

I must have been delusional, using one brother to make the other jealous.

The thing is, I don't want to be alone anymore and I'm not talking about some transitory passion masquerading as love.

Bobby calls me day after day and sometimes I talk to him and sometimes I don't. When I call him back he says, "When can I see you again?"

I wanted Bobby to tear into me passionately, filling me with his power and presence, pushing away any feelings I have for his brother. But once he was inside me I could hardly feel him at all. But...still...I like him. He has warmth and intelligence. He has a kindness and a sensitivity that I feel Jack is lacking. And I've reached a stage where I need kindness. (Dear God, I hope I'm not sounding like Blanche DuBois yet!)

Maybe if I had met Bobby first...

I have allowed a little romance to develop. Yes, it's sexual. Although

I don't feel same way for him as I do for Jack our romance has its own tenderness. But I don't want it to go too far.

It's funny though, the more I try to push Bobby away, the more obsessed he becomes with me. Just don't want someone and they're yours – that's a trick I've learned. But the minute you start wanting them, that's what sends them running for the hills. But if I mention Jack to Bobby I could see his face go stiff and all the color drains away.

I have to admit, I started to fantasize about what it would be like to be married to Bobby. He's better than nothing, and nothing is looming. Someday he might be president, after Jack, and I would be First Lady. And then….boy, would Jack be sorry. Bobby would have the power and he would have me too. And then Jack would realize all he lost.

July 2, 1962

It hurts a bit to say this, even though I always knew it all along I didn't have to think about it so seriously until now, once you've had a great success, people love to see you fail.

I know this is true of the journalists who once adored me. But it is just as true of the people who I considered friends.

When you're on top, there are "friends" who want to be near you, invite you places, praise you, but all the while they are envious in a way that's really poisonous. "Why does she deserve to be so famous?" "Why is she so loved?" It kills them a little on the inside. There is a lot of jealousy in this world. I think that I've felt this towards me. And yet, I did want to believe the best in people, so I blamed my suspicions on being hurt in the past, or maybe because of not having a family and other insecurities and so forth.

But no.

I realize now they were always waiting patiently. Longing for the day of my downfall. They feel it has arrived and they are gloating, but at the same time staying away from me. That's their way of showing me their happiness that I'm going through a bad time. "She's not worth an invitation. She's not worth a phone call." Now, I suppose, they can feel better about their own lives.

She's finished. Hooray!

July 3, 1962

Although I desperately want to, something inside me says: "Don't give up."

Fox is putting out horrible, nasty stories about me in the press every day. They are saying things like: "We had to fire Miss Monroe because she continuously and willfully broke her contract. On many days she did not show up for filming without any justification." Totally ignoring the fact that their own doctor, the studio doctor, told them that I was really sick and that they should postpone production until I recovered.

Well, I'm not going to sit back and let the studio make a mockery of me and dictate to the world that my career is over. They didn't make me. They don't own me. I worked long and hard to get to where I am. Alone.

I will go on a publicity campaign of my own and show them I belong to no one but the world.

Now that I'm not working and the world thinks that the studio fired me for being an unprofessional, lazy bitch, I feel it's really important to prove my value, my worth. So I've been keeping myself busy, being photographed and interviewed for all the big magazines – *Vogue*, *Cosmopolitan*, *Life*, to prove that I'm still desirable. I don't' know who I'm trying to prove it to. The studio? Jack? Maybe myself.

If they are going to say I'm over the hill, I'm finished, it's over, how should I respond? Roll over? Walk away? Let them win?

No, no.

I will show them I am still a star. A viable commodity. A world film favorite, as my recent Golden Globe award announced.

I am still Marilyn Monroe.

All I know is that when I leave Hollywood it will be on my own terms. And it does make me feel good that the magazines still want to do feature stories about me. I'd be lying if I said it doesn't.

Last week I was scheduled to be photographed for *Vogue* magazine at the Bel-Air Hotel. I didn't know what kind of pictures they would want me to do. I had never been photographed specifically for *Vogue*, and when I think of that magazine I immediately think: "high fashion." Well, that wasn't for me to worry about. I figured I'd just show up and play it by ear. It's *Vogue*, after all. They know what they're doing.

The photographer was Bert Stern. He's very big now and just came back from shooting Elizabeth Taylor on the set of *Cleopatra*.

When I arrived at the hotel, (*Vogue* had rented out a suite for the session) I saw that he had hung up white wall paper all over the place. It didn't look like a hotel room.

"You're beautiful," he said. "I made you a studio."

"This could be fun," I thought. But then, after further inspection, I asked myself, "Where is the fashion?"

Bert Stern had brought all kinds of see-through scarves and nets and beads and glittery things. There wasn't a single dress in sight. Obviously he wanted me to do nudes.

Here we go again!

I should have said, "No." Part of me is desperately wanting to move away from all that. "It's time to let that go," I say to myself.

I asked Bert, "You want me to do nudes?"

He was scared. He stammered a bit. "Well...uh...yes. I thought it would be nice. You look fantastic."

"What about my scar?" I asked. The scar from the gall bladder surgery is still very visible and I didn't have a body makeup expert, like I did on the movie set, to camouflage it. Nor did I know how the shots would be lit. On the movie set the cinematographer was very careful to light me so that my nudity was spotlighted in the most flattering way.

Bert Stern said, "Well, I can always retouch the scar. It will never be seen by the public."

I paused. Exposing the scar to a stranger made me feel very vulnerable. And I was terribly conflicted about posing nude once more.

Will I ever be anything more to them than a body? I remember when I was skinny dipping in the pool for *Something's Got to Give*, I said to myself, "This will be the last time, lady. Let's really give them something to remember your body by. Your naked last hurrah!"

But the other part of me, the stronger part, was saying, "Who cares about the nude swim? Maybe that movie will never even be released. Marilyn, you're thirty-six years old. Let's show 'em that you still got it."

And, against my better judgment, I listened to that part of myself.... again.

We shot photographs all night long. Drinking champagne. Here's a part of a poem I just thought of:

holding up scarves
covering up scars
and private parts
for the sake of the arts
and champagne was poured
until I showed more
that's what I live for
I get high for
that's what I die for

And I did show more. Ultimately.

"Fantastic!" Stern said.

But days later he called me again. "The photos are so beautiful, so gorgeous, so stunning, *Vogue* wants you to shoot more."

"More?" I asked. "We took thousands of pictures."

He said, "They want to shoot you in high fashion. They want to make you into a princess."

And I went back to the same hotel and the same photographer. But this time with a commotion of stylists and assistants and shoes and dresses and hats and furs. We shot photos for the *Vogue* fashion layout over the course of several days...and nights.

But guess what? On the last night I ended up naked again. Lying on the bed. With discarded fashion all around me. While Stern's camera went click click click.

July 5, 1962

I was watching him tie his tie and adjust himself in the mirror.

I was in an angry mood. Earlier in the day I had been at a meeting at Fox. After all the bad publicity the studio released about me, now they are calling me into meetings!

The studio wants me back!

They say, "There's only one Monroe. We made a mistake."

They want to rehire me. They offer me more money to finish the movie. They offer me a new director. They offer me the original Nunnally Johnson script I preferred. They offer me a new contract.

I'm so tired of people making me offers and then not coming through.

I turned my attention to Bobby in the mirror. I said: "If you love me, Bobby, as you say you do, tell it to the world! You want to be with me? Fine! Leave Ethel..."

"I will leave her," he replied. "When the time is right. You have to understand..."

"Look," I said, "I'm tired of understanding. I'm not a famous plaything to be passed around for the Kennedy boys' enjoyment."

Now he was getting mad. He raised his voice: "Stop acting, like the little dumb blonde the world thinks you are! I still have a career....and you still have a career! When the time is right.....”

It feels like everyone in the world keeps telling me, “When the time is right.” And the only thing that time is doing is passing!

“The time is right for me!” I shouted. “Right now. I'm not going to wait around until I'm fifty when you think that your political career will be over.”

“Marilyn,” he said, “Stay with me like this for now. When the right time comes, I promise, I will marry you.”

I could hardly believe that he called my bluff. “You'll marry me?” I asked, throwing his statement right back at him. “Yes, as soon as I could work it out.”

Oh how I want a home. A safe place. A protector.

“Soon,” I said then. “It has to be soon. After all, none of us really know how long we're going to be here.”

Fragment of a Letter to Dr. Greenson, Undated

I wanted to determine if it was a friendly crowd. Popping pills again. You say, “They take away all your personality.”

I say, “Good, that's what I want.”

July 8, 1962

There was a big show business party at the house of Gene Kelly the other night. Just so Hollywood would see that I'm still alive and that there's still some fight left in me I decided to go to this party. Before I left I took some pills and drank some champagne. Surprise, surprise!

The bottom line is, I am as afraid of people today as I was when I was a child. Sure, I could go through therapy for years and years and work through my fears and reach a point where I'm no longer afraid. But pills and alcohol work so much faster.

Because of all my experiences in all types of situations in Hollywood, I thought I could make myself appear to fit in anywhere. I was wrong. I was isolated and lonely in spite of my feeble attempts at being sociable. I should have known better. But I have bursts of optimism occasionally.

"Smile, it's not the end of the world. It's only a party. You're not acting in a Russian drama." This was said to me by Tony Curtis. Although he's still very handsome he's quite stupid and empty. His comment, though, made *me* feel stupid and empty as it was meant to….like a dizzy tart who is trying to take the world too seriously. He managed to break through my shield of "ready for anything" and hurt me.

Tony had the balls to talk to me after he told the press that kissing me, in our film *Some Like it Hot*, was like kissing Hitler. As if that wasn't supposed to hurt my feelings. He could have said it to me face to face. But instead he said it to the press because, you know…well…talking to the press makes a bigger play. You can get a lot of free publicity if you give a reporter a quote involving the name Marilyn Monroe.

Tony despises me because I was sick while we were making that movie. And I was totally unprofessional – I admit it. Although he didn't know it, I was pregnant at that time, but I lost the baby anyway and….oh, what difference does it make now?

I'm not particularly proud of the way I behaved on that movie. Or any movie for that matter. Because of my fears of performing, I was constantly late, and I was so sick all the time. That old story. But it's true!

I had difficulty remembering lines and I kept Tony and Jack Lemmon waiting around on the set in high heels waiting for me to show up and then to get it right. Part of me was pleased to be doing it to Tony. I hated his condescending manner and his lecherous oiliness. He's the type that views himself as irresistible to everyone, most of all himself.

Okay, so hate me. But don't go around to the press saying horrible things. And don't make up stories about me, please! For example, I heard that Tony is going around, fully equipped with his self-satisfaction and arrogance, telling a story about how Orry-Kelly, the great designer who did the costumes for *Some like It Hot,* supposedly said to me, "Marilyn, Tony Curtis has a nicer ass than you." To which I was supposed to have replied, "But he hasn't got tits like these." And then I pulled open my blouse, flashing my tits to prove it. Crass!

Now I could see how this anecdote could make for amusing dinner conversation, or lively talk show banter, but it never happened. But, because there's so much interest in Marilyn Monroe, he can always make up things involving my name and be assured that his chatter will be well received. Ouch.

For years to come, I am sure, he will make up lies about me and people will believe it because we starred in that movie together and they think he knows me. He doesn't know me at all.

Now, I could go around telling people certain truths around him, like, how he is losing his once lush hair and how he blackens his scalp with shoe polish so you can't see the thinning areas onscreen. Someday, I think, he will wear a toupee. There is no crime in that—but being the extreme narcissist that he is, this would certainly bruise his ego. But what would I get out of saying stupid things like this just for the purpose of hurting his feelings? That's the thing, I've never been able to do—hurt someone's feelings intentionally, even though mine have been hurt so often.

The party was filled with the kind of movie industry executives who have always scorned me. They look at me with a sly smile, trying to convey the notion that they know something about me that I don't. In actuality, I brought them to their knees. They're begging me to come back and finish *Something's Got to Give.* They need the money that a Marilyn Monroe film could bring in because the studio is nearly in financial ruin because of the waste of *Cleopatra.*

Part of me knows that already, at this age, I've accomplished more than most people can ever dream of achieving. But there is another part of me—the broken part—that tells me I'm inferior to them and I constantly have to prove myself worthy. This exhausts me because it means I always have to perform at a stellar level.

But after Tony's remark, I tried to smile charmingly so no one would guess I'm in a great deal of pain. Especially not him.

As I think I've written before, I've never been very good in big crowds or at big show business-type parties. Actually, come to think of it, that's how I met Marlon Brando. Years ago I was at this party in New York...full of Manhattan swells. But I could not find my place there. There was a piano in the corner and I figured if I sat down at this piano and made believe I was trying to play something, I would look occupied and wouldn't stick out like a sore thumb.

I concentrated and concentrated on "Chopsticks" which I could manage a little. If I appeared to be deep in thought, deep in concentration, no one would disturb me and I would be safe.

And I was sitting on the piano bench, just sort of hiding behind that big piano, and waiting it out, concentrating on my two-fingered "Chopsticks," when Marlon sat down next to me. He certainly was one of the handsomest men I have ever seen—and my favorite actor to boot.

He said, "Everyone is laughing and drinking and mingling and here you are sitting in the corner by yourself." So I had been noticed after all! Even after all the effort I had put into being invisible.

I said, "I'm not very god at parties," and that's how we started talking. He showed me a few tricks on the piano, but he wasn't much better at it than I was. I didn't tell him how much I admire him in *A Streetcar Named Desire*—which I most certainly do—because I figured he'd heard it a million times before and I didn't want to seem like everybody else.

He said, "May I call you?" And I gave him my number.

Marlon and I would talk on the phone pretty often. He was one of my favorite people in the world to talk to because he was as famous as I was and a better actor and there wasn't anything in the world he could possibly want from me except my friendship. We dated for a while, and chatted on the phone a lot, but we hadn't slept together until one night he called me and said, "I want to come over tonight. And there's no excuse in the world for me not to come, unless you really don't want me to."

I really wanted him to.

So I thought about my little affair with Marlon to help me get through this party. Our romantic affair didn't last long but something even more important did, a beautiful friendship. A true pal. Someone I really connect with on all levels. I really trust him. And we make each other laugh.

I sort of hoped someone would come and rescue me the way Marlon did at that New York party all those years ago…but no one did.

Written on a Paper Napkin

Was it a sick joke, God, to send me here as a stranger? To glare and recognize the inconsistencies of the others? Or is it that we are all born to feel this way about each other? Alone. Strangers among strangers. Unable to break through the mysteries. That, God, is truly sick joke.

July 10, 1962

Bobby has been calling me. Talking to me as if I was his sweetheart. I don't really believe he'd marry me, but that's beside the point. I could have him if I wanted him. But the idea of wrecking a marriage seems stupid if love is not involved. I'm talking about Bobby. He's in love with me, certainly. I know by now.

Or, if it's not love, it's a consuming passion which he has to label "love" because of his Catholic morality. I mean, to justify getting sexual gratification with me, he has to feel that he's in love with me.

He loves Ethel, that is for sure, but I don't think his passion for her is like what he feels for me. He told me that before they were married she almost became a nun and to this day she is very religious. Maybe for her, sex is only a way to have children. Oh, I shouldn't write that. I hardly know the woman. I'm sure she's quite lovely.

I don't want to be the cause of anyone's pain. Everyone deserves to be happy, and even though I don't know her at all, I wish Ethel happiness, too. But perhaps their marriage isn't a happy one. Perhaps they are both looking for a way out. There are all kinds of complicated things going on behind closed doors. Sometimes what you think is the problem is actually the solution.

For all I know maybe they have been talking about divorce for years. Maybe she is unhappy in the marriage. Bobby never reveals things like that.

Actually I really don't want to cause Bobby or Ethel any pain.

But I can't spend too much time worrying about hurting Bobby or crying over Jack. I have an immediate problem, much more urgent, that needs my attention.

I'm pregnant again.

July 12, 1962

What can I say to people? A woman of my age? A woman who is so recognized and even admired? A women who should be settled down and have some sense of permanence, some kind of a family?

I can't stand being with people and at the same time I can't stand being alone. I can't eat and yet I feel hungry and I'm worried about losing more weight. A couple of years ago I was in perpetual fear of gaining weight. Now I have to be careful not to waste away. I can't sleep and yet I'm exhausted. I can't concentrate and yet my mind runs a continuous cycle of despair. It seems all I am able to do is lie in bed and cry. And cry and cry.

I don't know where to turn or what to do anymore since I'm not being fulfilled socially, sexually, romantically, or creatively.

Peter and Pat invited me to come over and spend some time at their house on the beach for the weekend. Well, I had to weigh my options: either spend the weekend alone, drugged, with no sleep and crying. Or spend a few days on the beach with Pat and Peter wearing a mask of normalcy in the hopes that they won't see how I am really feeling.

I went to the beach house. I'm good at masks.

It didn't seem like a bad decision at first. I decided I wouldn't think about my pregnancy. I would decide what to do after the weekend. I needed to forget about my pain, at least for a few days, or I don't know what I'd do.

To help entertain me, the Pat and Peter had a dinner party and invited Natalie Wood. She was there with a new actor she has made a film with and with who she is now having an affair. His name is Warren Beatty. He is very handsome and is the brother of Shirley Maclaine.

During dinner Natalie asked me what was going on with, *Something's Got to Give*, and I told her I was in negotiations with the studio to go back to work to finish it.

They want me back and they offered me double the salary if I return. After all the hoopla about me being fired. Now they have to eat crow and pay me a fortune to finish the film. To top it all off they offered me another movie after this one is completed. In the end I'll walk away with a million dollars. I suppose it should make me feel victorious.

Natalie said she was eager to see me in a new film. She said, "Whenever I see you on the screen, I feel so protective of you. I want to take care of you. I want everything to be alright." I was very touched. It was sweet of this young, popular actress to say something like that to me. I had to think for a moment about why what she said made me feel so warm and comfortable. "Oh!" I thought to myself. "Her compliment has nothing to do with the way I look. And yet she still has good thoughts for me."

I talked to her about the *Vogue* shoot and all the things that I hoped were coming up but even with my bright chatter and practiced smile, Pat turned to me at one point and whispered, "What's the matter? You seem so sad."

All I could do is keep smiling and say, "I always seem that way. I guess that's just the kind of face I have."

Later, Warren said, loudly, that his biggest dream is to make a movie with me. He suggested *The Stripper*, which is a property that, as a matter of fact, 20th Century Fox did buy the rights for, with me in mind at one point (Warren probably knew this.) I was proud and delighted. He's a hot young star destined for great things. He is ambitious, and good looking, and charismatic, and canny. He reminds me of me when I was his age.

But on the inside I was filled with dread because the character that was offered to me in *The Stripper* is the "older woman" having an affair with a younger man. Even though it was a fairly decent part I can't imagine playing older women parts. Not yet. Not yet.

What's next? Bad "mother" roles?

"I'm thirty-six years old!" I guess I was so engrossed in these terrible thoughts that at first I didn't realize that I blurted this out loud. There was a sudden halt in conversation.

Natalie attempted to come to my rescue. She said, "I look forward to growing older. There are a lot of wonderful parts and it will be interesting to play women at different stages in life."

Despair!

"No! No! It can't happen to me!" I cried, suddenly blinded with tears. I covered my face with my hands. I realized I was falling apart in front of them—even after I had made a deal with myself to be happy and smiling all evening. I tried for a recovery.

I uncovered my face and smiled sweetly. "I'm not going to play character parts for years and years…and maybe even decades." And everyone laughed. I thought it was a pretty good fake. They had no idea how serious I was.

Still, by the time the guests left, I was feeling better. Pat and Peter and I talked for a little while longer and then we headed for bed—they walked me to the guest room. I hadn't slept in days but when I stepped into the

Lawford's guest room I finally felt ready to slip into delicious oblivion. It was a strange relief to be in a bedroom other than my own, at least for a short time. I was away from everything that was mine. It felt like the problems I had been carrying around with me for the past few weeks were stored away at my house. The problems in this house were not my own. Here there were no demands, no expectations. If the phone rang it wouldn't be for me. No one would be coming around looking for me here.

I was so relaxed and so exhausted that I took only half of my normal nighttime dosage. As I lay in the bed I devised a fantasy of staying in the Lawford bedroom for the rest of my life. Just lying there in the darkness. They could nail the door shut and just cut out a little flap to slide me in some food and water. I would never have to worry about looking beautiful again. I would never have to make a movie again—not with Warren Beatty or anyone else. I would never have to be in love again. Not with Jack or his brother not with him or that one or this one or the other.

Then I remembered the baby growing inside of me. Well, doctors had told me I could never carry a baby to full term. But if by some miracle I did, I would keep the baby here with me—safe from the press. The baby would be my own.

It was with these thoughts in my head, nestled in the lush, plush sheets, that I fell deeply asleep.

But a short time later I bolted upright in bed remembering the times that Jack and I had made love here. "Jack doesn't love me," I cried out.

Intolerable.

"Oh no," I said to myself, "Here we go again." I addressed the awful heartbreak as if it were an actual person. "Can't you leave me alone? Even for one night?" I asked the pain. The pain turned a deaf ear and did not answer.

It just kept right on hurting.

I put on my robe and stumbled out to the balcony. I wanted to feel the ocean air. I wanted to escape. I was looking out into the night, crying, when Pat found me there. "Talk to me, Marilyn," she said. "Tell me what's wrong. How can I help you?"

But how would I be able to explain it all to her. Sometimes an inexplicable sadness overwhelms me. It's like a grip. It could be for a good reason, as it was tonight. Or sometimes it could be for no identifiable thing at all. I could be talking casually to a friend and suddenly that friend doesn't seem so friendly anymore. I see ulterior motives. I feel I'm being used. I sense danger. I felt this right in the moment with Pat, but I fought the sensation off. Pat looked at me with tenderness and kindness. She has treated me as nothing but a friend and I don't know who else to talk to anymore.

"I'm terribly unhappy," I said. "All the time. And I don't know what to do about it anymore."

"Oh Marilyn," Pat said, "I made a terrible mistake."

Mistake? Funny she should use that word. That's the word I used to Jack on the night of his birthday celebration. The whole affair had been a mistake. I just looked at Pat and waited for her to explain.

"I didn't know," she said, and she was crying now too. "I didn't know how fragile you were. You know? Sometimes you seem so strong and self-possessed and I guess I thought that a fling with Jack would be okay. I didn't think it would do any harm. I allowed it to happen. I feel responsible."

"It's not your fault..."

"But don't you see? I was in awe of you. And your beauty. And your talent. It seems silly now but it's almost as if...as if...I wanted to reward you with something. I offered Jack up to you. I offered you up to Jack. I guess I was in awe of both of you. Two incredible forces in the world."

"I let this happen, Pat. The only one who is responsible is me."

"The thing is," Pat continued, "when we're all socializing, and there are men around, and we're drinking, you're so 'Marilyn.' You seem so strong."

I didn't say a word. I realize that the image I play is indelible and successful. I'm not surprised that even a close friend like Pat would fall for it.

"And I forget," she said, "that you're not strong. You're not strong at al. Out of all of us...."

She let it go but I knew she was going to say, "Out of all of us you're the most breakable."

Peter joined us with a tray of tea and he talked with us for a while.

At this dark and lonely hour it seemed like Pat and Peter were the best friends I had in the world. We drank tea out of bone, white china cups. Being out there with them on the terrace made me calmer—the closest thing I have to a family, at least for a short while.

But I knew I was not the first or even second to Peter when it comes to loyalty. Peter is more in love with Jack than he is with me or even Pat. He would do anything to protect Jack. Anything.

The thrust of Peter and Pat's advice was that I should just forget Jack. That it was wrong to think that there was a chance of any future together. That he would never leave Jacqueline. I knew that already.

"I'll do anything to help you get over him," Pat said mournfully. "I'll be there for you in any way I can. But when Jack's mind is made up, that's it. He doesn't change."

Then I dropped the bombshell on them. "I'm pregnant."

All the color drained from Peter's face. Pat began sobbing. She knew.

"W-w-who?" Peter stammered. "Bobby?" he added hopefully.

"I'm nearly two months," I said. "It has to be Jack."

July 13, 1962

I had been putting it off but I knew the time had come to deal with it. The problem was not going to go away. I picked up the phone and dialed.

I said, "Bobby I'm pregnant."

There was only silence on the other end of the phone. I could hear him breathing heavily. I could almost feel his astonishment push through the telephone wires and rush out of the holes in the ear-piece.

He cleared his throat. "What do you want me to do?" He said, as if it were some problem of the country that needed immediate attention.

I felt a torrent of tears in my eyes and my voice cracked and I spoke very quickly to get it all out. "It's not yours, Bobby. It's Jack's."

I said, "Bobby, you never told me much about your marriage. I understand there are your children to consider. But are you unhappy with...." (I couldn't say her name) "...your wife?"

"Marilyn..." he said. I waited for more but there was just dead air.

"Because if the both of you are unhappy. And you're actually thinking of divorce, then now would be the time. I mean, you said, 'when the time is right.' I wouldn't expect to create a scandal or anything. I'd go away to Europe. Come back in a year or so, and then...!" I stopped for a moment because I felt the tears coming. "...and then, I don't know. We can work something out."

"Marilyn," he said hoarsely, "I can't marry you. At least not for a very long time."

I guess I was expecting that. I don't know how I let things go so far. What was I thinking, playing one brother against the other? This isn't a movie I'm orchestrating. This is my life!

I swallowed. "Okay," I said. "But if you could...if you could just come be with me now. I'm so afraid of doing this alone."

"I can't come now, Marilyn. It's a complicated situation. I can't explain it over the phone."

I said, "I'm the one in a complicated situation. Can't you come be with me? Just out of humanness?" I was crying. I couldn't stop myself.

"I'm sorry," he said.

Then I got really angry. "You know what, Bobby," I said, "You can just..."

He cut me off. "Don't say any more over the phone," he cautioned. "As soon as I can, I will come and see you."

With each of these blows, every hurt, every cruelty, I die again and again—little deaths—building to a grand finale.

I feel hope leaving me like a lifeline through my grip. My hands are ripped and torn from holding so tight. What a comfort it would be to just let go and fall into whatever lay in store.

July 14, 1962

Not too long ago I wanted this so bad. But I had all those miscarriages when I was married to Arthur. I know I make it sound like it was all horrendous. But we had happy times. I *think* we had happy times. In our country house.

Once I was in a garden surrounded by flowers and birds and gorgeous nature. Arthur was in the house trying to write. I was going to have a baby.

And I thought everything would be all right.

Now I guess I will have to add another sin to my long list. I wonder if I'm forgiven. I can't worry about that now, though. God is God and I am only a human being. He is going to have to accept the difference.

July 16, 1962

It would have been nice if Bobby or Jack could have been with me. But...

It wasn't so bad being in the hospital again.

I gave up my history, my problems, and my identity. This time I did it willingly. I checked in Cedars Sinai under the name Zelda Zonk. I was being granted a legal abortion for medical reasons. Simple as that.

It was a relief to just lie back in the immaculate white bed, propped up by pillows, protected by crisp sheets, my eyes half-closed. The nurses, dressed in their clean, white uniforms, moved around me doing little things. Propping a pillow or bringing me a drink of water. I could have been anyone. The hospital staff fluttered around me like angels...

attending to me, readying me for my eventual ascent into Paradise.

I was in some peaceful Purgatory. Everything so white and bright and clean. I had no more movies to make, no more relations to resolve. If death is this peaceful there is nothing to fear.

But then an appalling thought cut through the huge, white peacefulness. The thought of someone who should have been born and will not be.

Ironic? I, who has been trying to have a child for years. But it had to be done. Bobby turned out to be a completely weak man. He could not get a divorce. It would mean ruination for all concerned, he said. He is so religious, so Catholic. He would never suggest I get an abortion. His brother's child? Never! He said I should have the baby. That the family would help me. Anonymously, of course.

To think I actually believed that he loved me enough to leave Ethel. That he loved me so much that nothing else matters. I mean, I know better. I always fall for it though.

I thought of going away to Europe, but my fame would follow me and so would the reporters. They would want to know the father. They would investigate. People are already hysterical with gossip regarding Jack and me. He would be destroyed. I couldn't do that. I couldn't do that to him or to the country.

That's not to say that I am not furious. Now it's the anger that cuts through my peace.

I have been lying in beds all my life, trying to recover from what others have done to me.

And most of all Jack! That bastard zeroed in on the wound of my loneliness and made me believe he responded to it and sympathized with it, a technique he used to render me helpless. He talked to me as if he admired my intelligence as well as my beauty and treated me with respect, which led me to believe that there was a chance for something lasting between us – at least in the future. Then he dumped me so heartlessly, so suddenly, that it made a joke out of everything I had worked so hard to accomplish and, in the end, made a fool out of me.

His manipulation is the most painful thing.

July 21, 1962

Out of the hospital. Holed up in my house. My house becomes a fortress. I have seen no one in person. I take calls. Frank. Marlon. Agents. I talk to the studio through my lawyer.

It isn't easy.

Alone with my thoughts. I have to start going out. Even if it's just to continue buying things for my garden. And things to fill up this empty house.

Even if it's just to buy new clothes. To start a new season.

July 24, 1962

Another day. And, also, yesterday...

It was one of those late Los Angeles afternoons when the sun is just starting to set and it makes everything look like it's touched with gold. I had been shopping in Beverly Hills looking at the new styles. After so many years of preferring black or white or beige I'm discovering color! The brightly colored dresses look so pretty now. I really don't need more clothes but sometimes buying new things to wear makes me ambitious about going out more often. I feel like time gets away from me and before I know it I've spent days locked up in the house.

When I buy something new I think to myself, "I'll wear this to dinner when I'm out with Frank in Las Vegas." I don't know if that will come to be or not but at least it gives me something to plan for.

So I find myself buying too many things, spending too much money. My lawyer will write me saying, "Marilyn, I feel I must warn you about your spending..." Or my accountant in New York will call and say, "If you keep on spending this way, I fear...." But I'm only broke on paper. I have all this money that will be coming in from my percentage of *Some Like it Hot,* and I own *The Prince and the Showgirl* which will make it to television someday soon. And if I sign the new contract with Fox I will make a bundle. Anyway, buying new things plants the seeds of plans in me and I do feel it's important to make plans.

Why am I so tired all the time?

Nowadays I almost always feel tired. Well, I mean, it's not surprising since I never really get a good night's sleep. But I NEVER got a good night's sleep before so why I am so terribly exhausted now? Is it simply age catching up with me? Am I sick? Melancholy? Why is it that by late afternoon, just from trying on clothes, I feel ready to go back to bed?

Anyway, that's just to start. More happened.

I was coming out of a dress boutique that I favor, JAX, carrying a bag with a new dress in it, bright blue in color, and this very young girl walked in as I was going out. Her presence stopped me in my tracks. Quite suddenly something deep inside me was touched. I felt she must be new in town. I had my dark glasses on and my hair covered with a kerchief but the people in Beverly Hills recognize me disguised this way by now. This girl did not know who I am. She looked at me in a vague, friendly way and held the door and half-smiled as we passed each other.

I don't know why. I can't explain it, but this woman, this girl really (she looked like she could be in her late teens) fascinated me. I mean she was really exquisite in a way that moved me.

Okay, I'll admit it, I'll write it down here and now that it's hard for me to see a woman so beautiful and so…fresh…and I don't know what else… and not feel some envy. I try not to feel it, believe me, because beauty is always in abundant supply in this town and if you start comparing yourself and worrying about it, it will eat you up and destroy you. Yet this girl's innocence touched my jealousy, quieted it, before it could swell up and anger me.

She didn't have to try hard. She was scrubbed and natural and I knew all the new styles would look so effortlessly good on her. Her hair was a light brown, the color of honey, really natural. I don't think she was wearing any makeup but she radiated health and, you know, youth and beauty. There's a particular glow in the skin of youth, it can't be duplicated with expensive facials or expert makeup. It's just part of who you are at the time and you have to learn to let it go as time goes by.

I walked back into the store and pretended that there was something else I wanted to look at but really I was watching her. I couldn't stop looking.

I can't explain why she fascinated me so. She did the ordinary things. She asked to look at a dress. A light yellow one. She held it up in front of her in the mirror. It looked lovely. She asked how much it cost and after she was told she said she may come back. I heard the salesman, who I know, say, "We'll look forward to it Miss Tate."

Then she walked out of the boutique. I went over to the salesmen and I said, "Thomas, who was that girl?" He said, "Oh Miss Monroe that's Sharon Tate. She recently arrived in town and she's trying to be an actress," and so forth.

It occurred to me, just this feeling, that she was very much like me when I was her age. So full of hope and light and surprise. Everything is possible. She has her whole life ahead of her. And her beauty will open doors—she will find the satisfaction in that. She probably hasn't even been in love yet. She will get noticed, I'm sure. She really has that certain something.

Of course she will be hurt too. If you're in the game that comes with the territory. But why did I feel such affection for her? It was strange. I didn't feel jealous. I felt protective. There was a vulnerability about her that was palpable. It made me want to put my arms around her, which is funny because that is what people say about me.

I left the store and looked down the street and there she was waiting at the corner for the traffic light to change. "No, no, no," I said to myself. "You mustn't do this." But I couldn't stop myself. I followed, walking slowly behind her. I started to feel sad. She was looking in shop windows. She was in no hurry. She has plenty of time.

The streets were not crowded at all. I was hiding behind my dark glasses and ducking in storefronts like a private eye. The sight of her flooded me with memories of the days of auditions and rejections and the joyfulness of finally getting a part. Any part. The hope of stardom in every tomorrow. Yes! She was me some seventeen years ago. In some ways it feels like a lifetime ago and in other ways it seems like last year. I know how quickly it goes by. Someday she'll know it too.

Once, years ago, when my contract was dropped at Columbia Pictures after just one movie with them I was desperately trying to get a contract with a new studio before I lost my nerve and gave up completely. I was having dinner with an important producer who had been out with thousands of beautiful girls, a different one every night, and all through dinner he didn't seem very impressed. He drove me home without much conversation and when he pulled up in front of my apartment he went to grab me roughly but then inexplicably changed his mind and took my face in his hand and kissed me lightly and gently.

Then he looked into my eyes and said in wonderment, "You really are exquisitely beautiful." The way he said it, with such tenderness, coming from one with such power, really meant something to me at the time. Sometimes all it takes is to stop and look at something to really see the beauty.

After a while, I found myself standing next to her looking at the diamond necklaces in a jewelry store window. She glanced over at me and recognized me simply as the woman she passed in the dress shop. I tried to silently signal to her all the secrets I know but that was impossible. She'd have to learn those things for herself, as we all do. She smiled at me fully now. The sun was going down saturating everything with the last of its gold. A breeze moved softly through her hair.

She was golden.

July 27, 1962

The idea was to get me away from my despair so "they" decided that it would be best for me to go to the Cal-Neva Lodge, the resort Frank

Sinatra owns. "They" being Peter and Pat, Frank, and the rest. A week-end of partying. A weekend of drinking. A weekend of forgetting. A weekend of "fun."

"Let's get her out of town before she starts shooting off her mouth," I could almost hear them collectively say. It's all about protecting the Kennedys, my dear, first and foremost.

Actually, I shouldn't be so pessimistic. Frank has come to my rescue again. Telling the press that he wants his production company to produce my next movie and telephoning me often. "Juliet Prowse was nothing to me," he says.

It was somebody by the name of Sonny's birthday and we were all supposed to meet in Peter's suite for a celebratory drink. Peter kept call-ing my room. "You've got to come, Marilyn. Please come, Marilyn. It won't be any fun without you, Marilyn."

And then I realized that this was going to be more than a little party for Sonny. Peter has always urged me to come to his sex parties, his orgies. I always refuse.

"I'm exhausted," I said. "I'm going to stay in my room tonight."

A little awhile later there was a knock on my room door.

"Hey Charlie," Peter said. He was very drunk or stoned or something – even by his standards.

I had already taken Nembutal. I was getting ready for bed. "Peter," I said, "I haven't changed my mind."

"This is a very special party," he told me. "Very interesting. You won't want to miss it. Take some of these," he said, handing me a prescription bottle with some pills left in it. "You won't feel so tired after a couple of these."

I looked at him with his silly grin, his mussed hair, and the fly of his pants wide open. "This is one of my best friends," I told myself. "No wonder I'm such a wreck."

But you know what the problem is? There's a part of me that wants to grow up and get on with things and straighten out my life, but there's another part of me that wants to play with the other kids – to float from one experience to the next – not caring about the consequences and not worrying about the future at all.

"Leave me alone for a while, Peter," I said. "I'll take a nap and see how I feel later. Maybe I'll stop by."

"Don't let me down," he said. "I really want you to be there. It won't be any fun without you." And he staggered out of my room.

Obviously my instincts had been right. This was going to be one of Peter's infamous sex party-orgies – that's certainly the reason he so wanted me to come. "Hey, let's get Monroe to come," I could hear them say, forgetting once again that there's a real person somewhere in here.

I took a couple of Peter's pills without even knowing what they were. The prescription tag had been removed. Or maybe these pills didn't even come in this bottle. I downed them with champagne, even though I had made a vow earlier that day that I was going to try and get through a day without any alcohol at all. Oh well. I'd try again tomorrow. After all, as my dear Scarlett O'Hara once said, tomorrow is another day.

My state of mind, I guess, can be demonstrated by the fact I swallowed Peter's pills without even knowing what they were. Is it my paranoia that has been making me think that my friend Peter may want to poison me? I believe now he is a latent homosexual and he wants to be a woman. Not just any woman. Me. That would partially explain his obsession with getting me to bed all these years. Not that I'm judging him for being homosexual. God knows some of my best friends are. Cole, for instance. But Cole has real talent and is living his life the way he wants, whereas, Peter would rather be a world renowned females sex symbol.

Perverse.

Strange.

My friends are strange. I guess that's why they're my friends.

Sex party. Sex party. Not a notion exactly unknown to me. But there's been talk about Peter's parties and the dark part of me was curious as to what would go on there. They've been pressuring me to attend one, "just to see." Still, I didn't really feel like going, but then again I don't feel like doing anything. I'm a zombie and I allow my body to be placed in this situation or that one.

"Maybe I'll go," I thought.

I sat down in front of the mirror at the dressing table. Strewn all around the vanity were powders, and creams, and lipsticks and eyelashes. The tools of contemporary beauty.

Lately, I've been studying my face very closely. I suppose I always have. But never with such a mixture of panic and intensity.

I looked and I looked hard. I've always been able to look at myself with absolute honesty. It's my business. I saw a face—still beautiful by normal standards—but I will never be judged by normal standards.

I can see in my face now where and how I will age. There is the beginnings of fine lines around my eyes and mouth. I took my finger and traced the lines as if my touch could erase them. They become deeper and more pronounced when I am smiling broadly. The famous smile.

There is nothing that money could buy, nothing in modern science that could bring me back the special glow of youth. Even for Marilyn Monroe. What could I do? I thought and I thought hard about what directions my image might take but all my thoughts led nowhere.

The image, which I worked so hard at creating, is so beloved. It is too indelible. When the world thinks of Marilyn Monroe they think of this child-like, voluptuous, innocent, sexual, available angel. That's what I created. Which was fine, even though it's not completely who I am, as long as I could give it to them. And I don't know how much longer I can.

It became most apparent to me that I am entering a new stage of "beauty" when I was examining the photographs that Bert Stern took of me for *Vogue*. He sent me a batch of the negatives and contact sheets for me to look over. Of course he expected me to send all of them back.

A few are certainly the best photos ever taken of me.

But there are others.

Wait! Should I write this...?

(Later)

...some of the other photos frightened me to death. Bert Stern's lighting is harsh. Almost clinical. His camera is cruelly probing.

Through his lens, I often look tired. Weary. Wan. And even though there is a wildness to the photos—in some of them the champagne was obviously pushing me to go too far—and I posed with a reckless abandon that might have worked ten years ago. My eyes have lost their light, the sparkle. They look dead.

In some harshly lit, close-up photos, with my wide, open-mouthed smile, I can see the crow's feet cutting deeply around my eyes—through the makeup. As I looked at them I had to catch my breath.

My heart was pounding.

I studied the body. I am certainly thin and toned. My stomach is flatter than ever. But all of the recent weight loss has made my breasts much smaller. In some pictures they look like they may be beginning to sag just a bit.

And the scar. Not yet retouched. Slashed across my body like a bright red magic marker crossing out an error.

"No! No! No! They can't publish photos of Marilyn Monroe looking like that! The people who love me will say, 'She's getting old!'"

I took a real magic marker and scrawled an X across the negatives that I really disliked so that *Vogue* could never publish them. But not satisfied with that – maybe they could remove the ink somehow – I took a hairpin and scratched deeply, angrily into the negatives, scratching at my face and body. Destroying the images beyond repair.

"What are you going to do with your life!" I screamed.

Enjoy youthful beauty. As you get older, you realize there will always be people who are younger, therefore more desirable. You have to learn how to deal with it, otherwise it will destroy you.

I can still, I know, look beautiful, when I meet someone new they always gush about how beautiful I am. But it's not like it used to be when it was just something I took for granted. Now I am conscious of the way I look all the time, obsessing over what the new batch of photographs will look like, or how I will look on the screen. That people think I'm beautiful delights and terrifies me. It's been a gift and a weapon but one that won't always be so potent. I've been trying not to lean on my looks so much. But when I look for somewhere else to lean I find nothing.

Once, I was the most beautiful woman in Hollywood – and that became my coat of armor. I can't help but obsess over what will happen when it's not so any longer. Right now I can still hold my own. But each day that goes by robs a little of that power.

But looking at those photos for *Vogue*, I felt something very scary in my mind telling me that Marilyn Monroe couldn't possibly exist for much longer.

Which brings up the question that I hate asking myself. Could there be a forty-year-old Marilyn Monroe?

I didn't put on any makeup to go to Peter's party. Instead I hid my hair with a kerchief and I dressed in loose fitting pants and a blouse. I wanted to fade into the background—not stand out as a sexual curiosity. I wanted to be a woman, not Marilyn Monroe.

I entered Peter's room, but it might as well have been the doorway to hell.

I'll admit that I've always had a secret fantasy of watching people do dirty things – silent and unnoticed in the background. There is a voyeur that exists in me right alongside the exhibitionist.

Now they feel me watching them. They look up and our eyes meet and they continue, knowing that I know.

There were bodies all over the room. On the two double beds, on the chairs, on the floor. Flesh on flesh. Body on body. Man on man. Woman on woman. Man on woman. Cock after cock. Was this what it meant to be rich and famous? Pushing ourselves deeper and deeper into a place where there are no boundaries, no consequences, no regrets.

I watched for a long time from a corner in the room. Frank was there. And quite a few other very well-known people. I won't mention their names, even here, in the hopes that they'll return the favor to me—which they won't.

I was in despair, yes! But Peter's pills were unleashing another part of me and I became excited. Being in the midst of this would allow me to feel something else for a moment.

I watched two handsome actors working on an up and coming actress, one was going down on her, the other was kissing her and their devotion and enjoyment of her was so complete, that I became jealous. I wanted to be worshipped. I took the kerchief off and shook out my hair. I went over to the threesome and I sat very close watching intensely until I was noticed. Soon one man started touching me. Then the other. They forgot about the woman, but soon she was touching me too. They were kissing my breasts, my stomach, and lower.

The more sexually excited I became and the more disgusted I got, the more I pushed myself to go further. In the blaring moments of sex, nothing else matters. Not age. Not career. Not money. Not love.

Soon I was rolling with the waves, and one body part led to another. And I became an animal of sex. We were all made up of sex. Throwing ourselves deeper and deeper into it. There were all kinds of famous people involved and I, in the middle of it all, Marilyn Monroe!

This is what I am made of: golden hair and delicate white skin, exquisitely precious and infinitely valuable to them all.

They all wanted me.

And I decided, through my sexual haze, that I was tired of being a woman. I wanted to see what it feels like to be a man.

With all this going on, I ended up near Peter. I had never had any sexual contact with him before, nor did I ever want to. But Frank was with me at this point and Frank and I had made love hundreds of times before, but this time it was different. Peter wanted to be degraded, and Frank, well, Frank has a secret loathing for Peter and he wanted to see me degrade him. I took the lead with Peter, forceful and demanding. I felt no inhibitions no shame with Peter, he's a nice guy but in this moment—I don't know, I despised him.

In my past adventures I've learned that most men, even the most masculine, the most heterosexual, love having a finger up their ass. I don't know why, some latent thing, I suppose. I put my finger at the crack of Peter's hole to test the waters. He moaned, which urged me to go on. Slowly...carefully, watching out for my fingernail – I didn't want to tear him – pushed my finger in.

I watched what I was doing in an almost detached way. Frank watched too, and he was gleeful. What I was doing felt good but I did it with a methodical coldness. Peter wanted me to call it a pussy, and when I did, he groaned with pleasure. My finger in there felt like power. I imagine it's the closest I will ever come to experiencing what a penis feels like inside of a vagina. While my fingers was there, I knew that I owned him.

And Frank became so excited by watching me exert this power over Peter that he grabbed me away from him, my finger plopping out with a quick "pop" like a champagne cork out of a bottle. Frankie wanted to be dominated a little too. So I threw him down and was kissing him roughly and we made love. Me on top. Wild. Passionate. Undeniable.

I was the one in control.

But when the orgasm was over there was no acknowledgement of the power I had exercised over him. Our roles went back to the way they had been before.

That's why I learned early on: "Get all their promises before an orgasm," because afterwards the power evaporates. Peter moved on.

We left the party together, Frank and me, although the sex was still going on full steam ahead, and Frank wanted to walk me to my bungalow. We were both a little embarrassed with each other now, but tender, and we went back to our roles by rote, I was the little girl and he was the lover, the father and the protector.

He wrapped me in his arms.

"I love you, Marilyn," he said. "Remember I said, 'when the time is right?' Well, I feel the time is right for us now."

Ah, my wonderful timing.

The moon was very bright, that I remember very vividly. And the sky around it was perfectly black, that I remember also. Once a reporter on the set of *The Misfits* said that looking away from Marilyn Monroe was like trying to explore the dark areas surrounding the moon. But even the moon fades as the sun comes up, and the dark areas become easier to explore.

Frank knew I was an emotional mess and that the Lawford's had brought me here to try to take my mind off of Jack and all my other problems.

He was saying that I had to pull myself together. That I was an important star, an artist, and I owed it to myself to straighten out my life, overcome my troubles, so I could still do all the great work I had in me. He said he was going to buy the rights to the play *Born Yesterday* and have it written as a musical for us to star in together.

He said that we should get married.

I feel Frank does love me. And I love him. But I realize now it's not in the way that two people in love want to spend their lives together. It would be wrong for us to marry. It's the kind of love that you feel for someone who you know will always be around, for a lot of laughs and good times, and when you need someone to lean on when you're in pain. Like a family.

Frank is something like family.

He said that I could start over, the way I have always done in the past. If only he knew that I couldn't see a future.

"Why bother?" I said. "I'm not going to be here much longer."

I surprised even myself by saying it out loud, but I knew in my heart it was true. I'm so very, very tired. I can't even pretend anymore.

"What are you talking about," he asked, alarmed.

And with the drugs and the alcohol and the sex and the loss – all combining in the pit of my heart all at once – I replied, "I'll be gone soon. But don't worry, Frank. I'll be seeing you in your dreams."

And I don't know why I'm telling you this except that the moment was important to me and I learned something from it and it seems worth telling.

July 29, 1962

It might not be such a bad place – death. Maybe it's all darkness and quiet and a continuing drowsy feeling, like the moments before a deep, wonderful sleep, where bad memories are unable to reach you and all that matters is the giant peacefulness ready to take you over in a matter of seconds.

August 1, 1962

What will they say about me after I'm gone, I wonder? When I'm dead they'll pick over my life as vultures would and they'll sell photos of my ruined corpse in the morgue – if it would mean a buck.

August 2, 1962

Sometimes I try to listen to Frank's advice and be optimistic and plan for the future. And sometimes it even works for a while. After all, I have come up from way down. Once becoming a movie star seemed impossible. Yet I achieved that. So I try to set my sights on the impossible again.

I say to myself: "I will use my fame and power and talent to completely transform myself. I will use all my future profits, still coming in from *Some Like it Hot*, (of which I own a percentage of), to form the "Marilyn Monroe Shakespearean Company." We will make films based on the classics and occasionally do stage work. I'll recruit Marlon and Monty and Even Elizabeth Taylor to join. Maybe I'll do *Macbeth* with Marlon, and *The Taming of the Shrew* with Richard Burton.

I know people will laugh at me for trying, but they've laughed at me before and maybe I'll win again. Who knows?

In a rush of enthusiasm and excitement, I called Marlon to talk about my idea.

"Hello Marlon," I said, "How would you like to have dinner with me? I have an idea I want to discuss with you."

And Marlon said, "Any idea you have, Marilyn, I'd be interested in. How about next week?"

And we made a date to meet.

Then I get nervous and think, "Who am I kidding." Well I'll just have to wait and see what he thinks about it.

August 3, 1962

Meanwhile…

I decided it would be best if I got dressed up and have dinner at La Scala. There's nothing like Italian food to cheer you up. But once I got there, I noticed the waiters didn't make the usual fuss over me – or so I thought. Was I imagining it? I'm sure everyone was staring.

My makeup felt cakey.

"This was a bad idea," I thought. "Never come out in Hollywood when you're feeling down. People will pick up on the bad vibes and avoid you like a plague."

I tried to raise my spirits again by going for a long walk and planning the "Marilyn Monroe Shakespearian Company," I mean, it's not as if I don't plan to work for it. I would pay Strasberg to train me for a year. I'd be his only student. Then I'd call Larry Olivier and study with him to give me the polish I'd need. Sure he hates me and I hate him…but we recognize each other's talent…and what we can get from being associated with each other.

But then the darkness fills up in me again. "Who am I kidding?"

My career won't save me this time. How much longer can I fight? They still see me only as a sex object and…I feel the luster fading now.

In the wings, in dark corners there are actresses waiting to take my place. Fresh and beautiful and wrapped in the excitement of newness. The thought of competing makes me very weary.

"You've had yours, honey." I whisper to myself. "It's someone else's turn now."

And I walked alone along Santa Monica Pier but the depression would not leave me. I felt the cool night breeze. I could smell the salt from the ocean. I looked up over a starless sky.

This was where we used to come together. Jack and I. We used to walk along the pier hand in hand. And I blew it somehow.

I continued to walk down the pier with my palms facing forward. When I felt happier, I would come down here at night and the air was filled with magic, but now it seemed only dark and dangerous. There were men loitering in the shadows and they watched me pass. Ruffians with eager eyes waiting to see what I was all about.

I wrote a poem in my head but I can't remember all of it now. Only the last lines:

...the sea, the sea
The infinite sea
Rude and laughing
Because it's bigger than me

I imagined myself being attacked by one or two or three ruffians. They would jump out of the darkness and force me down into shadows. They would rape me and beat me. I would not fight. Instead I would concentrate on each punch, each blow, and force myself to feel.

August 4, 1962

Peter called.

"Come down to the beach, Charlie" he said. "Bobby is here and he wants to see you,"

But I thought it was all said and done with Bobby! He didn't come when I needed him most. He is certainly no thread to Jack.

And now, instead of coming to see me himself, he has Peter call me and summon me. I know Bobby loves me but he's being very clever about it. He's making everyone think that I'm doing the pursuing. Trying to make me come across as the fool. The beggar. The needy one.

"Take a walk, is my advice to him," I said.

"I don't see what harm there is in talking with the man," Peter said feebly. I didn't view him as a friend at the moment. I viewed him as a pimp for the Kennedy's.

I said, "Peter, I'm very depressed today. I'm not in the mood for seeing Bobby or you or anyone."

"Natalie Wood might be dropping by," Peter replied. "You like her. And Warren will be with her."

"Who else?" I wanted to know.

And Peter named a couple of high-priced Hollywood call girls. How does he dare invite me to his house with those women present? He is trying to insult me. Allude to the past? I hung up the phone without another word.

Never being able to take "no" for an answer, Bobby showed up here this afternoon. Peter was with him, walking the usual two steps behind. I didn't ask them in. The three of us stood in the foyer.

Bobby said, "I need to talk to you, Marilyn." By now I had had it with him, his brother and all of the Kennedys and even the Lawfords.

"I'm very tired," I told Bobby. "And I have nothing to say."

Don't they know I'm preoccupied with Mr. Death?

I actually leaned against the wall to hold myself up. "Leave me alone."

Each unhappiness, each heartbreak robs something from you – a piece of your will but he didn't notice this, he thought I still had the strength to play along.

He said, "I love you, Marilyn. I know you don't believe that yet. But I want you to know I'm not giving up on us."

Suddenly, empowered I stopped leaning. I didn't need walls for support – I would use my life experiences instead.

"There is no *us*." I said firmly. "We we're both looking for something in each other that neither of us can give." And then in desperation, I guess, I got cruel. I added, "Bobby, I love Jack. And he wants nothing to do with me. So you stepped in. I'll admit, I allowed it. Even encouraged it. My mistake. I'm sorry…."

"Listen to me…." he said.

I was done listening. I said, "But when I needed you, you sidestepped my 'complicated situation,' so smoothly. You never planned to marry me. I feel passed around like a plate of caviar. You said you loved me! You've lied to me! Get out of here! I'm tired. Leave me alone."

He started to leave and then Peter whispered something to him. Something I couldn't hear, but Bobby's attitude completely changed. His eyes changed. His color drained. He started screeching at me. His voice became odd, high-pitched, panicked.

"Where is it? Where the fuck is it!"

Now I was really getting angry. "What are you talking about?" I demanded.

"The bugging device!" Bobby said. "You've been recording our conversations. Conversations with me and with my brother."

"Get the fuck out of my house now! Get out! Get out!!!" I screamed.

I was enraged. The nerve of him accusing me of something like that. I had never been so angry and the anger gave me strength. What does he think I am? A communist spy? Some blonde Mata Hari? Doesn't he understand I loved his brother? I'm not out to hurt anyone!

He pushed past me into the living room, followed by Peter.

I said, "My housekeeper is here and she will call the police!"

Bobby called back. "No she's not. She's out for the afternoon."

Had I been in a more lucid state of mind at the time I would have considered how he knew that.

Bobby started lifting up the phones and unscrewing the mouth piece, and tapping the walls and looking behind doors. Looking for God knows what. Now he was red-faced and frantic. If I wasn't so furious I might have laughed.

He was still yowling, "We have to know. It's important to the family. We can make any arrangements and give you anything that you want, but we must have it."

Apparently he was still talking about some kind of recording device. I should have demanded one million dollars and booted his ass out of there. But I don't know anything about any recordings. And I don't want his money.

Peter was saying, "Calm down, now. Calm down." But Bobby was still screeching and I was screaming for them to get out of my house.

At last, finding nothing, they left.

I immediately called Dr. Greenson, terribly upset. He came right over. Grim as a mortician. Or the Grim Reaper.

I still rely on him even as I plan ways to cut him out of my life. Conniving. Controlling. There's no doubt that his feelings for me are growing sicker. Making me sicker. I feel it. How could I have been so blind for so long? I must untangle myself of my dependency on doctors, on agents, on studios, on lovers, on friends. If I'm going to survive.

I am even questioning the Strasbergs. Lee and Paula. They know better than anyone about all my self-doubts. My fears.

My life has been such an exercise in terror.

I've always been terrified on a movie set. I needed someone to tell me they believed in me.

They praise me. They fill me up with confidence. All at a mighty big price. Paula on my movie sets, as my coach, is loathed. I never cared. I demanded she be there. My friends say, "They feed your ego, sure thing. But they are also feeding off of you." I pay them thousands to help me feel my worth. But money can't buy self-worth. I know that now.

Should I change my will? Should I cut them all loose? Even as Mr. Death is hovering.

Maybe. I don't know. Perhaps they really do….love me?

But I still have a night to get through. I told Dr. Greenson the entire story. He gave me a shot to calm me down. He is going out to dinner now. Me? I'm going to try and get some sleep.

As soon as Greenson left I did something I vowed never to do again.

With the tranquilizer numbing my veins, I called the White House. Jack was not in—or he did not take my call—but I left a message with his assistant, Kenny. I said, "Tell Jack to get his brother away from me. I'm tired of him using me." And then I said, "And tell the president to stay away from me too."

Fuzzy.

Peter and Bobby must have gone back to the beach house and stewed in their own juices because within a few hours Peter called to invite me over again. But, even though I was calmer now, I refused once more.

Peter said, "Bobby is very sorry that he accused you of anything. He loves you very much, Marilyn. Look, at least come here and talk to him."

I didn't even feel anger anymore.

"Tell him I said goodbye," I said wearily. "And say goodbye to the president and say goodbye to Pat. And say goodbye to yourself because you're a nice guy."

I'm thinking of Jack. Maybe he'll call me tonight. Maybe he'll get my message and return my call. Maybe he'll get drunk and think about me holding him. Maybe a tender moment he spent with me will come back to him and move him.

I should have done my hair.

I'm going to take another Nembutal to try to sleep.

God, if only I could get through this night.

I'm lying in my bed alone with nothing but my despair.

And a loneliness the size of an ocean – one of the big ones.

True, I have known love—but it has only brought me torment.

Tonight...

It's not my mother, leaning over me when I was a baby, with a pillow, with the intent of smothering me. Before I even started I'd be finished. Done! Before the disappointments. Rendering me nothing. Unimportant. Gone.

A father? I never knew him. Did he ever touch me? Did he want me?

"Who are you? Where are you going? What's your destination little girl?"

I was abandoned.

Love?

It's not one of the rich ones from my starlet days, with a cigar and a glint, waiving a script under my nose and promising me the sky for a kiss or a touch.

I have been passed from hand to hand and judged, coming up short. I have nothing left to give.

It's not one of my husbands who loved only the masks but couldn't, or wouldn't, look beyond to accept me for the imperfect woman that lay underneath.

Do my scars show?

Tonight it's John F. Kennedy. My Jesus. My destroyer.

I knew it was love because I didn't want anything from him except his love. And it was the one thing he wouldn't give me.

But as much as you could love a man…that's how strongly you could hate him.

He had to.

He had to recognize how lonely I was. That I was gullible prey for his horrible, insatiable appetite for sex and glamour and excitement. He could have used the others instead.

He knew well how much suffering I experienced in my life. I told him myself. But he used me anyway for whatever momentary thrill he could get out of me, and the ego boost of fucking her.

Marilyn Monroe.

Me.

It wasn't the first time I'd been exploited. There's a long, leering line of reporters, directors, actors and studio heads who hopped into my life… my susceptible bed…

…because I was beautiful.

But none of them had ever held me so tenderly. None of them had risked their own careers and lives to be with me…none of them had listened to my life story with such sensitivity and compassion and afterwards taken my face in their hands and looked at me with total understanding and saw me through the masks, the armor, the fakery, to the lost girl I am…and then betrayed me anyway.

But regret and hate will only rip away more of the quiet I have in me. And I have none to spare. If I take another Nembutal…one more…maybe I can put this book away, stop this writing, and sleep.

Oh Jack! You flunked the test. I thought you might have been the one. I thought you might think of me. The ocean of problems between us – nothing! I thought you might get drunk and remember holding me as if it meant something. Or I thought you might sleep with someone else and find out she didn't compare. But I keep thinking there *is* an ocean between us. And there are so many things to distract you from me. And the prospect of something new always looks better than something you've had.

I simply can't put my feelings away. I can't sleep. I dialed Jack's number. Not the office. The personal one he gave me a long time ago, when his feelings for me were still fueled by the excitement of newness. He answered this time.

I said: I'm sorry to call so late.

I said: Please, it's very lonely here tonight.

I said: My heart is very hungry.

He said: For god's sake, Marilyn, I'm with my wife...

I take another pill, another comfort, and try to dial my friends. But it's Saturday night and no one is home. They won't want to hear about it anyway. They're tired of hearing my problems.

I'm tired of hearing my problems.

I'm so very tired.

I say to myself: Just lay here quietly. It doesn't matter if not one single person loves you completely. The whole world loves you collectively. That should be enough.

Next month I'm going to go back to work and finish the movie. Then I'm going to make another one. I won't swim nude anymore.

The public? My fans. Can they accept a different version of Marilyn?

Playboy bought the photographs of me in the pool and I will appear nude. The issue of *Vogue* is coming out and I will be in fashion.

What about my scar?

Oh my God! How I long to be away from this confusion.

Sinatra is singing and he is telling of my despair.

Through the open window, a short distance away, I can see the night and it is very still.

Somewhere there is a Jesus and he loves me. This I know.

I'm going to go to sleep now.

Who's that there in the dark?

Mr. Death?

Jack?

...Daddy?

Somewhere deep inside of him there is a longing. A tender vacancy where no one has lived yet. I could reach this place and touch him there – if only he

25826014R00192

Printed in Great Britain
by Amazon